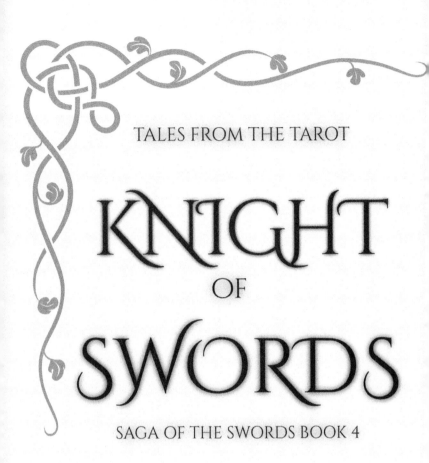

TALES FROM THE TAROT

KNIGHT
OF
SWORDS

SAGA OF THE SWORDS BOOK 4

CHRISTINE CAZALY

Behold! The Knight of Swords doth race, With mind as swift as steed in chase. He brings ye change at such great pace, Decisive action he'll embrace!
But, whoa! Too fast may lead to woe, As hasty winds do reckless blow. He might just trip o'er his own sword, For caution's whisper he ignored.
So cheer for speed, but mark this jest, Too quick to move is not always best!

Contents

PROLOGUE

Traitor's Reach, Iron Mountains, Epera, 1607

"For the North wind doth blow, and we shall have snow. And what will poor robin do then, poor thing?" Eng, Trad: 16thC.

Somewhere on the vast, weathered slopes of the Iron Mountains, a woman was singing. Her melody lifted in the wind. A cold, clear tone, like mountain crystal, suited to the rugged cliffs, the tumbling streams, and the deep, narrow valleys. At once beautiful and painful. It was a voice that could break hearts or shred souls. The plaintive song twisted about the strewn boulders and goat-cropped grasses, filled with yearning and unearthly regret.

Wheeling on the thermals, the birds heard it and followed the sound, their wings fleeting shadows on the ground as they drifted closer to earth, chased by the thin, northern sunlight. Even the inhabitants of nearby Traitor's Reach heard it. As one, they lifted rumpled heads from their daily chores to stare at the dark mouths of the mines. Exchanging grim, knowing glances with their companions, they huddled deeper into their threadbare cloaks and concentrated more heavily on their tasks. It was safer that way.

Way down south at the Castle of Air, Petronella, Queen of Epera, heard it. Tears drifted unheeded under flickering lids as she huddled in an uneasy doze, sweat beading her brow. Beside her, in an ornately carved wooden cradle, her newborn daughter, Theda, added her own tiny whimper to the unease. Petronella's ladies, Domita Lombard and Fortuna de Winter, exchanged anxious glances across the queen's heaped pillows. Domita rocked the wooden cradle with a gentle foot, cradling the queen's limp hand in her own. Fortuna laid the back of her own hand against Petronella's clammy forehead. Her heavy sigh said more than words.

High in his chilly turret chamber, Dominic Skinner, readying himself for a day's sword training under Sir Dunforde's eagle eye, heard it.

The song lit every nerve end and sent trickles of ice down his spine. Blinking in astonishment, he took a half step back as his recently purchased dagger danced to the edge of his bed and tumbled to the floor. Sunlight caressed the ornate pattern of archaic runes that flowed across the metal. His head filled with the wild, desperate song, he followed the point of the blade to his one narrow window and stared out. Gooseflesh crept between his shoulder blades as the melody played in his mind. Haunting but impossible to grasp. He blinked tears from his eyes as he traced the view north to the Iron Mountains. His fingers tightened on the chill stone sill, fighting a terrifying urge to push the window open and clamber out. "Follow," the song urged. "Follow me. Fly to me…"

"Felicia," he whispered into the cool autumn breeze. "Felicia, is that you?"

Chapter 1

Castle of Air 1609

Two years later.

"You'll not beat them on your own. Work as a team."

Muffled by the padding under his new helmet, Sir Hubert Dunforde's exasperation reached Dominic dimly through the confusion of battle. Dust from the melee ground swirled from the trampled earth and dried his mouth. Longing to wipe the sweat from his steaming face, Dominic shook his head free of Guildford's last strike. Despite the ringing in his ears, he glared at the old master at arms and planted his legs, determined not to fall and forfeit his chances. Sir Hubert looked him over, his expression sour beneath his own helm. Beyond him, the vast, grey battlements of the Castle of Air, crowned with Queen Petronella's falcon standard, stood sentinel at the head of the northern passes. At the perimeter of the melee grounds, the castle's occupants roared on their favourites, their combined voices underpinning the ring of steel on steel and the grunts of the combatants as they clashed. Sir Dunforde raised his own blunted weapon and poked at Dominic's chest guard. "Stop wool-gathering. Raise your guard and make a combined attack. I've told you all this before." Gritting his teeth and panting breath into his lungs, Dominic turned his gaze onwards to where two of Guildford's team raced towards their target, a mock castle erected in the middle of the field. The volunteer 'prize' for which they all fought, Fortuna de Winter, waited at its summit, her wide grin bright against her dark skin, cheering on the participants. Over to his left, Thomas Buttledon had pinned at least two of the opposition against the boundary, wielding his weapon with his customary, effortless grace. But apart from his efforts, Dominic's small force had scattered without hope. Even as he watched, Guildford's teammates toppled Alain of Winterbane, who rolled on the packed earth, drumming his heels on the ground, winded and unable to continue. Duana, his tall, dark-haired sister, dropped her own sword to give aid. Dominic winced as Jared Buttledon smacked her down with a blow from his own blunted sword and sprinted onwards in a cloud of dust. Sure of victory, Guildford raised his own weapon in an ironic salute, his taunting grin just visible through his visor. At sixteen, the illegitimate son of the former king stood two heads taller than Dominic—an illusion of golden glory, all radiance and warmth. "Come on, Sir Skinner," he jeered lightly. "Come and get us. Thought you wanted Fortuna a lot more than this." "Don't give up, Dominic!" Fortuna yelled, leaning so far over the flimsy wooden palisade of her mock tower that the whole thing rocked. "Jared Buttledon is a scurvy weasel who doesn't deserve me!" A wave of laughter from the crowds greeted her sally. Dominic rolled his eyes. That much was true, at least. Rolling his shoulders, he took a couple of deep breaths and bared his teeth at Guildford. Then he dropped his heavy sword and charged. Taken by surprise, Guildford took a second to adjust, but Dominic was off and running, blessing his Gods-given speed and his recent, hard-won strength. Two years of concentrated training under Sir Dunforde's harsh regime had honed his fitness and concentrated his mind. Guildford's strength was the might of a young bull. But, lithe and well-muscled, Dominic ran like a greyhound, flat out and sprinting. He took Jared by surprise with a flick of a foot and a well-timed push. Still armed, Jared stumbled and fell, cursing as his ankle twisted under him. The roar of the crowd, scenting a bid for victory, spurred him onward, away from Guildford's heavy-footed, determined pursuit. Fortuna's face, creased with laughter, filled his vision. Almost there. Ten feet. Five. Two...

"No, I don't want... please... please..." The young woman's mental voice filled his mind like a blaze of candles all lit at once and sent a shudder of ice crawling down his back. He skidded to a halt, whirling in a circle, searching the excited crowds for any sign of her. Spoiled of a race to the finish, the spectator's voices dropped away to a confused grumble. Guildford's pounding feet trembled on the earth as he approached, face red under his helmet, determined to win the prize. Blinking rapidly against the rush of sadness that attacked him, all thoughts of claiming Fortuna de Winter vanished. Dominic raised a hand to where Aldric Haligon, his squire, waited. The young man ducked under the narrow railing that demarcated the melee ground and sprinted to him, dodging the turmoil caused by Thomas Buttledon, who had yet to notice the battle was done. With no competition, Guildford jogged easily past, a question in his crystal grey eyes. He reached over the palisade to claim Fortuna and lift her down from her perch. She didn't look disappointed, but she brushed off Guildford's clutching hands and turned to Dominic as he greeted his squire. A fleeting frown crossed her smooth brow. "What is it? Are you hurt?" Aldric asked, scanning him for injuries. "Nay. Help me with the gloves." Aldric's nimble fingers skipped across the thick buckles attaching Dominic's hand protection to his armour. Released, Dominic jerked at his helmet, snatching it off and dropping it into Aldric's waiting arms. He turned on his heels to peer at the crowd once more, scrubbing his hands through his hair. After the confines of his helmet, the breeze felt chill against his burning cheeks. He strained his mental channels, scanning for Felicia's distinctive voice, to no avail. "Sir Skinner, can I give you aid?" Fortuna's rich, husky voice and the healing touch of her Gods-blessed presence swept over him in a

wave of honey and warm earth. Guildford rolled his eyes and waved at his own squire, Lionel Brearley. A moribund young man with a halting gait caused by a fall from his horse, Lionel hobbled across the field, taking his time about it. Guildford turned back to Dominic. "What happened? You could have won," he said, sheathing his sword and raising his visor. Dominic looked up at him. Those eyes! How could he ever forget her when he saw them in her brother's face every day? "Felicia," he said. Guildford's face creased into the same blank expression that always consumed him when someone mentioned his long-vanished twin. "Aye, and what about her this time?" he said, his voice rough. He gestured impatiently at Lionel, who accentuated his limp and slowed down. "I just heard her voice." Guildford snorted. "You couldn't. She's gone, Skinner. As dead as my mother." The words "No thanks to you" lingered between them, unspoken. All the same, Dominic flinched. He couldn't help it. Two years on, alone at night, he still saw the torn features of Arabella of Wessendean as she fell to her death, her shredded face a mess of blood, eyes wide with pain and shock. The Grayling's angry shrieking. Felicia's desperate leap into the whirlpool of dark energy summoned by his uncle, Terrence Skinner. Her disappearance. His frantic searching since. "I wish you would believe me." Another snort. "I don't hear voices in my head. Unlike you. About time," Guildford added to Lionel as the man finally closed the gap. He thrust out his fist. "Get these." "Yay, lord." Lionel performed his duties; narrow face closed, his thoughts concealed behind surprisingly fine green eyes fringed with long blond lashes. Guildford lost no time dragging off his helmet. His skin shone with a fine mist of perspiration. The weak sunlight dripped gold into his hair and highlighted his freckles. "You should forget her, Skinner. She's gone. Not coming back. It's done. Over." Dominic put his head on one side, surveying the younger man, listening to him as carefully as he did the voices of the precious birds clustered in the castle falconry. Guildford scowled. "What? You look like an owl. Don't stare at me like that." A half smile lifted the edge of Dominic's lips. "First, I can look at you any way I want," he said. "And second, you don't want to believe she's dead any more than I do. You might as well admit it." He raised an eyebrow, holding the younger man's gaze. Behind them, Sir Hubert called the bout closed. Thomas Buttledon lowered his weapon and pushed back his visor. His opponents leaned on their swords and gasped for air.

Guildford turned away first.

CHAPTER 2

A blare of trumpets heralded the entry of Queen Petronella and her husband, Prince Consort Joran of Weir, to supper in the vast Great Hall the same evening. Lowering sunlight lit the tapestries on the walls. The great hearth crackled with warmth. The air was heavy with the aroma of hops and wine. One of old Girdred's many sons plucked his harp and sang "Where the Wild Winds Blow," one of the Queen's favourite melodies. A riot of colour and the latest fashions, the Court of Skies rose, bowed, and returned to their benches on the usual avalanche of gossip. Seated at the high table, as befitted his status as Master of Falcons, with the Lord Chamberlain on one side of him and Fortuna de Winter, the queen's second lady, on the other, Dominic scanned the faces of the crowded hall for the one he most wanted to see. As always, he came up disappointed. Felicia of Wessendean was not there.

Across the room, Aldric Haligon had found a seat with Little Bird along the mid tables. Traumatised by the loss of her sister, Meridan, Little Bird had been inconsolable until Fortuna de Winter, head of the royal nursery, stepped in to help. Bird now held a prestigious position as nursery maid to the Queen's two children, Ranulf and Theda. Dominic's lips quirked as he watched her exchange a quip with Aldric that had the normally intense young man in fits of laughter. Aldric loved her company, but Bird still worshipped Will Dunn. Now a stalwart cadet in the Queen's Guard, Will took his supper with other young soldiers in the castle barracks. They had all moved on from their humble beginnings, orphans of the starving. Street thieves. Survivors. His jaw clenched. But not Felicia. She'd hurled herself into the dark maelstrom conjured by his bastard uncle, Terrence, and disappeared.

His knuckles tightened on the tankard until they turned white. Guildford didn't want to hear it, but the Queen would understand. He could tell her. He leaned forward to catch her eye. A light frown creased his eyebrows as the Queen mounted the shallow dais to be handed ceremoniously into her seat. Dressed in garnet red, shadows lingered under her navy eyes. Her pale skin shone like wax in the candlelight. Her hand, wearing the ring of mercy, rested lightly on her husband Joran's brocade sleeve, and he laughed as she made some comment as she took her place. But a lingering tension in her face reminded him of his first acquaintance with her years ago. She, a fugitive, running from her cloistered, dangerous life. He, a starving, ragged, young stable-lad, eager to prove his worth. He opened his mental channels as Petronella turned to greet her fellow diners.

"*Your Maj, are you well?*" he asked. Tense in his seat, he waited. Petronella had no requirement to acknowledge his telepathic request. If she'd closed her channels, she wouldn't even hear him. He crossed his fingers under the table, hoping that she would.

The Queen leaned forward and smiled at him across their fellow diners. "*I am fine, Dominic, just a little tired. Affairs of state, you know. Bad luck in the melee this afternoon. What happened? You were going to win.*"

As always, her soft voice in his head lifted his spirits. Hers had been the first telepathic communication he'd ever experienced. Up to that point, he'd never known himself Blessed by the Mage. He'd been a simple Citizen, son of a tanner. Good with animals, eager to please. Now. Well. He drew an earthenware decanter to him with a simple clutching motion of his fingers and watched it drift over the rough boards in his direction. Telekinesis. Telepathy. He poured ale into the tankard waiting for him by his plate and took a sip, savouring the light, apple-scented brew, wondering how to proceed.

"What troubles you, my friend?" she prompted.

"I heard Felicia's voice on the field today. She was frightened."

Down the row, Petronella's eyes widened. To his heartfelt relief, she didn't challenge him. *"Frightened? How?"*

Concentrating on their telepathic conversation, Dominic chewed his lip. The real-life voices of the company deadened in his ears. *"Someone was hurting her. Making her do something she didn't want to do. That's all I heard."* He paused, shoulders hunched as his imagination ran riot. *"My uncle might have got her. He could be hurting her."*

The Queen raised her glass to her lips and drummed her long fingers on the table. Silence bled across their mental connection. Dominic scowled into his small ale and hooked roasted venison onto his plate with the point of his enchanted dagger. He'd thought the Queen of all people would understand. Why did no-one listen to him?

"By the Gods, Dominic Skinner. Stop sulking." Caught by surprise, he gaped at her and cursed the blush that crept across his stubbled cheeks. Deeply respectful of her subject's privacy, the Queen utilised her own Blessed gifts so rarely it was easy to forget the ease at which she could penetrate a person's mental landscape to the emotions beneath it. Petronella tossed a mock glare his way. *"I'm thinking. Don't be so impatient."*

"But you believe me, don't you?" Dominic persisted. *"I know she's not dead. I know it. And what if Terrence has her? What if he's hurting her?"*

The Queen's slender shoulders lifted as she sighed. *"I know you believe it. I can tell you want to go looking for her."*

He shrugged. A muscle twitched as he ground his jaw. *"I do. What's so wrong about that?"*

Petronella raised a sardonic eyebrow. *"Remember what happened the last time you went looking for something? You could have died."*

Dominic half shrugged. A sudden vision of the swaying rope platform stretched across the space between the twin towers of Blade's greatest temple flashed across his memory. The darkness of that night, the icy wind, the yawning gap beneath him. His crawling, shivering, endless progress across the void to prevent the Wessendeans from lighting the signal fire that would topple Petronella's throne.

"But we won," he said, stubborn to the last. *"We stopped them."*

The caution in the Queen's tired eyes warned him before he heard her voice again.

"For which we thank you. Believe me, as a knight of Epera, Blessed by the Mage, you are worth more to the kingdom alive than dead. We need you and your Blessed gifts now more than ever. Don't go chasing rainbows."

Embarrassed at the unaccustomed praise, Dominic squirmed in his seat. He turned his knife on the table, watching the light flickering across the finely carved runes that chased endlessly across the wickedly sharp blade.

"There are not enough of us to weather the storm that's coming." Her voice was soft in his head, gentle even, considering the gravity of her words. *"We will need all our loyal subjects before this plays out."*

His head jerked up. "What do you mean?"

Petronella's sapphire gaze went right through him. From where he sat, Dominic could see the pulse in her ring as she connected with its power. The skin between his shoulders tightened in response.

Alerted by the flash of her diamond, Joran turned from his conversation with Guildford and caught the bleak expression on his wife's face. His aqua eyes narrowed as he opened his own formidable mental channels and joined the conversation.

"No-one gives you the right to question the Queen," he said, his telepathic voice colder than ice on a mountaintop. *"She has enough to concern her without worrying about you, too."*

"I didn't mean..." Dominic stuttered, mortified to the roots of his soul. He had never experienced Joran's mental voice before. The force of his reprimand tore his ego to shreds.

Petronella's navy gaze snapped back to the present. *"Nay, Joran. Don't berate him. He requested the conversation. I answered."* She took her husband's hand, directing his attention back to her.

Joran's lips thinned. *"I will berate him if he deserves it. I know you favour him, but he must remember his place as a knight. His vow of service and obedience to the Crown."*

Caught between a subject's respect for the Prince and his closer bond with the Queen, Dominic bit his lip to quell the urge to argue. Under the table, his hand coiled into a fist around his dagger.

Petronella shook her head and raised her hand as if she could still his anger. *"Peace, Dominic. I will not berate you,"* she said, her voice as cool and clear as the streams that cascaded over the rugged cliffs and hills of Epera's rocky terrain. *"Your concern for Felicia is admirable, and I understand it. You have no way of knowing for sure if she yet lives. I hope it is so. But while Dupliss eludes us, we need you here. I hope you will appreciate our wishes and not cause us to look for you."* She raised her eyebrow again, repeating the question.

Dominic bowed his head to her but raised stormy eyes to glower at the Prince. Joran met his challenge with the iron will all the courtiers had come to know since the rebellion, daring him to disobey. Pinned under his brilliant gaze, Dominic found his hand sweating on the hilt of his most expensive possession. He swallowed, his anger disappearing under the more immediate wave of self-preservation. Gods protect any who challenged Joran's beloved. His gaze drifted to the Prince's naked forefinger and then to the King of Epera's Ring of Justice that Petronella wore on a silver chain around her neck. He shuddered. By rights, Joran should wear that ring. He'd always refused. The Queen's Ring of Mercy amplified all her powers. Joran was already strong and well-trained. A battle-hardened warrior. A skilled telepath. Formidable. The charm bequeathed to him by his Oceanian mother softened his nature somewhat, but not by much, and certainly not in the last two years since Count Dupliss had attempted a rebellion. Staring into the Prince consort's stern visage, Dominic was suddenly relieved the man had not yet taken up the mantle of kingship that was his right and forged his bond with the land. He dropped his gaze to his tankard and took a shaky gulp, wiping the froth from his mouth with a hand that trembled.

"As you wish, my lord," he said.

Joran nodded brusquely and turned back to his conversation with Guildford—something to do with the hunt planned in a thrice of days. Dominic drank long and deep, hiding his burning cheeks, conscious of Aldric's curious gaze lancing in his direction from across the rowdy hall. The edge of his knife gouged the table as he struggled to order his thoughts. Thinking their conversation over, he jumped when his queen's musing mental voice sounded once more in his mind.

"We are dangerous, the Blessed," Petronella said. *"Our gifts are both a blessing and a curse."* She nodded at the dagger Dominic was turning end over end on the boards, the tip stabbing the ancient wood on every second strike. *"We are the knife that cuts both ways, for good or for ill. Gods grant us the wisdom to know how to use it."*

CHAPTER 3

"Dance with me?"

Starlight had claimed the night sky, and the evening meal was long over. The castle servants had removed most of the tables and shoved the benches back against the walls to make room for the entertainment. Tonight, a troop of acrobats from Battonia occupied the centre of the floor, mixing heroic feats of strength and flexibility with fire eating and a tribal war dance punctuated by the pound of drums and the wail of a bassoon. Clapping half-heartedly along with the rest of the company, Dominic had so far avoided Aldric, whose sharp eyes missed nothing. His squire was enjoying a game of dice with some others, their shouts of triumph clear above the general chat. Little Bird flitted, much like her namesake, from Aldric to Fortuna and back again, her golden curls reflecting the warmth of the hearth, a delighted smile stretching her wide mouth as her feet beat time on the floor and her sky-blue skirts swirled around her. Guildford had robbed Little Bird of Fortuna's company since the acrobats finished their performance. The two of them were now lining up for a country dance. Fortuna's head came about level with Guildford's shoulders. They made a pleasing contrast. Guildford, all burnished gold and warmth, Fortuna with her dark, sensual beauty, all curves, and a flashing smile. Guildford glanced over at Dominic, a challenge in his eyes, his expression smug. Yesterday, Dominic would have intervened. Tonight, he found, to his astonishment, that he didn't care. Felicia's plea for mercy replayed again in his mind. What had she meant? What didn't she want to do?

"Dominic. Aren't you listening? Won't you dance with me?" Little Bird grabbed his hands and tugged.

Apparently, it was now his turn for Little Bird's dubious attention. Dominic sighed. "Don't you have to go to bed?" he said, allowing her to pull him to his feet.

"Bed? What's that?"

"Where you should be, tucked up and asleep," Dominic said. "You are too young to be keeping such late hours." He drained his tankard and followed her to the middle of the floor.

Little Bird pouted. "I'm eleven, and I'll go when Fortuna does," she said, jostling for position in the line of dancers. Eyes sparking with mischief, she curtsied to his bow as the music started. "Don't you want to butt in?" she continued under the combined melody of pipe and lute. She jerked her chin at the laughing couple as they prepared to lead off. "Guildford's going to get her if you don't."

Dominic circled with the rest of their set, combining and recombining the figures in an intricate pattern as he pondered her words. Little Bird shot a quick, assessing glance at him as they met once more, hands clasped. Dominic spun her under his arm. Probably more fiercely than he should.

"You are nothing but a meddler, Bird," he said. "Too much time gossiping in the nursery with the other maids. It's none of your business what people do or who they do it with."

She shrugged. "Everyone wants to know who Guildford wants in his bed," she said.

Dominic rolled his eyes. "Ah, yes, Golden Guildford. I should have guessed it's all about him. What will I tell Will? Does he know your affections are now engaged elsewhere?" He'd meant it as a joke and was ill-prepared for the pain in his shin as Little Bird drew back her foot and kicked. Her blow caught the old injury to his calf, and Dominic winced. Apologising to his fellow dancers for breaking the formation, he limped to the nearest bench and massaged his leg, swearing under his breath. Little Bird followed at a safe distance, only marginally contrite. Aldric collected his dice and abandoned his game. He sauntered over, tossing a silver eagle from palm to palm as he joined them, amusement lighting his dark eyes.

"Strike Bird," he said. "Stow your talons." He took a seat on the nearest bench and amused himself, making the large silver coin dance across his knuckles. Little Bird ignored his attempt to distract her.

"It's his own fault," she glowered. "As if anyone could be better than Will."

"What are you wearing on your feet, girl?" Dominic growled, still rubbing his bruise. "You kick harder than Kismet."

"Serves you right," she said, putting her nose in the air.

"It was a joke. I know you love Will."

Little Bird smirked at him and crept nearer, hooking her fragile arm through his. "Will you forgive me if I tell you a secret?" she asked, blue eyes alight in the glow of the candles. Despite the neat gown and the lack of grime, her expressive face was still more street urchin than castle dweller.

Dominic narrowed his eyes at her. "I don't trust you."

"But it's the Gods-blessed truth. I swear it."

Aldric flipped the coin in the air and closed his hand over its face as it landed on his upturned palm.

"Heads, she's lying, tails, she's still lying," he drawled, holding his hand out to Dominic. "You choose."

Little Bird punched him on the arm. "Not fair. This is the actual Gods-blessed truth. I know who loves him." She nodded at Dominic, who glanced around for a spare tankard. He had the feeling he would need it to bear Little Bird's revelations.

"Bird..." he protested.

"It's Duana of Winterbane," Bird said, stifling a giggle. "Maria, the other nursery maid, said that she got it from Alain Winterbane himself. And if he knows, then their father knows. And we all know that what Duana wants, her father makes sure she gets. So you'd better start running if you don't want to be caught."

Dominic's mouth fell open. He put out a hand, which Aldric filled automatically with a cup of wine filched from the next table. Dominic took a huge gulp. "You are lying, aren't you?" he said. "Please tell me you're making that up." Over the cover of the rim, his eyes darted to the knot of well-born gentry currently gathered around the roaring fireplace. "I thought Winterbane was looking for a match with Simon Farrell. Look, they're all there. Talking." He gestured with the goblet, spilling blue Oceanian wine over his sleeve. Mistaking the gesture, the Winterbane patriarch lifted his own glass in a cheerful toast in Dominic's direction. Aldric tutted and took the drink away from him.

"Don't give him any ideas," he muttered. "Although there's nothing wrong with Duana. She's a fine maiden. Gifted with a sword. Sturdy."

"She's not a horse, Aldric," Bird said with youthful dignity. "She's the eligible daughter of a rich merchant and in love with our darling Dominic. Truly, really."

"Say no more, please," Dominic begged, his brain whirling.

"But there's so much to tell," Little Bird continued, remorseless as a winter wind. "All about how blue your eyes are...and how big your, what was it?" She put her head on one side, like a sparrow, pretending to think. "Oh yes, your majestic arms. That was it. Being the owner of the Queen's favoured tannery and the Master of Falcons doesn't hurt. Or that new land grant. Nor does the Gods-blessed ability." She stood up, hands on her narrow hips. "Better get used to it, Dominic. You're a man in demand at court. The Queen's favourite. A knight of the realm. Duana of Winterbane won't be the only one to come knocking at your door now you're eighteen. You mark my words."

Standing back, she surveyed both young men, smirking at their shocked faces, and then dipped a pert curtsey. "I give you good night, Sirs," she said. She turned on her heel, merriment trickling behind her.

Dominic stared at Aldric.

"By the Gods," he breathed. "We should have left her on the streets."

Aldric nodded. "She's relentless. It's like being knocked over by a hurricane," he said. "Gods help poor Will when she comes of age to be married. The poor bastard won't stand a chance." He handed over the wine and reached for another goblet, shrewd eyes scanning Dominic's face. "I don't know why you are so surprised, though," he remarked. "She's right. Duana of Winterbane is not the only one casting languishing glances in your direction. You are quite the catch of the court these days."

Dominic rolled his eyes. "Gossip," he growled.

Aldric chuckled. "The servants talk. Especially the ones with sisters in Blade..." He raised one dark eyebrow at Dominic's forbidding expression. "You know who I'm talking about, that dark-haired lass from Tressel's, Bettina," he said. "'T'is no bad thing, as long as she knows there is no chance of a wedding. Why so shy?"

"By the Gods, you are as bad as Bird." Heat flamed in Dominic's cheeks, already warmed by the consumption of strong Oceanian wine. "You're supposed to be my squire, not my mother."

Aldric shrugged. "A position I am most happy to fulfil, to be sure," he said.

"Which one?"

Another chuckle. "The rate you are going, probably both, although I quite like the title 'friend'." He took another sip. "And as your friend, I have to say you don't appear pleased to be the subject of all this noble attention, although some other ladies of lesser prospects already enjoy your favour of a night."

Dominic favoured Aldric with his best glare. "You know why I don't seek marriage," he said.

Aldric shrugged. "Aye. It's Felicia, isn't it?"

Staring moodily into his cup, watching the swirl of liquid in his glass, Dominic gritted his teeth. "I need to find her. I can't rest until I do. And when I hear her voice so clear like that..."

Aldric's gaze sharpened. "You've heard it before?"

"Not often. Sometimes, on the edge of sleep. I can hear whispers calling me. I think I heard her singing once, but today, in the melee... That was her. And she was in trouble."

"What does that mean?"

Over Aldric's shoulder, Dominic watched absently as Guildford swung Fortuna in an energetic measure that lifted her off her feet. She laughed, long braids flying under her gold-trimmed veil, her head thrown back. The lad's face was alight with amusement, bright with lust. If her brother harboured a second's doubt about Felicia's dreadful fate, Dominic had yet to hear it. In a different world, that could have been him dancing with Felicia. His fingers tightened on his cup.

"I've studied the books as much as I can," he said. "Admittedly, I'm no outstanding scholar. But the other telepaths say the same thing."

"Which is?"

"Telepathy doesn't work if you're dead. So either I'm going mad, or Felicia is still alive, and I must find her."

Grave as a judge, Aldric nodded, his oak brown eyes thoughtful. "Despite appearances, you are not mad," he said.

Dominic huffed a laugh. "Am I not? The Queen wants me to stay here. The Prince commands my obedience. I can hardly believe I'm thinking about betraying their trust by taking to horse and going in search of her." He stood, placing one hand on Aldric's shoulder in a gesture of thanks for the lad's understanding.

"You would never do that, surely?" Aldric said, startled. "That would be very..." He paused, his youthful face contracting in a fierce frown.

Shuffling his feet, Dominic waited for the younger man to complete his thought.

"By the Gods, very what?" he said, after a long moment when Aldric did nothing except stare at him.

"... Uncharacteristic," Aldric murmured, finally. "To disobey the Queen. Are you sure you're well?"

Across the room, the sweating musicians laid down their instruments. The dancers dispersed. In search of refreshment, Fortuna and Guildford drifted to the far end of the hall. Suddenly, the atmosphere was too close. Demanding. Oppressive. Shrugging his own confusion at Aldric, Dominic tugged at the neck of his embroidered brocade doublet, loosening buttons as he left. He shoved the heavy doors aside with a blast of telekinesis before the sleepy sentries could summon their wits to aid him. Beyond the noise and bustle of the Great Hall, the castle corridors stretched cool and watchful. He hurried away, nodding to the few people he passed, seeking the privacy of his chambers where he could be alone with his tumbled thoughts.

"Are you sure you're well?" He bit his lip as he recalled his squire's concern, taking the steep, winding stairway that led to his rooms two at a time. Slamming open the thick oak door of his study, Dominic pushed open a window and leaned out, heaving crisp autumn air into his lungs. It filtered past him to ruffle the parchment on his narrow desk, cluttered with ledgers from the tannery and accounts from his new holdings. A cluster of villages and a parcel of land gifted to him by Petronella as thanks for his actions in saving her throne. He'd yet to receive her permission to visit it.

Eyes bright, he scrubbed his hands across his cheeks and scanned the room as if seeing it for the first time. His gaze drifted across walls freshly panelled with the finest timber, a comfortable love seat positioned in front of the fire, the fine Argentian carpet under his feet, glassware from Oceanis available for his use. His once humble bedchamber on the tower floor above housed a comfortable, feather-stuffed mattress. He'd filled his once empty coffer with fresh linens and fine tunics.

Petronella. He owed everything to her. His wealth, his status, his allegiance. His nails dug into his palms as he clenched his fists.

So why? Why did he have a sudden, savage urge to smash the room and his entire life to splinters and kindling?

CHAPTER 4

T wo nights later, in a small, whitewashed room at the Sign of the Falcon in Blade, deep in the depths of Dominic's dreams, music played, and a woman sang.

He found he recognised the melody, the same wild, yearning tune that had so ensnared his senses two years ago. In the manner of dreams, he whirled in a circle, trying to place the singer. The tune taunted him. Her voice echoed down roughly hewn corridors, blacker than ink. Twined around sturdy pillars of chiselled rock left in place to support the weight of the mountains above, drifted above the inky, still waters of underground lakes populated with shoals of dead-eyed, silent fish.

At his hip, an unnamed instrument vibrated, strumming in time with the unseen singer's vibrato. Reaching his hand to still it, his dreaming self recoiled as he encountered his magical dagger in place of the expected lute.

The shock of it jerked him awake, and he lurched, panting, from his pillows, eyes wild with fright, blood heavy with lust, one hand tight around his enchanted knife, normally kept under his pillow, the other curled around his swollen member.

Sleepy at his side, his leman, Bettina, reached a hand backwards, patting his thigh. "Nay, sweeting," she murmured. "Pay the night frights no mind. Come to me."

Caught in a thick web of dark enchantment, Dominic needed no second bidding. Mind still humming with the disappearing threads of song, he reached for her warmth. The gently yielding tug and pull of her. She murmured soft encouragement, sleepy still but so beguiling. The homely aroma of the bakery clung to her. Long strands of her hair trapped the scent of freshly baked bread. The skin of her neck tasted faintly of sugar and salt. Groaning, Dominic sank into her again and again, rocking them both to a place where the nightmares vanished, and contentment reigned.

Bettina's soft moans of pleasure filled the narrow room. Afterwards, she drifted asleep, one hand still coiled within his much broader one, her rumpled head on his sturdy shoulder. Fully awake, staring blindly at the ceiling, Dominic used his gift to turn the enchanted knife end on end. The blade sliced the air in the darkness, its wicked edge a mere inch from his nose. Reaching out a hand, he stopped the motion and traced the carved runes with delicate fingers, following their intricate shapes, wondering at the language. The last fading whispers of the nightmare song played tricks with his inner ears. A light frown creasing his forehead, he raised his head a little from the pillow, balancing the knife across his palm. Deliberately, he cleared his mind. Gave no mental commands. Held a place of silence.

But still, the blade trembled against his skin, and its silver voice beckoned. "Come to me, fly to me. Come to me."

His fist closed on it. Gently, with infinite care, he withdrew his hand from Bettina's unconscious grasp and pushed back the blankets.

Outside, in the dim, yeasty chill of the tavern stable, Kismet grunted her disgust as he slid her saddle onto her back and pulled up the girth. Putting the inn and its sleeping occupants behind him, he rode out of Blade through the north gate and headed back to the castle. Kismet's hooves thundered on the turf as she stretched out. Dominic crouched on her back, lithe as a panther, cloak flying like a bird's tail behind him. On the narrow, cord-strung bed, he'd left Bettina a hefty purse. Enough to see her into a bakery of her own if she chose. Enough to look after her if there were consequences to their coupling.

He didn't look back.

Revelry and high spirits dominated the hunting party that clattered out of the west gate later the same morning. Outside the castle's confines, the fresh breeze stirred the smell of falling leaves and a hint of rain. Joran and Petronella led the group; the Prince mounted on his fine Battonian grey stallion. Petronella rode easily beside him on her own, smaller mount, the Grayling balanced on her free hand. Guildford's tiercel, older now and well-trained, stretched his wings, ready for action. Dominic had Felicia's merlin on his own fist, ignoring Guildford's teasing comments about the bird being a woman's choice. Owen Winterbane, rotund and jocund on a sturdy chestnut mare, rolled in Dominic's wake. Since Dominic's inadvertent greeting a few nights previously, the man had been seeking him out and asking some pointed questions about the size and nature of his holdings. Dominic's shoulders twitched in irritation at Duana's presence. Not for the first time, he cursed the gossip-hungry Court of Skies. Word must have already circulated that he'd parted company with Bettina. How, he couldn't guess, but usually horse shy, Duana rode closely behind, just a few strides away. He could feel her covetous stare, almost as if she held red-hot coals at his back.

As ever, Aldric rode at his side, keeping pace easily on his sturdy gelding. Son of a farmer but one time falconer's apprentice, Aldric loved nothing better than a hawking party. He nudged his horse forward to keep level with Kismet's slightly longer stride as Dominic sought to put more distance between himself and the avid Winterbanes.

"Bird was right. You are not running fast enough," he remarked as they followed Petronella's lead from the rutted path to the forested lower slopes. "How does it feel to be hunted?"

Dominic cut a glance at him. Aldric's light brown skin and black hair gleamed in the autumn sunshine, his dark eyes lit with pleasure as he scanned the surrounding countryside. At fourteen, the young man had lost little time finding his feet at court. He'd taken to education like a person starved, fonder of his books than many of his fellow squires. Dominic already relied on his shrewd head for figures and the practical common sense bequeathed to him from his Argentian mother. Growing in height and confidence, the lad was a far cry from the skinny waif Dominic had befriended in Blade two years previously.

"Let's just say I pity the hart and the hare," Dominic said wryly. "The man has been hounding me for days. I live in fear that I'll wake up one night and find Duana in my bed and my cock in her hand. If her father finds us thus, it's all over."

"Then you must run harder and faster," Aldric advised, struggling to contain his mirth. "Before you find yourself hauled in front of the priests and wedded and bedded."

"I want to tell him to leave off," Dominic hissed. "But how to do it without causing offence? That's the rub. I have nothing against Duana. I just don't want to marry her."

"A leave of absence from court to visit your new estates? Would that work?"

Dominic bit his lip, ducking to avoid a low-hanging branch. "Already tried it," he said gloomily. "The Queen won't let me go. Says I'm needed here. I think there's something wrong."

Aldric ducked the same branch. "How so?"

He shrugged. "I'm not sure. Petronella said something about all of us loyal to the Blessed being needed. The Prince stopped her talking to me before she could explain more. I am worried about her. She looks so tired these days, and Joran's even more protective than usual."

"Dupliss is still out there, somewhere. He's still a threat. And they know you want to go after Felicia, what with the Shadow Mage influence and everything else that happened. If Felicia is alive, maybe they don't want her back at court and around the Queen and the children. Have you thought about that?"

"Not want her back?" Dominic straightened his shoulders, casting a wounded glare forward at the Queen and Prince. Sunlight striped their thick hunting cloaks as they rounded a bend. "Base-born or not, Felicia's a child of the blood. Petronella would never deny Felicia her place at court. Joran, maybe. But not the Queen. And if she's hurt..."

Aldric stopped the tumble of words with a steady hand on Dominic's forearm. Felicia's merlin turned her hooded head in his direction. "We all saw how overtaken by the Shadow Mage influence Terrence was that night," he said, his voice low. "Petronella knows how dangerous he is. You can't risk bringing Felicia back here, Dominic. Not unless you are sure that she is free of its influence."

"She will be. I'm sure of it. She's too stubborn to turn," Dominic said. "But if she is, well, then I'll go with her. We'll go to my estate, somewhere far away from court, and I'll make it right. Somehow."

Aldric turned his face, his expression grave as he surveyed the undergrowth.

"What? You want to say something, just say it," Dominic said, catching the young man's hesitation.

Aldric sighed. "I wish you would leave this, Dominic," he said. "No good will come of this obsession you have."

A muscle clenched in Dominic's jaw. "What, you are against me as well, now?" he asked, his tone hard.

"I speak as your friend," Aldric murmured. "And I wish only for your happiness. But I agree with the Queen and the Prince on this. You are a sworn knight of the realm, tasked with its protection. I am your loyal friend and liegeman. And I know you, Dominic." He reined in, crowding Kismet off the narrow path so the others could pass them. Duana's head swivelled as if on a stick as her horse trotted on, her dark eyes intense with longing. Dominic scowled, turning Kismet in a tight circle.

"Whatever you think you know, don't be too sure," he hissed.

Aldric raised his chin. "I know you," he insisted. "And if you did anything that hurt the Queen, you could never live with yourself. You know it's true," he added. Dominic drew back as if he'd received a blow.

"I would never harm the Queen. Never," he said. Around them, the forest darkened as the sun disappeared behind a cloud.

"Then you have to trust her and obey her in this," Aldric said. "Please. Before all your good intentions turn to dust."

CHAPTER 5

B reaking from the autumn-scented forest to the wind-swept
higher ground beneath the crags and hilltops of the western
range, the hunting party scattered to fly their birds. One hand shading
his brow, Dominic watched Felicia's merlin circle high against the
sky, a dot amongst the thick grey clouds that gathered beyond the
mountains as she hunted. Over to his left, Petronella's ladies gathered
to watch the Grayling and his soaring speed as he scanned the ground
for prey. Guildford joined the Prince's group, where Joran flew his
great Gerfalcon, the men shouting encouragement as the magnificent
bird skimmed low and swift over the tussocks, hunting rabbits.

Thurgil, Dominic's friend and head of the falcon mews, found
himself in demand, stumping between the groups, whistling down
the exultant falcons, and instructing his staff to collect the bloody
kills. Petronella's pale face flushed with excitement as she cheered the
Grayling on. Out of sorts, Dominic sought his own company, leaving
Aldric with lure and jess to watch Felicia's hawk. Stomach rumbling,
he wandered to the edge of a stream and loosed Kismet's girth, one
hand on her neck. Her warm flank sheltered him from the brisk breeze
as his gaze slid idly from group to group.

The Winterbanes watched the magnificent play from horseback.
Neither father nor daughter indulged in the sport. Duana had already
bored with watching the birds. Conscious of her eyes on him, he busied himself unpacking his lunch, removing cloth, bread, cold meats,

and cheese from his saddlebag and spreading a soft woollen blanket across the rough grass. The view across the rushing stream eastward to the castle and south to Blade drew his eyes in a dizzying vista of angles and dips. He shrugged his cloak higher as a freshening wind found his collar and squatted to arrange the food. Hoofbeats behind him sent his spirits plunging. Winterbane, of course. A shrill squeak as the Grayling brought down a fat rabbit to the cheers of Petronella's ladies had him gritting his teeth. He kept his eyes on his task, cutting slices of cheese from the round he had brought with him, and tried to ignore the heavy footsteps as they approached. Two large shoes appeared in his peripheral vision—bright scarlet and edged with soft black leather. The older man's moon-shaped shadow loomed over the picnic cloth. He bit his lip, struggling with an urge to run and never come back.

"How now, Sir Skinner." Owen Winterbane's booming voice matched the rest of him for size and plumpness. Dominic heaved an inward sigh as he stood and bowed. Winterbane looked him over, at once mild and shrewd, his chest heaving slightly with exertion.

"I perceive you are avoiding me, sir," the elder said, his black eyes like currents in his round face. "I would continue our conversation. You know the regard my daughter has for you."

Caught. Dominic swallowed. He glanced across at the other groups, still calling encouragement to their birds. Aldric had dismounted to retrieve Felicia's merlin and the brace of larks she'd brought down. The lad looked his way and strolled towards him, much to Dominic's relief. Motionless on her mount, Duana watched. He could see the tension in her body even at this distance. For focus, she almost put the precious falcons to shame.

Dominic cleared his throat and straightened his shoulders, taking a moment to wipe the blade of his dagger against his thigh.

"I am sorry to disappoint you or Duana, sir," he said quietly. "I have no wish to marry at the present time."

"Ah." Winterbane took a shallow step back. Hope dropped from his face like a cloud passing the sun. He crossed his heavy arms. "My daughter is not good enough for you?"

"That's not the reason. I wish no offence," Dominic said. "Duana is a fine maiden, to be sure."

"Then why not? Come, sir, you must admit our fortunes will ride well together–the tin and the tannery." Winterbane's fur-lined sleeve swept out in an expansive gesture that took in a large sweep of hillside. "We are a wealthy family, sir. Famed for our skill in metal working. As are you these days. Why, that dagger you use so carelessly to cut your food–that is a Tinterdorn blade, is it not?"

Dominic blinked and looked at his knife, turning it over in his hand. "That is what I was told. What of it?" he asked.

Winterbane favoured him with a tight smile that did not sit well on such amiable features. "My wife, Emily, was a Tinterdorn. Her sister, Juliana, was a talent indeed. The best there was. May I?"

He held out a hand, fingers thick with silver rings. Curiosity churning within him, Dominic handed the dagger over. A pale shaft of sunlight kissed the silvered edge and highlighted the engraved runes. Winterbane held it close to his face, turning it this way and that. Clasped in his heavy hand, the lethal weapon looked almost dainty.

"Aye, this is Juliana's work, to be sure. Look."

He extended his hand. Aware that he'd possibly made an enemy, Dominic took a step back. The older man snorted. "I'm not about to murder you with your own knife, lad. Fear not." He waggled the point of the blade. "Look, there, near the hilt. See her initials?"

Dominic peered at the blade and nodded as he recognised the letters. "I hadn't noticed them before," he admitted. "I thought it was part of the decoration."

Winterbane raised a shocked brow. "These runes are not mere decoration, dear sir. Juliana was Blessed by the Mage," he said, voice as soft as a feather, pride in every syllable. "She could weave deep enchantments into her work."

The stiffening breeze found an exposed patch of skin. Dominic shivered. "The man who sold it to me said it is an enchanted blade," he said. "But I have yet to discover in what way."

"Aye, well, that's the thing," the merchant said. "Juliana could make a blade do many things. It could protect you. Lure you. Find you." He shrugged and gestured to the rug, panting slightly. "If I could sit?"

"Of course," Dominic waved his hand at the meal as Winterbane lowered himself stiffly to the ground. "Help yourself. Do you wish for wine?"

Winterbane's eyes brightened as he handed back the knife. "That's a good thought, lad."

"I'll get it," Aldric said as he approached, passing Dominic the merlin's jesses. "Hawking is thirsty work. By your leave, sir, your daughter has taken an escort back to the castle." He delved into the second saddlebag to retrieve the wine.

Winterbane's eyes jerked to the ride, where Duana's crimson cloak fluttered in the breeze as she left the party in the company of a groom, shoulders stiff. He huffed a chuckle as he received the goblet Aldric extended to him. "Aye, she can read the signs," he said on a half sigh. "No match today. Welladay. I tried on her behalf. That is correct, is it not?" He added, "You are not in the market for a bride. Despite the advantages the joining of our families could bring?"

Dominic took a sip of fruity red Argentine and allowed his shoulders to relax, dropping easily to the ground beside the older man. "Not much of a joining, sir. I was born the son of a humble tanner, that is all."

Winterbane's shoulders heaved as he chuckled. "Aye, and the Winterbanes were humble miners who got lucky. Self-made men. Citizens. Mostly."

"Apart from Juliana?"

"That's it. But the soldiers took her years ago, on Lord Falconridge's order." Dominic's eyes widened as the elder leaned back and spat his disgust into the stream. "Died in the mines, she did. Her Blessed skill with her. A crime and a sad loss to the trade and her family."

Reaching for a hunk of roast boar, Dominic chewed thoughtfully. "I am sorry to hear it. My uncle was the first taken. It's possible they knew each other. Can you tell what type of enchantment this blade contains?" he asked.

Winterbane grimaced. "Not I. That's a skill I do not have. But I think someone altered it from the original. Let's look again. I'll show ye."

Dominic stifled a grin against his cup as the older man fumbled in his pouch for a small pair of spectacles and perched them on his broad nose.

"This'll be you one day. You may well laugh," Winterbane huffed, taking the knife once more. "Look, there. See the rune for strength and the other for calling?" He tapped the dagger with a pointed, somewhat grimy nail. Not knowing the language of runes, Dominic nodded vaguely. He exchanged a sceptical glance with Aldric over the man's scarlet velvet cap.

Hunched over the dagger, the older man missed his expression. "See, someone's added something to the end of this. An extra sigil. Just there, look in between."

Frowning, Dominic bent over the knife. Winterbane's professional eye had seen the discrepancy in style that his own untutored gaze could not.

"Aye, I see it. What does it mean?" he asked.

Winterbane shrugged and tossed the knife back into Dominic's lap. "That, I don't know. Could be nothing. A previous owner, perhaps." He took a thirsty gulp of wine and sighed his pleasure, reaching for more bread, his brow creasing in sudden thought.

"But what I know is, you don't go changing an enchanted blade. Not unless you know what you're doing. That blade you've got. It's a rarity. Priceless, some would say. And you used it to cut your cheese." He shook his head, jowls wobbling.

Dominic frowned. He glanced over at Aldric, who shrugged.

"The Mage blessed me with telepathy and mentomancy," he said, spinning the knife in the air between them with a glance and a twist of his fingers. "Master Tingle, who sold this to me down in Blade, said it was meant for a person with telekinetic powers."

Winterbane watered his bread in the wine. Droplets dripped from his fingers to pool on the blanket like blood as he paused with the morsel halfway to his mouth. A smile lightened his heavy features as the knife turned before his eyes. "Still makes my heart sing to watch you Blessed do that," he said. "Never had the slightest touch of the Mage myself, but I am always loyal to him. Aye, I am."

"I think this enchantment talks to me. I hear it sometimes. It wants me to follow where it calls."

The elder shrugged. "That's possible if Juliana carved those runes," he said.

"The thing is," Dominic continued, dropping his voice, "should I follow where it calls?"

Sharp-eyed, his would-be father-in-law met his gaze with a questioning one of his own.

"Should you follow the call of a powerful enchanted blade, one that an unknown person has altered for their own purpose? Absolutely not."

Dominic's face fell. "That's what I feared you would say." He sighed. "I'm looking for Felicia of Wessendean. I think the knife wants me to find her." He let the dagger drop to the cloth and ran a gentle finger along the merlin's feathers.

"The missing girl. A Wessendean? Is that the one you have your eye on?" Winterbane grimaced, his eyes drifting across to the royal party and Guilford's commanding figure as he lounged beside the Prince. "Joran does right, keeping that lad close," he muttered. "No telling what those traitors will do. Best news I had when I heard Arabella met her end. Pity they never caught up with Dupliss. The Gods know what he'll do next."

Dominic kept silent, his memory full of the Grayling's angry screech and Arabella's blood-streaked face, gaping, eyes wide with fear and shock as she plummeted to her death.

Winterbane's black eyes scanned his face. "What you did, that took guts, lad," he said softly. "You were just a stripling back then. I remember ye, all eyes and heart. Thanks to you, Joran stopped the rebellion."

A half smile curved Dominic's lips. He snared the blade and stowed it carefully in its sheath, nodding at Aldric, who listened to their conversation with his head on one side, like a child hearing a bedtime story. "I had a lot of help," he said.

He glanced up at the spiteful slash of rain against his cheek and lifted his hood as the wind changed direction, blowing harsh from the north. His eyes widened as he scanned the sky. Black clouds roiled in the near distance, racing from the Northern ranges to strike the lowlands. Flocks of wild birds led the charge, their savage, alien cries greeting the storm as it advanced.

"Not much of a picnic," Aldric said, snatching an extra slice of meat and gulping his wine. "Pity the weather's changed." Working together, they bundled the foodstuffs into napkins and stowed them away. Winterbane groaned to his feet, aided by Dominic's sturdy elbow. Kismet tossed her head as the rain gained strength. Elsewhere, Joran threw Petronella to her mount's back, leaving her ladies to gather their food. Guildford had already turned away to face the ride back to the castle. Above their heads, thunder growled, the wind picked up, and the storm started in earnest.

Hoods pulled up against the weather, the party mounted and headed for the relative shelter of the gloomy forest. Overhead, the wind churned the branches. The horses shook their heads at the barrage of small twigs and cascading leaves wrestled from the heights by the gale.

Up ahead, Joran raised his hand. "Make all speed," he roared to the company. "This is no passing squall."

They cantered on. Riding full pelt, bending low against Kismet's sweating neck, Dominic followed the lead, heart beating fast with every new crack of thunder, his thirst for adventure beating time in his ears. Aldric rode beside him, glancing up every now and again as the branches whipped and the wind whined.

They were halfway to the castle when Joran called a sudden halt. Broken from his wild reverie, Dominic sat up, slowing Kismet to a trot. She threw back her head, scattering his face with water. Blinking, he wiped his eyes with a soaked sleeve and trotted her forward to the head of the line. Joran and Petronella had reigned in. Beyond them, a squarish figure atop a sturdy gelding splashed gamely towards them through the slick mud. Both horse and rider looked exhausted. The man wore half armour, liberally smeared with dirt and blood. The shield attached to his saddle bore the emblem of fox and hart. It was not a device that Dominic recognised. Its bright paint, splintered by fighting, revealed the raw wood and steel bracing beneath. Dominic's gaze jerked to his rulers. Joran's handsome face had settled into stern lines. His hand rested on his sword. Petronella's face was whiter than milk, lips pale, her brilliant eyes the only colour. His jaw clenched. A telepathic conversation was obviously taking place between them. Petronella's jaw tightened, and she nodded shortly to Joran. He hung back reluctantly as Petronella advanced to meet the stranger. Dominic ached to be privy to their conversation.

"Do you recognise that shield?" he hissed at Aldric under the cover of the wind-wrapped trees.

Aldric shook his head. His horse stamped and snatched at a wet patch of grass. "Not at court," he said.

"Take the bird."

Aldric took control of Felicia's merlin, and Dominic urged Kismet forward, drawing his own sword. Guildford closed the rank on the other side of the ride, grey eyes cautious.

The weary soldier dismounted and limped towards them down the path, boots sliding in the fresh mud. Too tired to move, his horse put its head down and grazed.

"Hold," Joran's voice rang out loud in the watchful forest. He trotted forward in line with Petronella, who favoured her husband with a glare that clearly said she was more than capable of dealing with one exhausted messenger without his help. Unrepentant, he joined her and slid his famous steel sword from its sheath with practised movement, elegant in its lethal simplicity.

The soldier's blue eyes followed the point of the sword as it lowered towards him. He shook his head, his fingers trembling as he removed his heavy, old-fashioned helm. Purple bruises, already fading to green, decorated his gaunt, whiskered cheeks. One eye was almost closed. "Nay," he croaked, his voice rusty with fatigue, "I am your loyal subject. I crave an audience with Her Majesty." He knelt in the mud, both hands clinging to the pommel of his own sword, using it as a staff to prop him up.

Joran did not drop his own weapon. "Speak then, and let us hear you," he commanded. "Who are you?"

The man's stare wobbled around the company, who waited in grim silence to hear what he had to say.

"My name is Jon of Hartwood, my lord. My estates run close by Frost Hollow, at Traitors Reach. We suffered an attack just days ago. Black-garbed demons armed with might and magic both. They struck at our granaries. Burned our mills. Raided at least one village and then vanished into the night. We request you send aid to protect us from these wild northerlings and stop their advance."

"Armed with dark magic? That can't be possible. What else did they want?" Petronella's tone rang like crystal as she straightened in her saddle. She dragged the hood from her hair. The frost of her diamond ring cast a blue light into the bleakness of the afternoon. Dominic shook his head to dislodge a sudden, high-pitched tone that resonated through his skull like a constant chime of finger cymbals. The dagger at his hip quivered in response. The Grayling shifted uncomfortably on the Queen's wrist, dropping his head to peck at his jesses.

Hartwood chewed his lip as he considered her question. "Nothing out of the ordinary, Your Majesty. We stopped them, for now, at some cost to my villagers and liegemen." His yellow teeth bared in a sudden, vulpine grin. "But we caught one. Made him talk."

The noise in Dominic's head grew louder. Insistent. Trembling within his very bones. His dagger vibrated in sympathy, and his shoulders clenched in sudden dread at what the man might say next. Petronella's shoulders also contracted under her heavy hunting cloak. One slender hand wandered upwards to press against her forehead. Glancing across, concern washing the fine lines of his face, Joran nudged his horse closer to her side.

"And?" The Queen's voice held a rare, ice-like quality, crisp as cut glass.

The hum in Dominic's head changed. Skin crawling, he recognised it as the same eerie, haunting tune he'd heard in his recent nightmare. Part lullaby, part lament. Petronella's face contracted in a fierce frown. All of a sudden, he wondered if she was hearing it, too.

"Speak, man." Joran's harsh voice brooked no disobedience.

"He said his orders were to head south, my liege."

"Who?" Joran demanded. "Who gave the order?"

Reluctantly, the man dragged his gaze back to Petronella, who sat on her horse as if turned to marble. "Count Dupliss, my lord. His forces are to gather supplies and then head south to the pass that guards the mines. To your family estates, my lady. To Falconridge."

The song swelled in Dominic's mind and broke into a cascade of wild laughter. He winced as Petronella uttered a single, sharp cry and slumped in her saddle. Startled, her mount took a quick sidestep, and the Queen tumbled earthwards. The Grayling soared from her wrist as she fell. Her head met the path with a sickening crack. Joran leapt to the ground, shouting his wife's name, and Dominic gathered himself enough to whistle. Blind in his hood, The Grayling took a moment to launch himself towards Dominic's glove. He landed in a ruffle of feathers, straining towards the Queen. Dominic urged Kismet closer, ready to dismount and go to her aid, but the Queen's household reached her first.

Her ladies threw their reins to the stableboys and clustered with Joran around the Queen's prone form, her heavy cloak pooled in the puddles, one leg twisted inelegantly beneath her. Long black eyelashes fanned her pale cheeks. Joran was patting her hand, her ladies reaching for smelling salts. Ignored and grey-faced with shock, Hartwood stumbled to his feet. In the absence of anyone else, his faded gaze met Dominic's angry, horrified glare.

"I'm sorry, sir," he stuttered. "We tried to stop them, we did."

CHAPTER 6

Faces sombre, the hunting party travelled as fast as they dared along the treacherous paths back to the castle.

Joran's face was the colour of skimmed milk. He rode with Petronella's limp form cradled in his arms, her dark head lolling against his shoulder. Tension shadowed his jaw. Flanking him on each side, alert and watchful, Guildford and Dominic scanned the scrubby bushes for any sign of danger. Petronella's household muttered their concern as they rode behind him. The Grayling had not settled despite his familiarity riding on Dominic's wrist. His noble head twisted constantly to Joran, his chatter loud and wild. The noise sent little rivers of alarm spiking through Dominic's senses. The wild laughter in his head and the strange, haunting melody seemed almost a thing of dreams. How could he ever have thought it was Felicia? Surely, she would never celebrate a turn of events such as this. He glanced across at the Queen. A slowly growing patch of blood bloomed against Joran's cloak, where she lay fragile as a lily in his arms. He opened his mental channels, just in case, but the Queen had lost all consciousness. Where her voice lived was an empty, cavernous space. He shivered at the thought that she might never regain her senses, his fingers tightening on the reins.

The Prince sent a guard sprinting for Fortuna de Winter as they clattered under the portcullis and into the stable yard. Petronella's other ladies fussed around her, and Master Mortlake, the castle physician, appeared almost by magic as if he sensed something amiss on this storm-ridden afternoon. Together, the group found a stretcher for the Queen, and Joran dismounted, his cloak trailing mud and water. His eyes narrowed as they landed on Jon of Hartwood, who had followed them back, plodding miserably at the rear of the procession. "Stay where I can see you," he said, his tone full of menace. Hartwood bowed, misery pressed deep into the lines of his forehead.

"Dominic, see this man housed and fed. We would speak to him more on this matter of the raid," Joran instructed as Fortuna de Winter approached at a run, her skirts lifted against the damp.

"Aye," Dominic jerked his head at Hartwood as he slid from Kismet's back and tossed her reins to the waiting stable boy. The Grayling pecked at his hand as he started back to the mews, and he paused, sensing the bird's intense distress at being parted from his mistress.

"My lord," he called, "I believe the Grayling wishes to stay with the Queen."

Joran glanced across at him, most of his attention on Petronella and her pale face streaked with mud and blood, "Bring him then, he may stay," he said. "But see to this man."

"Leave it to me," Aldric said. "I'll speak to the chamberlain. Find him something in the west wing."

"My thanks." Leaving matters in Aldric's more than capable hands, Dominic hurried after the stretcher-bearers as they bore the Queen to her chambers in the south wing.

Shadows seemed to crowd the corridors as they hurried onwards. Servants bowed as the group passed, their faces slack-mouthed with shock. The courtiers taking refuge from the rain in the long gallery gathered in jewel-toned clusters, questions on their lips, heads cocked, bright eyes alert, like a flock of nestlings. The rush of gossip started like the whisper of wind in the trees even before they mounted the shallow stairs that led to the Queen's wing.

In the queen's quarters, dim light percolated through the thick paned windows. The vast view to the south and west, all the way to the World's Peak, had grown hazy in the afternoon. Washed out by the drum of rain. A small, cheerful fire burned in the grate, a peaceful, homely sight in a world that had of a sudden grown bleak and watchful. Petronella's household bustled, transferring her gently to her mattress, finding bandages for her head and cloths to bathe her face and hands.

Dominic moved the Grayling's perch from Petronella's solar to a spot near her finely carved bed and removed the bird's hood, making a mental note to instruct one of the falcon mews staff to tend his needs. The Grayling's head turned, following the activity in the chamber as Fortuna and Master Mortlake conversed in low voices, discussing treatments for her head injury and broken leg. Joran stared down at his wife, where she lay motionless against her silken pillows, scrubbing his long, fine-fingered hand through the tangle of his hair. His mental channels were completely closed, but Dominic didn't need them open to witness the turmoil and confusion on his face. Anger flexed his jaw. Standing back a respectful distance from the carved four poster, with anxiety for the Queen clenching his chest, Dominic jumped when Joran turned to him.

"Dominic, gather Thomas Buttledon, Sir Dunforde, Guildford, the Lord Chamberlain, and Jon Hartwood. They are to await me in my office. You may attend also," he said, his voice harsh.

"Yay, lord." Dominic sketched a bow and withdrew, hurrying to his task. Turning his head at the last moment, he was unsurprised to see Joran on his knees at Petronella's side, her limp hand pressed hard against his lips. Magical senses prickling with tension, Dominic hurried to his own chambers, despatching various servants along the way to find the people Joran requested. Gooseflesh shivered his skin as he shed his heavy, rain-soaked cloak, hanging it on a hook to dry. Scraping his wet hair back and tying it with a strip of leather, he pondered the laughter he'd heard as the Queen fell from her horse. If that was not Felicia–and he couldn't, wouldn't believe that it was–then who? An enemy for sure, and one with powerful mind magic, but who could Petronella have so angered? And Dupliss. At large in the north, planning an attack on Petronella's own childhood home. Why? His brow twisted as he remembered the ghostly female presence hovering near Terrence Skinner on that fateful night two years ago. He and Little Bird had been the only people to see her. Maybe Bird knew something. He'd have to ask her.

Questions circled in his mind like buzzards above the hillsides. He marched to Joran's chambers, brushing past people who tried to stop him for more information. Traditionally, the Kings of Epera had always kept a suite of interlinked chambers in the North wing as a symbol of their sovereignty. Joran disdained both title and the weight of tradition as much as he refused to wear the Ring of Justice, preferring to keep to a simple suite close to the Queen and the royal nurseries.

"How now?" Thomas Buttledon said, his green eyes sparkling with anticipation as Dominic entered Joran's private office, brow lowered in thought. Seated in a padded chair, doublet loose at the throat, Thomas propped his feet on a small stone eagle that guarded the hearthstone, warming his toes. The small chamber smelled of woodruff and spices, cluttered with battered seats and a much-scarred desk. A portrait of Petronella and Joran hung on the oak-panelled wall over the stone fireplace, Prince Ranulf cradled in Petronella's arms, both smiling at the future. Dominic's heart contracted when he saw it.

"Well met, Tom," Dominic replied, taking the tankard of small beer Thomas held out to him and sinking into the nearest chair.

"So serious? What's to do?"

Dominic told him. Thomas's face slackened in surprise and then hardened. "Where is this Hartwood?" he asked.

"Coming. Joran wishes to see all of us together, including the Lord Chamberlain."

Thomas rubbed his hands together and took another swig of wine. "Joran's planning a mission, then. That's good news."

Dominic dragged his gaze away from the depths of his tankard. "He won't let me go, just you watch," he replied. "Both of them want to keep me here. They don't trust me."

Thomas frowned. "Not sure they don't trust you, Dom."

Dominic glanced at him, eyes narrowed. "That's what it feels like."

"You'll get your chance for action, lad. Don't fret."

"Complaining again, Skinner?" Guildford said as he slammed the door open and stalked in. His height dominated the small room. Dominic jerked his head at another chair.

"Sit down, Guildford. The ceiling doesn't require you to dust it," he snapped.

Guildford's lips twitched in response to Dominic's flash of temper. He reached up, stretching his long arms above his head to the panelled ceiling, and pretended to lift it above his head. 'T'is not my fault you are a midget," he said, taking a seat.

"At least I can grow a beard."

"Lads, lads," Thomas remonstrated. "Calm your pecking."

The room filled as Lord Colman, the Lord Chamberlain, entered, puffing like bellows, cheeks pink with exertion. Sir Dunforde followed him in—a sturdy, silent presence, craggy features grim with purpose. Jon Hartwood entered under armed escort, and the men gathered around the fireside quieted their speculation, turning to stare at him as he stood, twisting his hands. He'd taken time to splash his face with water, but fatigue rimmed his eyes with shadows.

"My lords," he said, "I am sorry for the Queen's accident. How is she?"

Dominic shrugged. "We do not yet know," he said. "She had not regained her senses when I left." The words left a bitter taste in his mouth. Underneath them, he was conscious of a dim panic, a sense that the world had tilted irrevocably without his permission.

They stood and bowed as Joran marched in and banged the door shut. He nodded shortly and waved a hand at the seating. Thomas held out a tankard, and the prince took it, tossing the contents down his throat without tasting them.

He took a place by the window and stared out for a few seconds before turning to the company, his shoulders broad and dark against the lowering afternoon. His aquamarine gaze fixed on the stranger, who sank to his knees like a vine cut by an axe, reading the threat there.

"Tell me," Joran said, his voice edged with ice, "exactly what happened!"

Jon of Hartwood's tale took a few moments and left the group exchanging grim-faced glances.

"Describe this dark magic to me," Joran demanded. "What form did it take? What did it do?"

Hartwood's fingers trembled on the tankard he held. "It was dark, my lord. There were nobbut a few mages. A tall, thin, older man and several others, younger. I didn't recognise them. They struck on a moonless night, all in black. We're used to dealing with thieves and bandits. That's common, so close to the mines, where the living is grim, and the rations short. We can cope with them. Take 'em down if we must. 'Twas the whispering that did us in."

A trickle of unease traced icy fingers down Dominic's spine. "Whispers?" he said, thinking of the haunting melody that coiled seductively around his senses, sowing a sense of confusion and dread every time he heard it.

The older man shrugged irritably. "I know you'll think it nonsense, but there are folk on my estate blessed with mage magic, and they swore they could hear whispers. Voices. Telling them they were trapped. There was no way out. That their neighbours had given them up for dead and deserted them. Near on caused a riot, it did. No-one heeding anyone else. And the sadness..." He paused, bewilderment clouding his gaunt features as he scrubbed at the sparse hair under his cap. "Nay, I can't account for that. Not at all. It's like we almost gave up before we started fighting."

"But you fought, that's something," Thomas said. He leaned over and topped up the old soldier's tankard. "Come, sir, drink up. You lived to tell the tale. These are ghost stories, surely, bred by panic and darkness."

Alert as a hound scenting a hare, Joran sat forward and stared at Dominic, his eyes like ice. "Sound familiar?" he asked. "You've gone white as snow."

Dominic fidgeted with the sheathe of his dagger. It lay harmless at his hip. No sign of its previous agitation. "It's like the night Felicia went missing," he said slowly. "We were trying to get to the Grayling. My uncle had him. He was trying to change him. Chanting a song or a spell, I don't know which. And it was so hard to move forward. Like walking through mud, chased by our worst nightmares. We all felt it. Little Bird hated it. She's a telepath. Even Will, and he's a Citizen, through and through."

"Your uncle, eh?" Joran took a thoughtful sip of wine. "Master Terrence Skinner. Tall, thin. Older. Another one who vanished, never to be seen again. Until now." His piercing gaze stabbed Dominic like a dagger. Challenging, accusing.

Dominic stiffened in his chair, understanding all at once the source of Joran's deep mistrust. "You think I let him get away that night?"

Joran raised a thick eyebrow. His lips thinned. "You did."

"I threw a dagger at him," Dominic protested, suddenly aware of Guildford staring at him from across the room. "Felicia jumped into the vortex, and I stabbed him. That's what broke the spell. And then there was mayhem." He jerked his head at Guildford, whose grey eyes filled with his own set of memories from that fateful night. "He was there. Terrence nearly killed him. Would have done with a bit more force, except that he had used most of his energy conjuring the dark magic."

Eyes turned to Guildford as he chewed his lip, considering his reply. He nodded shortly to Joran. "Much as I hate to say it, Skinner has the right of it, my lord," he said.

The Prince's eyes dropped momentarily to his own goblet as he reflected on their words, and Dominic huffed in a breath of welcome air. He glanced across at the younger boy, but Guildford was glaring into the depths of his cup and refused to meet his gaze. Joran rose and paced the chamber, striking one fist against the other, eyebrows drawn together in a fierce scowl. Dominic grimaced and took a bolstering sip of ale. The Prince Consort's temper had been on a short fuse for months; only the Queen was ever able to offer comfort to her frustrated husband as he sought Dupliss up and down the country. And now this.

"I have felt the influence of the Shadow Mage," Joran said. "Similar to Dominic's experience and yours, Master Hartwood. The dread. The stifling of your abilities. Doubt. Confusion."

"Shadow Mage? Are we really talking about this?" Sir Dunforde clapped calloused hands to his sinewy thighs, his thick grey beard jutting in exasperation. "The Queen banished that force, did she not? We are a nation united under the Mage. Or would you now have us believe differently? We fight like men these days, not wizards."

The Prince grimaced. "Apparently, the Shadow Mage is no longer banished," he said. "By the look of the thing, Terrence Skinner's actions have re-awakened his influence. He and Dupliss are both clearly involved in this northern raid, working together once more." He stood, raking a fist through his hair. "I need you to form a small troop, Sir Dunforde," he ordered. "You will move with all speed and guard the pass to Traitor's Reach. Make your base at Falconridge. There is room there for your force, with a large estate in which to hunt. Send out search parties. Question everyone you can. I want Dupliss, alive and in my custody. Do what you have to dissuade any rebels." His eyes glittered in the dull afternoon light as they scanned the group, who had risen along with him. "You will depart on the morrow, so make haste and gather what you need. I leave it to you to decide who to take. In the meantime, double the guard here and in Blade."

"My lord." The old soldier saluted, fist to his heart, as he bowed and hurried out. Following suit, Thomas and Guildford scurried after him, clearly eager to be included in his plans. The Lord Chamberlain added his agreement to the preparations, his jowly cheeks rolling. "I will arrange supplies, my lord," he said, heaving his bulk out of the chair with some difficulty.

Joran nodded his thanks. "Master Hartwood, I thank you for this intelligence," he said. "You will depart with my forces and share as much information as you can about the countryside and terrain. Get some rest and prepare to travel. I must speak to Sir Skinner."

"Aye, my lord." Hartwood left the room, with Lord Colman closing the heavy door carefully behind him.

"Dominic."

Alone with the Prince, Dominic watched Joran as he strode the length of the narrow chamber and back, restless as the wind that threw rain-like pebbles against the windowpanes. Waiting for instruction, his own mind drifted inexorably to the anxious bedchamber, where the white-faced queen lay unable to take control, as she had done every day for the past six years. Cautiously, he opened his mental channels, testing the older man's trust in him. *"My lord?"* he said, *"What do you want of me? Surely, you know I am the queen's man to command?"*

A half smile pulled at the corner of Joran's wide mouth but did nothing to lighten his expression. At the other side of the hearth, he stopped, a powerful presence full of contained power.

"But are you at my command, Dominic?" he asked, his voice as soft and deadly as an assassin's blade. "You, who would leave us and fly off in search of a traitorous Wessendean? You, whose uncle summoned the Shadow Mage from the depths of slumber and disappeared into the night? Who commands you, really? As far as I can see, you do as you want, do you not?"

He took a couple of steps closer, and Dominic took a defensive step to the door, itching to reach for his dagger. Not daring to. This was not the Joran he'd known in the past. Shorn of Petronella's softening influence, this was a cold-blooded noble nursing the sharp edge of an ice-cold rage. His mind tumbled in free fall. The ghostly female presence who appeared when Terrence called on the power of the Shadow Mage, Arabella's face as she fell to her death. His last-ditch attempt to stop the signal fire that would have brought about the end of Petronella's reign. Fury quickened within him. By the Gods, he'd succeeded. Joran stood here, king in all but name. The Queen was still the queen, injured or not. Somewhere in his hot, prideful heart, the anger of a child thwarted rose to smite him. He stretched to his full height, short though that was against Joran's intimidating stature, and raised his gaze, biting off his words.

"You should wear the ring of justice, my lord," he said. "Why do you not?"

The Prince's eyes widened fractionally in surprise and then narrowed. He didn't move, but Dominic strained every nerve not to quail. The older man's long, imposing shadow seemed to tower over him. Silence stretched between them, broken only by the crackle and hiss of wood in the grate. The rattle of the rain at the window.

"Your task is this, Sir Skinner, if you wish to prove your loyalty to me and to the Queen," Joran said, the quiet menace of his voice somehow more frightening than a full-blown bellow. "Prepare yourself and your squire to leave with the troop at dawn on the morrow. Find your uncle and bring him back to me. He has raised the spectre of evil once again in our land against the Queen's will and wish. I want him dead at my feet. And you will be the one to do it."

CHAPTER 7

T he rest of the afternoon passed in a whirlwind of activity. Pacing his chamber, Dominic loaded his old pack with the essentials, concentrating on provisions, weapons and the most sturdy and water-proof clothing he owned. Underneath the activity, anger beat alongside fear at the role Joran had appointed him to. Assassin. Murderer of his last remaining kin. His jaw clenched as he remembered the horrible sucking noise from two years previously as Terrence withdrew Dominic's dagger from his own shoulder and flung it down. He bit his lip. Joran was right. He could have killed his uncle then. Wanted to, even. What did that make him? The better man? Or a stinking coward. A traitor?

Grinding his teeth, he flung a last pair of warm woollen hose into his pack and pulled the straps tight. His old hiding place under the bed frame still existed despite the sturdy chest in his study downstairs. Dominic knelt and prised the loose flag away from its position, pulling out a stash of coin to add to his pouch. There was much more these days than his sixteen-year-old self had once rejoiced in. The pouch felt heavy in his hand, but he could be gone a long time. Better to take enough than regret it later.

The light was fading, and the temple bells pealed for supper as he quit the quiet chamber and clattered down the spiral stairs in search of food and Little Bird.

To his annoyance, Bird did not attend the main meal. Instead, her fellow nursery maid, Maria, had perched herself next to Aldric. The smell of pottage and roasted meats sent Dominic's empty stomach into a frenzy of anticipation as he entered. Gossip was in full flow as he passed the crowded benches. The two central chairs normally occupied by Petronella and Joran stood empty, their servers still standing at attention behind them despite the monarch's absence. Fortuna de Winter was nowhere to be seen. Only Guildford and some of Joran's senior household occupied the long royal table tonight. Disdaining Guildford's company, Dominic nodded a greeting at Owen Winterbane at the next table and squeezed in next to Aldric. The lad glanced up at him over his stew, some relief showing in his dark eyes at the interruption. Maria giggled at her own joke and favoured Dominic with a ready grin, lively interest sparking in her topaz eyes.

"Welladay, Sir Skinner," she said, budging up to make room for him. "Are you hobnobbing with us peasants today?"

"I was hoping to see Bird," Dominic said, reaching for a platter and some stew.

"She's on duty in the nursery tonight. Fortuna is with the Queen."

"I need to see her. Will you take a message from me?"

"Aye, of course. I'll spell her for a while after supper."

Dominic nodded. "My thanks. Tell her to meet me in the stables." He bent over his dish, spooning up thick gravy and aromatic meat like a starving man. "Have you made ready?" he asked Aldric, under the wash of conversation and the plaintive melody of the harpist strumming his instrument in a far corner.

"Kismet is waiting. I'm bringing Hamil. I've packed their feed into the supply wagon. Saw Will in the stable courtyard. He's champing at the bit. Can't believe Sir Dunforde included him. They even got him a horse."

Dominic's eyebrows raised. "He's a might young, isn't he?" he said.

Aldric laughed. "He's one of the best fighters in the army, so he says. Single-minded, that's what Sir Dunforde told him, apparently."

"Single-minded is the least of it. Blind rage is more the case, as far as I could tell." Dominic said, helping himself to bread.

"Aye. He's a fair lad to have with ye in a scrap," Aldric agreed.

"Does Bird know?" Maria interjected, a tankard halfway to her lips. "She'll take a fit if her precious lad's put into danger without her to watch over him like a mother hen."

"Bird's daft. We all know that," Aldric said. "He's joined the army. Of course, he's going to be in danger. That's the whole point."

"Who else are we taking?"

"Guildford, of course. Sir Tom. You, for your magical abilities. Dunforde's rapping out orders left, right and centre. There's a score of foot soldiers. One of Master Mortlake's best physicians, Mistress Trevis, as a healer. Gervase Hoppington is the quarter-master. He's being trusted with the rations. And me. I'm a good tracker."

"Right." Still caught up in his conversation with Joran, Dominic spooned the rest of his stew automatically, his forehead twisted into a heavy frown. Aldric carried on a half-hearted conversation with Maria. She finished her bowl and bobbed a curtsey as she left, muttering something about going to find Bird.

"You're not saying much. Are you well?" Aldric demanded as her skirts twitched through the heavy doors.

"The Prince thinks I let my uncle escape," Dominic said, wiping his gravy-stained cheeks with a napkin. He crushed the linen in his fist and turned to face the younger lad, resentment burning in his chest. "Joran thinks I'm a traitor to Petronella. He wants me to prove myself to him. I'm to kill Terrence and bring him back. Not necessarily in that order."

Aldric's dark eyes widened. His lips pursed in a mock whistle, glancing round to ensure their conversation went unheard in the din of conversation.

"Kill your own uncle? Your only living relative?" he breathed. "Petronella would never ask you to do that to prove yourself to her, no matter what she thought he'd done."

"Aye, but Petronella is not in charge right now, is she?" Dominic reached for his tankard and drew his hand back when he saw how much it shook. "After everything we went through, I can't believe Joran mistrusts me so much."

"Could you do it, do you think?" Aldric's voice hushed to the merest whisper, his steady gaze soft with concern. "If you had to?"

Dominic hardened his jaw and pulled a deep breath into his lungs. His eyes drifted to Guildford, chatting easily to his neighbour at the top table, his crystalline eyes in the candlelight so like his sister's it hurt to look at him. He huffed a short laugh. "If Guildford could get near him, he'd do it without even stopping to think," he said ruefully. But Terrence is a powerful telemantist. Guildford would never get close enough to do any actual damage."

"But you could."

"Aye. I could at least get close. We are closely matched for power these days. I rarely display it. I have no need to," Dominic admitted. "And I have telepathy, while my uncle does not. It's a slight advantage. But could I kill him?"

He used his gift to pour a goblet of strong wine, pulling it easily through the air towards him with a subtle gesture of his fingers. The alcohol bit the back of his throat as he gulped it down but did little to dispel the block of ice that had hardened somewhere near his heart and felt suspiciously like terror.

"Well, could you?" Aldric pressed, reaching for his own tankard.

Dominic swirled his wine around, inhaling the aroma of fruit and oak as he took another, more measured sip. He shrugged. "I don't know," he said.

Little Bird was already waiting, drumming her heels on a mounting block in Kismet's stable, when Dominic marched in. Lamplight illumined her cheeks, rosy with health, and picked out the gold lights in her loosely bound hair. As ever, mischief sparkled at the back of her eyes. The warm, musty air smelled of oats and dung and the heavy breath of horses. Dominic breathed it in, feeling his shoulders relax for the first time in weeks.

"It stinks in here. I should be in the nursery. What is it?" Bird whispered, clutching the folds of her serviceable cloak more securely against her slender form. "Fortuna will be furious if she finds me gone. She's worried sick about the Queen."

By way of mollification, Dominic held out a sweetmeat, purloined from the kitchen on his way through to the service yards. Bird glared at him but took it, anyway. "Well, go on," she said through a mouthful of marchpane.

"I wanted to ask you about that night," Dominic began, unsure quite where to start. The mischief died in Little Bird's eyes. She jumped from the mounting block and dashed her hand across her mouth, leaving a trail of crumbs and sugar.

"I don't want to talk about it," she said, her navy eyes brimming with tears. "I can't. Don't make me." She turned on her heel and headed for the door, intent on flight. Dominic's heart went out to her.

"I understand, Bird," he said softly. "I know how much you miss Meridan."

"You can't," Bird said flatly, her back to him. "That bastard Pieter, he murdered her. Stabbed her in the back. He's a disgusting, snivelling coward. I hate him. Hate him." She shuddered, rocking herself in agitation, her voice squeezed into the moist air as if she couldn't find breath enough for the words.

"Will killed him for you, Bird," Dominic said, taking a cautious step forward, gentle as he was when coaxing a young falcon to his fist.

"But Will's going with you, isn't he? He sent a message. What if he dies, Dominic? What will I do?"

She turned to face him, her delicate face as woebegone as a snowdrop crushed under the heel of a careless boot.

"I couldn't bear to lose him. To lose any of you. Please don't go, Dominic. Please. I'm scared."

"Oh, Bird." He took the two remaining strides to her and enclosed her in the warmth of his arms. She resisted only for a second before sobs engulfed her. He stood where he was, rocking her gently, his cheek pressed against the top of her head. Her hair smelled of almonds and milk.

"Will has to come. He's a soldier, but I'll try to look after him for you, I promise," he said when the first storm of weeping had passed, and Bird was still against his chest. "Come and sit down." He led her gently to a pile of straw and stretched out along it, a twisted smile across his lips.

"I used to sleep in here, did you know that?" he commented as she shuffled into the straw alongside him, staring up at the cobwebbed rafters above their heads.

"Really, did you?" She wiped her nose with her sleeve.

"Aye, right up 'til Queen Petronella escaped the castle on her own adventure. I helped her. Drove her out of the castle hidden in a cart alongside a dead horse with Princess Alice. I was only a bit older than you."

"I didn't know that. I thought you were rich when I first met you. What with the tannery and everything."

Dominic chuckled. "The tannery comes from my father. I've been lucky," he explained, "but nothing comes easy, Bird. Not for anyone.

We all fought battles that night. You did, too. Remember rolling across the ground with Rosa, like a pair of fighting cats?"

A half smile crept across Bird's mouth as she remembered before grief shut it down again. "But Meridan," she said.

Dominic rolled to face her. "Meridan was a soldier that night. The bravest protector. She looked after all of us, even me," he said. "And she would want you to be brave now. For all of us. Can you do that? It's important." The straw rustled as Bird rolled her face to look at him, the sheen of recently shed tears glazing her cheeks in the lantern light. "I'll try," she whispered.

"Well then. 'Tis about that woman we both saw. The one who looked like the Queen."

Little Bird's eyes narrowed. "She was smiling. Glad to hurt the Grayling. I could see it in her face," she said.

"Hmm," Dominic grunted, churning through his tangled impressions. "Do you think she was there? In the chamber with us?" he asked. "I couldn't work it out."

Bird frowned. "Me neither. I thought she was a ghost. Your uncle didn't even know she was there. Just me and you, I think."

"Both of us telepaths," Dominic murmured. "But was she a ghost? What if she's real? Who is she? What does she want?"

Bird shrugged and sat up. "I don't know, but that's what I saw. I think she made your uncle do those things, but I don't think he knew." Her navy gaze bored into his as her chilled, nail-bitten fingers grasped for his collar. "You must be very careful, Dominic. Promise me you'll look after Will."

He put his hands over hers, warming them with his own. "I told you I would, didn't I?" he reminded her. She pulled away and busied herself brushing straw from her cloak. "Help me," she commanded as she stood, "I can't go back to the nursery looking like I've had a tryst in a haystack."

Biting his lip on a smile, Dominic used his gift to banish all signs of the stable, spinning Bird about in the air and harnessing a breeze to blow the dust away. Unusually, Bird let him, trusting him completely to keep her balanced as her feet left the ground.

"You made me fly!" she said, her small face lit with delight when he turned her in a final, careful circle, inspecting her clothing for evidence. "I didn't know you could do that!"

Dominic returned her smile and nodded to the door. "Go on, Bird, it's getting late," he said. "Remember to keep up with your studies while we are gone. Especially the telepathy. Keep your channels open for me so I can tell you what's going on. Let me know how the Queen is."

She jerked her head in response, her eyes solemn. "Good fortune, Dominic," she said. "Mage go with ye."

Brow creased in thought, he kept an eye on her as she vanished into the night, swallowed by shadows. In the distance, somewhere on the path that led north, an owl hooted, lonely and full of portent. Power surged at his fingertips as he raised his hand in the same direction, sending a message across the ether into the night dark mountains and whatever evil force dwelled within them.

"Whoever you are, know that I will find you," he whispered in his mind. *"And if you've hurt Felicia, Gods help you when I do."*

CHAPTER 8

Dawn had barely lightened the edge of the eastern ranges when the troop gathered in the northern courtyard the next morning. Rushlights and torches flared at intervals around the small courtyard walls. Breath clouding the air, the horse's hooves rang on the cobbles. Bits jingled as they tossed their heads, scenting adventure. The foot soldiers mustered on either side of the heavy castle gates, muttering grumpily to each other, their pale, unshaven faces still creased with sleep. A doubled guard patrolled the battlements above their heads, looking north, their broad-shouldered silhouettes deep shadows against the still-dark sky. A candle or two illuminated some windows in the castle, but most of the inhabitants slumbered on, unaware of or ignoring the bustle below them.

Dominic leapt atop Kismet's broad back and turned her in a circle, surveying the activity with a grim smile spreading across his face. He'd donned half armour for the journey. His sword hung at his side, the enchanted dagger beside it, and his old dagger was handy inside his boot. His saddlebags contained dry clothing, a warm blanket, and supplies for the road. Aldric clattered from the stable yard on his own gelding, rolling easily with his gait, his dark face alight with anticipation. He carried a bow across his shoulders and was leading another placid gelding behind him. "Guildford's coming," he said as he reigned in at Dominic's side. "The idiot insisted on wearing a full suit of armour. Sir Dunforde ordered him to remove it."

Dominic rolled his eyes, noting the preparations with interest. As a puny twelve-year-old, he'd been a simple soldier, tolerated in the lowest ranks of the infantry for his known skill with horses. No-one had asked him to join the army. But at the time, it had seemed imperative to do so, not least because the arm was receiving most of what remained of Epera's depleted food stock. But mostly, it was because he was sure Petronella needed him. He turned his head with the thought of her, but the Queen's wing was far away on the other side of the castle, facing the sunlit south. There had been no word of her progress. Her mental channels were closed and empty, as they had been since her accident.

A creak of heavy wheels heralded the approach of two large supply wagons, each pulled by a brace of sturdy dray horses. Thomas Buttledon followed behind, a night's worth of stubble still lining his jaw, brushing off the clinging attentions of his current paramour, Geraldine de Grym.

Dominic exchanged a telling glance with Aldric as Tom drew nearer, irritation plastered across his normally good-humoured features. "Go back to bed, Geraldine. I must leave," he said.

"I don't see why," Geraldine returned, grabbing hold of his elbow. "What will I do while you're gone?"

"My dear, you will fill your bed with someone else," Tom said, removing her pale hand from his serge sleeve with some determination. "Now go on, you'll catch your death out here in the chill." He gave her a little push to get her feet moving and swung himself into the saddle of the mount a sleepy-eyed stable boy brought to him. Eyes sparking with covert interest as Geraldine undulated sulkily away, the foot soldiers levered themselves to reluctant attention as Sir Dunforde arrived through a low archway that led to the barracks. He steered young Will Dunn before him, yellow teeth bared with the effort to keep the lad facing in the right direction. Will's feet dragged, his head constantly turning back to the castle, dark eyes determined in his square-jawed face. "You said you'd let me say goodbye to her," he muttered, trying to detach his sleeve from Sir Dunforde's iron grip.

"Ye're a soldier now, lad," the old soldier grunted. "If you want to be a good one, you'll do as you're told."

Will wrenched his arm free, dodging the mild cuff Dunforde aimed at his head. "Bird!" he yelled, his voice echoing from the damp stone walls loud enough to raise the dead.

"By the Gods, he'll wake the entire castle!" Aldric shoved both sets of reins into Dominic's hands and slid from his mount. "Will. Will!" he said, closing the gap between them.

"Bird, are you awake?" Dominic sent his mind to the south wing, where Bird slept in the narrow chamber she shared with Maria. He rolled his eyes when the girl herself appeared at a small side door that led into one of the many storerooms around the service courtyard. Her hair stood on end, smooth cheeks smeared with a mixture of dust and tears. Clutching her cloak around her against the bite in the air, she sprinted across the cold cobbles and launched herself at Will. Aldric shook his head and returned to his horse.

"Should have guessed," he said, vaulting lightly from the ground to Hamil's back. "Looks like she's been in that storeroom all night. She would never stay abed and miss him going."

Even grim Sir Dunforde looked somewhat abashed as the two youngsters clung together for a telling second, Will's rough hair dark against Bird's blonde curls. He cleared his throat and marched off to bully the foot soldiers instead.

"How old is Will, again?" Dominic asked, half turned away from the pair as they embraced.

"Thirteen," Aldric said. "Old enough to bear arms on the queen's behalf. He wants to come." They watched out of the corners of their eyes as the farewell continued with much sniffling on Bird's part and more gesticulating on Will's. His fellow soldiers looked on with scant interest, fond farewells being a thing of the past for most of them.

Thomas joined them, glancing backwards over his shoulder. Geraldine put her nose in the air and threw him one last glare as she disappeared into the comfort of the castle. "Welladay," he said ruefully, scratching his stubbled jaw. "She'll be courting Jack Tressel before the cock crows. You just wait and see."

Dominic laughed. "Plenty more flowers in the meadows for you to pluck, Tom. Where's your squire?"

Thomas grimaced. "Won't come. Guess who I've got instead?"

"Not your brother?" Dominic said as Guildford strode into the courtyard with all the swagger of a seasoned warrior, trailed by both Lionel Brearley and Jared.

Thomas heaved a sigh that raised his shoulders to his ears. "Aye. Found out Guildford was part of the troop and harassed Sir Dunforde until he gave in. He's a lazy bastard, too. Such larks." His tone left little doubt that Jared's presence was unwanted. "Hie," he shouted, waving his hand to get his younger brother's attention. "You are holding us up. Grab your horse, and let's get going."

Sir Dunforde mounted his huge grey stallion and swung around in an irritated circle. "About time, Wessendean," he barked, his stentorian tones ringing across the courtyard. "Will. Mount up. Young lady, go back to bed. The time for goodbye is over. The sun is up. We must be away."

Will prised Little Bird's fingers from his cloak and tugged her hood up. "Go on, Bird," he said roughly. "I must go now."

The young girl's jaw stiffened. She shot Dominic a hot blue glare, almost as if she blamed him for the entire affair and took a reluctant step back. Will straightened his tunic and raised narrowed brown eyes at the mounted knights towering above him. "What?" he said.

Dominic concealed his grin with difficulty, and Aldric held out the reins of the gentle gelding he'd picked out for the younger boy. "Here you go," he said cheerfully.

Will stared suspiciously at the placid Hartley, who turned his chestnut head and gave the lad a nudge. Will's face broke into an unwilling smile. "I can't ride," he informed the company at large.

"You'll learn," Dominic said. "Come on, get up."

"If he falls off, I'll have your hide, Dominic Skinner." Bird's shrill voice pierced the gloom like a knife, raising a chuckle from the soldiers. Will blushed and grabbed a handful of mane.

"Use the mounting block," Aldric said, nodding to the bench by the courtyard well.

Settling themselves, they waited, some more patiently than others, as Will clambered gracelessly aloft, clutching the pommel of his saddle with whitened knuckles.

"Finally," Sir Dunforde said as they arranged themselves in formation, knights at the front, soldiers in the middle, and the heavy supply wagons following behind. He nodded to the sentries at the gates, and they waited, anticipation rising for the journey as the portcullis rattled upwards.

A chill breeze sifted through the open gates, stirring the hair on Dominic's head. It brought with it the scent of autumn leaves and the first hint of winter. Kismet snorted, dancing sideways, eager to be on her way.

At the head of the troop, Sir Dunforde raised his burly arm, and the column jolted into action. Despite his misgivings, Dominic exchanged a grin with Aldric as they clattered through the dark archway of the north gate and gained the narrow road that led through the pass into the foothills. A thin line of daylight brightened the jagged peaks to their right, touching the peaks with hints of rose and gold. The soaring cry of the castle starlings accompanied the jingle of bits, the creaking of the cartwheels, and the soft whistle of a soldier down the line somewhere as he started the chorus of "Where the wild winds blow."

Rolling easily with Kismet's flowing stride, they were gaining the first slope to the pass when a tingle of telepathy tugged Dominic's gaze backwards to the castle. It sprawled against the mountainous backdrop, heavy as a fist, crowned with Petronella's blue and grey pennants. His eyes lingered on the battlements and lodged on the tallest figure standing there, watching their onward progress. Joran. Hands on his hips, cloak billowing in the wind.

The Prince's voice was caustic as lye as it echoed inside his head. *"Remember your duty,"* he warned.

Swallowing heavily against a flare of resentment, Dominic's hands tightened on Kismet's reins. He jerked his head around, eyes narrowed, and tightened his heels against her smooth bay flank. She trotted on, obedient to his wishes, unaware of the rebellion churning like acid in her rider's breast.

CHAPTER 9

F ive days later, the troop had settled into a semblance of army routine. Inns and other lodging in the scattered villages dotting the foothills afforded rough beds for the knights and even rougher shelter for the infantry. The group grew used to Master Gannymead's low-voiced swearing as he coaxed his dray horses to magnificent efforts hoisting their supplies over the rough terrain. The frustrated musician amongst the infantry turned out to be a tow-headed youth called Clem, whose brother was one of Petronella's favourite minstrels. His melodic voice added a touch of gaiety to the long marches. The soldiers accompanied him tunelessly as they tramped along the rough road that led to the Iron Mountains. Carts laden with ore rumbled past them at regular intervals, along with many more filled with half-made tools and weaponry, bound for Blade, where master craftsmen and women took over to bang them into shape.

True to his mission, Sir Dunforde questioned many a carter, quizzing them on where they had been, what they had seen. But the carters worked in relays, each traversing a narrow section of road between villages a mere twenty miles from their homes, and those this far south had little to report about events further north. Scowling, Sir Dunforde muttered to himself under his bearded cheeks, his weathered gaze scanning the hillsides, his hand ever clutched around his sword against imminent attack.

"By the Gods," Guildford said on the morning of the sixth day, with the sun hot overhead in the clear autumn sky and the horses plodding up a steep rise into the hills towards a tiny hamlet where they would stop that evening. "Look at the man. His hand never leaves his steel. What does he think will attack us way out here? Death by eagle, perhaps?" He tipped his head back, golden hair rich and molten, pretending to scan the sky. Jared mirrored his movement and tittered his agreement.

Deep in thought, Dominic barely heard them. He'd tuned out Guildford and his inanities long ago. Eyes half closed, almost stupefied by boredom and heat, he took a swig of water from the flask at his waist, offering it automatically to Aldric. The infantry straggled behind them, the slope steep enough to prevent even young Clem from attempting a tune. Still awkward on his mount, Will rode behind, cursing his saddle soreness and complaining loudly to Tom Buttledon, who was advising him on the best way to overcome it. In the near distance, yet another carter approached, his conveyance cresting the hilltop and jolting slowly in their direction. Trees stretched away from the road in every direction, tightly packed, a virgin forest. Cool and shaded.

Stomach grumbling, Dominic cast a yearning glance towards it, but Sir Dunforde had better use for him.

"Find out if that man has heard anything," Dunforde ordered, fixing him with a fierce and battle-hardened eye that missed nothing and had certainly noted that Dominic was almost asleep in his saddle.

Glad of something to do, Dominic and Aldric trotted forward. Ears pricked, Kismet stretched out, enjoying the opportunity to lengthen her stride. Behind them, their leader called a halt, and the weary troop juddered to a standstill, taking the chance for a drink and a small snatch of food from their pouches and pockets, crowding under the slim shade afforded by the trees.

"Ho!" Dominic rode with one hand on his sword, but closing the gap, he could see nothing in the carter's demeanour to cause alarm. Two sturdy oxen pulled his cart steadily over the rutted road, heads down, snorting slightly in the unseasonal heat. The carter nodded to them shortly but did not stop.

"Hold, in the Queen's name," Dominic said, drawing Kismet up in front of the oxen and forcing the man to halt or run him down.

Aldric took up a position behind him and casually unslung his bow. The man dropped the reins of his cart into his lap and slammed on the brake. He glared at them, black eyes glowering from under his hood. "Well, and what do you want?" he grunted. "I'm late getting this to Flaxby."

"A moment of your time, no more," Dominic said. "We are seeking news of a raid out of the Iron Mountains in the hamlet of Hartford .Have you heard of it?"

The man's eyes flared at the question. He shifted his weight in his seat and glared at them again. "And who wants to know?"

Dominic held his stare and fingered the hilt of his dagger. "I do. Sir Dominic Skinner, knight and queen's man." He tapped his breastplate,upon which Petronella's house colours and badge gleamed in the sunlight.

"That supposed to impress me?" the man demanded, hawking a wodge of tar-coloured phlegm into the dust at Kismet's hooves.

Eyes narrowing, Dominic's fingers tightened on his dagger. He pressed Kismet closer. "What are you carrying?"

"What I always carry. Ore."

"Mind if we look?"

The carter snorted. "Don't have much choice, do I, seeing's how you brought an army with you," he said. "What you lot doing, running about these parts?"

Dominic ignored the question and gestured to Aldric, who shouldered his bow and twitched the tarp from the wagon bed. The carter was at least true to his word. Sack after sack of iron ore filled the wagon to bursting. "See," the man said as Aldric replaced the tattered covering. "I'm just doing my job, like any other good Citizen." He pushed back his hood, spat into the dust once more, and then convulsed into a fit of violent coughing. Black spittle flew from his mouth to splatter the dusty road.

"You have yet to answer my question," Dominic said as the man regained some composure, eyes red-rimmed and streaming. "The raid in Hartford. I perceive you know of it. What can you tell me?"

Resentment washed over the carter's gaunt features. Up close, lines of dirt pressed deep into the skin of his cheeks and forehead. Shadows crowded the hollow spaces under his fierce black eyes; perspiration beaded his brow.

"We don't talk of it," he said as the silence between them lengthened, and Dominic continued to wait, his steady gaze fixed on the older man with hawk-like intensity.

"Why not?" he asked, genuinely curious. In a world where gossip spread on the wind faster than it left people's lips, to learn some people did not discuss everything that happened was a complete novelty to him.

The man's eyes drifted from his to his lap. He fidgeted with the reins, sliding them over his hands, tying them in loose knots and then undoing them. A frown crossed Dominic's forehead. He glanced at Aldric, who raised a dark eyebrow and gave a shrug of one shoulder.

"Well?" Dominic prompted. Perspiration dripped down his neck to dampen his collar. He dropped Kismet's reins and pressed a hand against his empty stomach to prevent its gurgle. "I'm still here."

"Welladay, so you are," the carter agreed, favouring Dominic with a rictus grin that bared black stained teeth. "And so am I, and so are we all. Can't sit about, must be off." He tightened his hands on the supple leather and clicked at the two oxen, flicking their backs with a swish of his whip. The oxen removed their heads from the cropped turf at the roadside and glared at the two horsemen with small, empty eyes. The carter released the brake on his cart. "You'll move on now," he advised, "if you know what's good for ye."

Startled at the man's sudden change in mood, Dominic gave up fingering his dagger and drew it from its sheath. Sunlight danced off the blade, the runes a shifting symphony of blue light. He frowned as he felt it vibrate in his grip. The carter's dark eyes locked on it, mesmerised. "Where did you get that?" he demanded.

Dominic's lips thinned in a mutinous line. "I'm the one asking the questions," he said, guiding Kismet closer with a subtle squeeze of his knees and pulling his sword from its scabbard. "In the Queen's name, you will tell me what you know."

He advanced until the point of both blades contacted the man's scrawny chest. Up close, the carter's breath was foul. As acrid and black as the spittle that peppered the road. "You have little time left," Dominic said, lacing each syllable with as much menace as he could muster. "We are on a mission from Prince Joran and the Queen. Tell us what you know or suffer the penalty."

The carter surveyed him from a hand's span away, broad shoulders shaking. "You..." he said, locking both his hands around his own throat. He coughed again. A hacking, awful sound dredged from the depths of his chest and then he gasped, choking on the vile ichor erupting from his lungs. "You won't beat her. You won't."

"Won't beat who? Tell me!" The image of Felicia rose inexorably before Dominic's mind's eye. Transfixed at the point of his blade, the carter choked with each successive, heaving breath. The heavy black substance gushing from him was changing in front of Dominic's horrified gaze. Not the black ink of dried blood now, but fresh, crimson. Almost as if his blade had already pierced the man's heart. Swallowing bile, he reined back, aware of Aldric's appalled gasp from behind him.

"Dom, he's dying!"

"I didn't touch him!"

"We must get help." Aldric turned, craning back at the distant troop, where Mistress Trevis, the medic, travelled alongside the wagon master. He raised his arm to signal, but the troop had deserted the hot road in favour of the trees. No-one was watching.

Hands shaking, Dominic sheathed both weapons and leaned forward, grimacing with disgust as the man's blood flowed over his fingers. A river of vermillion, rank with disease.

"By the Gods," he muttered, struggling to support the carter's weight from where he sat on Kismet's back. The horse snorted, ears flattening, and kicked out with a hind leg.

The older man's remaining lifeblood left him in a rush, pooling at his feet and dripping through the roughly nailed planks to the dusty ground. Eyes dimming, his stubby hand closed on Dominic's sleeve. "That blade..." he whispered, harsh with regret and bitter memory. "I remember that blade."

Much later, crowded round a sulky fireplace in a flea-bitten tavern, the knights hugged their tankards, discussing the turn of events in low voices.

The hamlet of Bearbank had little to offer in the way of comfort. The tavern was a tumbledown building, more shed than an inn. A wiry fellow with a stained tunic and a greying beard did duty as an innkeeper. The serving maid, well-scrubbed and comely in her patched dress, moved slowly amongst the soldiers, dodging their advances with practised ease. Tom and Guildford followed her progress with interest over the rim of their cups. Where its usual clients had fled with the noisy arrival of the queen's troop, Dominic could not guess. At present, they had the place to themselves. Clem,already lubricated with the ale pressed upon him by his weary fellows, had begun a lively tune, accompanied by much banging of pewter and stamping of feet on the greasy flags.

"Could it have been lung rot?" Tom said, his green eyes locked on the swing of the tavern maid's hips.

"That's what the miners get," Sir Dunforde said grimly. "Probably accounts for it. I suppose we'll never know."

Stomach churning on an uneasy meal of greasy stew, Dominic glanced at his hands. He'd dunked them into the stream bordering the road as soon as they reconvened with the troop, but the carter's blood still rimmed his fingernails. Remembering the gush of crimson and the disgusting smell that accompanied it, Dominic's gaze drifted to Will. On the edge of the group, the butt of teasing by the older men, Will stared miserably into his drink, his back pressed hard against the rough wall. He'd cast his accounts at the sight of the carter's blood-stained corpse, loaded haphazardly atop his own wagon and brought to Bear-bank for burial. Dominic could only guess at the memories it stirred. His own were no less bitter.

"Will!" Dominic gestured to him through the smoke of Sir Dunforde's evil-smelling pipe. "Join us."

The young recruit cast a wary glance at his colleagues, clustered around the few knocked-together tables, their faces flushed with good cheer, exchanging banter and jokes, many of them aimed in his direction. His lips screwed together as he levered himself from the wall and limped across to the fireplace. Sprawled in front of the fire, Guildford smirked at him and moved his enormous feet enough for Will to squeeze past.

"What's ado?" he asked lazily, taking a sip of the fine wine he'd ordered Lionel to produce from his own stash in the first supply wagon. The subtle aroma of Blue Oceanis tickled Dominic's nostrils. Guildford smirked at him over the rim, taunting him with the luxurious brew before setting his sights back on Will. "Some soldier. Spewing up at the sight of blood."

Tongue-tied in front of the young princeling, Will hunched his shoulders and squashed himself onto a splintered bench next to Aldric. "Nothing's ado, my lord," he said, his voice already low and rich despite his relative youth, but his hands trembled where he had them twisted in his lap.

Dominic glared at Guildford before tilting his head towards the two younger men.

"Perhaps it's time we sought some fresh air. A stroll might clear our heads," he suggested, standing up. Exchanging glances, Aldric and Will followed him as he strode to the door, passing Jared and Lionel, who had snared a small table on the other side of the room and were playing cards with fevered intensity. They didn't look up.

Outside, the tiny village sprawled haphazardly around the single well. Apart from the sign of the Bear and its warren of sheds, stables, and outbuildings, it contained little beyond a few tattered market stalls, closed for the night, a blacksmith, and a shrine to the Mage. The elegant stone building looked well-tended. Unusually so, amid the general wear and tear displayed by the other buildings. The still evening air was crisp as the bite of a tart apple rimmed with frost. It tingled against Dominic's magical senses. Above them, stars cloaked the night sky in a haze of silver spangles. The pregnant harvest moon hung belly-full over the mountain tops. From somewhere nearby, a stream rushed on its way to join the Cryfell. An owl hooted, and Dominic's shoulders stiffened, aware of the dagger at his hip as it vibrated in response. He shivered, covering the movement under the guise of pulling his cloak further around him. His right hand closed on his sword of its own accord.

Their footsteps crunched on the dirt road as they strolled away from the busy tavern, their combined breath rising in the night air.

Aldric loped at Dominic's right-hand side, head up, his dark eyes taking everything in, snuffling the air like a foxhound. Will moped on his left, head down, kicking random stones from his path with increasing irritation. At the brook, they crossed a moss-covered wooden bridge and took a path towards the forest.

"How are you faring, Will?" Dominic asked as the lad pulled his sword and swiped moodily at the nearest vegetation.

Will shrugged. "It's alright. Mostly. Better than stealing for a living."

"What happened this afternoon..." Dominic bit his lip, tiptoeing carefully over his words. "That must have been a shock, I suppose?"

Another shrug. "'T'weren't the blood, if that's what you think," he said scornfully. "I've seen enough of that."

"What then?"

Will took another savage swing at the bushes. "The suddenness," he said after a moment. "Like one second you can be here, the next..." he revolved his sword and hacked at a bramble. The vibrant strand tumbled to the dark earth. "Gone, like that. Like Meridan. No warning. No time to prepare or say goodbye."

Dominic nodded, "Aye. Death can outrun all of us, that's true," he said. "That's why it's important to enjoy your life, don't you think? Just as it is, warts and all."

A crooked grin crept across Will's freckled face. "Plenty of warts," he said. "Mainly horse shaped."

"Welladay, then," Dominic said, "Let's consider ourselves more blessed than cursed. What say you?"

"Seconded," Aldric said, clapping Will on the shoulder.

"Thirded, I suppose," Will muttered, sheathing his sword as they passed under the boughs of a huge old oak and into the depths of the wood.

Dominic blinked in the sudden darkness, eyes taking a second to adjust. The skin between his shoulder blades prickled with tension, and he turned his head, aware they were being watched. He shrugged the thought away. Sir Dunforde had posted sentries, as he did at every stop. They would announce themselves soon. The frost-bitten leaves shuffled in shallow piles under their feet as they marched onward down the well-trodden path. He imagined it was a forager or a hunter's trail. Tense at his side, Aldric swung his bow from his shoulders and loaded an arrow. "There's someone following us," the young man whispered.

"Aye." They drew to a halt, looking around. Far to the left, the brush rustled. Will drew his own sword. "What's that?" he asked. "Too big to be a fox."

Country-bred Aldric raised his bow. "Deer, boar, or bear," he said. "Only one of those is good news."

"Where are the sentries?" Will said. "Dunforde put Arnold and Merriman on the first watch."

Tense as bowstrings, they swivelled on their feet as the bushes rustled again, closer this time. An earthy, musky smell drifted towards them, born on the whisper of a breeze that sprang up amongst the trees. Part mud, part wet leaves. Aldric's arrow wobbled a little. "Boar," he choked out. "We should probably go back."

Dominic's sword rang as it left the sheathe. He stood poised, ready to fight if he had to, telekinesis already tingling in his left hand. "Get behind me, Will," he muttered.

"I've never seen a boar, except at a distance, on a platter with an apple in its mouth." Will rejoined stoutly, squaring his shoulders.

Aware Will needed to reclaim his dignity, Dominic forbore to argue with him. As one, the three waited for the boar, their breath wreathing in mad circles around their heads.

The rustling stopped, dying away.

"Where is it? Has it gone?" Will murmured.

"Ssh," Dominic warned, straining his senses in the darkness. He could hear nothing apart from the distant trickle of the brook and the sigh of the dry leaves overhead. Around them, the forest lay totally still.

The sudden pounding of two pairs of feet approaching at a run through the undergrowth on both sides of the path had them spinning on their heels, following the progress of two dark shapes just visible in the gloom. Barely seen, their panicked panting accompanied the snap of breaking twigs and the dank, fertile smell of freshly turned leaves as they fled for the village.

Dominic swallowed, turning to the massed greenery, ready to face a marauding beast.

"So much for the sentries," he muttered, glancing sideways to Aldric, who was squinting into the Stygian depths of the dense woodland with a furrowed brow.

"That makes little sense..." the young man said, his shoulders trembling with the effort of keeping his bow tight on the string. "If I was an angry boar, I'd be chasing them."

A high-pitched scream of terror shot ice in frigid rivulets across Dominic's senses. All his magical channels open and alert, he sprinted into the dark, leaving the narrow path for the closely packed undergrowth. Fighting his way into the unknown, he tripped and stumbled on unseen brambles and knotted roots, one hand raised to protect his face from the twigs and branches that conspired to block his way. With Aldric and Will just a footbeat behind, he hurried onwards as a woman's voice shattered the silence once more.

"Get away from me, you brute!"

Bursting from a tangle of vegetation, Dominic ground to a halt at the edge of a small clearing. The woman lay in a puddle of mud, one leg tangled in a complicated mess of stones and branches, propped uncomfortably against a rotting log. She'd wrested a branch from the ground, but the boar lingered, half in shadow on the other side of the clearing, snapping its jaws, its head lowered, and furious. It stamped its feet and crouched back, taking weight onto its haunches, ready to race forward and claim a kill.

The woman's head turned, her face a pale oval in the moonlight, her hair a spill of dark blonde in the moonlight. Dominic blinked, struggling to make out her features. "Felicia?" he breathed, taking a quick step towards her.

The boar turned its head, long, sharp tusks lowered, its snout glistening with moisture and dirt. "Don't move, Dom," Aldric said. "I've got it."

He took his shot, his arrow lancing through the space to hit its target. The enormous pig uttered a shrill screech of pain and vanished into the trees. Sheathing his sword, Dominic raced towards the fallen log, his heart in his mouth, Felicia's precious name on his lips.

He collapsed to his knees in the mud, folding back her hair with a shaky hand, cursing the darkness that played tricks on his eyes. "Are you well? Tell me!" he breathed. He took hold of the woman's hand, wondering at its unexpected roughness, and the woman tipped her head to smile her thanks.

His overfull heart plummeted to his boots as the clouds parted and the moon gathered strength to light the woman's face. Long, dark blonde hair she had in abundance, but her eyes were brown as acorns, her figure lusher than Felicia's slender form. A full, soft bosom peeked coyly from the loosely tied laces at the neck of her homespun gown. She stretched out her hand, her grip powerful in his. A servant or artisan, then.

"I give you my thanks, good sirs," she said, her accent far from Felicia's high-born tones. "You have saved my life."

CHAPTER 10

S wallowing down his abject disappointment, Dominic aided the woman to her feet. She clung to him briefly as she wobbled, twisting to extract her ankle from the tangle of fallen branches and briars that ensnared it. He was aware of the subtle press of her bosom against his tunic, the clutch of her fingers. Awkwardly, he waited as she regained her composure, pushing back the whirlwind of dark blonde hair that cascaded around her shoulders into her hood. In the moonlight, her face was attractive. Somewhat sharp-featured but with fine brown eyes, fringed with dark lashes. A full, pink mouth. Will removed himself to a respectful distance, fingering his army-issue sword. Aldric surveyed her with one dark eyebrow raised and then turned on his heel to the edge of the clearing, where the boar had disappeared. "Help me, Will?" he requested as he covered the space. "If I killed it, we could gift it to the innkeeper. It might help pay our tab."

Dominic nodded his approval at the plan and turned his attention back to the woman, sliding his arm from her grasp.

"Are you well, mistress?" he asked. "What are you doing out here alone? How are you called?"

Brushing mud from her cloak, she glanced up at him from under her long eyelashes. "Celia is my name, sir. I was hoping to reach Bear-bank and the main road before nightfall, but I got lost in the forest.

And like an idiot, I turned my ankle. Am I close?" Her voice was soft and lilting, a country accent, gentle on his ears.

"Aye, to be sure, 'tis just a step away," Dominic assured her. "We will escort you to the inn. You are safe now."

"I thought the boar would attack." Celia pulled her cloak closer around her shapely form and shivered. "'Tis a good thing you were nearby."

"Aye, to be sure," Dominic repeated, glancing across the clearing to where Aldric had followed the boar into the depths. "Can you walk? Try your ankle."

He watched as she took a couple of limping paces forward. "It's fine," she said, setting her jaw. "Just a twist, that is all. You don't have to walk with me. I can manage."

"Nay, we're going back to the inn. Our healer, Mistress Trevis, will check your ankle for you."

She surveyed him in the moonlight, taking in the gleaming breastplate and Petronella's standard. "You're with the army, then?"

He favoured her with a quick bow. "Sir Dominic Skinner," he said. "Of the Queen's Guard."

"The Queen?" her eyes rounded. "What business do you have up here?"

"The Queen's, of course," Dominic said lightly. A light frown crossed his forehead. In the distance, the familiar timbre of Aldric and Will arguing drifted out of the woods.

"You heard it squeal. You know I hit it!" Aldric said.

"Well, where is it, then? Thought you were a tracker?"

"By the Gods," Dominic muttered. He raised his voice. "Have you done, you two? There's a woman here who needs a warm fire and something to drink."

Aldric strode across the clearing, fingering his bow, his even-featured face dark with irritation. Will limped lopsidedly in his wake, rubbing his thighs. Dominic's lips twitched. "You should get Mistress Trevis to give you a rubdown," he said. "Iron some of those kinks out."

Will glowered. "You're as bad as Sir Tom," he growled. "If I never have to get on the back of a horse again, it will be too soon."

"You'll get used to it. A few more days, and you'll be as good as the rest of us," Dominic assured him. "Come. Early start tomorrow."

"Where are you bound?" Celia asked, bending down with some difficulty and retrieving a sturdy branch to aid her progress.

Dominic could find no reason not to share the information. "Further north, to Falconridge."

A few steps further along, Celia turned to stare at him, her eyes shining in the moonlight penetrating the thick canopy.

"Falconridge, truly?" she breathed. "I was going to hitch a ride with a carter. That's where I'm bound. They're expecting me."

"Well then, you can probably ride in the supply wagon with Mistress Trevis," Dominic said. "But you'll have to ask Sir Dunforde. 'Tis not up to me."

He offered his elbow again as they started back through the forest, carefully keeping her away from his body. The enchanted blade trembled against his hip. Subtle but continual, like the hum of a bee against a closed window. Her scent tickled his nose. An enticing combination of hay and meadows with a light, salty undertone. Beneath his hose, his member twitched to life. It seemed a long time ago since he'd last lain with a woman. Gritting his teeth, he quickened his pace and wrested his elbow from her grasp. Glancing sideways, he caught the glimpse of a smile hastily masked as she dropped her head to the rutted ground. His jaw tightened as he glared ahead where the village met the road, eyes piercing the gloom for the flare of torchlight that marked the entrance to the Bear. He'd yet to see his chamber there, but suddenly, a night in the stable, surrounded by the Queen's guard, felt like the better idea.

CHAPTER 11

After the haunting quiet of the moonlit road, the level of rowdiness at the Bear hit him like a fist between the eyes as they entered. Dominic blinked hard against the pipe smoke. The tang of hops competed with the welcome aroma of roasting meat and rose to meet them in a wave. Clem had found an old lute abandoned in a corner. Some of its strings were missing, but he was doing the best he could, leading the drunken soldiers in a round of "Where the Robin Roves"—a lewd ditty, belying its seemingly innocent name.

Celia's eyes sparked in the dim lamplight. She dropped her cloak from her shoulders, revealing the creamy skin beneath. Dominic rolled his eyes as both Tom and Guildford took one look and started forward like rutting hounds after a bitch. Aldric stood rooted to the spot, jaw clenched, as Guildford's long legs beat Tom to the prize. The young man towered over her like a giant and brushed a frond of greenery from her head. "Who is this winsome stranger with a garland in her hair?" he said. "Tell me all, fair maiden."

"By the Gods, Guildford, give it a rest." Tom strode forward, elbowing him out of the way. "Sir Tom Buttledon, at your service," he said.

Celia blushed prettily and bobbed a curtsey. Aldric growled his displeasure at the posturing and grabbed a plate of roasted meat.

"What's to do?" Dominic said, Aldric's glare fixed on the flirtatious tableau spread out before them.

"She shouldn't be here," he grunted in response, swallowing his mouthful with some difficulty. He wiped his full lips on his sleeve. "We should have left her."

Sir Dunforde peered at Dominic from under his brows and gestured him over. "What's this?" he demanded, wiping froth from his upper lip and jerking his thumb at the distracting newcomer.

"Found her in the forest. Saved her from a boar," Dominic explained, watching out of the corner of his eye as Guildford and Tom argued over which of them would buy her the first drink. Celia tossed her head and laughed. The sound slid over his skin like rich silk. She appeared to have forgotten about her twisted ankle. "She says she's on the way to Falconridge to work, but got lost in the dark."

Dunforde grunted and waved him to the seat recently vacated by Guildford. "She did, did she?" he said. "And what do you make of that?"

Dominic shrugged, stretching his toes to the hearth. "I have no reason to doubt her," he offered. "It's surely possible."

"A woman like that, alone?" Aldric interjected. He glanced at Sir Dunforde, aware of the elder's more senior rank. "By your leave, sir?" he added hastily.

Dunforde shrugged his heavy shoulders. "As you will, lad. No need to stand on ceremony with me."

"That boar I hit," Aldric continued, shooting a glance at Dominic, "we could find no trace of it. No blood. No tracks."

"It was dark. The forest is dense," Dominic said, fingering an empty tankard warmed by the fire on one side. His dagger still trembled in its sheath.

Aldric scowled, unwilling to concede his point. "We had a good look," he argued.

"Have another look in the morn." Dominic stretched his arms and yawned. "I'm for bed," he said. Tipping his head, he grinned as Celia started a lively dance with Tom in the small space available amid the crowded tables. The girl had the attention of every man in the place, raising her arms above her head, long hair drifting seductively across her high cheekbones. The tattered tavern wench eyed her with distaste, hands on hips.

"She's trouble," Aldric said shortly, following his gaze.

Dominic shrugged lazily. "Aye, but she's not my trouble. 'Twill be fun watching Tom and Guildford fight it out between them. My money's on Guildford. What say you?"

A reluctant smile tugged at Aldric's lips. "Tom."

"A crown?"

"Done." They shook hands. Across the tavern, Will had rejoined his comrades and joined in the song. Someone clapped him on the shoulder and passed him a drink.

"He'll have a sore head tomorrow," Dominic said.

"You don't need to worry about him," Sir Dunforde muttered, noting the concerned look in Dominic's eyes as he watched the young man settle back against the wall. "Born to be a soldier, that boy. They tease him, but he's well-liked."

"He has a good heart," Dominic said. "I've just got to return him in one piece, or Little Bird will have my hide."

Dunford snorted. "That young maid has a strange idea of life in the army. Let the lad enjoy himself. There's not much rest between here and Falconridge. The country's rougher, and the ale here is surprisingly good, considering." He crooked a grizzled eyebrow, a half-smile twisting his thin lips under his beard as he watched Guildford and Tom tie themselves in knots for an ounce of Celia's attention. Laughing, she spun away, raising her tankard to them both. "Women," he grunted. "Will be their downfall. You do right to stay away from that one."

"She wants to travel with us," Aldric cut in. "On to Falconridge."

A rare chuckle erupted from Dunforde's thick chest. "I should not allow it. Amusing to watch though it would be."

"With both Tom and Guildford frothing at the mouth, I don't rate your chances for a peaceful life if you refuse her request," Dominic said, rising. "I give you good night, sir." He bowed and wove his way through the mess of bodies, heading for the door. Aldric followed close behind.

"Not up for the game?" Tom asked, stopping him with a hand on his elbow as he dodged the tavern wench and her cluster of tankards. "Come, it will be more sport with three. You should give us some competition." Dominic peered at him through the haze of smoke. Tom had his leaf-green eyes fixed on Guildford, who had taken a seat but still occupied more space than anyone else. The younger man's eyes sparkled in the dim light, broad shoulders flexing impressively under his fine cambric shirt. Celia took him in with wide eyes, entranced.

"I'm of a mind to let her know the lad is only sixteen," Tom said irritably. "Seems only fair to tell her she'll be bedding a callow youth barely out of the schoolroom."

"I'm not sporting with you," Dominic said. "It would spoil our wager."

Tom blinked at him. "Your wager?"

"Aye. For what it's worth, my money's on Guildford."

"And I'm rooting for you," Aldric said, clapping Tom on the shoulder. "So, by all means, tell her what you like. What are you waiting for? A man of your charm and intelligence? I've a crown on you to win."

Startled, Tom threw back his head, rocking the rafters with his ready laughter. He rubbed his hands together. "Welladay, lad," he said. "You've backed the right horse." Squaring his shoulders, he armed himself with a fresh decanter and re-entered the fray.

"You've started something now," Aldric said as Dominic shouldered the battered door. "Gods know which of them will come out the victor. She wanted you first, though. I could see it in her face."

Glancing around at the quiet courtyard, silver and black under the moon, Dominic closed his eyes, picturing another girl with dark blonde hair and eyes like crystal. Her ready wit and lively intelligence. "Wanting's not having," he said, with a wry twist to his lips. "I should know."

A single lantern illuminated the rough stone walls and low ceiling of the tavern stable. The troop members ordered to stand guard through the night snored like piglets wrapped in their thick cloaks, awaiting their watch. The scent of dry grass perfumed the air with the memory of summer. Sensing his presence, Kismet snorted a welcome. Dominic crossed to her automatically, running a hand over her smooth flank, checking her legs for unusual heat. Kismet turned her head, nudging him, and he handed her a wrinkled apple from his pouch. Tossing her head, she crunched the treat. Aldric leaned against the edge of a stall, picking his teeth with a blade of straw. Above their heads, the murmur of the next on watch drifted grumpily from the hayloft as they roused.

"Wonder where they went," Aldric mused, twirling the straw between his fingers.

"Who?"

"The sentries that ran past us in the woods. They weren't in the tavern, and I don't think they came back, or these fellows would have taken over by now."

Yawning, Dominic scratched his bearded chin. "That's true enough," he said. "Maybe they got over themselves and are still on patrol. That's where they should be. If not, Dunforde will have their hides."

The short ladder leading to the hayloft rattled as the next two soldiers climbed down for their watch.

Squinting in the semidarkness, the younger of the two rubbed his eyes. "You're not Arnold and Merriman," he stated. "Are we early?"

Dominic shrugged. "Last we saw of them, they were running in this direction," he said.

The young soldier blinked owlishly. "Running? What's ado?"

"Nothing but a boar in the forest. Seemed to scare them both more than it should," Aldric said. "Have they not been back?"

"How would we know?" The deep voice of the older soldier rumbled like a grumpy bear in the gloom. "Asleep, weren't we?" Fastening his sword about his waist, he shrugged his cloak further to his ears. "Come, we'd better check for them," he said to his companion. "That Arnold spooks easy, so he does. Full of tales of ghosts and goblins."

Nodding his respect, he turned on his heel. The younger man scurried in his wake, still rubbing sleep from his eyes. Dominic yawned again and eyed the hayloft. "That's for us," he said. "Quick, before anyone else comes to their senses and bags it."

He shinned up the ladder, rolling easily from the top into the half-flattened mound of fragrant straw, and poked his head back down to the stalls when Aldric didn't follow. The young Argentian remained where he was, still twirling the straw thoughtfully between his fingers, his dark brown gaze piercing the rough planks.

"It's been a long day. You need rest," Dominic said.

Aldric shrugged and headed for the door. "In a while."

CHAPTER 12

As predicted, scores of heavy heads, the smell of vomit, and a general bad-tempered malaise settled like a fog over the company the next morning. Sir Dunforde barked orders, reprimands, and requests, many of which involved the refilling of his water skin. The soldiers responded with little enthusiasm and delicate movements. In the dimness of the stable, strapping Kismet's saddle to her back, Dominic hid his amusement behind her broad shoulders, grateful to have escaped the worst excesses of the previous evening.

Clem's face in the early morning light resembled the colour of melted wax, his famous voice reduced to a harsh croak as he bartered with the serving wench for ownership of the battered lute. Tom and Guildford were apparently not speaking to each other. Grim-faced, Tom saddled his mount with his back turned to the young princeling. Guildford leaned casually against the stall with one fine leather boot propped behind him as Lionel prepared his own handsome grey. Guildford, at least, wore a smile. Although, in his case, it was the smirk of triumph. Watching from a distance, Celia sauntered across the courtyard from inn to privy. Only the barest hint of a limp hampered her flowing stride. The pale morning sunlight suited her soft colouring and brought flashes of gold to her hair. Her eyes turned continually to Guildford, the hunger in them obvious. Tall and well-rounded, she exuded an earthy allure that needed little embellishment. Seeing her in this environment, her thick tresses bound roughly with a cotton kerchief, Dominic frowned as he slid Kismet's bridle over her head. Even in the moonlight, how could he have mistaken her for Felicia? The only similarity was the colour of their hair.

Hooves clattered as Aldric led Hamil forward and bent down to check his feet. Dark shadows crowded the hollows beneath his eyes.

"Did you go back to the tavern?" Dominic asked. "I could swear the cock crowed before you got your head down."

"Nay, I went back to the forest. Took a torch."

Dominic stared at him with a furrow forming across his brow. "That's a lot of trouble for one lost arrow," he ventured, slinging one of his saddlebags over Kismet's sleek rump.

"It wasn't about the arrow," Aldric replied. "But if you want to know, I found it."

"You did? Well, that's good." Dominic scratched his nose, more perplexed than ever.

"But I didn't find the boar," Aldric continued. He wadded some straw into a crude brush and rose to curry Hamil's coat.

"Bad luck. The arrow must have fallen out."

"Nay. That's the strange part. I found the arrow embedded in a tree stump." Aldric stopped brushing Hamil and leaned against his warm flank.

"So you missed. It was dark."

Aldric straightened, hands on his narrow hips. "You heard it squeal. We all did. I hit it."

Dominic scrubbed at his hair, trying to quell his exasperation. "You might have just injured it. By the gods, Aldric, what is this about? We all know you are a good bowman. What do you have to prove?"

"I just want to know what happened." Aldric's jaw tightened into a stubborn line. "Was there a boar, or wasn't there?"

"By the gods, what does it matter?"

The younger lad shrugged and continued his brushing. "I just think it's strange, that's all. Boars forage at night, but they're shy. They don't attack unless provoked. It could have been in rut, perhaps. That would make it more dangerous, but it's early in the season." His gaze narrowed across Hamil's back as Celia took another turn around the busy courtyard, hips swinging. Eyes lazy and lusting, Guildford levered himself from his comfortable position against the wall and strolled after her, a charming smile plastered across his face.

"And then she arrives," Aldric muttered under his breath, throwing the makeshift brush to the dung-spattered cobbles. "And rutting is all there is on anyone's mind."

Eyebrows raised nearly to his hair, Dominic stared at his squire. "What?" he said. "I hope you are not referring to me."

Aldric shrugged, hunching in on himself, a picture of misery as Guildford's long arms wrapped around Celia and tugged her in for a lusty kiss. Dominic frowned, forcibly reminded of the fragile waif Aldric had once been. Beaten, defeated, bullied.

"Ah," he said as realisation dawned. Ducking around Kismet, he laid a hand on Aldric's arm. "Not me, you're worried about, is it? It's him."

Aldric shuffled his feet and ducked his head. "He's the sun, and I'm just the dirt beneath his feet," he mumbled, addressing his dusty boots. "But I can't seem to help it."

Dominic sighed. "That's common enough. I still feel like that about the Queen. Have done since I was a lad of about eleven, the day I first saddled her horse."

"Really?" Aldric raised a curious gaze, unshed tears sparkling in the chocolate-brown depths. "What happened?"

"Not much. The stable master told me to get her horse ready, and I held her hand to steady her on the mounting block. She thanked me. It was nothing, but there was something about her. So beautiful, but so sad..." He shrugged. "I just wanted to help her. She was all I could think about for days. Hers was the first telepathic voice I ever heard, as well. I suppose there's something in that."

"So what about Felicia, then?"

A wry chuckle escaped Dominic's lips. "Aye, well, that's where everything changes. Petronella for me, Guildford for you. They're perfect, aren't they? Unobtainable, like eagles or gods, flying so high above our heads. She might feed my dreams, but I can't imagine living life at Petronella's side. How do you compete with that? Felicia, though..." He grinned, remembering. "She's real life. Sarcastic, and brave, and clever. Felicia, I could live with. That's why I've got to find her." He clapped his hand against Aldric's stiff shoulders. "Chin up. There will be someone like that for you. Never fear."

His moment of weakness apparently passed, Aldric snorted like a dray horse in self-mockery. "I can only live in hope," he said, dashing a hand across his face and scowling at the dampness he came away with.

At the sound of raised voices, both glanced around at a fresh altercation taking place in the inn yard. Sir Dunford, Tom Buttledon, and the innkeeper were engaged in a lively discussion about the contents of the bill. Guildford had disappeared with Celia. Scowling, Lionel Brearley finished up preparing Guildford's horse and joined Dominic and Aldric as they sauntered across, glad of the diversion.

"You owe me for four quarts of Argentian," the tavern owner said, hands on hips. "And I'm standing here 'til you pay up."

"We didn't have the Argentian, did we, lads?" Thomas called as they approached.

"I didn't have the Argentian, nor did Aldric. Whether you did is another question entirely," Dominic said. Up close, Thomas' normally good-natured face held a definite tinge of green. "By the look of you, the Argentian may have been your downfall. In quantity as well. What happened? I'm guessing Aldric owes me that crown?"

Sir Thomas ripped the bill from the innkeeper's hand, scowled at the total, and dragged out his purse. "Don't talk to me about young Guildford, that cockster," he said, plunging his hand into the depths and withdrawing several shillings. He slapped the coins onto the parchment and folded it around them. "There, good fellow, let that be the end of it."

"There the rooms as well," the barman insisted, his small round eyes hard as marbles. "Who's paying for them? I've got a chamber each for all you gentry. I'll need to replace the straw in the stables. Feed for your horses."

His voice droned, soporific as a bumblebee, but with the additional sting of being in the right. Sir Dunforde grumbled his own purse open and thumbed out coins. Dominic held out his hand to Aldric. "That crown you owe me?" he prompted, the corner of his mouth twitching into a grin.

Aldric huffed a sarcastic laugh. "What a glorious morn this is turning out to be," he said.

"Not my fault you lost the bet," Dominic countered mildly. "Sir Tom must be losing his touch." He dodged the mock punch Thomas threw at his head.

"Watch your manners, young Skinner," the older man said, his green eyes screwed up against the light. Dominic took a couple of light steps away from Tom's long reach and offered him a bow.

"Apologies, Sir Buttledon. It must be a grievous blow, losing to a youngling such as Guildford. Aldric, I can wait for the money." He reached into his own purse and tossed coins to the tavern master.

Aldric shook his head, his black curls dancing. "Nay, I can pay you. I'll just win it back from Jared. The man is completely useless. As a matter of fact..." He turned to Thomas. "As you pay Jared his wage, and I'm just going to beat him at Hazard and win back the money I owe Dominic for our wager that you caused me to owe by failing to beat Guildford for Celia, we could save lots of time, if *you* just pay Dominic that crown." Aldric's eyes sparkled in the early morning sunshine, a picture of innocence.

Thomas scratched his rumpled head and blinked at the young would-be swindler. "What?" he said.

Aldric planted his hands on his hips, drew a deep breath, and started again. "As you pay..."

"By the gods, he's a born merchant," Dominic said, trying and failing to hold in his laughter. Sir Dunforde's craggy features cracked into a rare grin. He rocked back on his heels, surveying the activity with the air of a man content with his world, and felt for his pipe.

Bit by bit, the hungover company gathered themselves for travel. The privy door stopped banging. Rolling stomachs did better with some food inside them. Fresh air, exercise, and the pure, crystal water of the inn well aided many a sore head.

Aldric kept his face turned away from Guildford, who swept into the courtyard, pulling his shirt over his head, and called for Lionel to help with his armour. Celia slid out of the inn behind him a few minutes later, her hair freshly braided. Mistress Trevis, grim-faced, eyed the girl with dislike as she made room for her on the seat of the second supply wagon.

"Company, mount up," Sir Dunforde finally roared when the sun had crested the eastern range and flooded the courtyard with sunlight. "We are already late."

Dominic swung himself easily into his saddle, reigning Kismet in her usual circle as she cavorted underneath him, eager to be on her way. Fearing for his health, Aldric had left off baiting Thomas and waited beside him.

They'd almost taken the first step when the innkeeper approached from the kitchens, wiping his greasy hands on his jerkin. "Wait, wait," he yelled.

"By the Gods, what's to do now?" Sir Dunforde growled into his beard. He looked down his nose at the man as he shuffled up, panting.

"What am I to do with that?" the tavern master said, jerking his head to the most shaded corner of the yard and the looming shape of the carter's wagon, upon which lay the corpse of its previous owner.

Only loosely covered by the tarp, the body was already attracting flies by the dozen. "Can't your men bury him?"

"We brought him back to the village. What happens to his remains is not up to us," Sir Dunforde said, settling his rump more firmly into his saddle. "Perhaps you should make enquiries locally – see if you can find anyone who can name the man's kin?"

Caught by a subtle movement at the corner of his eye, Dominic turned his head to see Celia sliding from her perch. "I could look," she suggested. "My family is from around these parts."

A deeper furrow dug into Sir Dunforde's creased forehead. "Are you sure, mistress?" he asked. "'Twon't be a pretty sight."

Skirts rippling in the slight breeze as she crossed the cobbles, Celia shrugged away the older man's concern. "'Tis of no matter," she said.

Tack jingling, the horse's hooves stamped impatiently against the flags as the company waited for her pronouncement. Dominic took a quick swig of water from his flask. Guildford threw the reins of his mount to Lionel and vaulted down to accompany her. Dominic's eyebrows lifted at this show of chivalry. Head and shoulders above her, the young giant reached easily into the cart to pull the tarp back. Celia took his hand and used the cart wheel as a ladder to get a better look.

Overhead, birds sang, their gentle, melodious cries at odds with the watchfulness that crept over the company. Blinking, Dominic realised that the bird calls were echoing inside his head, as well as from the nooks and crannies of the outhouse rooftops.

Celia paused for a long moment, her back to them. She didn't move.

"Well, mistress? Do you know him?" Sir Dunforde's tone was gruff. "We need to get on."

Celia pulled the tarp carefully over the dead man's face and put her slender hand into Guildford's, letting the lad help her down. Her face contained little expression as she turned towards them, her mouth set in a hard line.

"Nay, good sir. He is unknown to me," she said.

"Well, and good. Over to you then, good fellow," Sir Dunforde said cheerfully to the scowling innkeeper. "But I wouldn't wait long to bury him. And that ore needs to get on its way."

He raised his hand to move the column out. Guildford vaulted into his saddle, and Celia regained her seat next to Mistress Trevis. Collecting Kismet to follow the lead, Dominic glanced back at her. The young woman stared grim-faced ahead, toying with some small object she held in her lap. In his head, the bird song swelled, and his dagger vibrated in sympathy, adding its metallic voice to the strange melody filling his skull.

Rubbing his hand against his own chest, where an ache of sadness blossomed, Dominic blinked as he rode out of the humble tavern yard, following the road where it led uphill into the mist-covered mountains. He glanced across at Aldric, who returned his look with a sceptical one of his own. Dominic nodded. He set his jaw, one hand on his dagger as it continued to buzz annoyingly against his hip.

Celia was lying. But why?

CHAPTER 13

A rising breeze swept across the rugged terrain as they journeyed onwards into the first range of foothills that hugged the lower slopes of the Iron Mountains. The wind brought with it an underlying dampness, scented with notes of pine and cypress and a hint of the harsh chill winter to come. The remote north road was busy with carts carrying supplies to and from the small villages that peppered the region, hugging the shallow vales and sheltered valleys as best they could. Heavy snowfall would cut them off for days, leaving the villagers relying solely on what foodstuff they had preserved in the preceding months. The air rang with the blows of unseen axes deep in the forest. Thin, spiralling threads of smoke drifted in the wind from the solitary charcoal burners. Gervase Hoppington had been busy with a glib tongue and bulging purse at every village they stopped in over the last three days. His supply wagons, laden with salted meat and sacks of dry goods to augment the stores at Falconridge, lumbered in the wake of the soldiers, the oxen sweating and straining over the stony ground.

Jogging easily on Kismet's sturdy back, grateful for her strength, Dominic scanned the hillside for threats. Buzzards circled like sentinels over their heads, riding the winds in front of the blue-black clouds of an incoming storm. Thunder rumbled in the distance. Saddle and footsore, the weary troop grumbled their way upwards, striving to put the latest slope behind them before the weather broke.

"How far to Thorncastle?" Dominic yelled to Tom as they rounded yet another corkscrew bend in the road that wound ever upward as if it led straight to the home of the Gods. He shivered in the increasing breeze, pulling his hood around his bearded cheeks.

"This is the worst part. Thorncastle lies in the hollow on the other side of this pass," Tom called back from his position at the front of the straggling column. 'Tis a goodly town, with a reputation for fine ale."

"Oh, good," Aldric muttered. "Just what we all need. More ale and wenches." Dominic tilted his face to look behind him. Hunched in his cloak, chin tucked against the wind, Aldric rode with a hard look in his eyes that had not been present before Celia joined the company. Casting his gaze further back down the train, Dominic watched as Guildford swung Celia from her uncomfortable seat next to Mistress Trevis into a warmer one in his lap, where he huddled her to his chest under his cloak. Dominic could hear her protesting the cold steel of his breastplate in a breathy tone that prompted Guildford to throw back his head. His rich laughter echoed from the craggy hillside.

"Fussy maid," he said genially to the company at large. "Given a warm perch, she still has cause to doubt my care for her comfort." Dropping the reins, he lifted the girl easily away from him. "There, sweeting," he said. "Find the edge of my cloak and fold it, so."

Laughing, Celia did as he suggested, forming a small pad against the chill of his armour upon which to rest her head. He settled her back and wrapped her up in its further edge once more. "Happy now?"

"Aye, my lord," Celia said, settling herself against him. "'Tis a chill day, to be sure."

"Not with you around, lass," Guildford said. He gathered his mount's reins and spurred the horse into a jog to the head of the train. Thomas glared at his back as the lad trotted past to place himself at Sir Dunforde's side.

The senior man looked down his nose at Celia, who avoided his gaze and snuggled closer to her benefactor. "Much good as a guard, you'll be with that woman astride your sword hand," he said, eyes narrowed and streaming as the wind gained strength.

Guildford rolled his eyes. "To date, good sir, there has been no need for a guard. Gods be thanked," he said.

"Yet," Dunforde said ominously, "were I ye, I'd give the woman an extra blanket and take her back to the wagon. Wenching will serve us ill amid an ambush."

Dominic bit his lip to keep himself from comment, but Tom's leaf green eyes gleamed with amusement as they exchanged glances. It was rare Guildford received a reprimand from the older man.

"She can dismount as easily as she mounts, good Sir Dunforde," Guildford said, dismissing his words with a good-humoured shrug and a sly wink.

Dominic's eyes widened. He glanced at Celia, who kept her expression neutral, although the corners of her lips tightened at his words.

Thomas Buttledon was less circumspect. "By the Gods, Guildford, do you besmirch your leman so?" he growled. "Fine feathers do not make a fine bird, it seems. Take back your words."

Guildford's thick, golden eyebrows contracted. "By the Gods, I will not," he said. "I mean nought by it. Celia knows."

"Does she?" Tom said, his eyes narrowed. His hand crept to his sword. "You seem determined to show your ownership of her. I'm sure the lass is more independent than you would have us believe."

"Of course she is. When did I ever say she wasn't?" Guildford said, glancing at Tom with genuine bewilderment spreading across his face. "Come, Sir Tom, we've had this argument. 'Twas Celia's choice back in Bearbank. I did not force her into my bed."

Shaking his head, Dominic dropped behind, leaving them to their discourse. The two men had been at odds from the minute they contended for the young woman's attention. Celia herself did nothing to stop them, listening to their harsh words with a wry twitch of her lips she thought went unnoticed. Their rivalry had worn on for the last three days, and he was tired of hearing it.

The group continued onwards, Guildford's voice rising against Tom's as the column wound its way to where the tree line disappeared to reveal a narrow pass that hugged the jagged cliff edges.

"Don't like the look of that," Gervase said as Dominic and Aldric joined him beside his wagon. The quarter masters' steel-grey eyes glinted in the faltering light as the rain finally closed in. He gestured with his whip at the narrow, crumbling path that clung to the cliff. A distant, savage drop awaited any who tumbled from its edge. "Animals won't like it either," he added. "Slow going, though it be not as steep. You'll take care now. Lead your mounts if you must."

With hoods raised against the spiteful slash of rain, the group marched grimly on. The horses put their ears back, their sweating coats steaming. Single file, as the road dwindled to a mere track, the foot soldiers muttered anxiously, casting terrified glances at the vertiginous drop on their right. Will hugged the wall, one tanned, square hand tracing a grimy path against the rocks. Small stones and pebbles, dislodged by the storm, plummeted to the depths. Biting his lip, Dominic slid from his saddle. He'd never fully come to terms with his fear of heights. His fingers tightened on Kismet's reins as he slid them over her head. Better the horse found her own footing.

"It is better to dismount?" Aldric said, his voice high with nervous energy.

"Just want to give her every chance, just in case," Dominic muttered. He took a moment to unstrap his saddle bag, slinging it easily over his own shoulder. "I couldn't bear for her to fall," he said.

"Wait for me, then." Aldric jumped down and mirrored Dominic's actions, shoulders slumping slightly under the weight of his own pack.

"What have you got in there?" Dominic asked as they set off once more in the wake of the slow-moving wagons. "Rocks?"

Aldric grinned. "Books," he said.

Rain drenched their cloaks before they made it halfway along the goat-cropped path. The rain slashed at them horizontally, driven by the rising gale. Kismet walked daintily as a dancer, head down, picking her way carefully over the rocky ground. Too aware of the yawning gap waiting to claim them, Dominic winced every time her hooves slid on the pebbles. Up ahead, the lead wagon rocked slowly. Gervase had jumped from his seat and had taken to pulling the oxen behind him, coaxing them to follow with a handful of hay snatched from a feed bag. Behind Dominic and Aldric, Mistress Trevis, in charge of the second wagon, sat erect on her seat, her long blonde hair dripping water, disdaining the rain. Something in her air of confidence filtered to him through the gloom. She would go down, wagon and all, if she had to. But it was obvious that she didn't consider it a possibility. Glancing behind him, Dominic's respect for the woman increased tenfold as she clucked to her team, the warmth of her healing presence calming them somewhat against the roll of thunder echoing around the cliff tops. Her oxen plodded, shoulders straining, small ears flicking back and forth in response to her urging. Lightning flickered all around them, slicing the air like the fingers of fate as it bounced around the mountains. Thunder followed swiftly behind. Her breath panicked, Kismet huffed in Dominic's ear, and he reached a hand back to steady her. "Easy, girl, my beauty," he murmured. "Just a little further, look. Nearly there."

Sir Dunforde, Tom, and Guildford had navigated their way to a broader pathway where the cliffs overhung the road. One by one, the troop followed, swearing, muttering. Clem was humming a low ditty, at odds with the wildness of the tearing wind. Gervase coaxed his oxen over the last few paces, gesturing at the soldiers in front of him to clear the way. "Move!" he yelled. "If you want to eat. All the meat's in here!" The foot soldiers shuffled obligingly aside. Dominic felt his shoulders relax as the end of the treacherous path loomed in front of him. His stride lengthened, and he glanced behind. Mistress Trevis' wagon was the last, yelling to her oxen as they finally baulked, scared out of their wits as blue light struck the cliff straight above them.

A cascade of earth and small rocks warned them of the danger to come. Appalled, Dominic snatched his gaze upwards, where an enormous boulder had shifted from its mooring. "Hurry!" he yelled, gesturing furiously at Aldric and Mistress Trevis. Aldric ran, hauling Hamil behind him. The horse, scared and trembling, fought the drag on his reins. The boulder was shifting. Moss, stones, and earth hurtled down to the path. Mistress Trevis raised a hand to shield her head, and Dominic tossed Kismet's reins to whoever was nearest.

Sprinting towards the wagon, he reached out a hand to help Aldric tug Hamil onward. Aldric's face was a mask of gratitude, his brown skin pale with fright as Dominic clapped the horse's rump, startling him into an erratic trot. A heavy clod of earth bounced off his shoulder, and he raised his head to meet Mistress Trevis' thin face as she stared upwards at the boulder that loomed over her like the fist of a god.

"I can't make them move," she said.

"Jump. Come on, I've got you," Dominic said. "Leave them."

Her jaw tightened. She took up her whip and gave each oxen a mighty belt. The oxen took the punishment, but not the hint. They remained where they were. Stoic, determined. Immovable as the rocks sliding above them were not.

"By the Gods, Mistress, jump!" Dominic yelled at her. "That boulder is coming down!"

The healer stared at him, her lips a thin, forbidding line, as stubborn as the oxen she drove. Over her head, the grind and screech of rock against rock warned them both of the imminent danger. The boulder shuddered, loosened from its centuries-old bed, propelled by the tremble of the thunder and the lightning lancing all around. Setting her jaw, Mistress Trevis gathered her skirts to jump.

Too late. The boulder fell.

Horror struck deep into Dominic's chest. Power blazing, he threw out his hands, enveloping the huge rock with all the force his Blessed gift allowed him. He stumbled with the weight of it against his mind, only just able to slow its descent. Startled out of their funk, the oxen bolted. Panting with the effort, he lurched out of their way as they stampeded down the length of the track, the wagon jouncing behind. Mistress Trevis clung to the seat. The boulder crashed to the ground. Dominic felt the shockwave tremor beneath his boots. Hauling breath into his lungs, his eyes widened at the path fissured around it. The fault line followed the cart, and he jumped back to the cliff face, clinging on with rain-slick fingers, conscious of the terrible drop beneath his boots. He yelled a warning as it caught up with the terrified oxen. Unaware, Mistress Trevis could do nothing when her wagon wheels disappeared beneath her. The oxen bellowed their distress, hooves hammering at the solid pathway in front of them, sliding backwards along with the heavy wagon. The abyss yawned under Mistress Trevis. She lost her seat and tumbled into the bed of the cart with a scream of terror that clutched at his own stomach. Barrels and sacks catapulted over the rear edge. One crashed straight through the hindboard, smashing the frame like so much matchwood. A sack of grain followed and dangled in midair, caught on something inside. Sir Dunforde added his own bellow to the company. He sprinted forward on stiff legs, reaching for the wagon harness. Tom yelled, catching hold of his leader and yanking him away as his boots skidded in the mud. Guildford dumped Celia to the ground and vaulted from his mount to help.

His back to the cliff edge, Dominic flung his hands out once more, calling on the Mage to help him, struggling to balance the over-weighted cart bearing Mistress Trevis, their remaining supplies, and the shifting, maddened mass of two fully grown oxen.

"Hold!" he yelled as the track disintegrated. "Leave it all. I have it." Hearing his own words out loud steadied him. He breathed air into his lungs, slowing his heart rate, pumping power from his hands through the sodden afternoon air to encircle the cart. Stones and pebbles rained down from the cliff face all around him, but he stood his ground, arms held out, regarding the tableau as objectively as he had once dealt with the maths problems set by his uncle, safe in the castle. *"Here,"* his mind whispered. *"And here. Look, where that front wheel is... If you push here. And look, the lead ox, he's not as frightened. A nudge. Just a little. There. The wagon. Lift it now, gently... A little more..."*

Bit by bit, the wagon steadied, held straight and firm by the strength of his mind, back wheels standing in the air. He had it. Sweat ran into his eyes, waiting for Mistress Trevis to emerge from the cart bed. Locking eyes with Aldric across the chasm that separated them, he read the panic there. He lurched as the remaining sliver of ground under his feet crumbled. There was no sign of the healer.

"Mistress Trevis!" Aldric's voice bounced off his ears, so deep was his concentration. The lad started forward, determined to go to the older woman's aid. Tom stopped him, staring at Dominic across the void, his face white. There was only one way out, and Dominic took it. He launched himself into the bed of the cart, not daring to remove his mind from balancing it. From somewhere, he knew dimly that the soldiers were organising themselves to haul the oxen onto more solid ground. But here, in the cluttered gloom of the covered wagon, his gaze clashed with Mistress Trevis. She was clutching the cart's edge with whitened fingers, her feet tangled in a mess of rope that had once tied off the neck of a heavy sack of grain. The sack that still dangled from the yawning gap at the back of the cart.

"Please, I daren't let go," she rasped, blue eyes wide and staring.

Dominic grabbed for the trusty old dagger he kept strapped to his leg, inside his boot. Bending, he sawed frantically at the rope that kept Mistress Trevis captive, aware that his control would only last so long. Already, his exertions were sapping his telekinetic powers. The wagon tipped, its contents sliding inexorably to the broken tailgate. The healer's fingers tightened, her mouth clamped in grim determination. Distant shouting indicated the oxen were under powerful encouragement to move. Unfortunately, because of Dominic's control of them, they couldn't. And he dared not take the time for adjustments. Not now.

Mistress Trevis' face was a picture of fear, overlaid with a stoic mask of inevitability. Dominic could feel her hope pouring into him. Her strength. The woman closed her eyes, forcing more of her own healing essence into his aura, helping him at cost to herself. Her breath came in small pants of distress. Perspiration popped out on her brow. He sawed harder, cursing the neglect of his old blade in favour of the new one. It was blunt, and the ropes were fibrous and tough. The wagon tilted further, the rope around the healer's ankle tightening painfully as gravity took over. He reset his footing and tried again, sweat blooming on his own forehead, struggling to keep the cart balanced. Finally, the ropes gave, along with the old knife itself. The blade snapped off in his hand. The sack of grain vanished into the rain-sodden ravine. He grabbed both blade and handle, prised Mistress Trevis' bony hands from her death grip on the wagon side, and heaved.

They tumbled painfully onto the rocky path, and the soldiers blundered in pursuit of the panicked oxen as Dominic's telekinesis gave out and the broken cart lurched after them. Somewhere, Dominic was aware of Aldric's dark, terrified face, and then, strangely, Celia's hand drifted across his cheeks. He could smell the dust and sweat on her skin, the warmth of her breath as she unfurled his fingers to see the pieces of his broken dagger.

"Well, by the Gods," she whispered. "Blessed by the Mage. You kept that close, Sir Skinner."

After that, there was nothing.

CHAPTER 14

S ubdued, weary, and soaked to the skin, the troop navigated the
corkscrew descent into Thorncastle in unaccustomed silence.
The soldiers eyed Dominic from under their drenched hoods, muttering to each other, divided between awe and suspicion. Bird song
and the last of the sunlight accompanied their entry into the bustling
town. A stone wall encircled the outskirts, manned with local militia
in a motley selection of uniforms and armed with a startling array of
ancient weapons. Dunforde raised a grizzled eyebrow at the state of
the defence. The local militia stood in stony silence as the bedraggled
group passed under the narrow gateway and into the town environs,
their lips curled at the wealth of steel, broadcloth, and armour on
display. Their entry had a similar effect on the citizens, who stopped
what they were doing to stare.

Riding pillion beside Mistress Trevis, his head almost on her shoulder, Dominic saw the narrow stone buildings and slate rooftops
through a grey blur of fatigue. Aldric trotted alongside the wagon,
leading Kismet. After the events on the cliff path, he had remained
within touching distance, huge dark eyes consumed with worry. Mistress Trevis, pale-faced herself from her narrow brush with death,
placed one hand on Dominic's arm from time to time, giving him a
boost of her own healing strength.

She glanced across at Aldric as they clattered across the surprisingly
clean cobbles and into the main town square, where the people were

preparing in anticipation of the autumn fair. A bonfire, yet unlit, dominated the space. The townsfolk had erected stalls around it at a safe distance and were busy loading them with goods, shouting across each other as they laboured in a rush against the failing light. Despite the lateness of the hour, potential buyers were already circulating, poking at the cabbages and turnips, testing knife blades. In one corner, a puppeteer had attracted the attention of the youngsters. Across the way, a fiddler and a bassoonist were arguing over their scores. The doors of the taverns breathed the hearty aroma of hops and wine. Linkmen were busy with their torches, giving light to the lanthorns, bathing the scene in tones of red and gold.

"Festival tomorrow," Aldric said, leaning across and poking Dominic in the ribs. Again. Dominic grunted in protest, and Mistress Trevis fixed the young squire with a beady eye. "Leave him to rest, lad. He won't die on you if he goes to sleep," she said.

"He looks too pale," Aldric complained.

"I'm not surprised. He used a great deal of magical energy to do what he did. It will take time to replenish. You would know this if you included healing in your education and not just economics."

"I'm not a healer," the young man protested.

"I think you are," the woman countered. "With a lot to learn."

Eyes closed, Dominic's mouth twisted in a wry grin as their argument continued without him. His mind drifted, lifting him from the hard wooden seat, padded roughly with a saddle blanket. The inside of his head, where his telepathy usually lived, felt like an empty room. His thoughts echoed and floated across the absence, like dusty leaves tossed aimlessly in the wind. The telekinetic power normally available as a surge of energy in his hands barely registered. It was like the day two years ago when he'd killed Aldric's master, and the Mage had stripped him of his ability. Suddenly, he was normal. Vulnerable as any other ordinary Citizen once more. Head spinning, he sat up, bracing himself with trembling hands against the cart's edge as it lurched into a pothole.

"How long will it be before my abilities return?" he asked the healer, plucking her sleeve to get her attention.

"A day or so, mayhap. I'll give you something to help as soon as we stop, but you must rest. Don't overtax yourself," the woman warned, glancing at him.

"I never had to use that much at once before," Dominic murmured.

Mistress Trevis chuckled. "Testament to your abilities then, young man," she said. "Few could have juggled all that. Even your uncle would have found it difficult, and he was a master."

Dominic's grip on the wagon tightened. "Do you think my uncle is an evil man?" he asked, glancing across at her, almost too scared to hear her response.

A brief frown crossed the healer's face. She paused before she answered, considering her words, before she turned to meet his gaze.

"Not by choice, Sir Skinner," she said. "The Terrence Skinner who taught me my basic magic skills was a formidable mage, that is true. An exacting tutor with some original teaching methods. He never mentioned his past, but a shadow of it would cross his face from time to time. As a young healer, I felt that from him. His internal struggle. His deep grief." She clucked at her oxen and navigated the corner of the square, joining the troop as they lingered in front of the largest inn. Tom had disappeared inside in search of accommodation. Hauling the oxen to a halt, she shook her fair hair free of her hood, fingers coaxing the snarls.

"So evil, no. I wouldn't say so. Conflicted. Driven. Wounded, definitely."

A memory of his uncle rose in Dominic's mind. The cavernous blackness in his eyes, that long ago day in the castle library when Terrence had pinned him against the bookshelves like a beetle. "The

Shadow Mage still has my soul in his claws. I battle him to stay in the light every day of my life," he'd said then.

"Prince Joran wants me to kill him to prove my loyalty to the crown," Dominic said, keeping his voice low. He picked at the wood under his fingers, tearing small slivers and shredding them until nothing but dust remained. Mistress Trevis watched him fidget and closed her eyes. The oxen put their heads down, and Dominic found his chin on his chest. He blinked, struggling to lift his gaze to her.

"What?" he croaked, battling for the will to even lift a finger in his own defence.

"Breathe," Mistress Trevis instructed. "Don't think. Just breathe."

Unable to do anything else, Dominic did as she instructed. A wash of warmth swept over him, comforting as a blanket heated in front of his fire. It reminded him briefly of Domita, long absent from court on urgent business of her own. He realised suddenly how much he missed her. Her cheerfulness and positivity, her boundless enthusiasm. Even her cataclysmic dancing style. Over his head, Mistress Trevis let out a huff of laughter. "Aye, lad. Let the memories come. 'Twill do you good," she whispered.

Dominic swallowed. "I don't want..." he began.

"Breathe," Mistress Trevis instructed. "Let things be as they are. You don't have to fix everything right now."

"But—"

Mistress Trevis' hand snaked across to pat his own. "Always so busy, young Dominic," she said. "So many questions. So much going on in that head of yours. Take some time, lad, before you go rushing off. 'Tis important."

The wave of healing spiked in his aura, almost against his will. He slumped against her. Mistress Trevis put her arm around his shoulders and waved at Tom as he came out of the tavern, his eyes alight with anticipation at the delights on offer inside. "Sir Skinner needs rest," she said. "Help me with him".

The vibration of the enchanted dagger under his cheek and the soft sigh of its Gods forsaken melody dragged Dominic awake much later that evening. Struggling to open his eyes and faint nausea gripping his belly, he found himself in a narrow cot, heaped with blankets, in a chilly chamber lit by a single candle. The unmistakable signs of revelry on the ground floor trembled the legs of his bed through the floorboards.

Sitting up, he blinked away a wave of dizziness. A glance around the dormitory-style chamber showed a few hunched shapes and the sound of heavy breathing, but most pallets were empty yet. Sliding his legs from under the blankets, Dominic reached for his clothes, shrugging into his warmest tunic, and plunged his feet into his boots. He winced as he slid the left one on, stifling a curse. The two pieces of his old dagger tumbled onto his blankets as he upended it. Grimacing, he squinted at the blade where it had snapped in the worn hilt. Even broken, the grip still felt solid and familiar in his hand. Its heft and weight promised strength and solidity, unlike the enchanted blade that sighed and sang and trembled like a maid at a wedding. The pommel of that knife poked coyly from his pillow, where someone, probably Aldric, had left it. He eyed it with distaste, wondering why he'd ever bought it. It seemed to bring nothing but bad luck. His lips tightened as he strapped it around his waist. Enchanted or not, he still needed a knife. Tugging his boots back on, he left the sleeping chamber for the rowdy taproom, following the urging of his stomach, tucking the remains of the old dagger into his pouch as he went.

To his utter astonishment, the entire taproom went completely silent as he entered. He paused mid-step, almost unbalanced by the absence of conversation. Strangers stared back at him, their eyes dark and hollow in the dim light, tankards halfway to their lips. The piper stopped playing, tapping his instrument on his thigh. The rattle of industry in the back kitchen continued unabated, along with an off-key ditty sung by a tuneless cook. Dominic felt the hairs on the back of his neck stand up. He'd never been more conspicuous in his life. He wasn't sure he liked it.

"That's him," he heard someone mutter. "That's the lad that can move stuff with his mind." A low murmur of debate spread like a plague throughout the taproom.

"Yay, Sir Skinner, the telemantist," Guildford yelled from across the room. "That's the man. Saved the day. Again." Sarcasm laced his tone. Dominic rolled his eyes. Seated at the fire, Celia perched on his knee, Guildford was already awash with ale. She laughed, drawing eyes to her.

Cheeks flaming, he squinted into the gloom, searching for a friendly face. The crowd parted miraculously for him as he took a hesitant stride in Aldric's direction.

"Well, that didn't take long to get around, did it? Proves my point that no-one gossips better than a soldier," Aldric said as Dominic joined him at a table near the door. It was the only spot available. Gradually, the noise level crept back up. The entire taproom was full to bursting, swollen with customers ready for the festivities the next day. Faces flushed with heat and alcohol leered on every side, the air heavy with packed bodies, grime, and ale. Guildford glanced across at him, exchanging a sly quip with Jared, who almost choked on his drink. Even dour Lionel glanced up from his seat, the corner of his mouth twisting.

Dominic glanced at Aldric. The lad rested easily against the wall, drumming his fingers on his tankard in time with the melody straining to make itself heard over the din. He waved a hand at the pitcher. "I got a tankard for you. Help yourself," he said. "How are you feeling?"

"Hungry." Dominic sampled the beer before taking a longer pull. "Good ale, this," he said.

"Aye. Food's not bad either," Aldric said. He grabbed a rosy-cheeked serving wench by the arm as she passed with a fistful of empty cups. "Supper for my friend here, lass. If you would," he said.

The girl eyed Dominic with more than passing interest and squeezed through the crowd to attend the request.

"Mistress Trevis said to let you alone, thought you'd sleep the night away."

Dominic managed a half smile, still aware of the many pairs of eyes boring into the back of his skull. "I nearly did. Where's Sir Dunforde?"

Aldric shrugged. "Went off to see about mending the wagon and to find a dovecote to send his report to the prince. He'll be back, I don't doubt. Tom went with him."

He scowled as the table lurched, and the tankards slopped some of their contents.

"Go on, do some magic," someone said above their heads. "We want to see it, don't we?"

Dominic glanced up from his ale at the lanky frame taking up space in front of them. The man stood nearly as tall as Guildford, although much slighter in build. A shock of dark hair crowned a freckled face twisted by malevolence and alcohol. His companion stood slightly behind him. Almost completely bald, something about his bright button eyes and shiny nose put Dominic instantly in mind of a piglet. The man stunk like one, too.

"Leave us alone," he said. "We just want some food and a quiet drink."

"But we want to see some magic, don't we?" the drunkard said, waving his arms at the crowd, who quieted once more. "Don't believe what your friends are saying. No-one can lift a cart like that. Or a boulder, can they?"

"I'd be happy to oblige," Dominic said mildly, despite the annoyance that was spiking his heart rate. "But I used most of my energy already this afternoon. Why don't you people strengthen and widen that road? We could have lost the entire troop today."

The newcomer spat his disgust at the stone floor. "Queen's men. What do we care about you up here?"

"By the Gods," Dominic said, losing his patience along with his temper. He shot to his feet, one hand on the enchanted dagger. Across the room, Guildford unfolded like a giant from his stool, grey eyes sparkling at the thought of a scrap. Celia laughed again, a low, throaty tone, at once avid and sultry. "Go on then, my love," she said.

"How now, outside, outside," the tavern wench approached, a steaming bowl of pottage in one hand, a grubby cloth in the other. She flapped it at the taller man, like a farmer's wife shooing a chicken.

The man looked down his long nose at her. "I want to see some magic," he said. "And I bet you do, too." He peered at Dominic again. "Come on, Mage. I'm waiting. Magic. Or you'll feel my fist on your noble jaw."

Dominic sighed. "That wouldn't be the worst that has ever happened to me," he said. "But if you want to see some magic, how about this?"

Despite his air of confidence, he'd never been more grateful when a flick of his wrist jerked the bowl from the serving maid's hand to crash against his assailant's face. The man yelped with shock, clawing the steaming gravy from his eyes, staggering backwards into his pig-shaped friend.

"You've blinded me, you bastard!" he snarled.

"Sorry. Too hot?" Dominic said, raising the pitcher with a flick of his other wrist. The crowd watched, roaring with laughter as he tipped it deliberately over both their heads.

"You scurvy knave!" the taller of the two roared, dirty hands rubbing frantically at his face. "You'd better watch it. I've got my eye on you!"

"Yay, well. Come back when you can see," Dominic said, standing back as the man blundered out of the door, barrelling into Tom Buttledon, who was coming in.

"Welladay. I leave you alone for one moment, and that's the mess you get yourself in?" Thomas said, aiding the man's onward progress with a boot to the backside. Pigman sidled past him, giving Dominic a wide berth. Around them, the customers settled back with their ale, roaring their mirth. Guildford strode across the room to join them, Celia in his wake. She crept under his arm, amusement sparking in her dark brown eyes. At the sight of her, Aldric gritted his teeth and took another swig of beer.

"Well done, Skinner. You've a wit when you want," Guildford said grudgingly, tipping his wine glass in Dominic's direction.

"I got lucky there. Honestly," Dominic said, sitting down with a bump as his legs gave out. "Good thing I didn't have to fight. My dagger broke. I've got to get it mended or buy another."

Guildford nodded to the hilt of the enchanted blade at his waist, a frown plastered across his freckled forehead. "You've that other one," he said. "You could use that."

Dominic shook his head. "I've never used it for anything much," he said. "It's a strange weapon. The Gods alone know what enchantments are woven within it. I daren't use it, especially against a Citizen, just in case the Mage takes his favour back again."

Guildford grinned. "Just for show then! And I thought I was the bird with the fine feathers around here." He nudged Thomas, who was flirting with the serving maid as he ordered more food.

Thomas eyed Celia from under his well-marked brows. "There are a few fine birds on the premises tonight," he said, "but I see you have the best already." He slid into a seat next to Aldric, who had yet to shift his dark brown stare from the bottom of his beer.

Celia dragged her eyes from the dagger at Dominic's waist and favoured Tom with a smile. "I thank you, good sir," she said. She turned to Dominic. "Sir Skinner, do you have your broken blade? I have some skill in that area. I could mend it for you." She held out a hand. Strong and capable, marked with callouses.

Dominic glanced at her and shrugged. "I was going to buy another, but you can try if you will," he said, passing the pieces to her. "My thanks to you."

He sat back to make way for the girl bearing another bowl of stew. The piper and bassoon had struck up a tune, and the clientele joined in with gusto.

"Don't," Aldric whispered suddenly, jerking his gaze away from his cup. He stared his own daggers at Celia as she took the knife, turning it over with a practised air, examining the broken blade. Dominic glanced from her to him.

"Why not?" he mouthed back.

Aldric's mouth worked. He shrugged helplessly, his face a picture of misery, glancing from Celia to Guildford and back to Dominic. Dominic rolled his eyes.

"Aldric," he murmured, "just because she's with Guildford..."

Aldric shook his head, stubborn as the oxen pulling Mistress Trevis' smashed cart. "I don't understand it. 'Tis not that," he insisted, dropping his tone to the barest whisper.

Dominic glanced at the girl as she continued to examine the knife. "Look, you can see where the blade wore out," she said, showing it to Tom. "I'll take it to the nearest smith on the morrow and mend it for him. 'Tis the least I can do after today."

Her face was turned away from Dominic, and she took no notice of their conversation. But, judging from the tight line of her back, Dominic had the sinking feeling that she had heard every word.

Chapter 15

Lionel Brearley poked Dominic awake the next morning. He emerged from the cocoon of his blankets, conscious of an overwhelming thirst and a headache worse than a pounding from Guildford's heavy fist. The pockmarked visage of Lionel looming over him did little to aid it. He groaned in protest.

"Here, wake up." Lionel thrust a pitcher at him. "Mistress Trevis said to give you this."

Blinking, Dominic struggled upright, glancing at the neighbouring pallet. Empty. "My thanks, where's Aldric?" he asked, taking the flask and sniffing at the contents. Valerian. A mild dose. Enough to soothe.

Lionel shrugged. "With the horses, I don't doubt. Like always," he said. "You should get up if you can. Sir Dunforde says we can have the day here. Mistress Trevis will remain also, but we are to catch them up with all speed. The troop cannot wait too long, and your skills are required."

Wincing, Dominic nodded. "Why are you here?" he said. "Is Guildford with you?"

Lionel smirked. "I'm to escort Celia," he said. "And watch over her."

Dominic raised his eyebrows and shrugged. "As he wishes," he said, brow quirking in bemusement. He waited until Lionel had limped through the door before lurching to his feet. The room reeled around him. Shaking his head, he took a grateful swig from the jug. The familiar taste of valerian swept him instantly to a memory of Felicia and her potions. If he closed his eyes, he could still see her leaning over him, her hair a tangled mane concealing her anguished expression, her beautiful lips sewn shut by her own mother as she forced her brew into his mouth. He swayed where he stood, skin prickling with desire and aching loss.

His mental channels were still dull with fatigue, but he sent his greeting to her anyway, as he did every day upon rising. "Where are you, Felicia? Tell me... I miss you."

He waited, but just like every morn, there was no reply. His mouth tightened.

After taking another swig, he dressed, swinging his cloak over his shoulders. The tavern master glowered at him as he passed through the noisy tavern and into the bustle of Thorncastle's autumn fair. Crisp sunlight highlighted the bright faces of the townsfolk as they headed to the market square. The women wore baskets over their arms and determined expressions. Their menfolk sauntered, eyeing the tavern, heading for the livestock pens, marked by the mournful bellow of a bull and the trail of dung mapping its location.

Children stared, open-mouthed and snotty-nosed, at a troupe of jugglers forming a human pyramid, at massive risk to life and limb. Hawkers and stall holders called their wares. Dogs barked, and chickens added their cackles to the general hubbub. Soothed by the potion, Dominic felt his heart lift a little as he dodged the colourful crowds and went in search of the stables. His lively little mother would have loved this. All the bustle and excitement. The noise and the colour. The cut and thrust of bargains made and the weight of her basket on her arm.

He found Aldric sitting on an upturned bucket, head propped on his hands, surveying the activity with boyish excitement. The stable was empty of all signs of the soldiers. Beyond Aldric, a sulky lad forked hay and dung into a barrow, casting covetous glances toward the market. Aldric grinned as Dominic joined him.

"Welladay, thought you'd never waken," he said, jumping to his feet. "Dunforde waited as long as he could. They've only just got going."

"We can follow them now if you want," Dominic said, wandering over to Kismet's stall and running a hand through her mane.

Aldric rolled his eyes. "Orders are to stay here. Recover. Besides, there's someone else who wants to see you. Over there." He nodded at the town square. "Celia wants you to meet her at the smithy," he said. His mouth twisted. "Can't wait to see what skills she has in the metalworking area."

Dominic grinned. "Apparently, Guildford's instructed Lionel to watch over her."

Aldric smirked. "Aye. Dunforde insisted Guildford came with them. He didn't want to leave her. Not that secure in his ability to hang onto her if she's left in your vicinity, obviously."

Dominic grimaced. "By the Gods, I don't want her," he said. "And I'm sure Celia doesn't want me. She seems perfectly satisfied with her present arrangement."

Aldric shrugged and nudged the bucket out of the way against the wall. "Still think you shouldn't get anywhere near her," he mumbled.

Dominic frowned. "You really have got it in for her, haven't you?" he said, fingering the pieces of the dagger he'd stowed safely in his pouch the night before. "She's Guildford's leman, a passing fancy. That's all."

Aldric sighed. "Mayhap. I hope you're right. Come on then," he said, with the air of a man going to his own execution. "Let's go."

Squeezing through the buzzing throng was harder than it looked. Pulling Aldric away from the sweetmeat stall harder still. Distracted by the festivities, munching on marchpane, they found the smithy halfway down a quiet back street. The smith himself was nowhere to be seen—probably part of the strong-arm wrestling match they'd just watched as part of the ongoing entertainment. The warmth from the forge smothered them as they ducked in.

"How now," Celia said, turning to face them, a broad smile stretching her lips. "I'm glad you came."

Backlit in the light from the fire, her hair glowed chestnut. She'd donned a leather apron over her normal garb. The narrow room looked like any other smithy across Epera, crowded with tools, workbenches, and a huge anvil heavy enough to support a mountain. Perspiration beaded Lionel's forehead as he pumped the bellows. The familiar tang of iron and coal hung in the air. Celia held out a hand. "Let me have a look at your dagger again," she said. "I need to decide whether to repair it or reforge it."

"I could just buy another," Dominic said, hand halfway to his pouch. "You don't have to go to so much trouble on my behalf."

Celia blinked. "But that's yours," she pressed. "You've had it for years, haven't you? Was it your mother who gave it to you?"

He half shrugged. "Aye..." His forehead creased into a frown. "How do you know that?"

She huffed a laugh. "I could tell, last night. It means a lot to you. More than that over-decorated thing you're wearing now." She jerked her chin at the enchanted blade strapped at his waist and took a step closer, her warm, womanly scent mingling with the aroma of hot metal. "And you saved my life and Mistress Trevis' life. I want to do this for you. Please."

Up close, her wide brown eyes had flecks of gold at the centre. Mesmerising. Aldric hissed like metal dunked in a bucket of cold water, and Dominic stepped back, blinking. Numbly, he handed over the two parts of the blade, ignoring the younger man's hard stare boring into the back of his neck.

Celia took the pieces from him, stepping to the better light at the door to examine them more closely.

"I can mend this," she said after a pause. 'Twill be good as new. Do you agree?"

Dominic spread his hands. "I'm a falconer, not a smith," he said. "Do as you will."

Celia gave Lionel a nod. "More heat," she said.

Lionel pumped the bellows. Head cocked, Celia examined the broken edges of the blade, holding them lightly in her grip. Dominic exchanged glances with Aldric, questions sparking in his mind. To date, Celia had displayed no signs of any kind of magical ability. But, to his inexpert eye, she appeared to be almost listening to the metal, rocking slightly as she turned the pieces in her hand. A prickle of unease trickled like sweat down the length of his spine. His hands tingled with the gradual return of his telekinesis.

"What are you doing?" he asked. "Are you using magic?"

Celia laughed. "Nay, not me. Just feeling the weight, working out what it's made from, so I get the temperature right." She glanced across at the forge and nodded to Lionel. "That's hot enough," she said.

Picking up a cloth, she wiped the two broken edges of the blade clean. The forge blazed white hot as she thrust both ends into the blaze of the fire, humming lightly under her breath. Shifting uneasily from foot to foot, Dominic watched as the metal glowed angrily in the furnace's glare. Celia glanced at him from under her lashes.

"You don't have to wait, Sir Skinner," she said. "This will take time. I've got a day's work ahead to make it anew and as strong as it ever was."

Dominic's eyes widened. "So long?"

Celia shrugged. "This was a fine blade, once. It's only fitting that the repair matches the quality," she said. "Your mother knew a good knife."

Dominic raised his eyebrows in acknowledgement. "I come from a long line of tanners," he said. "I suppose it goes with the territory."

Celia nodded as if this was what she'd expected. Humming, she strode across to the anvil and laid the metal across it, carefully aligning the two softened ends.

"Where did you get that other dagger? Surely that's too fine for everyday," she said as she began creating the weld. The forge rang with rhythmic blows from her hammer as she worked, her eyes narrowing in concentration.

Fascinated by the sureness of her movements and the play of muscles in her arms and back as she turned the blade over and began anew, Dominic told her how the dagger came to him.

"I've never used it, except to play with," he said at the end of his story. "Sometimes I think it sings to me, but more often it's just annoying, trembling away. I'll be glad to get my old one back, to tell you the truth."

Lionel rolled his eyes from his position at the bellows. "Sings to you," he scoffed. "As if."

Satisfied with the first part of her weld, Celia thrust Dominic's knife back into the furnace and straightened, brushing a tendril of hair from her perspiring face. "Some blades can do that," she said. "I've heard some are bound with enchantments. Like yours. I've heard tell of one blade that can sever souls, but that's just a story smiths tell their children to get them to behave."

Dominic grinned. "That might have worked on me, to be sure," he said lightly. "Pity my mother didn't know it."

Celia smiled, and Dominic blinked, caught by the full force of her charm. He dropped his eyes hastily, aware of the swell of unwilling attraction. Aldric cleared his throat, and Dominic took a step back as his squire tugged at his sleeve. "Are we done here?" Aldric asked tightly, "There's a mummer's show I'd like to see."

"Aye," Dominic mumbled. He bowed slightly in Celia's direction, but she'd plucked the knife from the forge and was bending over the anvil, the curve of her hips clear beneath her gown. Straightening, he caught the knowing smirk in Lionel's green eyes. The man lounged against the wall, propped against it with one foot.

"Don't miss the fair," Lionel said, nodding at the door.

"You can buy me dinner, Sir Skinner," Celia said, glancing up from under her well-marked brows as they left. "Shall we meet at the tavern after sunset?"

Caught by good manners, Dominic nodded reluctantly as he reached the door. "Does the owner of this place know you are here?" he asked as he shouldered it open.

Celia's leaf-brown eyes glinted with amusement. "I made him an offer he couldn't refuse to stay away," she said. She glanced across at Lionel, who snorted with laughter. "He won't disturb us."

She raised her hammer again and brought it down smartly on his dagger. The noise of the ricochet found a strange response in his blood. At his hip, the enchanted blade trembled to life, along with other parts of him that had long gone wanting.

He paused, suddenly unwilling to leave her, his feet mired to the cobbles. She didn't look up, but the rhythmic tap of her hammer did the work of suggestion for her. Dominic watched her, his mouth dry, his blood rising with every successive blow.

Dark eyes sparking with alarm, Aldric gripped his elbow.

"Dominic," Aldric said more urgently. "Come on." He bundled Dominic out of the door and into the fresh air. The noise of the festival rose all around them. Normal. Healthy. Turning his head, feet dragging, Dominic's longing gaze clashed with Lionel's as the squire followed them to the door. Green eyes bored into his with a lazy, smirking indifference. The sound of metal on metal drifted into the busy street like a promise. The man nodded once and then pulled the door shut.

Still fogged with thwarted lust, Dominic allowed the younger man to drag him back into the bedlam of the fair. Face set, Aldric bypassed the sweetmeats and stopped at a drink stall. He thrust a flagon of small ale into his hand. Dominic took it, thankfully.

"By the Gods, what was that?" he said, glancing over his shoulder at the smithy. "One minute she's mending my dagger, the next..." Cursing the blush that swept over his face, Dominic scrubbed his hand through his hair, conscious that his heart still pounded like a drum.

"Told you she's trouble," Aldric said, his jaw set. "And you wouldn't listen. Can't you see she's playing with you? First, Guildford and Tom. Now you. She wants all of you at odds with each other over her. If I was at all interested in girls, I bet she'd try it on me, as well."

Gesturing to the stallholder, who was listening to the conversation under the guise of serving other customers, Dominic bought another couple of drinks. His brow furrowed. "Guildford can have her," he said, with a shudder of his shoulders, handing one to Aldric. "I would have forgotten everything if you hadn't dragged me out. Felicia, the troop's mission, Joran's instructions. All of it, just for one second with her. I don't know how she did it. Why did I tell her about the enchanted blade? It's as if I couldn't help myself."

Aldric sniffed in derision. "She's just a knowing wench who knows how to tempt. And now she has your dagger," he said, his tone sour. "And she expects you to buy her supper. No-one needs farsight to work out how that will end."

Dominic stared at him. "I'm not meeting her. You are," he said as his fiery blood cooled enough to allow reason to assert itself.

Aldric paled. "Not I," he said. "I don't want to get anywhere near her."

"You don't have to eat with her. Just give her the money for a meal and get my dagger back."

"But..."

"And in the morn, we'll set off without her. Leave her and Lionel to find their own way to Falconridge. Will that satisfy you?"

A reluctant smile crept over Aldric's face.

"Aye, although you'd better hope she absconds with Lionel," he said. "I don't fancy your chances if she turns up at Falconridge, knowing you left her here to fend for herself. Hardly the honourable behaviour of a knight."

Another shiver crept across Dominic's back. Across the noise of the crowd, the rhythmic chink of hammer on metal from the smithy drifted in the breeze. Cold and chilling. Gripping Aldric's elbow, he steered the younger man deeper into the throng.

"Honour be damned. Celia can look after herself," he said. "Better Lionel than me."

CHAPTER 16

S leep still blurring his eyes, Dominic strapped his freshly repaired
  blade to his waist and buried the enchanted dagger deep in his
pack, glad to be free of its constant barrage of vibration and distant humming. Nightmares had haunted him the night before. He'd
looked for Felicia in his dreams as he always did, but somehow, her
delicate face had merged with Celia's. Impossible to tear them apart.
Images of his uncle, broken and white-faced, picking his way through
some dark tunnel drifted across his mental landscape. He'd woken
with the confounding impression that he'd travelled somewhere far
away overnight and that part of him was still there. Yawning, he leaned
over and nudged Aldric awake.

Slumbering in the aftermath of revelry, the town barely stirred as
the two young men crept out of the inn and hurried towards the
stable. First light tangled with dew-spangled cobwebs and sparkled in
the depths of shallow puddles. Upturned barrels littered the market
square. Awnings, damp with dew, drooped from the empty stalls.
Crows pecked at the cobbles, seeking scraps. The remains of the enormous bonfire still smouldered, filling the air with the scent of ash.
Storm clouds were already piling in the north.

Kismet stamped her welcome on the cobbles as she spied their
approach. Mistress Trevis drew her oxen away from the water trough,
tilting her head in greeting. A wry smile twisted her lips, and she placed

her finger there, shaking her head before Dominic could utter a word. He frowned, following her exasperated gaze behind her heavy wagon.

"Gods greetings, Sir Skinner," Lionel said. He limped from the darkness of the stable, squinting in the light. "Are you ready to leave? We are."

Guildford's squire kept his face almost entirely expressionless, but Dominic's heart sank. Already tired from a night of fitful sleep, his mood took a decided dip. He exchanged glances with Aldric, who was glaring at his fellow squire with something akin to hatred.

Dominic nodded shortly. "Brearley," he said.

Greeting complete, he ignored the man and concentrated on feeding and watering Kismet for the journey, avoiding Celia's curious gaze as she wandered into view. The young woman surveyed him with her hands on her hips, brown hair rising in the breeze, her cheeks rosy with health.

"How now, Sir Skinner. All recovered?" she asked, picking up a blade of straw and biting the end.

Dominic cleared his throat, annoyed at the blush that was gaining ground under his tunic. "Aye," he said, pulling up Kismet's girth. The horse grunted as he tightened it. "I thank you for your trouble in mending my blade," he said awkwardly, as Kismet tossed her head. He wrapped an arm around the horse's neck, taking comfort in her solid strength.

Celia took a moment to survey him before she replied, twirling the straw idly between her fingers. "It was my pleasure," she said, her voice low. 'Tis a pity you could not join us at supper." Her eyes drifted over him, noting the old dagger in his belt. She smiled. "Does the repair meet your approval?" she asked.

"It is without fault," he admitted. "You are talented indeed."

Avoiding the lure of her smile, Dominic turned to Kismet's bridle, slipping the bit into her mouth and tightening the chin strap. Over her sturdy shoulder, his gaze clashed with Aldric's. The lad was saddling his own horse with stiff shoulders, his generous mouth one straight line of disapproval. Dominic sighed. Some journey this was like to be! He opened his mouth to say something, but Mistress Trevis interjected before he could. She strode forward, hefting her own pack higher on her shoulders.

"Are you rested, Sir Skinner?" she asked, merriment twinkling beneath her concern for his health.

"Aye, followed your orders to the letter," he responded, following her lead.

The older woman strolled over and took his hand, one hand on his brow. He relaxed under the warmth of her touch. 'Tis well," Mistress Trevis said. "I'll give you another draught when we halt at midday." She turned to Celia, eyeing her with distaste. "You'll travel with me, mistress," she said. "Wrap up warm. There'll be a shortage of laps on this ride. If you are cold, you can bide in the wagon."

Celia bridled. "Is Sir Skinner not the leader of our group?" she said, annoyance pinking her cheeks.

Mistress Trevis raised a well-marked eyebrow. "Sir Skinner will lead," she said, "But I was in the army before I followed the healing profession. Make no mistake, young lady, I know what I am about." Her tone brooked no disobedience. Biting her lip, Celia lowered her eyes. She climbed onto the wagon seat, clutching the folds of her cloak around her. A furious scowl disfigured her features.

Dominic stifled a laugh as Mistress Trevis winked at him. "Shall we depart?" she asked, stalking toward the wagon.

Vaulting to Kismet's back, he tightened his thighs as she flirted with the cobblestones. He avoided Celia's stare as he reined his mount to stillness, waiting for Mistress Trevis to stir her oxen to move. Settling into his saddle, he turned to the north, the wind rising in his face.

A morning's ride saw them cresting the brow of a steep hill. A broad track snaked towards the mountains, better maintained than the crumbling mountain pathway that had nearly claimed them a couple of days before. Birds called and circled overhead, and a light rain tapped gently on the covered wagon. Jaw set, Celia had retreated inside its shelter, having spent the last few hours wrapped in stony silence next to Mistress Trevis, who had more to say to her stalwart oxen.

Jogging ahead, wrapped in their cloaks, Aldric and Dominic stayed alert as they tried to close the gap between themselves and the troop. Lionel rode within talking distance of Celia, walking his mount alongside the wagon. Dominic's skin prickled the further they travelled away from the relative safety of the town. There was little habitation out here, apart from the odd woodcutter's camp. He rode with one hand on his sword, ready to respond as the path narrowed. They were a ready target for thieves and bandits.

The midday meal was a subdued affair. They ate in the slim cover of a stand of silver birch next to a bubbling stream, a steady breeze building to buffet their faces and pink their cheeks.

"The weather is closing in. How soon before we can catch them up?" Lionel asked from his position, crouched on a fallen log. He searched the ground for a twig and used it to pick at his teeth.

Dominic shrugged, swallowing his cheese. "Without the wagon, much faster," he said. "But I won't be leaving Mistress Trevis without an escort, don't even think it."

Grimacing, Lionel looked around. Mistress Trevis had unhitched the placid oxen and led them to the brook to drink. Celia remained in the cart. Dominic swallowed a last mouthful and stood, scrubbing his hands on his britches. The wind ruffled his hair as he turned his head to the cloud-tossed sky.

"You are right, though. The weather is changing. We should be away. Aldric!" he yelled, his voice carrying clear across the brook and into the hushed depths of the surrounding trees. "Come on, we're going!"

He frowned when Aldric failed to respond, exchanging glances with Mistress Trevis, who looked up at his shout.

"Guard the cart and the women," Dominic said to Lionel over his shoulder. He marched into the trees, still calling Aldric's name. The lad had only gone to answer a call of nature. Brow quirking with annoyance, he drew his sword, comforted by the steady ring of steel as it left the scabbard. A couple of muddy footprints on the track marked Aldric's passage through the forest. Squirrels scurried from his path, watching his progress with bright, avid eyes. Crows cawed at the tops of the trees, balding with the advent of winter. Tugging his cloak closer, Dominic scanned the bushes and the hollows beneath rotting logs.

"Aldric, where are you? We need to go!" he yelled. But his voice bounced off the ancient trunks, swallowed by the drifts of rotting leaves tumbled at his feet. The scent of charcoal touched his nose, drifting through the vegetation.

"Dominic!" He stopped, whirling in a small circle, head cocked, trying to trace the distant shout.

"Where are you?" he bellowed again. Gritting his teeth, he focused his telekinetic powers. The sign of the Mage in his left palm tingled as the power gathered there. He grimaced as he turned again. Less power than normal. He was not yet at full strength.

"Over here!"

Casting a glance backward at the stream, Dominic sprinted deeper into the forest. Tugging his cloak free of a holly bush, he blundered into an unexpected clearing. Grey light illuminated a small field of tree stumps. A roughly thatched hut dominated the scene, surrounded by evenly placed charcoal pits. Smoke trickled steadily into the air. Another stream trickled behind the hut. A tributary of the one they had stopped by.

"Hello?"

He approached the hut, cautious, all his senses on alert.

"In here, Dominic. Quick!"

The lad sounded frantic. Abandoning all caution, Dominic charged in.

He blinked in the gloom of the smoky, ill-lit interior. A rough chimney breast crawled to the roofline. The small fire outlined a bench and a table along one wall. A single cot against the other. He tripped over an axe dropped to the earthen floor. Crouched next to the cot, Aldric looked up from beside the prone figure of an old man, his youthful face twisted with concern.

"I found him outside. He'd slipped with the axe, I think," Aldric murmured. Glancing down, Dominic winced at the blood dripping freely from the man's ankle, clamped by Aldric's hand. Thick blood oozed over his fingers. The discarded boot lay ruined at his side.

"Can you find something to bind this?" Aldric said. "It's deep. I daren't let go."

A quick glance around the simple chamber revealed nothing much of use. Reaching into his pouch, Dominic dragged out a linen kerchief. "Here," he said. "This might do if we tie it tight enough. We must get him back to Mistress Trevis."

The man groaned as Aldric wadded his own kerchief into a thick pad and pressed it against the jagged wound. Dominic wound the cloth around it as tightly as he dared. "I don't know if this will be enough," he muttered. "Look how much he bleeds."

"'Twill have to do," Aldric said. "Do you think we can get him to Falconridge?"

Dominic shrugged, bending over to shake the man's shoulder.

"We can try. Master, waken," he said. "You cannot stay here."

The man groaned, head rolling against his pallet. His grubby face was pale, a light perspiration shining on his wrinkled skin. Dominic's lips tightened. He slammed his sword into his scabbard and heaved the injured man over his shoulder. "Support his leg," he said to Aldric, coming to his feet in one swift movement. Despite his advanced years, the man's body weighed like several sacks of coal on his shoulder. For an instant, he regretted Guildford's absence. Transporting the old man on his own would not even raise a sweat for one of his strength.

Aldric scrambled to obey, squeezing through the door after Dominic. "Couldn't you use your magic?" he asked, quickening his pace to keep up with Dominic's stride.

"I might have to. He weighs more than he looks," Dominic said through clenched teeth, shifting the man higher on his shoulder. "But I'm not fully recovered yet."

Staggering slightly under his burden, Aldric alongside, hand still clamped to the old man's ankle, the way back to the horses seemed to take much longer. Halfway there, Dominic turned his head; ears pricked at a distant shout and the ominous sound of a skirmish. Kismet's high-pitched, angry wicker filled the air.

"By the Gods, what's that?" He surged forward, panting with the effort, and jerked his chin at Aldric. "Go. See what is happening. If it's bandits, stay out of sight and wait for me."

Aldric winced as he let go of the man's leg. Fresh blood dripped steadily through the makeshift bandages.

"Aldric, go!" Dominic's command was harsh. Biting his lip, Aldric sprang away, snatching his bow from across his shoulders and loading it on the run. The shouts grew in intensity, accompanied by the thwack of fists on flesh. The short hairs on Dominic's neck raised at the sound. Gritting his teeth, he broke into a sprint, the old man's head bouncing uncomfortably against his spine on every step, already reaching for his sword.

CHAPTER 17

Panting for breath, Dominic jerked to a halt at the edge of the forest, scanning the chaos taking place beneath the stand of birch as he lowered the injured man to the ground.

With blood dripping from a gash across her forehead, Mistress Trevis was defending the wagon from a couple of ragged attackers armed with cudgels and daggers. She wielded her short sword with wicked, vicious strokes, forcing the two men back from the rich pickings within. Dominic glimpsed the white oval of Celia's face as she peeked out, only to disappear again. His mouth thinned. Sword raised, Lionel stood near the foot of the wagon. His pale eyes clashed with Dominic's across the space.

"By the Gods, don't just stand there, you idiot!" Dominic yelled. He strode forward, shaking his head as Lionel jabbed half-heartedly at the nearest ruffian. His hesitant efforts did little to dissuade the man. A patched elbow lashed backwards, and Lionel stumbled to the ground, a thin thread of blood staining his cheek. His assailant grabbed the sword from his hand and whirled on Mistress Trevis. Aldric's arrow stopped him in his tracks. It lanced across the space and buried itself in the rough boards of the cart, right in front of the thief's nose. The man jerked around, searching for the bowman. His distraction cost him dear. Blood boiling, Dominic sprinted onward, launching himself into the fray. Their swords rang as they engaged. Eyes narrowed, Dominic took a firmer stance and mounted an attack. His opponent had received some training in the past. That much was obvious in the first rushed seconds of their encounter. Blue eyes alight in his grimy face, the man dropped back away from the cart, giving himself more space. Jaw set, Dominic closed the ground between them. Mistress Trevis fought beside him, her face a mask of concentration. Out of the corner of his eye, he was aware of yet another thief sidling towards Kismet and her laden saddlebags. His heart clenched with fear as the man took out a knife. The wicked blade glinted in the afternoon light. Kismet threw back her head, snorting her annoyance as he crept closer. The bandit held his knife hand behind his back, his free hand reaching for her bridle. Dominic grunted as his opponent took advantage of his momentary lapse of concentration. Another strike, and another. His breastplate took the blows, and he dragged his attention back to his own fight, struggling for purchase on the damp grass. Heart pumping like a piston, he lunged and parried, struggling to concentrate on two things at once. All his wealth was in those bags. Including the enchanted dagger. It would seem like a fortune to this downtrodden group. Not to mention the danger to his beloved horse.

Turning at the last second, he thrust his palm out to her. He dared not risk using his gift against a Citizen, but there was nothing to stop him encouraging his mount. "Kismet, up!" he yelled at the top of his lungs. The surge of power collected under the irate mare. Ears flat, eyes wild, she reared, lashing out with her front legs. The thief's skinny chest caved in with a sickening crack. He catapulted backwards into the stream and remained there, water cascading into his gaping mouth.

Facing Dominic, the swordsman's eyes widened with fear. "Blessed!" he said. He dropped his guard for an instant. It was all Dominic needed. Eyes narrowed, he closed, forcing the man's chin back at sword point. The man arched backwards away from it and dropped his weapon onto the slippery grass.

"Pax," he wheezed. "I yield. Please, do not kill me!"

Aldric loosed another arrow that pierced the foot of one of Mistress Trevis' attackers. He winced, stumbled, and Dominic rounded on him with the back of his arm. The blow was enough to knock the man to the ground, where he stayed, yelping with pain. Mistress Trevis finished the last thief with a roundhouse blow of her free fist that took him completely by surprise. He crumpled at her feet, and she stood over him, face grey with exertion and grim determination, her hair a mess of crimson snarls, gown stained with her own blood.

"Thank the Gods you came back," she remarked between breaths, swiping a hand across the cut on her forehead and glaring at the stain on her skin. "I'm getting too old for this."

"Aldric, get some rope from the cart," Dominic ordered. "A night out in the open will teach them all a lesson." He glanced at Lionel's long form where it lay at the foot of the wagon. The squire groaned as he sat up, massaging his jaw.

"A lot of use he was," he muttered. "My apologies, Mistress Trevis. I thought him made of sterner stuff than this."

Mistress Trevis snorted a laugh, her expert gaze taking in the fresh bruise on the young man's face and his crestfallen expression. "Well, now we know for next time," she said, sheathing her sword. "Are you hurt?"

"Nay, but there's a man over there in desperate need of aid, Mistress," Dominic said. "A collier has all but chopped off his foot with his own axe."

The healer nodded shortly and bustled to her wagon. "Get out of the way, wench," she snapped. "I need to reach my supplies. Fine lot of help you were."

"Celia was frightened," Lionel protested, staggering to his feet.

"Humph," Mistress Trevis grumbled with a disbelieving shrug of her shoulders. She gathered her satchel and headed for the trees.

Aldric dropped to his knees with a length of rope, rolling Dominic's captive over with a swift kick and binding his hands behind him. Still terrified of Dominic, the man laid entirely still, his grubby cheek pressed flat to the dark earth. He was wearing a roughly carved necklace, a humble piece, mere wood and leather, carved with the mark of the Mage. It peeked out from beneath his frayed collar.

"You are devout," Dominic said, spying it.

The man's thin face twisted. "I was a soldier once," he said. "One of Dupliss' men. We all were."

Dominic scowled, one hand creeping to his dagger. "Dupliss," he said. "He's the man we seek. What do you know of him?"

His captive snorted, struggling to sit up against the wheel of the cart with his hands tied behind him. "Touched by evil, he is," he said, his tone clipped with anger. "Has some kind of plan to raise the north against the Queen. Threatened to kill us, he did, when we refused to raid our own kin at Hartwood and came over to the Queen's side. We ran for it rather than risk his wrath. But no-one wants to employ us, so here we are. Robbing."

"So, you don't know where he is?" Dominic pressed. "There's a price on his head. A good one. I'm sure you could use a windfall like that."

The man looked at him, his sapphire gaze hard. "Aye, we could use some good fortune. 'Tis a hard life, this. Dupliss is around here somewhere. Wish I could tell thee summat useful." His eyes drifted over to his fallen comrade lying motionless in the rushing stream. Free of unwanted attention, Kismet grazed peacefully on the bank. Bird song sounded once more in the watchful forest. "That's Robbie," he said quietly. His mouth quivered. "He was my brother."

Dominic bit his lip. "I am truly sorry," he said. "But this is no life for a man of skill. Would you work for the Queen?"

The man frowned, blinking furiously. Dominic glanced aside, unwilling to intrude upon his grief. "Think about it," he urged. "There is a place for loyal soldiers in our troop. We are seeking Dupliss to face the Queen's justice. 'Twould be a chance for you to start anew. All of you."

Raising his hand, he concentrated his power on lifting Robbie's broken body from its watery grave. Another wave of his fingers unwrapped the rope that bound his captive's fists. "Bury him," he suggested. "'Twill take you a while. There are tools in the collier's cottage down the path over there. And then find us at Falconridge. I will vouch for you."

"I just tried to kill you all and steal your saddlebags. Would you trust us so far?" the thief said, shaking his shaggy head. A tear trickled down his bearded cheek. He rolled his shoulder to brush it away.

"I know misfortune when I see it," Dominic said. "Everyone is worth a second chance." Glancing down at the man once more, he turned on his heel, suddenly filled with more questions than answers.

Reaching the rear of the wagon, he flung the cover back. Celia peered at him from the depths, her face smudged with dust. He frowned, struggling to reconcile the bold maid of the forge with the cowering figure she presented to him now. Aldric joined him, his shoulders tense with dislike.

"Is it done? Did they rob us?" Celia eyed him from beneath the curtain of her hair.

"I hadn't thought you a faint-hearted maid," Dominic noted, one eyebrow raised. "With all your spirit, I would have thought there would at least be a hammer involved."

She ignored the jibe, wrapping her arms about her waist. "They came out of the trees. Said they would take everything." She shuddered. "The wagon, the horses. Me."

He scowled at her. "With no thanks to your precious escort, they failed," he said. "All our goods are intact. You are safe."

Celia's shoulders fell. A fleeting frown crossed her brow. "That's good then," she said, drumming her fingers on the wagon side.

Dominic's brow quirked. She didn't look pleased at the news. Righteous indignation swelled within him, but Aldric, bristling like a bantam cock, took the words right out of his mouth.

"What are you about?" he demanded, "sheltering in here while an older woman goes to battle on your behalf, and only worried about our goods? Mistress Trevis took on three thieves whilst you were hiding out in here. They could have killed her, and then what would have happened to you? Lionel was worse than useless. Not much for fighting for your virtue, are you?"

He threw her a final scowl and stalked off to where the healer was leaning over the injured collier, his curses turning the air blue behind him.

Celia's mouth tightened as he left. She watched the lad's retreat with her chin raised, radiating tension. Anger trembling within him, Dominic glared at her, his eyes cold.

"Seems we've mistaken the shade of your true colours. They darken with each cowardly shadow you choose to hide in." With a dismissive flick of his hand, he turned and walked away, leaving a grim silence in his wake.

CHAPTER 18

T he sun was setting as Dominic led his small group down the overgrown ride and across the moat to Falconridge two days later. The shadow of the gatehouse set in the thick outer walls loomed over them as they exchanged the dank wildness of the verdant forest for old grey stone and the chance of a decent meal.

"How now. About time, too. Dunforde was sure something terrible had happened to you." Will Dunn hailed their arrival at the manor, waving at them from the top of the gatehouse as they approached. "Wait, I'll open up," he called. The sloping roofs of the manor dominated the scene behind the lad's head. A jumble of slate and timber with tall, fanciful chimneys hinting at much wealth. But the walls sported moss and small plants seeding in the masonry. Petronella's flag flew listlessly on its pole. Dominic knew Petronella had left her childhood home fifteen years ago. He doubted she had ever returned.

Sliding from Kismet's back, he waited for the lad to open the studded iron door, stretching muscles weary from the long ride, longing for food and a bath. Aldric joined him, his shrewd gaze travelling, as Dominic's had, over the signs of gentle neglect on the outer walls.

Mistress Trevis let out a sigh of her own as she left her high wagon seat, rubbing her abused haunches. Celia clambered down from the wagon bed where she had been keeping out of the way, ostensibly nursing the injured collier, and joined Lionel. Her piercing gaze swept the manor with some disdain. Since the bandit raid, they had both stayed at a safe distance from the other three. Ignoring the pair as much as she could, Dominic had hastened onward, eager to gain the manor, hampered only by the slower pace of the cart. But he dared not leave Mistress Trevis to fend for herself. The going had been rough. The cart, already battered, would need several repairs before it was fit to make the return journey. At his back, Kismet tossed her head, as impatient as her owner to rest for the night.

The door opened slowly in front of them, and they moved into the confines of Falconridge, staring round in wonder at the size of the residence. A large, cobbled courtyard greeted them, serviced by a well. The manor house itself comprised a ground floor with stone walls. A further gatehouse led directly under the living spaces, rising another two floors above it. Dominic guessed the ground floors contained the manor great hall, kitchens, still rooms, and storage. Tilting his head, he admired the timber-clad walls and the honey-red brick of the living quarters. The sign of the falcon decorated the massive front door and was repeated in complicated designs carved into the timber. The manor glowed in the light of the setting sun. He looked around for a stable boy and found one waiting at his side, looking up at him in some wonderment. Dominic turned Kismet's reins over to him and watched the lad take them in his grubby fist, leading Kismet away. The horse went with the boy willingly, her hooves clattering across the cobbles. Dominic turned to Will, who had clapped Aldric on the shoulder and was exchanging news.

"Bandits!" Will said, his eyes rounding. "We never saw action all the way here. 'Twas the most boring time."

"Gods greetings, Will," Dominic said, joining him. "Where's Sir Dunforde? I need to make my report."

"On patrol to the north. Tom's group is scouting east. Guildford's got another group scouting west. So far, all is clear," the lad reported. "They'll be back afore dark. Come, I'll take you to the steward. He'll get you settled." He glanced at Celia, lingering on the edge of the group. "Are you to work here, Mistress?" he asked.

Celia moved a shoulder in a half-shrug that might have been agreement. Her eyes glinted with resentment as she turned them towards Dominic. "Mayhap," she said shortly. 'Twill depend on my lord Wessendean's wishes, I don't doubt."

A fleeting frown crossed Will's freckled forehead. Shrugging, he headed for the magnificent entrance. "Come with us, then," he said. "Master Ash will have to place you."

A short flight of steps, flanked by a low balustrade crowned with falcons carved from granite, led them through a further door and into a wide passageway dominated by a huge candelabrum hanging from the vaulted ceiling. Cool air brushed softly over Dominic's face as he gazed around, taking in the tall, panelled walls decorated with dusty tapestries. A display of armour dominated the left-hand wall. Portraits of former Falconridge family members took pride of place on the richly carved staircase. He took a step for a closer look, drawn by their vibrant colours and out-moded attire, but stopped at the approach of a small, wizened old man who bustled forth, rubbing his hands together with what looked like immense satisfaction.

"My lords, my lords," he said, sweeping a bow so low his long grey beard brushed the flagstones. He winced as he creaked upright, but his face still wore a merry grin. "We have been expecting you hourly. My apologies for not welcoming you. Kitchens, you know. Never a dull moment! Master Ash, Steward, at your service!" He bowed again.

A smile tugging at his lips, Dominic blinked, taken somewhat aback by the steward's spritely energy. 'Tis a pleasure, sir," he said. "My name is Dominic Skinner." He performed the introductions, but paused when he came to Celia. The girl brushed past him, pert as a sparrow.

"Celia Smith, sir," she said brightly. She threw back her hair, her skin glowing like satin in the light of the candles. "My lord of Wessendean's companion."

Master Ash looked her over, his expression tightly controlled. "Ah, yes," he said, somewhat stiffly. "My lord mentioned you. I will show you to his quarters." He stood back and waved them up the stairs, recovering some of his former gaiety. "Come, come. Plenty of room for you all. Falconridge bids you welcome. We will make merry tonight, to be sure!"

In short order, Master Ash allocated rooms, promised more wood, water, and candles, and bustled off to round up some servants to do his bidding. Dominic roamed the chamber, shaking dust from the curtains around his ornately carved bed. He turned the sheets from the mattress and passed a hand over it. Dry. That was a blessing, at least.

Aldric poked his head round the door. The chamberlain had given him a small chamber adjoining Dominic's larger one. "Do you think they provide baths?" he asked. "I stink like a skunk."

"I hope so. If not, a strip wash will have to do." Dominic toured his chamber, trailing his fingers across the hastily dusted surfaces. A carved oak trunk pressed against one wall waited to receive his meagre wardrobe. The tall, diamond-paned windows looked north, over the stable courtyard to the rear of the manse. From where he stood, he could see the edge of another well and the roof of the stable block. Ridges of mountains crowded the view further north, the lower slopes a blaze of red and gold, interspersed at higher ground with the dark green of pines and spruce. Snow crowned the tips of the tallest. The sun was dropping, and he shivered. Turning to his pack, he tossed a clean tunic and hose onto the bed and took the enchanted dagger from its sheath. As normal, the blade vibrated within his grip, the carved runes flashing blue in the candlelight. He stared at it, the familiar melody plucking at his senses, and stifled a shudder.

'Tis a minor miracle to find so many servants," he said, tapping the scabbard against his palm. "I thought there'd be no-one here but a steward." Biting his lip, he glanced around the chamber, looking for a place to hide it. Better to place his valuables somewhere less obvious if they were to be here for a while.

"Joran must have sent a message by pigeon or telepathy, warning them of our arrival," Aldric said. "Are there any Blessed here?"

Closing his eyes momentarily, Dominic opened his mental channels. A smile curved his lips as he registered the brisk energy of the tiny chamberlain. "Master Ash," he said. "He's a telepath. A handy thing, in the middle of nowhere. No wonder they are so well prepared."

He frowned as another mind brushed against his, only to retreat, fleet like a deer, before he could grasp the connection. "There's someone else," he said. "But they are very cautious. Mayhap, we'll find out who it is."

Turning to his bed, he concentrated his power on lifting the heavy mattress from the heavily carved box frame. He handed the dagger to Aldric and nodded at the narrow gap between the bed frame and wall. "Shove that in there," he said. "It will do for now." Aldric grabbed the blade with some distaste registering in his mobile features as he felt it tremble in his grip.

"I hate this thing," he said as he hid it in the shadows behind the bedhead.

"It's not my favourite blade either," Dominic said, dropping the mattress back into place and moving forward to smooth the blankets, "but I know it's important."

He glanced round at a knock on the door. Tall and stony-faced, a manservant, eyes small and sparkling beneath beetling brows, stood at the entrance, accompanied by a group of servants lugging a wooden bath and heavy pails of steaming water. A young maid of around ten brought up the rear, bowed under the weight of linen towels and washcloths tucked under her chin. A bar of soap and a vial of some sort of oil poked from the pocket of her apron.

"My name is Cedric, deputy steward. This, for your comfort, sir," the man said, ushering his staff into the room. He turned to Aldric.

"Let us know when you are ready, and we will bring fresh water for you." He nodded to another young maid laden with a bucket of wood and coal, who scurried to the newly lit fireplace. The servants busied themselves organising screens to trap the heat around the fire and prepared the bath. Dominic exchanged a grin with Aldric. At the Castle of Air, despite his status as a nobleman, baths were something he organised and prepared himself. As like as not, a strip wash normally served, shivering at his ewer with the bite of a stiff draft at his neck from his ill-fitting window. Or a plunge into the Cryfell in the height of summer. This was luxury, indeed.

"Do you require assistance, my lord?" Cedric asked, his heavy face impassive. At Dominic's negative, he bowed, his assessing gaze roving the room to ensure all was well. "Then we will leave you. Dinner is at eight bells in the Great Hall," he said.

He withdrew, closing the heavy door gently behind him. "By the Gods," Dominic said, stifling a peal of laughter. He eyed the tub, where the steam rose gently from water scented with a liberal handful of lavender. "The height of decadence."

"Well, go on then," Aldric said, wrinkling his nose. "Enjoy your luxury. I'm off to explore before I get clean. See if I can find a fresh scent. I don't fancy your lavender."

Eight bells from the manor temple saw the company in the Great Hall, feasting on roast boar and venison. The wind was freshening outside. Smoke blew back from the enormous chimney, which was long overdue for a clean. Clem's lyrical tenor rose above the hubbub to serenade the group with lays and legends of times long past. Master Ash dined at the top table with the knights. Heartened by hot water and freshly shaven, Dominic had spent most of the evening plying the man with questions, fascinated at his knowledge of the family in former years. At the other end of the table, Guildford feasted his eyes on luscious Celia, who had somehow found a fresh gown of deep crimson red edged with brown. The combination set off her dark blonde beauty, and her light laughter echoed from the rafters of the great hall. Deep in his cups, Lionel loomed gracelessly at her side, casting silent, jealous glances at the golden princeling. Sir Dunforde presided in the centre of the table, his dour gaze taking in the excited household. On his left, Mistress Trevis ate quietly, face thoughtful in repose. The fresh bandage across her forehead lent her a rakish air. Tom had lost little time in finding a willing bedfellow. His wit sparkled at the middle of the lower table, where a local widow listened to his tales of derring-do with scepticism written large across her comely face. Aldric was joining in, adding his own dry asides to underline Tom's tall tales. Their section of the board rocked with laughter.

Surveying the merriment, Master Ash sat back in his chair, hands clasped over his stomach. "Welladay, that's enough food," he said. "Me belly's as tight as a drum." Sighing with pleasure, he reached for his wine. "'Tis a long time indeed since Falconridge saw such company," he said. "Right pleased I was when I received the Prince's instructions, much though the need for it causes me pain. How is the Queen? Have you heard?"

"I've heard nothing from the Prince," Dominic said. A light blush swept across his cheeks at the question. He was deliberately blocking any attempt Joran might make to nag him about their progress. Dunforde had been painstaking about the use of pigeons to send word back to the castle. Dominic had been relying on Bird for news of the Queen, but so far, their communication had dwelt mostly on Will's welfare and on Bird's struggle with young Prince Ranulf, who delighted in hiding in obscure places for extended periods of time, especially when lesson time loomed. *It's a good thing I'm a telepath,* Bird had reported with a giggle. *He does not know what blocking is, so he gives his hiding places away for free. He's always confused when it's me who finds him."*

Smiling at the memory of their last conversation, Dominic turned his glass in his hand. "As far as I am aware, the Queen is awake but very weak," he said. "Her leg causes her much pain. Mistress Fortuna is doing her best to strengthen her."

Master Ash nodded gloomily. "Aye, that was my last news as well," he said. "I wish her well, poor lady. She was ever the more delicate of the sisters, as I recall."

"I know little of her sister, Jana," Dominic admitted. "Except that the Queen looked up to her and missed her terribly when she died." He took a sip from his glass.

"She did that. An awful time, it was, to be sure. Lady Briana was beside herself. Sent her almost mad with grief, losing the girl. We almost lost Petronella. Lass refused to eat. Couldn't sleep. My lady would follow her around the manor at all hours, praying to all the Gods the girl wouldn't throw herself out of a window or down the courtyard well. I found her standing on the edge of it myself, one freezing night. Picked her up and brought her back to bed. Blue with cold, she was." The little man stared into the depths of his goblet. "She kept gabbling something about her father, but he'd long left the manse by then. Rarely returned, except to collect her when it was her turn to make the journey south." He sighed. "I couldn't work out what she was talking about. Something about a cave up in the hills. A place where she and Jana used to go, before..." He broke off, his jaw tightening. "Welladay," he said softly into his cup. "I'm talking too much. Time moves on. And my lady is queen now, with a family of her own. We must wish her health and healing." He raised his goblet and stumbled to his feet. "Hie!" he shouted at the company, who stopped mid-sentence to stare at him in bewilderment as he stood before them, drink raised. "To my lady, the Queen!" he yelled.

The diners raised their drinks high before swallowing the contents and calling for more. Only Dominic noticed that Celia merely picked up her cup, a small, secretive smile playing across her expressive mouth as she mimed taking a sip. Eyes narrowed, he settled back in his seat, his mind returning to the evening of their first acquaintance in the chilly forest at Bearbank. "They're expecting me at Falconridge," Celia had assured him then.

But the steward had not acknowledged her at all when he first made her acquaintance this afternoon.

"Master Ash," he murmured, under the din of conversation, "do you know that young woman?" He nodded over his cup to where Celia sheltered within the curve of Guildford's brawny bicep. His bulk made a dainty maid of her that was less apparent when she stood on her own, without the burly shadow of his presence.

The older man's wizened brow wrinkled as he glanced down the row and then back at Dominic. "Nay, sir, I don't, except as my lord of Wessendean's leman," he said, stretching a blunt-fingered hand to a bowl of sugared plums. "Should I?"

"When we first made her acquaintance, she said you expected her here. She's an accomplished smith. Were you waiting for such? Or an additional servant, mayhap?"

Master Ash pursed his lips as he nibbled at the edge of a plum. He shrugged. "We have all the staff we need for your visit," he said. "I organised it as soon as the Prince informed me of your journey, and that was nearly a sennight ago. 'Tis good to see the old place come to life again." His gaze wandered across the company, his expression tinged with sorrow. Turning, he looked up at Dominic with the wise, sad eyes of a performing monkey. "'Tis you I've been waiting for, Dominic Skinner." Wiping his fingers on a napkin, he touched them to the carved wooden falcon Dominic wore on a leather thong around his neck. "Mistress Eglion told me you would come. The lad who wears the falcon on his breast and in his heart." His voice brushed against Dominic's magical senses. Trembling and softer than goose down, he whispered, "To my fear and sorrow, I have something I must give to you. The time has come. Meet me at the temple at midnight."

Scraping his heavy chair away from the table, the old man wobbled upright. He bowed to Dominic and withdrew from the crowded hall, the tail of his over-long cloak trailing him across the freshly lain rushes. Tugging a goblet towards him with a gentle twist of his fingers, Dominic sat back in his chair, one hand toying with his necklace, the simple wooden figure carved for him so long ago by his long-dead brother Gavin. A draft crept across the long room as Master Ash closed the door behind him. Dominic shuddered at the frost on the breeze as it touched his skin. *"Master Ash,"* he called in the privacy of his mind. *"What do you mean? What do you have to give me?"* But the old man's channels were closed. There was nothing there but silence and the taste of winter on the wind.

CHAPTER 19

A spectral mist haunted the edges and corners of Falconridge's central courtyard as Dominic made his way to the manor chapel later that night.

His boots crunched on a crisp layer of frost, and he huddled into his cloak, blinking in the near darkness. Sir Dunforde had called a halt to the evening before any heavy drinking could begin. Falconridge lay wrapped in slumber. Stars wheeled above his head, and the moon wore a halo of ice. Dominic's shoulders tightened at the flight of a midnight owl as the bird swooped before him, wings bright under the cold eyes of the night. The distant distress of its prey was loud in his ears. The courtyard smelled of frozen foliage and the distant tang of pipe smoke from the open window of the gatehouse, where the sentries were changing guard. Opening his mental channels, Dominic searched the ether for Master Ash's lively energy. He found it easily, frowning as his mind brushed once more against another telepath. One who cloaked their thoughts nearly as well as his queen.

"In the temple, lad," the old man's voice croaked within his skull, cheerful and alert despite the lateness of the hour. *"Hurry, it's freezing,"* he added.

Dominic grinned, increasing his pace, and then all but jumped out of his skin as the bite of a familiar, imperious tone echoed in his skull.

"Dominic, report!"

Joran; evidently awake and scanning the ether for any sign of Dominic's open mental channels. He gritted his teeth and stamped on his guilt, realising too late he'd made a severe error of judgement in trusting the speed of the nation's pigeons.

"My lord," he returned, striving for neutrality. Frozen to the spot, he waited. A sudden vision of the prince pacing the battlements, ever turned to the north, pricked his conscious. *"How does the queen?"* he asked, biting his lip.

He winced at the level of ice in the prince's mental tone as he replied. *"She would be better with news of the troop's progress. Are you at Falconridge? Have you found Dupliss or your uncle?"*

Dominic leaned on the nearest wall. The weight of the stone against his back was comforting. *"There is little to report yet, my lord. Bandits attempted an attack on one of our supply wagons on the way here. Absconders from Dupliss' forces. They refused to fight against their own kin at Hartwood."*

"And? What about Dupliss? What are his plans?"

"It is as we were told, my lord. He is planning an uprising in the north. To date, that is all we know. Sir Dunforde is seeking more information daily, but Falconridge is, as yet, safe. We will guard and protect this land as you wished, my lord, to the best of our ability."

Silence bled down their mental connection. About to close his mental channels, Dominic jumped again when Joran's voice sounded in his mind.

"Sir Dunforde wrote you saved the lives of Mistress Trevis and the supplies for Falconridge on your way there." The prince's tone was grudging, struggling to relinquish the ice of his anger.

Dominic smoothed the wool of his cloak, tangling his fingers in the folds, and stamped his feet on the cold ground. He didn't reply. His mind supplied him with a sudden, stomach-churning memory of the lurch of the wagon as his control slipped and the knowledge of the yawning drop that waited to claim them if he faltered.

"The Queen and I thank you and wish you well," Joran said after a long pause.

"May I speak with the Queen? Please, my lord. Let me speak with her," Dominic replied, his mental voice quivering on the request.

Another long pause. He waited, nails digging trenches in his palms, longing suddenly for Petronella's calm, wise presence. The security of her affection. For a moment, he thought the Prince might relent. But only one sentence carried back to him. Quiet, relentless as falling snow.

"Remember your task," Joran said.

The connection closed. Dominic bit his lip and bruised his fist on the wall at his back. Hot-eyed, he turned his gaze to the clear night sky, blinking in confusion as he registered snowflakes in the air, dancing, flying like tiny ice sprites in a non-existent wind. He held out his hand, expecting the delicate crystals to melt against his skin. But, to his surprise, his hand remained empty, glowing faintly blue with the power of the Mage that rippled constantly in his palm. He clenched his fist and brought it to rest against his chest, where the ever-present loneliness lay like a boulder on his heart. Snow in a clear sky.

"Felicia," he thought, grinding his teeth until he thought they might break. *"Where are you?"*

The iron handle of the temple door carved in the familiar sign of the Mage turned easily in Dominic's hand as he stepped across the threshold. Master Ash had lit the candles clustered at the temple altar. Dominic's gaze crept upwards automatically, searching the vaulting timbered rafters. There were falcons flickering in the candlelight everywhere he looked. Carved into the ancient wood, clustered at the tops and bottoms of the soaring stone columns that supported the structure. Huge tapestries in shades of blue and grey adorned the stone walls. Wide-eyed, Dominic's gaze leapt to an enormous depiction of the Mage, one hand raised to the sky, the other pointing to the earth. It dominated the wall behind the altar. Dominic lingered at the temple entrance, locking his eyes on the Mage. The God's presence trickled into him like a benediction, softened with incense, soothing his battered emotions with the promise of divine intervention. Scrubbing a hand across his damp cheeks, Dominic turned his attention to Master Ash. The tiny man knelt at the foot of the altar, his back to Dominic, his slight figure hardly denting the shadows. He appeared to be scrabbling around on the floor. Dominic moved to his side, his boots ringing on the ancient slabs, and snatched a candle to better light the scene.

"A little help here, lad," the old man grunted, taking a grip on a heavy crowbar. He pushed, and the ancient stone, worn smooth by years of shuffling feet, lifted slightly from its bed.

"I'll do it," Dominic said, passing the man the candle. A combination of pressure on the crowbar, with a little extra help from his power, eased the stone from the floor. Sliding it to one side, Dominic knelt down as the steward glanced over his shoulder, his sparrow-like eyes darting around the temple, shoulders hunched.

"Is all well, Master Ash?" Dominic asked, the skin between his own shoulders prickling in response to the man's caution. Master Ash's gaze bored into him. 'Tis the first time since my Lady Briana ordered this hidden," he muttered. "Even now, there are folk who would be interested in what she had to say. Can't be too careful."

He reached both hands into the dark hollow under the floor, feeling around with a frown plastered across his brows. "Where is it now?" he murmured, his voice hard with tension. "I know this is where she left it." He reached further. "Ah, here. I can feel the edge." He sat back on his heels and brushed dust from his cheeks, puffing slightly as he massaged his stiff joints.

"I can't quite reach it. She's given the thing a fair shove. Can you try?" He stood, and Dominic took his place, reaching one long arm into the hollow. His questing fingers closed on the rough edge of a fustian sack. Bemused, he tugged the prize free. "What is it?" he asked, gaining his feet.

Master Ash chuckled, his voice grim in the chilly air.

"My Lady of Falconridge's journals," he said.

Mouth dry, Dominic stared at the elderly steward. He held the bag out to him. The contents weighed heavily on his arm. There was more than one volume. "This is not for me," he said. "Surely these are private. Not meant for prying eyes."

Master Ash shrugged one shoulder, his face gaunt in the twisting light. "You fit the description Mistress Eglion gave me before she left," he said. "She was deep in the Mage's presence, standing right here in front of his altar on the day we buried my Lady Briana." His mouth twisted. "She said a young man would come, distant kin to the Queen herself." Dominic gaped at him, instant denial springing to his lips.

The steward smiled beneath his beard and held up a forbidding hand. "She said you would doubt me," he continued. "And I am bid to tell thee these books are precious. More than you will ever know. You are to guard them with your life."

Confusion mingled with trepidation reached deep into Dominic's chest and clutched at it with icy fingers. He shivered in reaction to the light breeze at his exposed neck that brushed his flesh like the touch of gentle fingers.

'Tis for you... Take them." The voice in his head was a sigh. The merest whisper. A female voice. That's all he could tell in the brief snatch of time as it resonated against his magical senses. Was it Felicia? He looked around automatically, forever searching the shadows for her delicate face, the ripple of her blue cloak. Nothing.

Master Ash tipped his rumpled head back to regard him, his expression a mixture of pity and compassion. "Aye," he muttered. "My

Lady Briana is here. As always. Guarding her treasure as best she may."
He stooped and slid the stone back into position with a grunt of effort.
The grate of its passage across the flags was loud in the heavy silence
of the temple. He took a moment to brush the dust back around the
disturbed mortar, rubbing his hands against his cloak as he rose.

"What...When?" Dominic moistened his lips and tried again to
marshal his spinning thoughts. "How did Lady Briana die?" he asked,
settling on a question that had never been asked. Not by Petronella
or anyone else, to his memory. The other revelation, that his humble
family were related to the greatest in the land, he discounted. How
could that be?

Master Ash lit a fresh candle from the guttering remains of another
and placed it reverently in a vacant holder. He bowed his head for a few
seconds, lost in prayer, and Dominic clutched the heavy sack closer
to his chest. He bowed his head as well, mirroring the elder's gen-
uflection. The soft candlelight underlined the sadness in his hollow
features. Another guardian, Dominic thought, and perhaps one not
long for this world.

Master Ash raised his head, the glint of tears sparking in his hooded
gaze. "Aye, lad," he said harshly. "Too long I've been here, waiting
for you. 'Tis your burden now, this treasure I pass to you. Mind you
guard it well." He paused, one hand wandering to caress the dusty
sack. "You'll find what you need within those pages, lad," he said. "The
answer to your question, and many more you have never known to ask.
Mayhap you'll find a path to your lost love. Who knows?" He cocked
his head, one grizzled eyebrow lifting at the surprise on Dominic's
face.

"Aye, I can see her, as you do when you think of her," he said. "A
lively lass, is she not? With a brain and wit to match. Beautiful eyes."
He turned, shuffling to the door. "A far cry from her oafish brother, if
you don't mind me saying."

Dominic smiled at the man's words. "Felicia's a telepath and a seer. She hid her Blessed status from her family for years," he said. "Guildford is a powerful young man, to be sure. But a Citizen only. No Blessed gifts I can discern."

With one hand on the massive door, the smaller man turned. "Yet you will not discount his influence," he said, stern as a judge. "Young Guildford has much to learn and everything to gain. He treads a perilous path, one foot in both camps, though he knows it not. He is a lost soul in need of guidance. Watch him well and keep him close. I charge you."

Frozen into place at Master Ash's assessment, Dominic nodded slowly. The bundle he clutched at his chest felt heavier, somehow. As if the knowledge it contained weighed more than mere paper and ink. As if it could change everything. His fingers tingled with power. A sudden urge to thrust the books away from him made his arms tremble. Master Ash tilted his face.

"Trouble is brewing, Sir Skinner," he warned. "The north wind is rising, as it did once before. Your task has only just begun. Keep your wits about you."

He pulled the heavy door open. A chill wind blasted the temple with the inexorable breath of winter. Dominic wrapped his cloak around him and dipped his chin against the icy tendrils of dread tugging at his heart. Pulling up his hood, he followed Master Ash into the storm.

CHAPTER 20

"**B**y all the Gods, where have you been?"

Closing the door to his dimly lit chamber, Dominic blinked at Aldric.

The younger man shivered in the chill as he clutched the enchanted dagger to his slim chest. A growing bruise darkened his jaw. Dominic crossed to him, letting the heavy bundle of journals slide to the tangle of blankets atop his mattress. He frowned at the mess, sure he had ordered his bedclothes more neatly than that upon rising that morn.

"What happened? Are you well?"

Aldric swallowed and held the dagger out to him. "Here. Take this horrible thing. I think this is what she was after."

"Who was after it? Here, sit." Dominic pushed the younger man into the single seat by the fire and took the blade from him. As ever, it trembled in his grip. He tightened his lips as its sibilant song wound through his senses. He could feel its agitation.

Relieved of his burden, Aldric scrubbed his hand on his breeches, his mouth twisting. Dominic dragged a blanket from the bed and tossed it over to him. "What happened? I'll have their hide," he said.

Aldric shrugged. "I don't know," he said, wrapping the heavy wool around him. "I went to check on Master Hadrian, the collier. When I came back, there was a girl in here. Just a young thing, but by the Gods, she took me by surprise." He fingered his jaw, wincing as he traced the bruise.

Dominic poured wine from the decanter on the heavy, ornate table and handed a draft over, his face grim. "And you think she wanted the dagger?"

"She was turning the room over. Never thought I'd see a slip of a girl heft a mattress that size," Aldric said. "I yelled at her, and she ran straight at me, elbowed me in the face and out the door." He shook his head, dark curls dancing. "I'm ashamed," he said. "I should have stopped her, but I was that startled, and she was so quick, like a mouse." His lip curled. "And I hate mice."

"Lucky you came back when you did," Dominic said, taking a gulp of wine. The alcohol warmed him. He eyed the dagger and placed it on the table. The blade continued to tremble, threatening to tip the decanter of wine over. Biting his lip, he retrieved it again.

"Gods blast this thing," he said. "It's never still. I suppose I'll have to keep it on me after all. Who was this girl? Would you recognise her again?"

Aldric shrugged. "It was dark," he said. "But no-one we've seen at the manor so far, I don't think. Where did you go?"

Dominic nodded at the sack. "To the temple. Master Ash gave me Lady Briana's journals," he said. "Apparently, Mistress Eglion, our Queen's grandmother, foretold our arrival, and I am now the guardian of them."

Aldric's eyes rounded. "But you hate reading," he said.

Dominic scowled. "I don't hate it. I'm just not very good at it. Started too late," he said. "Give me maths any day."

Aldric grinned over his cup. "Good practice for you, then," he said. "I'll enjoy watching you decipher the daily life of the mistress of the manor."

Dominic raised his eyebrows. "Judging from what Master Ash explained, I think they contain rather more than the household accounts," he said.

"Aye, well, I've had enough of magic and madness for one evening." Aldric stood, dropping the blanket from his shoulders and massaging his jaw. "I'll give you good night. Enjoy your bedtime stories."

Curiosity burning through him, Dominic waited as Aldric finished his wine and grumbled his way to his pallet.

Lighting a fresh candle, he sprawled on the mattress, ignoring the call of the dagger as it trembled at his side like a whipped puppy, begging for his attention. He glanced at the door as he drew the sack towards him and reached inside, wondering about the late-night intruder. Someone who knew about the enchanted blade and was prepared to ransack his room to find it. Brow quirking, he squinted at the heavy volumes spread out before him. Their pages were ruffled from much handling. Random snatches of parchment stuck out from the main content in places. His fingers drifted across the paper and came away grubby. His mind lingered over the obvious possibilities, snagging on Celia Smith and Lionel Brearley. But Celia had seemed disinterested in the blade when she saw it. Made light of his attachment to it. And she was far from the mouse-like figure Aldric described. His lip twisted with distaste. Undoubtedly, the woman would be abed with Guildford, cuddled up to his warmth and sleeping like a cat.

Hitching himself further onto his elbow, he dismissed the problem for the morning, tilted a random journal closer to the light, and turned to the first page.

He read until his tired eyes drifted shut and fell asleep with one of Briana's diaries draped across his chest like the flattened wings of a dead bird. Her long-ago daily concerns and fears stalked him in his dreams. She'd been a lady of much wit, with a questing mind, all underpinned by the deep distrust she felt for her oft-absent husband. The enchanted dagger sent its subtle song through the bedcoverings and into his mind. Free of the earth, his spirit roamed to Felicia. He flew to her like a hawk. Forever searching. Beneath his piercing gaze, the landscape undulated and peaked, all sharp edges and deep, shadowed valleys. The night air was cold and brilliant, like crystal against his senses. Stars lit his way. His dreaming mind passed one of Dunforde's sentry patrols, camped for the night in a secluded dip half a mile from the main track. Over another rise, the Iron Mountains loomed on the near horizon. The steep cliffs sweated ebony shadows. He circled high above them, at once attracted and repelled. The song grew louder, and he turned, chased away by the humming notes of its Gods-forsaken melody. Drawn back to Falconridge, standing proud in wild, once magnificent grounds. The Queen's standard drooped on a single flagpole. A lone candle lit a shallow window. Guards patrolled the perimeter. He circled the gardens once more, soaring on the wind. The manor was grand indeed. He could make out the silent chapel. More buildings and stables clustered at its rear. Far-flung farms, windmills, and beehives. Self-contained. Remote. A little like the Queen herself. In the manner of dreams, his vision shifted with the thought of Petronella. In a blink, he flew over the Castle of Air, where Joran roamed the battlements, much as Dominic had last seen him. Lonely and haunted as a ghost. Restless and worried, waiting for news.

The mountain melody hummed louder in his mind. Agitated, he rolled his head, fighting against the pull to the north. He dreamed of the enchanted dagger, still trembling, deep in his pack. Celia's face loomed over him in the darkness, her mouth full and pink, her eyes golden brown. He felt the brush of her kiss against his lips, the tickle of her long hair against his skin. Felt the stirring of his body. He whimpered in protest, trying to claw his way upwards to wakening. Trying to replace her image with Felicia's delicate features.

"Sleep," he heard her said. "Sleep now."

Felicia or Celia? He couldn't tell. Their faces blended, aching loss at the very centre of him. Pain, soul-deep. A woman sobbed somewhere in the night. And after that, nothing.

The urgent blast of a trumpet in the courtyard beneath his frosted window shouted him awake in the early hours of the following morning. Shocked from his broken slumber, Dominic cracked his eyes open, palms tingling with ready power, and prised himself from the warmth of his tumbled blankets. His toes shrunk against the chill flags as he felt for his clothes, donning them as quickly as possible. Curses from the adjoining chamber showed Aldric was experiencing the same dismay at being dragged from his bed before the sun crested the hilltops. The trumpet sounded again, its piercing clarion call urging haste.

Shoving his arms into his doublet and reaching for his breastplate, Dominic glanced at the scattered journals, looking around for a safe place to put them.

"Aldric!" he said. "Are you fit?"

"Aye," Sleep slurred Aldric's voice. "One moment, only."

Hair on end, he emerged from his room and tightened the straps on Dominic's breast and back plate with a skill born of long experience. Together, they navigated Dominic's preferred light armour, saying little. It was too early for conversation.

Only minutes passed before Dominic greeted his fellow knights in the courtyard, scattering hens before him, clutching a fist full of yesterday's bread and a hunk of left over mutton. Tom, already mounted in the courtyard's corner, and looking daggers at Jared as the lad slumped in his own saddle, tipped his head in acknowledgement.

"What's to do?" Dominic asked, as more foot soldiers emerged from their quarters, hands still busy with straps and laces. Their communal breath clouded the frozen air.

"Plenty," Tom said, shortly. He nodded at a pile of hay stacked neatly against one wall, where Clem huddled, holding his head. Mistress Trevis crouched at his side, her tray of bandages and salves next to her. Dominic could hear her tut of disapproval from where he stood.

"There's a group of rebels," Tom said, his voice hushed to a whisper. "Took Clem's group by surprise just an hour ago. They need reinforcement. We'll ride out to meet them. Are you ready?"

Heart pounding, Dominic nodded. Aldric hurried past, heading for the stables, his shoulders laden with additional weapons and supplies.

"A few moments. Aldric knows what he's about," he said.

He strode over to Clem. "Anything we need to know?" he asked, as Mistress Trevis prepared a clean bandage and pressed it to the man's forehead. Clem winced, pulling his tow-coloured shock of hair out of the way. A trail of blood trickled slowly down his cheek. His dented helmet lay discarded next to him.

"About ten of 'em, from what I could see," Clem said. "We put a few to the sword, but there are more out there, yelling threats against the queen, intent on coming here, to Falconridge. Make haste, we must go back."

"Was young Will Dunn with you?"

Clem looked up, his face white under his soldier's tan. "Aye, he were. Fights like all the demons of the Shadow Mage were after him. 'Tis a wonder to behold in a lad so young. Pity his horse had other ideas. They parted company, but that lad's a born foot soldier. I wouldn't worry about him."

Brow clenched in a scowl, Mistress Trevis flapped her hand at him. "Get you gone, Sir Skinner," she said. "I'll get this lad sorted to lead us out. Guildford is on his way."

Face hard, Dominic handed the wounded man a portion of his breakfast. Clem nodded his thanks and chewed with relish, wiping crumbs from his face. Mistress Trevis batted his hands down so she could finish the job.

"Lucky, you were," she said, tying a last knot. "An inch over and you'd have lost an eye."

"As long as I can still sing," Clem said, a hint of colour returned to his drawn cheeks.

A clatter of hooves and Kismet's familiar whinny drew Dominic away. He swung himself into the saddle, waiting impatiently for Guildford. who arrived on his own, eyes alight with the prospect of battle. "Gods know where Brearley is," he said, scowling back at the manor. "Strapped me into the armour and took off like a scalded cat. Suppose I'll have to fetch my own mount." He strode towards the stables, bellowing for assistance.

In short order, the group formed up under Tom's command. The light-hearted charmer disappeared. In battle mode, Sir Thomas Buttledon's emerald eyes radiated fierce purpose and a steely resolve. He glared round at the company, and then wheeled to the gatehouse, where the Falconridge guard remained. "Lock up tight, lads." he yelled.

"Aye." The guard returned his salute with a pounding of their pikes against the stone.

A spare horse led by a tattered stable lad appeared for Clem. He mounted somewhat dizzily, screwing his eyes up against the glare of the sun as it peeked over the treetops. "I feel sick," he said.

"No time for that," Tom said. "How far out were they? Tell me the lay of the land."

Leading the group forward into the dawn light, he listened carefully to what Clem had to tell him. "Knot's Hill, then," he yelled back at the soldiers as they put the manor at their backs and headed north over the moat. He waved at Dominic and Aldric. "Ride forth and scout ahead," he commanded. "Clem will go with you. He knows the land better. Report back. If you can, try to lead them to Knot's Hill. The foot soldiers will head there."

Spurring their mounts to action, Dominic and Aldric gathered themselves and raced ahead, alongside Clem, their horses' hooves drumming on the hardened soil. The wide ride spread away from them uphill, flanked by oak and beech crowned with frosted leaves in rich shades of red and gold. Crouched over Kismet's sleek back, hair streaming in the wind, Dominic glanced across at Aldric. The lad rode easily, his bow and arrows strapped within easy reach across his chest, his expression determined. Rested from their long journey, the two horses stretched out, only slowing as the path narrowed and steepened before them, twisting northwards into the mountains. Clem kept pace, his face pale, his fingers tight on his mount's reins.

"Keep going at the end of the ride," he called. "Straight up. It's narrow, but we'll get a good view across the countryside from there."

A growing sense of familiarity pricked at Dominic's senses as the path narrowed and wound ever upwards away from the stands of oak and beech. The trio entered a more sombre world of pine and juniper. The sharp, balsamic scent thrown up by the pounding hooves of their mounts filled the air. Crows cawed harshly overhead. The path jinked and turned, rocky and treacherous, with a steep drop to one side. Ferns crowded the edges of the paths, their fronds drying and russet brown with the onset of winter.

He frowned in recognition as he recalled a passage from Lady Briana's diary, written in haste on the day following her beloved Jana's death. Something about a steep pathway, and Jana's fatal fall from her horse. Briana had attributed the appalling damage to her younger daughter's hands to a frantic scramble into the gully that claimed the life of her sister. But more alarming had been Petronella's complete absence of explanation for what had happened. 'I cannot comprehend it,' Lady Briana had written. 'Jana knew the paths to the cave so well, and her body is so broken and battered I only recognise her by her hair and her new riding habit. Petronella cannot – will not, tell me what happened.'

Dominic had winced as he scanned the blotched pages, fragile with time. Their ink faded. In later entries, the lady of the manor had vented her fury and deep grief at the loss of her daughter, but in the first report of Jana's death her shock and disbelief were still raw. His gaze roamed the terrain to each side, scanning for hiding places or ambush points, but the most he saw was the frantic scurry of squirrels gathering pine nuts for the winter. Clem raised a hand to get his attention and jerked his head to a fork. He pointed east.

"This way," he called. "The path to Knot's Hill lies this way."

Nudging Kismet to turn, Dominic's sharp eye caught a furtive movement in the opposite direction further up. What was that? The tail of a cloak disappearing through the trees? Or just a trick of the shadows? Chewing his lip, he sat back in his saddle, slowing Kismet's stride, and drew his sword, squinting into the gloomy forest. Aldric slowed and threw him a questioning glance.

"What is it?" he asked.

"There's someone there, in the trees." Dominic stared past Aldric's shoulders, and then turned his head, chewing his lip. Clem's battered helmet and the hindquarters of his steed disappeared around the next bend as he carried on to Knot's Hill.

Aldric tutted, peering into the tangle of branches and vegetation. "There's no-one there. Come, Dominic. 'Tis urgent," he said. "The others need us. Leave it."

Mouth set, Dominic shook his head. "I must look. It could be important. Carry on. I'll catch you up."

"I'll go with you."

"No point both of us in trouble with Dunforde. Go. I won't be long." He pointed east. "Go, Aldric."

"I don't like it." Aldric said, jerking Hamil's head around. "This is not our mission."

Dominic heaved an exasperated sigh. "Our mission is to scout. I'm scouting. Go."

He barely watched Aldric leave. Hamil's hoofbeats marked his passage to the battlefield. Dominic's gaze hardened as his conviction grew. There was someone there. He could feel it.

CHAPTER 21

Alone, Dominic opened his mental channels and drew on his helmet, feeling the power in his palms surge at the prospect of action. Birdsong swelled around him. Kismet shook her head, harness jingling, and jogged in place. Dominic smoothed her neck and followed his instincts along the higher path, all his senses on high alert. Kismet's hooves ground a steady passage across the stony ground as the track steepened further still. He continued to climb, gazing around with a mixture of admiration for the beauty and wildness of the mountain forest and trepidation at what lurked amongst the trees. High above the valley, the air was fresh as crystal, tinged with frost. The rising sun cast long shadows before it, gilding the mist with hints of gold. He tilted his head as the faint sound of voices wafted towards him on the breeze, accompanied by the smoke of a campfire. He took a better grip on his sword. At his hip, the enchanted dagger jerked and leapt in its scabbard like a badger on a wasp's nest.

The path opened suddenly to a plinth of granite, standing like a platform at the mouth of a generous cave. A thin thread of smoke drifted towards him from its interior. Power spiralling in his palms, Dominic slid from Kismet's back and looped her reins over the branch of a nearby bush. The view was astounding. Remote Eperan countryside rolled away on every side, a tapestry of mountains and valleys, shaded in red and gold, alive with birdsong. Human voices carried further in the clear air. Creeping closer, he opened his mental channels but could sense no telepathic communications in the near vicinity. If he tried, he could pick up Master Ash as he went about his business at the manor, but apart from that, there was nothing to hear.

Only feet away from the cave entrance, heart in his mouth, he almost jumped out of his skin when Lionel Brearley appeared. The man met his astonished gaze with his familiar smirk. "Welladay, about time, too," he said. "We're waiting."

He stood to one side and raised a hand towards the dim recesses of the cave. "After you, Sir Skinner."

Dominic arched a brow. "I'll stay where I am. What are you about? Why are you not with Guildford?"

Brearley smiled. A mirthless expression that did little to lighten his expression. He eyed Dominic from his under his brows. "Guildford can look after himself," he said shortly. "I have other people to be concerned about." Dismissing Dominic, he wandered off to the edge of the platform and turned his back, fumbling with his breeches. Dominic, watching him with disgust, jumped at the sound of another voice.

"Well met, Dominic." The low voice was gravelled with age. Instantly recognisable. Mouth dry, every hair on his head standing on end, Dominic waited, his hand trembling on the hilt of his sword, as Terrence Skinner's tall, narrow figure detached itself from the shadows and stood forth in the dawning sun.

Shock crawled spider-like across Dominic's skin. The passing years had claimed more territory on his uncle's saturnine, once handsome, face. Shadows circled his deep brown eyes, and more white hair than black grew upon his head. But his expression was still calm and proud. He wore his tattered robes with dignity despite the stooping of his shoulders and the slight tremble of his hand on the staff that supported his weight. Memories flashed in chaotic fashion across Dominic's mind as they observed one another. Terrence Skinner, his last remaining family member. Scholar and teacher. Uncle, mentor, friend. Former prisoner. Killer. Traitor.

He was supposed to kill him.

He couldn't.

Questions crowded his tongue, but his reeling mind could not settle on any of them. He searched his uncle's piercing gaze for any sign of the blackness that showed the Shadow Mage had control of him. Terrence smiled slightly. "Nay, 'tis I," he said, transferring his staff to his other hand. Dominic noted the stiffness in his uncle's shoulder as he performed the action, and his mouth thinned. Felicia had sacrificed herself two years ago to prevent his uncle from claiming the Grayling in the name of the Shadow Mage. Back then, Dominic's knife had found a home in his uncle's flesh. Apparently, the man still carried the after-effects.

Suddenly, he knew the question he needed to ask.

"Where is Felicia?" he demanded.

"First things first," Terrence said mildly. He held out his hand, fingers clawed, knuckles swollen. "You have something that once belonged to me," he said. "It has led you here. I want it back."

Unbidden, Dominic's hand crept to the elaborately carved sheath that housed the enchanted blade. He frowned as his fingers closed upon it, realising that the dagger had gone completely still. "This?" he asked stupidly.

Terrence rolled his eyes. A familiar gesture at his pupil's apparent slowness. "Aye, young Dominic, that. 'Tis mine, given to me by my mother many seasons ago and decorated by the hand of a master craftswoman."

"Juliana Tinterdorn. Aye, I know of her," Dominic said. A rising breeze ruffled his hair. His telepathic senses awakened at the warning brush of a delicate mind against his own. He didn't stop to wonder whose it was. "I was told she died in the mines."

Terrence's eyes glinted. "Juliana was my love," he said quietly. "And she died giving birth. She carved that blade for me. Said I would always find her when she called. 'Tis mine. A keepsake."

Confused, Dominic frowned. "A love token?" He removed the blade, tracing the runes with gentle fingers. Terrence took a convulsive step towards him, and Dominic backed off, shoving the dagger back into his sheath. He raised his hand, power rising like the head of a falcon sighting prey. The Mage's symbol on his palm cast a blueish glow over his uncle's pale skin.

"I can use my abilities against you, Uncle," he said, relishing the security of the Mage's power as it tingled in his hands. "And I will if you come anywhere near me. I am not the ignorant child you once taught."

Terrence's dark eyes narrowed. "Nay, you are not," he said. "But I can give you your heart's desire. Think on that."

Dominic's soul lurched. "Felicia is alive? You know where she is. Tell me!"

Terrence lifted a grizzled brow. "The blade?" he prompted.

Torn with indecision, Dominic's hand tightened on the hilt of the enchanted dagger. It lay dormant beneath his questing fingers. At rest, now that it had reached its owner.

"Tell me where she is," he said. "And you can have it."

Terrence stood steady as a rock, hand still outstretched. "Give it to me, and I will tell you," he countered. "What do you have to lose? This blade means nothing to you and everything to me."

Eminently reasonable, as ever, Terrence's question bounced around his mind like a stone skimming across a pond. Joran's stern command to prove his loyalty echoed through his consciousness. Dominic clenched his teeth at the memory of the humiliating scene in the prince's study. Petronella's fragile features, pale as ice against the ivory of her sheets, swept through him. Aldric's face clouded with concern, advising caution. Reminding him to abandon his obsession with Felicia's disappearance.

"She'll die if you don't give me the blade." Terrence's mild-mannered tone insinuated itself into the treacherous thoughts circulating like a flock of vultures within Dominic's skull. He wet his lips, swallowing against the dryness of his throat.

"What do you mean? Tell me where she is!" He raised his sword, along with his voice, the edge flashing like the bite of his anger in the morning sunshine. He took a swift step forward and twisted his fingers, gathering the power there. Pulsing with his will, he felt it coil and tense within him, seeking an outlet.

Terrence took a step back. His own hand turned over. Mesmerised, Dominic flinched at the sign of the Mage pumping deep within Terrence's narrow palm, matching his own. Horror rose within him as he registered that, in Terrence's case, the sign of the Mage was a blur of ebony. Even as he watched, his uncle's eyes darkened.

"I will kill her," Terrence said. "Do not doubt me."

"Don't do it!" Felicia's scream ricocheted in his skull. Unmistakably her own. Defiant, determined, and gasped grimly through some distant, unimaginable pain.

"Remember the stable in Blade!" Her soft, beloved voice filled every part of his being with gratitude, even through the agony behind her words. *"Don't give it to her!"*

Caught up in the relief that flooded his senses, her words made no sense. Dominic's gaze snapped to his uncle, who glared at him across the slim gap that separated them. He whirled at the subtle clutch of fingers at his waist and plunged his fist deep into Lionel Brearley's gut. Whirling, he followed the punch with a savage kick to his narrow chest that took the man down.

"What do you mean, her?" he gabbled across their mental connection.

"Celia. She's a shapeshifter, Dominic. Like Briana was. The gift of transformation and illusion."

Heart in his mouth, he raised his blade against his uncle once more, face a grim mask of determination. "Celia?"

Between one blink and the next, his uncle vanished, and Celia stood before him, rosy-cheeked, buxom and angrier than a starving buzzard denied a meal.

"Celia," she spat. "My name is not Celia. But that blade is mine. Mine. Give it to me!"

"My Lady Felicia says no," Dominic said, ice settling over his heart. He lunged with the sword but pulled back instantly as the figure of Celia morphed into another familiar figure, tall, slender, with dark hair and eyes of sapphire blue.

"Petronella?" he said hesitantly, his skin crawling with disgust.

"She's not the Queen, Dominic. She's..."

Felicia's words ended in a scream of pain so raw it scorched Dominic's nerves. He dropped his sword with a clang that rattled against the stone. The woman before him laughed, high and mocking. "Recognise me, do you?" she said. Her eyes narrowed on him. Pitiless, cold. "I can be anything I want. Whenever I want," she hissed. "I can make you believe you saw two soldiers chased by a pig. I could make you think that black is white, and you will never question it. Stupid, just like my Lord Guildford." Her voice altered on the last sentence, dropping easily into the gentle country burr that had characterised Celia's breathy tone.

Dominic stared at her, perspiration blooming on his forehead. "It was you beneath the temple the night Felicia disappeared," he whispered.

The woman's eyes narrowed. "Aye, that it was," she sneered. "Cerys Tinterdorn. You will do well to remember my name, Sir Skinner. I will reclaim what is rightfully mine. You can do nothing to stop me."

A flare of his power and a twist of his fingers retrieved his sword from the floor. Disgust writhing beneath his skin, he lunged, driving his power and his blade towards her. She laughed again; the sound echoing in his skull and reverberating around the mountainside. The enchanted blade trembled once more at his hip as he thrust, strong and true. He stumbled over his own feet, his blade sinking into thin air as Cerys vanished.

Shuddering, icy sweat cascading down his back, he scrubbed his fists over his face, his heart yearning for Felicia, terrified for her safety. Her scream still sounded in his ears, and his last view of Cerys Tinterdorn's own eyes had bred terror through him as she dropped all disguise. Tall, slender. So like the Queen, it was uncanny. But for her eyes. Mocking, evil. Black as night.

Chapter 22

"Tinterdorn. She's Juliana Tinterdorn's daughter." He whispered the words as parts of the puzzle clicked agonisingly into place. Her skill with metal work. The constant trembling of the dagger at his hip as it sought its owner.

Someone groaned behind him, and Dominic spun around, sword raised in his sweating grip. He'd forgotten Lionel Brearley, but the man was little threat. The squire lifted his head and sneered at him from the stony ground, clutching at his ribs where Dominic's boot had landed.

"You're a fool, just like all the rest," he said through a gasping breath. "She's been playing you all this time, and you fell for it."

Dominic advanced until the point of his sword pricked the delicate skin at the neck of Lionel's sturdy tunic. His eyes narrowed. "Doesn't care too much about you, either, does she?" he said. "Or she'd be seeing to your comfort."

Lionel huffed a half laugh. "I doubt she's ever known how to care," he said, struggling to raise to an elbow, "but at least I know who she is."

Blood stained the tip of Dominic's sword as he pressed it deeper against the man's throat. "Don't mistake my youth," Dominic said, hatred coursing through him. "You are a traitor and deserve a traitor's death. It will be my pleasure to despatch you to whichever God you serve. "What does she want?"

Locked deep into his own anger and fear, he slid the sword in a delicate arc from one side of Lionel's neck to the other. The older man's eyes widened, and he winced as he shuffled painfully backwards to avoid the icy slice of its dance across his skin. Dominic followed, keeping up the pressure. Felicia's scream still twisted like the shriek of a hunting hawk in the very bones of him. "She has Felicia a prisoner somewhere. You will tell me what you know or die here, like the snivelling coward you are," he threatened.

Face grey, Lionel backed up almost to the edge of the platform. Kindness lost behind the stone wall of his anger, Dominic loomed closer. Part of him noted Lionel's eyes matched the verdant green of the pines that stretched across the magnificent landscape behind him. He waited. The breeze twisted around the two men, frozen into a tableau of conflict. Lionel's breath hissed through his teeth, his skin pale.

"Please, I can't breathe," he said.

"Punctured lung. I broke your ribs. You need Mistress Trevis," Dominic returned. "But you won't live that long unless you tell me what I need to know. Where did Cerys go? Where is Felicia?"

Lionel scrabbled a little further backwards and halted suddenly when he realised he'd reached the edge of the cliff.

"You've got nowhere to go except down, with your throat cut," Dominic said past his clenched jaw. He swallowed heavily, some of his anger leaving him at the sight of Lionel's sweating, pallid face. The role of torturer sat ill with him. "'Tis a pity, but at least you can enjoy the view."

The older man flinched, shoulders hunched. He coughed, blood staining his chin.

"You're not yet far enough north," he muttered. "You'll have to go to her home at Traitor's Reach, where she grew up."

Dominic scowled. "How do you know that?"

Lionel's gaze softened suddenly. "She were a babe, left at our door one freezing night," he murmured. "My pa took her in. Traitor's Reach smith, he was. We both learned our trade from him. I took it over when he got the lung rot, but Cerys' skill went way beyond anything I could ever do. Uncanny, it was."

Dominic's blood ran cold. His free hand clamped on his newly mended blade.

Lionel pressed his hand to his chest. "Oh, don't worry about that. There's no magic within it," he said between painful pauses. "She wouldn't waste her skill on you." His eyes drifted to the tooled scabbard at Dominic's hip. "That other'un, now. That's different," he said. "She marked that long ago. By the Shadow Mage, she did. It scared him, my pa. He took off that night, never came back. Took to carting. You met him just a few days ago."

Remembering the carter's last words, Dominic shook his head. "I know that blade," the carter had whispered at the sight of the enchanted dagger. He glared at Lionel. "She lied. So she did know him." he said.

Lionel glanced sideways, noting the distant drop below him. He took another gasping breath, its wet, rattling sound loud in the gentle sigh of the wind in the trees. "He brought her up. Gave her everything he could. Please," he muttered, his eyes wet with tears. "Help me. I can't breathe."

Shaking his head, Dominic flung down his sword. Perspiration dotted Lionel's forehead. He shifted restlessly. "Hurts," he said. "You've killed me."

"Please, you must tell me everything you know," Dominic said. His voice broke at the request. Cerys' mocking laughter trickled through his mind, sizzling like salt on torn flesh. "Who owns this blade?"

The former smith's eyes burned into his. One calloused hand crept out to clasp Dominic's sleeve. 'Tis your uncle's blade. That's true. His blood that marked it first. Then Cerys' mother, Juliana, when she added her enchantment to it. They were lovers, so your uncle said. In the mines together. Prisoners. Cerys would go to him for stories of her as a little scrap, that's how she knew." The last words left Lionel in a rush, forced out of him along with a rush of blood.

Dominic's eyes widened. "So my uncle is Cerys's father?" he said, the words like stones in his mouth. His whole being revolted at the thought they could be related.

Lionel grimaced, pressing his hand to his wounded chest. A faint blue tinged his lips. "So he thinks," he said. "But he's wrong. She's Darius of Falconridge's get. Born under the light of the Shadow Mage. You'd only to see them standing together to know." He glanced sideways again into the yawning drop beneath him and then rolled his head to stare deep into Dominic's eyes. "She wants the throne. You'll not stop her," he muttered. "No-one can."

Too late, Dominic realised the man's intent. Lionel closed his eyes and rolled over the edge.

There was nothing he could do. Shoulders hunched, he winced at the sound of Lionel's fall down the jagged mountainside. Below him, Kismet snorted and stamped her alarm as the man's body crashed to the deep recesses of the valley floor.

Dazed, Dominic stumbled to the edge of the platform. There was no sign of the former squire. In his place, the wind sang aimlessly around the rocky outcrop, stirring a drift of russet leaves to a frenzy at his numb feet. Somewhere at the back of his mind, he thought he heard the light touch of a girl's distant laughter. He shook his head, dispelling it. Without Cerys' dominating presence, the cave claimed his attention. Rubbing his arm across his forehead, he retrieved his sword with shaking fingers and moved into its quiet, damp interior, away from the judgemental sun as it burned away the morning mist. Instinctively seeking solitude.

"By the Gods," he muttered as he squinted around the walls, mottled with moisture and the musty aroma of wet moss. "She's the Queen's half-sister. What have I done?"

Head pounding, he slumped to a rough seat on a handy boulder, staring blankly at the campfire, still crackling in a rough circle of stones. Lionel's knapsack rested beside it. He nudged the bag with his foot. It didn't move. Warmth from the flames bled into his chilled skin. He stared deep into the blaze, wondering momentarily what Domita would say if she could see him now, as weak and trembling as his younger boyish self. "Knight of Epera," he said, rubbing a hand over the hollow weight of dread in his chest. "And look what I've brought to us. A monster, born from the night."

Cerys' enchanted dagger trembled at his hip. He slid it from its leather bed, holding it by the very tips of his fingers, and searched the curving runes for the additional rune Master Winterbane had mentioned. There, cunningly laced together and joining two other symbols. A curling tracery, etched with an arrogant flourish. He could almost imagine the woman calling her power into being as she dipped her fingers in her own blood, surrounded by the might of the Shadow Mage. In his mind, her dumbstruck father watched, perhaps from a distance, maybe through the mean window of a humble cottage, as his fosterling summoned the darkest of blood magic to forever curse the blade.

The knife must have hissed and sung its own enchanted song as it shivered under her touch. He wondered at the young woman's emotions as she worked her enchantments deep into the metal. What had possessed her to take her mother's love token and poison its pure heart? He couldn't imagine.

But no more.

Releasing his physical hold on the blade, he held it in place with the power of his own Blessed gifts, tip down over the fire. Mouthing a prayer to the Mage, he thrust it deep into the space between the logs, holding it there with the force of his will, willing it to melt. To writhe, to die.

The blade steamed and smoked. Flames licked the carved surface and tasted the runes. Its familiar song wound through his head, higher and higher. Heartened, he rose to his feet. Hands held out, he forced it as deeply as he could into the heart of the fire, leaning over the blaze until his own cheeks burned. Despite the heat and the pain embedded in the angry notes of its melody, the blade remained stubbornly solid. Only the hilt charred.

"Enough, enough. Let it die," he begged the Mage.

But his God was silent, withholding his judgement.

Not so Felicia. Deep in a contest of wills with the blade, he was unprepared for her precious voice as it filled his mind again.

"Dominic. No!"

Her command shocked him to life with the force of a hammer landing on his foot. He stumbled, almost falling into the fire himself. The blade landed beside him and spun like a devil. He skittered away as it screeched its displeasure into his mind, its song warped and twisted with anger. It came to rest, trembling, with its narrow point aimed straight at him. Dominic rolled over and retched onto the floor. Despair clawed at him. The need for sleep thrummed through his body with the draining of his power.

"Felicia, I'm sorry. I will find you." He sent the thought to her without hope that she would hear it.

To his surprise, she replied, her mental voice panting in the aftermath of pain. Hushed, as though she feared being overheard.

"Your companions need you. Do not seek me. Do your duty to the Queen."

Chapter 23

Fatigue crawled through Dominic, and the journey to Knots Hill seemed to take forever. He rolled in his saddle, guiding Kismet with his knees, praying for his strength to return quickly. He'd thrust the enchanted blade deep into his saddlebags once more, disgusted at the very touch of it. Its presence seemed to weigh on his senses like a stone around his neck, filling his thoughts with guilt and rage. He cast a glance at the height of the sun over the pines, biting his lip at the time that had passed since his time in the cave. Too long. His heels squeezed Kismet's flanks, urging her to more speed.

The battle was all but done by the time he arrived, trotting downhill through thick woodland, following the deep hoof prints left by Clem and Aldric as they charged into the fray. The churned-up ground was a mess of dead and wounded, littered with army-issue swords and pikes. His stomach whimpered in protest at the sight of this, his first real battlefield. The metallic tang of spilt blood assaulted his nostrils. Late-season flies were already swarming the staring corpses, buzzards and crows circling, waiting for a meal. The groans of the injured punched holes in his heart as he rode by, Kismet picking her way, delicate as a dancer between the bodies. He swallowed his gorge with effort, searching the fallen for Aldric and Will, guiltily grateful not to see them. Painted with blood like some sort of sacrifice, helm battered and dangling from one brawny arm, Thomas Buttledon conversed with Sir Dunforde under a stand of birch at the edge of the clearing.

Both men looked at him with sheer anger on their faces. Surrounded by soldiers with lighter injuries, Mistress Trevis glared at him from her station. Aldric circulated at her command, bringing water, bandaging limbs. Even he looked at Dominic with a complicated mixture of relief and rage. Dominic bit his lip and nodded, ashamed beyond belief. He deserved every inch of their disgust.

"By all the Gods, where have you been?" Sir Dunforde snarled as he approached. "We'd have been over and done in half the time were you here to take on the rebel Blessed. As it was," he gestured angrily around the bloody field, "a disgusting waste of good men on both sides."

"And still no sign of Dupliss," Tom added. "Please tell me you found him, and his body lies yonder in the forest." He frowned as Dominic swayed. "By the Gods, you're pale," he remarked in a slightly softer tone. "What happened?"

Still numb with the events of the morning, Dominic shook his head. "Lionel Brearley was a traitor," he said, forcing the words out through his parched throat. "Just in case Guildford wants to know where his squire went." He glanced across the battlefield to where Guildford was roaming the field, despatching the badly wounded with short, efficient strokes, his young face a study in duty and pity.

"Brearley? That numbskull? You spent all your time with him when you could have been here?" Dunforde leaned over and all but dragged Dominic from Kismet's back, ignoring his protests. "We needed you here. How many times do I have to tell you?" He drew back his fist, and Dominic reeled under it. He didn't even try to defend himself as it slammed into his jaw, with all Sir Dunforde's considerable might behind it. Kismet nickered in protest, and Aldric dropped his tray of bandages to stare.

"Nay, nay," Thomas caught Sir Dunforde's arm as he lunged again. "The lad's done in, like before. You can see, look." He beckoned to Mistress Trevis. She glanced at her charges and shook her head, her lips set in a stern line. Tom waved again, commanding her to him. "Punish him later," he said, his voice grim. "Something happened."

Sir Dunforde dropped his fist, staring at Dominic with disgust in his eyes. "Aye, well. Magic, of course," he said shortly. "But Blessed or not, I'll still give him a proper flogging come the morn. 'Tis only what he deserves." He gave Dominic a shove that sent him to his knees in the noisome mud. "I don't care what you think you were doing. You've let us down, lad," he said, his voice as harsh as a crow. "I won't forget it, and after tomorrow, nor will you."

The journey back to Falconridge took place in forbidding silence. Dominic rode with his head down, conscious of the glares boring into his back. There were a few missing spaces in the troops. A tattered string of prisoners roped together trudged behind them. His only blessing was that Will marched alongside, uninjured, his tired face grimed with a mixture of dirt and blood. Mistress Trevis handed Dominic a flask of valerian and pointed to the stairs as they arrived. She had not uttered a word to him. Sir Dunforde headed for the great hall, bellowing for food, and the manor servants jumped to do his bidding. Master Ash met Dominic at his chamber door, his face creased with alarm.

"Welladay, you look rotten," he said with rough sympathy. "Where's your squire?"

Dominic shrugged. Aldric had deserted him in the stables, muttering something about tending the horses. His chamber offered a dim, comforting sanctuary. The old oak panelling glowed in the candlelight. "My fault," he muttered. He took a swig of valerian and staggered to his bed. "I used too much time and magic trying to destroy that Gods-forsaken dagger. Lionel Brearley is dead, and Celia is not Celia."

Master Ash frowned. "Explain, if you can," he commanded, settling his narrow frame into a chair. He leaned forward, stroking his beard, deep in thought, as Dominic blundered through the day's events.

"Celia knew what she was doing when she lured me away," he finished. "Cerys, I mean." He shook his head, struggling to focus. "She's got the gift of illusion, and she wants that dagger, and not because it's a love token. Why?"

Master Ash sat back, drumming his long fingernails on the arms of the chair. "So, she's a transformist, just like my Lady Briana," he mused, "although Briana never used her magic in all her time here. She dared not. Too scared of her husband and the Shadow Mage."

"Lionel said Cerys is Darius' daughter, with Juliana Tinterdorn. Did Lady Briana know of that?" Dominic asked.

Master Ash jerked his chin at the space behind the bed where Dominic had placed the journals before he left that morning. "If she did, 'twill be in her books," he said. "But somehow, I doubt it. Darius kept his secrets close, always. Even as a child."

"So, Petronella doesn't know she has a half-sister?"

"That's about it, lad." Master Ash fell silent, frowning across the room at the flames dancing in the shallow grate.

Dominic bit his lip, staring into the gap between his drawn-up knees. "Joran and the Queen think it's a rebellion, pure and simple," he murmured. "And they think Count Dupliss is heading it." He raised his face, staring at Master Ash with dawning horror trickling like ice in his veins. "But he's just a tool, like everyone else. Cerys is behind it all. She uses her gifts to control people. Like Guildford. Like me."

Master Ash's bushy eyebrows lifted. "'Twas always the most powerful and rarest of skills," he said. "With a terrible temptation attached. Too easy it is for those Blessed with illusion to get what they want. Lady Briana was nought but a shadow of herself after she gave up her magic. Caught by the Shadow Mage the first time she wore Darius's betrothal ring, she was. Even Mistress Eglion couldn't break the bond.

All my lady could do was take heartsease, to keep the evil at bay, and she took it for the rest of her life to keep her family safe." He shuddered. "That gift at full strength, ruled by the Shadow Mage... Doesn't bear thinking about."

Dominic nodded, fighting the descent into slumber. "I must warn the Queen," he said. "As soon as I can get my energy back."

Master Ash nodded, creaking to his knees. "I'll send a tray up, try to explain things to Sir Dunforde," he said. "Although the man is stubborn as a mule and as deaf as one, too. Can't risk a pigeon with this information."

He shuffled to the door, pausing with one hand on the latch. "And I'll back you up if Prince Joran will not listen," he added quietly, his ancient face drawn. "We'll both tell him what we face. Might and Shadow Magic, both. As soon as we can."

CHAPTER 24

T he door closed with a dull click as Master Ash bid him good-
night.

Weary beyond words, Dominic reached for the decanter of valerian
Mistress Trevis had given him. The liquid swirled as he tilted it, and he
inhaled the familiar, herbal fragrance, longing for the warm embrace
of oblivion.

"...What we face, might and Shadow Magic, both." Master Ash's
words lingered in his mind. Frowning, he placed the jug to one side,
turning his palm to stare at the delicate tracing under his skin. At

a low ebb, the sign of the Mage glowed with the faintest blue light. His eyes traced a path from his palm to the corded muscles of his sun-kissed forearm, hardened with battle training. He clenched his fist. Easy, it was now, to swing a sword, ride for days. Protect himself and others. His mouth thinned. His gaze wandered to the courtyard window where, in a few brief hours, Blessed or not, Sir Dunforde would see him stripped and flogged. Humiliated before them all. His jaw clenched along with the chill across his shoulders, anticipating the icy sting of the lash.

"Your majesty, Petronella..." He sent his mental voice to the queen with a desperate urgency, knowing she wouldn't receive it. His energy was too low, even if her mind was open to communication from him. Only silence drifted where he longed to hear the Queen's cool voice. He pounded a fist on the woollen coverlet in frustration.

"But Felicia lives," he said out loud, a thin attempt at carving some sense of victory from the day. "I know that now. It's worth a flogging." Despite the bravado, the words were hollow. He flinched inwardly at the memory of the bloody battlefield. The hard faces of his comrades. The weight of his savage, fatal kick against Lionel Brearley's narrow ribcage. Cerys, causing mayhem and vanishing. Escaping. He reached for the sleeping draught again. Huffed a laugh at the similarity and put it down. Despite his exhaustion, he couldn't sleep. Buried deep in his subconscious mind, he was aware of a growing urgency. As if something important had shifted just beyond his sight. He glanced at his saddlebags, where the enchanted dagger vibrated. Even buried deep in the folds of his spare doublet, it buzzed like an angry wasp against a window, whispering tales of revenge and cruelty. His lip curled. "Gods rot the thing," he muttered to himself. "There must be some way to get rid of it." Gritting his teeth, he flung himself from the soft mattress. Putting his back into it, he shoved the bed away from the wall, grunting with the weight without magic to aid him. Briana's diaries lay where he'd left them that morning, stacked neatly atop each other in the shallow space behind the oak panelling. Nudging the panel shut, he shunted the bed back against the wall and picked up the nearest journal, squinting at the dates.

Briana's writing was an elegant scroll of plume and ink, and she painted a vivid picture of her life at the secluded manor. Dominic's need for sleep dissipated as he immersed himself in her world. A narrow, lonely world, to be sure, but one lightened by her delight in her two daughters, born eight years apart. She'd enjoyed her successes in stillroom and gardens, took pride in her management of the estate during her husband's lengthy absences. He smiled at her description of reuniting with her mother despite the need for caution. His eyebrow lifted at the constant battles that took place between them. Mistress Eglion argued for allowing them their magic, Briana fiercely opposed. "For all her Farsight, she doesn't understand," Briana had penned one evening in 1586. "Jana's worse than me at that age. I can't trust her not to use it in front of Darius. She'd do it just to spite him and hang the consequences. For all our sakes, we must keep it secret if the kingdom is to survive. And I can't trust the servants not to talk."

Scanning that extract, Dominic bit his lip and massaged his jaw. He knew firsthand exactly how Darius of Falconridge reacted to the reality of true magic. The kind that arrived as a blessed gift. The Lord of Falconridge had both hated it and yearned for it in equal measure. Lacking any Blessed gifts, lusting for its power, he'd forced it under his control by invoking the cunning might of the Shadow Mage. The swelling bruise Dominic wore, courtesy of Sir Dunforde, matched exactly the one Darius of Falconridge had dealt him on the day of Petronella's triumph six years previously. Fingering the knot under his skin, he allowed himself a small smile and continued reading. At least this time, he'd remained conscious.

The mood of Briana's diaries turned increasingly bleak as the years trickled by. Dominic could sense her growing mistrust and dread of her husband, her own constant fight to keep the Shadow Mage at bay. There was even one diary in the stash that looked to be kept specifically for recording the banal minutiae of her life, with little sense of the vibrant personality behind it. He wondered whether she'd penned that deliberately, as a blind to fool her husband, should he ever take the urge to pry. At the times Darius was present at the manor, her private entries thrummed with fear. She mentioned how her skin turned cold whenever she caught her husband poring over his own small, black-covered journal. "He changes when he reads that," she'd confessed. "And I know exactly what has hold of him, even if he does not. The same dreaded force I fight every day." And then another entry, written in haste just a week later. "He's planning something. I wish I knew what it was. I need to destroy that book. It contains so much knowledge. Perhaps even a way to rid us of the Shadow Mage's influence on our souls. But he guards it close, and I can't get near it. Jana's powers are growing despite our efforts. We give her heartsease. She pretends to drink it. She thinks I do not know. Thanks to the Gods, Petronella gives us no sign the Mage has Blessed her. At least, not yet. I pray it remains so."

Lost in Briana's world, Dominic managed a snatch of sleep when his candle died just before dawn. He tossed and turned on the woollen blankets, his restless mind crowded with images of daggers and lashes. Black books and spells and parchment. Briana's deep, abiding fear, embedded in every drop of faded ink, chimed with his own creeping dread.

Morning came too soon. Bowel churning as he awaited the summons, Dominic washed in the freezing water left in his ewer and threw another log on the fire. He gathered Briana's precious diaries and hid them once more. Mouth dry, he cast a glance out of the window to the gloomy courtyard. He'd never had cause to notice the whipping post before, but there it stood. Sturdy, intimidating. Silent as stones, the troop gathered around it, saying little, heads downcast in the morning gloom. Rain poured down outside to match his mood. He jumped when the door banged open. Thomas Buttledon stood on the threshold, his normally merry face held in iron control, a length of rope in his hands. His grass-green gaze clashed with Dominic's, then darted away. "Come," he mumbled, biting the words out. 'Tis time. Give me your hands."

"You don't need to bind me," Dominic said, striving to keep the tremor from his voice.

"I'm sorry, but I do," Thomas said. "Sir Dunforde's orders."

Biting his lip, Dominic forced his hands out. Thomas lashed them together and gave the bonds a light tug to ensure they held fast. His troubled gaze searched Dominic's. "It gives me no pleasure to do this," he said.

"Welladay, that's good, then," Dominic replied, failing to keep the sarcasm from his tone. "Let's all obey orders, to be sure."

Sir Thomas shook his handsome head. "See, that's the attitude that always gets you into trouble," he said. "I'm sorry for it, but perhaps this will teach you a better way."

Dominic stared at the floor. "If I told Dunforde that Celia is really Terrence Skinner's daughter, out to take the throne, do you think he'd listen?" he said, bitterly.

Thomas paused, one hand on the latch. "Master Ash tried to explain last night," he said. "And you are right. He didn't listen."

He preceded Dominic along the richly decorated passageways, through the kitchens, and out into the service courtyard. Dominic tried to keep his head up and his gaze steady, even as his spirit shrunk from the hard faces of the manor's inhabitants. They murmured behind their hands as he passed. The whipping post loomed in front of him. Wet straw clustered at its base. Off to one side, Aldric waited, a bowl in his hands, with a cloth draped over it. His dark eyes raised to Dominic's in fearful sympathy, shaking his head. Dominic had rarely seen him look so miserable.

Braced like a golden god in his armour, Guildford stood to one side, accompanied by Jared Buttledon. Pink with anticipation, Jared stood on the balls of his feet, rubbing his hands together. Guildford met Dominic's stare with an embarrassed one of his own. He scraped a hand through his wet hair, fidgeting, and then turned his face to the iron-hard sky, removing himself from the scene.

Dominic stumbled slightly as Thomas ushered him forward and jerked his bound hands over his head to a hook embedded in the post that waited to restrain him. The ripping sound of his shirt tearing was loud in the courtyard. The voices of the onlookers hushed. Rain cascaded down his naked back, peppering his shrinking skin with gooseflesh.

"Dominic Skinner, you stand before us charged with dereliction of duty and failure to muster at the appointed time for the battle at Knot's Hill." Sir Dunforde's strident tones behind him stiffened every muscle in his body. He pressed his cheek to the harsh wood post, willing himself to be strong. "Your tardiness, caused by your failure to fulfil your sworn military obligations, has endangered our cause and brought shame among our ranks. For this grievous offence, you will receive fifty strokes of the lash. Let this be a lesson to all who might shirk their duties in times of war."

Fifty strokes! The crowd muttered, shocked.

Dominic was ashamed of the fit of trembling that swept over him at the man's words. He had no time to process it further. The knotted rope sang through the air and landed in a shocking blaze of pain that scraped a moan from his throat. He bit his lip until it bled, arching away, fighting the bonds. Sir Dunforde's blows were efficient and remorseless. Again and again, the rope whistled, and the crowd groaned, first in agreement and then, as Dominic's skin broke, bled, and bruised, into murmurs of sympathy. Dominic screamed at the tenth lash. By the fifteenth, he lolled at the ropes, all his senses occupied by the pain that ground through every nerve. He'd lost control of his bladder. The whistle of the lash sang through the air, playing a savage song with his senses. At the twentieth blow, he all but lost consciousness, barely aware of swift footsteps behind him and the familiar sound of Guildford's voice, loud and clear as he strode forward.

"Sir Dunforde, I must speak to you," the lad said, drawing an avid gasp from the crowd.

Still expecting the agonising slice of the next blow, Dominic waited, head hanging, his entire body on fire, struggling against rising nausea.

"You will not stand in the way of a just punishment, Sir Wessendean," Sir Dunforde said, heaving a breath. "Much as it pains me, it is my duty to carry out the sentence."

Face pressed tight to the whipping post, the only thing solid enough to prevent him from collapsing where he stood, Dominic could barely understand what was taking place.

"With the greatest respect, Sir Dunforde," Guildford said, his voice carrying across the courtyard, "we need Sir Skinner's skills and abilities. He is the only Blessed member amongst us and has already acted to save lives at the risk of his own on our journey here."

"I note your point," Sir Dunforde responded gruffly. "But his offence was great. I cannot simply dismiss this punishment."

"Nor should you," Guildford said. "Let this stand as a reminder to Sir Skinner of his duties but allow him to serve us now when we need every capable warrior. His punishment will continue should he fail again."

The only sound in the courtyard was the drumming of the rain as the witnesses waited for Sir Dunforde's judgement. Dazed and broken, Dominic heaved much-needed air into his lungs, grateful for the water that cascaded over his head and down his face. It meant he could cry in privacy. Eyes blurred, all he could do was wit, every nerve on his back on fire. Water from the overflowing gutters pooled at his feet, stained with his own blood.

"Punishment postponed," Sir Dunforde grunted, finally. "Cut him down."

Pins and needles rushed down Dominic's arms as Thomas cut the bonds around his wrists. His legs crumpled beneath him, the harsh straw agonisingly rough against the lacerations striping his back.

"Here, let me." Guildford's voice, rough with uncommon emotion, filtered into his battered mind. He was aware of the lad crouching at his side, his powerful arms lifting him easily from the ground to dangle across his wide shoulder. His stomach reeled.

"Clear the way," Guildford said. "Back to work. Mistress Trevis, Aldric. Come."

The crowd parted, their muttering dim in his ears as Guildford transported him across the busy courtyard into the shadowed mansion. The princeling took the stairs two at a time, nudging Dominic's chamber door open and easing him carefully to the feather mattress, face down.

Dominic groaned, confusion mixing with pain, unable to control the shivers that convulsed him. "Why?" he managed in a hoarse whisper, meant for Guildford's ears alone. Guildford crouched at his side, his crystalline gaze so close that Dominic had to blink to focus on it.

"You saved my life once," Guildford said, "when you could have let me die. Fifty lashes would have killed you. Let's just say we're even, eh? All debts paid." He made to rise. Dominic reached out to grasp the lad's wrist. "We have to talk... Soon," he murmured. "There is much I have to tell you."

Guildford jerked his head in acknowledgement. A blush rose to colour his skin. "If 'tis about Celia, I already know," he said ruefully. A shadow passed across his freckled face. "Master Ash told me last night. I know what she is. How she tricked me. You are not the only fool here."

"Did he tell you Felicia is alive?"

Trepidation crept across the younger man's features. A fearful hope tempered by years of disappointment. He stood, a towering figure pressed against the low ceiling. "I'll have to see it with my own eyes," he said. "I can't just believe it if you say it."

"Yes. I understand." Dominic's eyes flickered closed.

"Let us tend to him now, my lord," Mistress Trevis' voice took over. "We must bathe his wounds lest infection sets in."

"Aye, let him rest," Guildford said. "We will speak later."

He turned on his heel, his heavy footsteps fading as he left. Still trembling, Dominic pressed his cheek into the bolster. Mistress Trevis' hands dipped into view as she placed a wooden bowl by his bed. The scent of onions invaded his nostrils.

He bit down on the pillow as she bathed his back. The rhythmic trickle of water as she wrung out the cloth was infinitely soothing after the violence inflicted on his spirit. He winced as she applied the onion mixture to his wounds.

Mistress Trevis chuckled. 'Tis a mash of onions and honey," she informed him. "It will clean the wounds. I've comfrey here to mend your skin and willow bark for the pain. Lie still now. Let me help you."

The gentle touch of her healing gift washed over him. Aldric stood awkwardly behind her, chewing his lip. "I'm sorry, Dominic," he stuttered, his voice over-loud. "I shouldn't have let you out of my sight. Not for a minute."

The pain in his back eased by the slowest of degrees. Dominic's mouth lifted. 'Tis not your fault," he said. He turned his head with difficulty, his voice muffled by the pillows. Aldric shuffled his feet, his gaze clouded. "But" he began, "I'm your squire. I should have been by your side."

"You were following my orders. 'Tis mine. My mistake. The troop would have fared even worse had you not joined them." He stopped, a hiss of pain escaping him as Mistress Trevis tended to a more savage cut.

"Aye, this will hurt for some time," Mistress Trevis said, wiping her hands on her apron. "You will be stiff and sore for a few days yet. Give me the comfrey, Aldric."

The comfrey stung. He writhed in response. "I know," the healer soothed. "But 'twill ease in a moment. I could do more, if you wish, to relieve your pain." She moved her hands to his shoulders, their touch cool against the fire in his skin.

"You could take the pain away?" Hope blazed through him. The thought was terrifying and impossible.

"If the Mage wished it, through me," she whispered, leaning low over his back to cover her words.

Temptation sang a siren song in Dominic's soul. About to agree, he ground his teeth, pressing his face deeper into the pillow. A fleeting memory of Joran's suspicion brushed the recesses of his mind, his telepathic words stinging perhaps even more than the cold air against his savaged flesh. "I will punish him if he deserves it. I know you favour him, but he has to remember his place as a knight. His vow of service and obedience to the Crown." And then there was Guildford's unexpected intervention, reducing the severity of his sentence by no small degree. He heaved a sigh and rolled his head on the pillow, trying to catch the healer's eye. "A little," he said. "I need to be mobile, but I need to feel it still. As a reminder. For my sake."

"As you wish." Mistress Trevis gestured to Aldric. "Prepare an infusion of willow bark, as I instructed you, if you please."

"Aye." Aldric withdrew to the narrow table, fumbling with bowls and pitchers, humming under his breath.

"Quietly."

The humming stopped. Mistress Trevis pushed back her sleeves. The mattress dipped as she perched at his side, hands on his shoulders. "Breathe with me," she instructed.

The air softened around him with the gentle tingle of her power. Her hands warmed against his naked skin, infinitely soothing. He closed his eyes, transported momentarily into a vision of clear, blue sky. Shades of azure and sapphire gathered and rotated, lazy as a summer breeze, freshened by the touch of autumn. Cooling. He relaxed under it, aware of the tingle of his own returning power buzzing through his fingertips. The torn skin on his back itched as it knitted, leaving behind the tightness of scar tissue.

"Enough," he murmured into the pillow. "That's enough now, and my thanks to thee."

"Aye, that will see you through. The stiffness and bruising will remain." Mistress Trevis rose, brushing a hand against his hair much in the same way his own mother once had. "We will leave the willow bark here. You'll still need it come the morn. Rest now."

Gathering her utensils, she ushered Aldric away, hushing his low-voiced protests with firm, good humour.

The door closed behind them, and Dominic's eyes flickered shut, taking refuge in sleep.

CHAPTER 25

The sky beyond his window was fully dark by the time he woke, blinking in the light of a single candle. Aldric must have returned at some point to replenish the fire. Muffling a curse as his muscles protested, Dominic rolled awkwardly onto his side, reaching for the willow bark tea. He grimaced as he swallowed the bitter, earthy liquid, wiping his mouth with the back of his hand.

Drawing his pack towards him with a gesture of his fingers, he propped himself to a seated position on the edge of the mattress, jaw firmed with determination. His dreams had ranged far and wide, starting with the disappearance of Cerys in front of his eyes and ending with a vision of the Iron Mountains and the guarded entrance to their infamous mines above the remote mining village known as Traitor's Reach. He yawned as he fumbled through his pack, searching for clean clothing and his warmest doublet. There was no doubt in his mind now. Cerys was determined to draw the cream of the Queen's troops north and let them remain, kicking their heels while she moved her own forces into better positions to make her assault on Petronella while she was vulnerable and injured. She was using Felicia; he was sure of it. The maid had reached her majority only a few short weeks ago. Her Blessed gifts would have settled by now. Farsight and telepathy. More powerful and much more reliable than before, much like his own. The ideal combination for someone who needed to keep one step ahead. A shudder chased down his spine as he struggled to pull a fresh cambric shirt over his head. Felicia's protest on the day of the tourney, her birthday, made so much more sense now, in the light of what he knew.

He winced as he stood, strapping on his sword and sliding his trusty dagger into its sheath. The enchanted blade performed its usual dance against his hand as he buckled it around his narrow waist. Swallowing against his dry throat, he marched as strongly as he could to the Great Hall, where, by now, supper would be served.

All eyes turned to him as he slammed the door open. Falconridge's famed tapestries brought much-needed colour to the whitewashed interior. Accompanied by their hawks and hounds, the lords and ladies of yesteryear watched his progress from the wall. A long line of pale, embroidered faces. Conversation died to a whisper. He was conscious of the judgement of his companions as he strode the length of the room to the dais, where Sir Dunforde dined with Tom on one side of him and Master Ash on the other. Guildford met his gaze with an amused smirk of his own, as if he'd half-suspected Mistress Trevis' timely intervention. Seated at a lower table with round-eyed Will, Aldric grinned. Dominic nodded as he passed, taking his usual seat on the dais with as much of a flourish as he could manage, considering the savage ache in the muscles between his shoulders. Sir Dunforde glared at him from beneath his grizzled brow. "Thought you'd still be abed," he said, his tone sour. He stabbed his knife into a haunch of venison and hacked off a chunk, still slightly raw at its heart.

"Mistress Trevis' skill with herbs has no equal," Dominic replied. He slashed at the venison with his own knife, filling a trencher of bread with meat and gravy, conscious of his audience. The company muttered to each other, leaning forward to witness the conversation at the head table.

"Welladay, we were just discussing strategy," Dunforde said. "We need to establish a better guard around the perimeter. One prisoner confessed Dupliss was the man in command. He makes his base at

Fletcherton. We will take a group there on the morrow and flush him out." He sat back, chewing heartily, looking around the company with satisfied eyes. "We have enough men to do the job, I believe," he said.

"Aye, if the prisoner was telling the truth," Guildford interjected. "How can you be sure? Could be a trap designed to tempt us. I know my stepfather."

Sir Dunforde's beard jutted. "I must fulfil Prince Joran's wishes," he said. "And he wants us to find Dupliss. If the man is there, 'tis nothing more than my sworn duty to find him or die trying." He eyed Guildford with his head on one side. "Time for you to display your loyalty, I believe," he remarked. "Your stepfather or the Queen. Your choice."

"My loyalty is my own affair," the young man said, his voice taut with tension. "I believe my actions today proved that to you. Whatever our personal views on the idea of magic, it can yet aid us." He nodded down the row to Dominic and lifted his glass. 'Tis good to see you, Sir Skinner," he said, his voice, as ever, carrying effortlessly over the buzz of conversation.

"Aye, aye." Many of the company followed Guildford's lead, drumming their tankards on the crowded tables. A few abstained, Jared Buttledon noticeable amongst them. Clem took up his lute as the company resumed their seats, strumming gently to warm up his fingers. Dominic's shoulders hunched with embarrassment at the tribute.

"My thanks for your service, my lord," he said, remembering his manners. His brow creased in thought as he returned to his meal, half-listening to the swell of music as it gathered volume. In the absence of Cerys, Guildford's manner had altered almost overnight. More adult, less oafish. His mind returned to the words of Master Hartwood in the days before the troop headed north. He'd mentioned how his people had believed themselves deserted during the skirmish. Their thoughts their own and yet not, tinged with doubt and dismay.

He remembered a day two years before when he and his companions had struggled against a tide of increasing desperation in their bid to rescue the Grayling, Cerys' ghostly presence lingering on the edge of their conscious sight. The manipulative might of the Shadow Mage, turning their own thoughts against them. Revolving his knife in his hand, he pressed the tip deep into the old wood. Perhaps that was how it worked, bringing out the worst in people. Laying bare their deepest fears and increasing their basest urges. He grimaced. It was a chilling thought. His gaze wandered around the company, scanning for unfamiliar faces. With her ability to shapeshift, Cerys could be anyone. Watching. Waiting.

"Master Ash, how much did you tell Sir Dunforde about my meeting with Cerys?" he asked.

He glanced down the row as Master Ash's eyes widened. *"I wonder if the man comprehends the threat she poses,"* the steward replied, his words dry as dead leaves. *"To be sure, I told him. What he took from my words is hard to discern. I am inclined to believe he thought you a liar and a coward."*

Dominic squared his aching shoulders under his doublet, bristling like a hedgehog. *"Oh, he did, did he?"* he said.

"Of course, I dissuaded him of the idea," Master Ash added before Dominic could bristle further. *"I told him you are a Blessed Knight of Epera; a somewhat different beast to the foot soldiers it is his unhappy lot to nurture. I think that did the trick, although he cannot stomach this idea of the Shadow Mage. The man sees only as far as the point of his sword, and what he can pierce with it, it seems."*

"My thanks for your efforts on my behalf," Dominic said. He washed his meat down with a mouthful of wine. About to say something else, his mental conversation with Master Ash clanged to a halt with the interjection of another familiar voice.

"Dominic! At last, you're there. How's Will?"

He rolled his eyes. *"And good evening to you, Bird,"* he said.

"Your channels are always closed. You never talk to me. What's happening? Are you at Falconridge? What's it like?" Bird's familiar gabble dominated his channels. *"The Queen is awake but weak, thanks to the Gods. Prince Joran has at last stopped growling at everyone. What are you doing up there? When are you coming home? 'Tis lonely without you. Fortuna wants Guildford to come back. She won't admit it, but she does."*

Dominic closed his eyes at the barrage and took another sip of wine while he ordered his own thoughts. Better not to alarm Little Bird unduly, or she'd set off by herself. *"We are well,"* he said. *"A skirmish fought the other day. Do not fret. Will is unscathed and making you proud of him."* His gaze wandered to the young foot soldier, conversing merrily with Aldric, tankard in hand. Will glanced across, sensing his stare, and Dominic tapped his head with his finger. "Bird," he mouthed. Will grinned, giving him a thumbs up. He mimed a heart shape.

"Will sends his love," Dominic said, *"and, what was that? Oh, something about how it isn't true what they say about the girl in Thorncastle."*

Bird's outraged shriek caused him to cringe, breaking into laughter as her language worsened. Will glared at him with narrowed eyes. *"Pax, I'm teasing you, Bird,"* Dominic said. *"There is no girl in Thorncastle or anywhere else."*

He waited as Bird's feathers smoothed. *"I have got a question, though,"* he said. *"Serious, this time. The woman we both saw that night in the temple. She's real. I need to speak to the Queen. Is she well enough for me to speak to her? Can you get a message to her for me?"*

"Mayhap. I will try." Bird said although doubt lingered in her voice. *"If Fortuna will let me enter her room. What is it? Can you say?"*

"My apologies, Bird, not to you," Dominic said. *'Tis for the Queen alone. And Joran, if she wishes it."*

A pause. He could sense Bird fighting her desire for more information. *'Tis state business or I'd tell you,"* he offered. *"Don't worry if you don't hear from me for a bit. I might have to close my channels, just in case."*

Bird uttered an unladylike mental snort. *"I barely hear from you now,"* she pointed out. *"What's the difference?"*

He stifled a grin as she closed the conversation, quietly pleased at her progress. Bird's need to hear about Will had had the desired effect on her studies. Her telepathy was progressing handily. She would be a phenomenal force on her sixteenth birthday if she kept it up. Still... His gaze roved around the company, alighting on Master Ash, who had turned to converse with Sir Dunforde. Petronella had been correct in her Gods-blessed vision. There were so few of the Blessed left these days. Younger, less experienced people like himself and Bird were gradually displaying their gifts as they grew to adulthood. But, thanks to the years of bitter persecution, the adult Blessed available to teach them were thin on the ground. Older, wily individuals like Master Ash had kept out of the way. Unfortunates, like his uncle and grandfather, had paid the price for their own power. Lady Briana had dared not use her gift, lest her husband find out or the Shadow Mage took her over. Petronella had grown up in total ignorance of her own, thanks to her mother's dreadful fear.

And then there was Cerys. An unwanted child born in fear and darkness. An empty soul that the Shadow Mage had delighted in filling with his own version of the Blessed gifts. His mouth twisted at the thought. Patient, like her father. Happy to linger in the shadows like some sort of poisonous spider, to emerge when the time was right and inject her venom.

Lost in his thoughts, he frowned as Clem's rich tenor floated around the room, accompanied by his bartered lute, now restrung, polished, and restored to its former glory. "The Prophecy of the Sword," he announced.

Clem's skilled fingers drifted over the strings. Skin crawling, Dominic broke from his reverie. He recognised the melody as it wound through the smoke-tinged air, like the very breath of the mountains themselves. Horror-struck, he stared at Clem from across the room. The young man cradled the instrument on his knee, his head bent as he concentrated on the song. Dominic knew nothing about music, but he guessed its minor tones and shifting keys took a master musician to manage. One by one, the company stilled as Clem's voice lifted and traced the air. Mesmerised, Dominic listened like a man possessed in a fever dream. He'd never thought the melody that haunted his nightmares might have words to go with it.

"In shadows deep where whispers weep,
A blade of fate lies cast,
Aequitas, the soul's eclipse,
A curse from love's lost past.
A token turned to fate's cruel hand,
To sever bonds unseen,
Beware the heart that wields this blade,
For night and day convene.
Aequitas, the knife that cuts both ways,
In balance, true, its power sways,
A whisper dark, a beacon bright,
It holds the realm's own fragile light.
Prophecy in ancient lore,
Foretells of times to come,
When kingdoms rise, or kingdoms fall,
Beneath the blade's cruel hum.
The bearer walks a path unknown,
Through shadows, thick and thin,
For light and dark both mark the path,
Where destinies begin.
Aequitas, the knife that cuts both ways,
In balance, true, its power sways,
A whisper dark, a beacon bright,

It holds the realm's own fragile light.
To wield this blade of fateful edge,
A heart must find its peace,
For good or ill, its secrets spill
And bring the world release.
The runes that bind both kind and cruel,
Hold truth within their lines,
In hands of those who understand,
Its power intertwines.
Aequitas, the knife that cuts both ways,
In balance, true, its power sways,
A whisper dark, a beacon bright,
It holds the realm's own fragile light."

Clem's voice held the last note and faded into the mesmerised hush of the collected household. For a few moments, the spell of the song held them in thrall, like folk caught in a pixie ring, hardly able to move. Dominic stared at the singer. Unable to believe his ears.

Chapter 26

Despite the crackle of the log-piled hearth, Dominic's blood ran colder than the icy heart of the Cryfell in the dead of winter. His hand crept to the scabbard that housed the enchanted blade. As usual, it trembled beneath his clammy palm. He stared at the meat on his platter, fat congealing and stained with blood. Nausea roiled his gut, and he shoved the plate away, staring at Clem. The musician finished his song with a flourish and a bow. The company roared their applause, breaking the atmosphere, calling for something merrier.

"Surely not," Dominic whispered to himself under the din, afraid to speak the words out loud. "This can't be it. It 't be." As if in answer, the blade stilled for a few seconds beneath his sweaty grip. Heart pounding, Dominic reached for his goblet, swallowing the contents in a swift gulp, terrified beyond measure. This blade couldn't be Aequitas, the blade of legend, spoken of in prophecy, accompanied by a voice that had haunted his dreams for years. He put down his cup as the knife shivered, and its haunting melody sighed across his mental landscape.

But what if it was? He glanced down the row of diners to Sir Dunforde as the man took his supper, locked in his limited world of duty and obedience. His jaw tightened. Only one way to find out.

"Sir Dunforde, I need to speak to you. Might I have a moment alone?"

Dominic pitched his voice loud enough to carry over the hubbub of voices, but Sir Dunforde chewed stoically on, one hand tapping to the rhythm of Clem's jaunty melody, the plume of his hat nodding in time. Teeth clenched, Dominic sat, feeling like a fool, his very skin tingling with embarrassment as he realised the older man was intent on demonstrating his complete contempt by ignoring his request in public.

Annoyed beyond words, Dominic stood, scraping his chair back from the table. He ignored Aldric's alarmed expression and waved his hand in Clem's direction. The minstrel yelped as his precious lute floated from under his grip to hover in mid-air over the banquet boards. "Hold a moment, Clem, if you please," Dominic said. "I have something to say."

Muttering, the soldiers crowded at Falconridge's tables waited. Pale, bearded faces blurred in front of his eyes. The lute rotated languidly under Dominic's control, its red ribbons trailing.

"If you will not hear me in private, I will speak aloud. I believe you are wrong in your assumption that Count Dupliss is in Fletcherton," Dominic announced boldly. Sir Dunforde lifted his head from his meal. His expression dared him to continue. Dominic raised his chin. His voice carried across the hall. "I was late to the skirmish yesterday because I encountered the true villain behind this rebellion. A woman named Cerys Tinterdorn. She is a telepath and metal smith. Beyond that, she has a power that none of us can match. That of illusion and transformation. I witnessed it myself."

He paused, scanning his audience for their reaction to his words. Expressions ranged from polite interest to downright scorn. A couple of people watched him with open mouths, circling their chests with the sign of the Mage as a symbol of protection. Someone else snorted in derision.

Sir Dunford spat a lump of gristle onto the floor. "Sit down, Sir Skinner. Your tales have no bearing on military matters," he said.

"Tis no tale. I heard her ambitions from her own lips and her history from Lionel Brearley before he died. She is Darius of Falconridge's bastard daughter, Queen Petronella's half-sister. And she wants the Crown of Epera. We must stop her. Find her, and the rebellion will end."

Dunforde glanced up at him, his faded blue eyes almost lost under their wrinkled, lizard-like lids.

"Are you disobeying my orders, Sir Skinner? Think again. Your punishment still stands. We can resume at any point."

The muscles in Dominic's back clenched reflexively at the older man's words. He screwed his hands into fists. "I ask that you allow me a party of a few men to help me find Cerys Tinterdorn and bring her to the Queen's justice," he pressed.

Sir Dunforde snorted. "What, split our forces and allow you off on a wild goose chase in these hills? This woman could be anywhere. How will you find her?"

"She is holding Felicia of Wessendean. A Gods-blessed telepath. I am in contact with Felicia. She will help us." He bit the inside of his cheek. He hoped Felicia would help them. There was no guarantee.

Guildford raised a golden eyebrow. "You said that before," he rumbled. "How do you know for sure? Perhaps that voice you hear is just Cerys trying to trick you. Not Felicia at all."

The company fidgeted, caught uncomfortably in a discussion that, by rights, would never include them. Shrugs and frowns abounded as they debated matters amongst themselves.

"I don't know if it's her or not. Why are you asking?" Blurred and overloud, a lowly soldier seated nearby scowled at his neighbour. "I don't have to know. I just do what they tell me."

Sir Dunforde's fierce frown hardened. His eyes flashed, and he stood, a commanding figure still clad in his half armour and heavy, mud-stained cloak. Petronella's falcon symbol blazed proudly on his brawny chest. "You will come with me," Dunforde said. "We will talk. In private. Now."

He gestured to Tom and Guildford, stalking out of the room with pure fury emblazoned on his brow. Tom shook his head. "Not well done, Dominic," he said as they left the dais. "He's already climbed down publicly once today, courtesy of my lord of Wessendean."

Dominic nodded his head at Clem's lute as he made his way stiffly to the door. The instrument drifted into the musician's lap, gentle as thistledown. Clem clutched it to him, staring at Dominic with wonder in his eyes.

"'Tis his own fault. He needs to listen," Dominic said through gritted teeth. "He didn't have to ignore me in front of everyone."

"Welladay. You surely know how to get attention," Tom drawled. "By the Gods, I'll be glad to get back to the castle. This mission is going to the dogs quicker than the drop over Goldfern Falls."

Flanked by both Tom and Guildford and watched blankly from the wall by the painted ranks of Falconridge ancestors, Dominic traversed the broad staircase to the upper floor. Sir Dunforde had appropriated the lord's solar as his office for the duration. Several sheets of parchment containing musters and rotas scrawled in thick black ink littered the finely carved table. Books and ledgers crowded the narrow shelves. A tiny fire flickered weakly in the narrow hearth. Dunforde turned on Dominic as soon as the door shut behind them.

"What do you mean by it, questioning my orders?" he spat. "Have you not had enough pain for one day? Must I give you more? And what are you doing downstairs, anyway? The hiding I gave you... You should not be able to leave your pallet."

Dominic sighed. "Mistress Trevis has other skills than just mixing the odd potion and a deft way with a splint," he said. "I am surprised you do not know this."

Sir Dunforde snatched up a metal tankard and hurled it at the fireplace so hard it bounced off and hit the opposite wall. "You Blessed and your blasted magic," he said, face white and taut with rage. "Think yourselves so fine. You are a Knight of Epera under my command. You are not free to choose your own missions."

"Alright then," Dominic returned, his voice hard. "If you won't take my word about what we truly face, what about my lord Joran's personal mission? For my ears alone?"

Dunforde scowled. "What mission? What is this?"

"Joran commanded me to find and kill Terrence Skinner. I believe Terrence Skinner is hiding at Traitor's Reach, in the mines where he was held prisoner. Those are my orders. I therefore beg permission to leave your command and carry them out."

Dunforde's glare spoke volumes. Dominic returned it with an icy one of his own. "After all, you don't need me and my magic to kill a few rebel Citizens, do you?" he taunted. "And I've provided you a couple of additional soldiers from Dupliss' original army who can help you smoke them out. Quite handy with their weapons. With their own grudge against Dupliss." He bared his teeth in a mirthless smile. "If you won't provide an escort, I will leave on my own."

Guildford and Tom exchanged glances. Guildford shifted uncomfortably from one foot to the other. "Nay, don't," Guildford muttered, staring at the floor. He poked at the sulky fire with his boot, nudging a log deeper into the embers. "You shouldn't leave on your own." Hands outspread, Tom turned to his commander. "Surely you will not send him away without support against this Cerys or the mage, Terrence Skinner?"

Sir Dunforde shrugged and helped himself to a glug of wine from the decanter on his desk. "He wants to go," he said. "If he wants to go alone, that's his business. My duty is to my men and my queen." He wiped his mouth on his sleeve, eyeing Dominic as if he were a bothersome insect to be swatted. "Go, and good riddance, Blessed Knight of Epera," he said shortly. "But I'll spare you no men. You'll go alone."

The warmth of the Great Hall enveloped Dominic like a sweaty hug as he returned, boiling with rage at Sir Dunforde's stubborn nature. The noise level had intensified in his absence. He picked his way between the knotted groups to the fireplace where Clem sat, stretching his fingers between tunes. "I need to know more about that song," he said.

The musician yawned and scratched the wound under his bandage. "Which one?" he asked. "I know hundreds."

"The one about the knife that cuts both ways." Tapping his foot, Dominic resisted the urge to haul Clem from his stool and shake the information out of him. His hands curled into fists at his sides. He glanced at Aldric as the lad ambled over, stuffing coins and dice into his battered pouch with the air of a satisfied winner.

"Play another, Clem," someone shouted from across the crowded benches, his voice smudged with drink. "We've yet to hear 'The Drunken Fiddler'."

"Aye, bide awhile." Clem's brow twisted as he looked up at Dominic looming over him like a vengeful god. "The Prophecy of the Sword? It's an old tune from the North. The miners had it first. Why? Did I not sing it true?"

Dominic paused, biting his lip. Frustration burned him like fire. "I know the melody, but not the words. Is it a true story? A legend?" he asked. "What does it mean?"

Brow quirking, Clem shook his head. "'Tis just a lament with a pretty tune. I hadn't remembered it at all until this eve," he said. "It just popped into my head. Made a change from all the bawdy tavern tales."

Dominic huffed a sigh. "But it must mean something," he urged. "It must have come from somewhere." He scrubbed his hands through his hair.

"Why is it important? What did Dunforde say?" Aldric asked. "Do you think the song has something to do with..." he glanced at the elaborate scabbard Dominic wore on his hip and broke off in the face of his warning scowl. "Oh," he said.

Clem's confused gaze wandered between them. He shrugged. "I know the song is old," he offered. "I can tell that from the music. My brother's old tutor taught me. He told us the words, of course." He lifted the lute. "I can play it again."

"Nay. Just tell me the words," Dominic said, pulling up a stool. "I'll get my scribe here to write it down."

"Scribe?" Aldric said, his eyes narrowed. "Now I'm your scribe as well?"

Dominic waved an impatient hand at him. "Just listen. You'll remember it better than I," he said. "You can write it down later."

Aldric rolled his eyes. "As you wish," he said.

They waited as Clem recited the words once more. At the close of his rendition, Dominic felt in his purse for a coin and passed it across. "I thank you," he said. He turned to Aldric. "Come," he said. "We've got work to do."

"Welladay, 'twas a pleasure," Clem said, gawping at the silver in his palm. Leaving the man to pocket the coin, Dominic pulled Aldric after him into the depths of the manor.

"By the Gods, Dom, you don't have to drag me. What's the rush?" Aldric protested. "I'll go wherever you want."

Lurching into his chamber, Dominic yanked his saddlebags from under his bed and tipped the contents onto the mattress. A jumble of coins, grubby clothing, a heel of stale bread, and a wrinkled, half-eaten apple made a mess of the woollen coverlet. "You may not want to come this time," he said. He glanced at the younger man from under his hair. "I wouldn't blame you."

"Whatever you are doing, you won't be doing it on your own," Aldric responded stoutly. "Not again." He frowned as Dominic shook out his clothing and refolded it roughly before jamming it back into his bags.

"What are we doing?" he said.

"Going after Cerys Tinterdorn," Dominic said through gritted teeth. "She's behind all of this. She's using Felicia's gifts of Farsight to aid her plotting. If we get Cerys, and if Dunforde finds Dupliss, we win. Free Felicia. End the rebellion. Simple."

Aldric blinked at him. "But what about your position in the troop? And didn't you say that Count Dupliss is not at Fletcherton?" he said.

Dominic shrugged. "As far as Dunforde is concerned, I am released from my duties to him. Joran and the Queen have an army of loyal Citizens who can fight the likes of Dupliss at Fletcherton or anywhere else," he said. "And you can wager your purse that Joran has been deploying them whilst we are away." He stomped across the room, gathering Briana's diaries together. "As far as ordinary fighting is concerned, I'm just one man with average skill. The Mage bans me from using my Blessed gifts against Citizens like Dupliss. Cerys, now..." He smiled wolfishly at his friend. "Cerys, I can and will kill with the utmost pleasure."

"Cerys Tinterdorn, the woman who tricked you, Guildford, Tom, and everyone else?" Doubt clouded Aldric's face. "She has Shadow Mage gifts. How will you even find her?"

Dominic threw the stale bread into the fire, watching it char. "I have a secret weapon," he said.

"What? Felicia? But if she's working for Cerys, telling her what will happen, where to be..." Aldric began.

"Nay, my friend," Dominic interrupted him. "Cerys can fool many people, but there was one person she didn't take in, isn't there? Someone who disliked her on the spot and never trusted her for a second."

He smiled at the dawning realisation on Aldric's face. "You."

Chapter 27

Dominic and Aldric left Falconridge at first light, well wrapped against the frosty dawn, riding north on the well-trodden path towards the mist-wreathed mountains. Ice nipped their cheeks. They were but silhouettes against the fading stars, and early birds circled the sky. Aldric rode easily at Dominic's side, leading a packhorse laden with supplies. Unhappy at leaving the warmth of his stall, the nag dragged at the rein.

"Still say you should have told the Queen," he muttered, his breath clouding the air. "Did you send a pigeon with a message?"

Reliving his mental conversation with Little Bird, Dominic's mouth curled into a half smile. "In a manner of speaking," he said. "Bird said she'd ask the Queen to contact me. It's impossible the other way around. Believe me, I've tried. Both she and Joran are too good at blocking." He yawned. He'd burned through a couple of candles the night before, perusing Briana's diaries for any mention of the Prophecy of the Swords. Frustratingly, he'd come up with nothing of interest. As usual, the dagger vibrated at his hip. He massaged warmth into his frozen cheeks as he rode, deep in thought, through the damp chill of the northern forests.

"Do you really think that blade you carry is the one in the song?" Aldric asked, breaking the silence. "Seems far-fetched to me."

His words only emphasised the tangle of doubt in Dominic's mind. He shrugged, the action causing a knife of pain across his abused back.

"I have no way of knowing for sure," he admitted. "Of course, it could just be a story."

His neck muscles had tightened overnight. His hands clenched into fists on Kismet's reins as he turned to Aldric. "I can't waste time kicking my heels under Sir Dunforde's command anymore," he muttered.

Aldric raised an eyebrow in acknowledgement. "Hardly surprising," he murmured. "After what he did to you." He paused for a few more hoof beats. "Does this mean we are using this as an excuse to run away?" he asked. "Because we don't really know where Cerys is. If she can transform herself, she could be anywhere or anyone."

"If this dagger is really cursed, it will lead us straight to her," Dominic replied, ignoring the first question before he could brood over it. "She wants it, so she'll either come and get it or let us find her. That's her plan."

"Yes, but why does she want it?" Aldric persisted. "She's evil, Dominic. In the cave under the temple that night, she wanted the Grayling. We don't know why. She's told you she wants the throne. This is a dangerous game to play. And what if she is playing with us? What then?"

Dominic narrowed his eyes, his expression stony. He faced forward once more, his gaze set to the north, and pressed his heels to Kismet's side, urging her into a trot. "I can't sit and do nothing. While she has Felicia, she can play as many games as she wants," he said, his voice hard. "As long as she remembers, I can play too."

By midday, the pair had crossed the border of Falconridge lands, marked by a standing stone carved with the familiar avian symbol. Wilderness stretched before them. They travelled through forests alive with the whirl of frost-kissed leaves. The sun shone weakly against a bank of clouds gathering in a pale blue sky, a far cry from the blistering temperatures of just days ago. Aldric leapt from his mount's back to gather mushrooms clustered like elf stools amid rotting logs, stowing them carefully in his kerchief for later consumption. Eyes fixed ahead,

Dominic scanned his mental channels for Felicia's distinctive voice, alert for danger. He took regular drafts of willow bark to ease the pain of his striped back. Unaware of her master's discomfort, Kismet trotted gamely on, her ears pricked and alert.

They ate as they rode, following the tumble of a stream as it cascaded downhill to join the Cryfell. The terrain steepened as they left the mighty forest, gathering itself in a series of folds and curves in preparation for the precipitous slopes beyond. The Iron Mountains loomed ever closer in front of them, slashing the pale horizon with harsh, ragged diagonals. They saw no-one on the northern road. Not even a carter lugging ore, but the landscape was alive with wildlife. Rabbits scattered at their approach. Eagles and buzzards whirled on the thermals. Away from the looming tension of Falconridge, Dominic breathed more easily, revelling in the vast solitude as he always had. At his side, Aldric was a cheerful, practical presence, his bow ready on his back. Not for the first time, Dominic gave silent thanks for the day they met.

"Do you know where we're heading?" Aldric said, breaking a long silence as they watered the horses. On their left, the sun disappeared, swallowed by clouds as the afternoon lengthened. Frost already rimmed the edges of the rutted cart tracks stretching before them. The wind rose, tossing the first flakes of snow before it.

"I believe we are on Hartwood land now," Dominic said. "After Hartwood, Traitor's Reach. Perhaps we can find more news on the raid and what the villagers saw…"

He broke off at the sound of Master Ash's voice as it drifted into his mind. *"Dominic, you were correct,"* the old man said, his tone a complicated mixture of vindication and dread. *"The soldiers are back from Fletcherton with no sign of Dupliss. Tom is as mad as a trapped wolf. Been arguing with Dunforde ever since they returned, saying he should have listened to you."*

Eyes wide, Dominic stared at Aldric, his mind whirling. Aldric, hunched in his cloak against the cold, recognised the signs of a telepathic conversation. Scowling, he stamped his feet on the iron-hard ground. "That had better not be Bird wanting to chat," he said. "We don't want to get caught by the weather out here." Concentrating on the steward's words, Dominic tuned him out.

"What's the outcome?" he asked.

"Wait, Guildford's joined in now."

"Are they arguing in front of all?" Dominic's brow quirked at the thought.

Master Ash chuckled. *"Nay, in my lord's solar. But they shout and curse loud enough for the entire manor to overhear. 'Tis not hard."*

"Especially if you are standing right outside the door?" Dominic suggested. His spirits lifted at the thought his closest allies were arguing their case on his behalf.

The old man's amusement bled down their mental channel for a second. *"I'll let you know what's decided,"* Master Ash said. *"Be wary, Dominic. My heart tells me Dupliss is closer to you than to us. And that blade you carry..."* His conflicted thoughts came across as a swirl of conflicting emotions. His mental voice weakened as if he was gathering himself for some great battle. *"I trust it not,"* he said. *"Do not let your desire lead you from your path. The Shadow Mage is treacherous beyond belief. His greatest triumph, the capture of the brightest spirits, like my lady Briana. I would hate to see you caught in his web."*

Hearing the words, Dominic's jaw tensed. A vision of Felicia's voice and the thought of her in pain stabbed through him. *"I must follow this through, Master Ash, wherever it leads,"* he said. *"If I can get to Cerys, I can at least weaken her or delay her plans. At best, I will see her dead at my feet. Her threat to Petronella ended. Do not doubt my resolve."*

The older man's sigh brushed his soul with the same icy fingers that pinched his frozen cheeks. *"I do not doubt your resolve,"* Master Ash said sadly. *"Just your wisdom."* He paused for a few seconds, and then his voice sounded once again. *"'Tis decided. Tom and Guildford are to follow you. Watch for them. Do not set foot in Traitor's Reach without them."*

Dominic closed his eyes. Relief at Master Ash's words warmed him like a hefty slug of mulled ale. *"Give them our thanks. Tell them to travel prepared for snow,"* he said. *"Gods blessings to you, sir,"* he added.

"Travel safe," Master Ash's farewell faded into the darkness as the older man closed the connection.

Dominic winced as Kismet nudged his back. He put a hand up to feel her skin under her thick mane, "Aye, lady, I know you're cold," he said. "Let's move."

He nodded to Aldric. They remounted, urging the horses to a trot on the hard ground. "Looks as if Tom and Guildford are on their way to us," Dominic said. "They didn't find Dupliss at Fletcherton."

Aldric grinned through chattering teeth. "A blessing, to be sure," he said. "But a greater one would be to find some shelter."

The bitter wind drove powdery snow into their faces as they continued, stinging their skin with icy fingers. Dominic bit his frozen lip. Aldric was right. There was no other shelter in this vast, open landscape of rocky slopes and silence. Not a patch of woodland or a handy cave. Faces down, they trudged onward as the sun continued its descent and the storm picked up pace.

"I can smell smoke. If we're lucky, that's Hartwood over the ridge," Dominic said, his lips numb with cold.

Spurred by the thought of shelter, they urged better speed out of the tired mounts. The pack horse baulked, forcing them to slow. It was fully dark by the time they had wrestled it to the crest of the hill. Dominic breathed a silent sigh of relief at the distant lights of a quiet village nestling in the valley, enclosed by a pale stone wall. Surrounded by well-tended fields stripped of their harvest, it had an air of quiet prosperity. Torches flickered from the high barricade. His stomach rumbled at the scent of roasting meat drifting towards him on the breeze. If this was Hartwood, it was a far cry from the jumble of shacks his vivid imagination had conjured from the tale told by Master Hartwood himself.

"Rich pickings," he said as they jogged downhill, genuflecting automatically as they passed a shrine to the Mage on the side of the road. "No wonder it's a target for thieves."

Up close, the rugged town walls rose to a forbidding height above their heads. Snow swirled around them as they lingered at the heavy wooden gate. Dominic's mouth turned down when he realised the gate guards had already bolted it fast for the night. Dismounting, his back aching, he banged on the frost-gilded planks with the hilt of his sword.

"Open up! We're on the Queen's business!" he yelled, hopeful that a surly guard lurked somewhere and would let them in. At a price. Huddled against the horse's flanks, they hunched their shoulders against the penetrating cold.

"Be gone. 'Tis after curfew," a deep voice called from above. "We don't open for strangers after sundown."

Dominic glanced up, shielding his eyes against the sting of snow. A large round head, heavily wrapped against the chill, peered from the gatehouse window. "We are part of the Queen's troop from Falconridge," Dominic explained. "And we carry her might and will. Open up! 'Tis cold out here. This is not the welcome Jon of Hartwood promised us!" He rolled his eyes at Aldric. The lad grimaced.

"Master Hartwood never promised us a welcome at all," Aldric said in hushed tones.

"They don't know that," Dominic hissed.

The man's head withdrew. Aldric dismounted, shivering. "By the Gods, 'tis cold," he said, huddling as close to Hamil as he could get.

Silence. Dominic gazed back at the remote hillside, whitening now as the snow gathered pace. He pulled his cloak tight around him, his face pinched with cold. "They'd better let us in," he said. "We'll surely perish right outside their Gods-blasted gates if they don't."

Stamping their feet, huddled in their cloaks, hours seemed to pass before the gate finally creaked open. The moon-faced man glared at them, sword raised, his mouth pursed with suspicion. "Prove who you are," he said. "'Tis more than my head is worth if I let you in and find you're those dark devils sent to rob us."

Dominic shrugged. "We are part of the Queen's army sent to guard this region at your request," he said. "Here's the Queen's device upon my breast shield." He let his cloak gape wide to show the Queen's falcon. "This is my squire, Aldric Haligon. I am Dominic Skinner, a Blessed Knight of Epera. I can take this village apart stone by stone if you wish." He raised his palm. The guard backed off at the sight of the Mage's mark. "All right, all right," he huffed. "I believe you. At least 'tis not stained black, like those others."

Exchanging relieved glances with Aldric, Dominic led Kismet forward. The guard ushered them through, peering into the snow-crusted landscape uphill as if he expected an invading army at any moment. Putting his shoulder to the gate, he heaved it shut. He shouldered the heavy bar across it with no help, thick muscles bulging with effort against his coat sleeves. He looked them over, sniffed, and gestured up the street. "You've a choice of tavern," he said. "Queen's Head, on the market square, where the ale is good, the wenches pretty, and they'll fleece you fast as look at you." He pointed to the left. "Or you can try the Beaten Drum down there. My brother owns it, and we can promise you good food, a clean bed, and a decent night's sleep. Also, our stables are second to none."

"Good stables. No contest," Dominic said. "Your brother is the better off tonight." He placed a coin in the man's gloved palm. "We thank you for your kindness," he said.

The guard bit the coin, testing it for soundness, and dropped it with a jingle into his own pouch. "Aye, well," he said. "My name's

Cedric. My brother is Oswin. Tell him I sent thee and that I'll be in for a nightcap shortly. 'Tis a perishing cold night."

Bidding the man a good night, they turned down the street, the horse's hooves resounding from the neat cobbles. Lamplit windows turned the falling snow gold, but accustomed to the rowdiness of other taverns and towns, little sound escaped the shuttered windows. "'Tis a weird place, this," Aldric said, more cheerful now some comfort was in sight. "So quiet."

"Aye," Dominic glanced round, "Is that the curfew or the snow, do you think? Or are folk not allowed to breathe in Hartwood after dusk?"

"Mayhap 'twill be different indoors," Aldric said as they stopped outside the Beaten Drum. It stood two storeys high, a neat establishment with a hitching rail outside and well-scrubbed stone walls. Snow already dusted its windowsills. A dull murmur of conversation issued outwards from the shuttered windows.

"You find the stables," Dominic said. "I'll get us some food."

Yawning, Aldric nodded, gathering the reins into his hands and leading the weary horses down an alley beside the tavern.

Dominic watched him go, glancing once more at the quiet street, a perplexed frown screwed into his forehead. He kept one hand on his sword as he opened the door of the Beaten Drum and walked in. His cheeks tingled at the touch of warmth radiating from the blazing hearth. The patrons were mostly labourers. A motley mix of artisans and some grubby-faced miners, their faces seamed with encrusted dirt. They stared at him and then averted their eyes. Without a doubt, it was the quietest tavern Dominic had ever encountered. A group of citizens huddled around the fireplace were playing Tarocchi, a small pile of coins in front of each, their concentration on the game absolute. The innkeeper, as round-faced as his brother, stomach stretching the bounds of his apron, polished tankards, humming a lament under his breath. His eyes darted at Dominic, telegraphing alarm, and then shifted away. Dominic paused. The low room reeked of tension under the familiar tang of hops and spiced meat. Every nerve end thrumming, he peered around the space, wondering at the nerviness of the occupants, and came up short.

Propped in a corner, huddled over a goblet like a spider, he spied a familiar figure. Thin. With clawed fingers and long, greying hair. A gaunt, dark-eyed face filled with sadness and immense power. His blood turned to ice. "No," he whispered.

The shadowed figure half smiled. Every instinct told him to run.

"Good evening, Dominic," his uncle said.

CHAPTER 28

"**Y**ou!" His shocked voice bounced off the rafters, cutting through the quiet tavern like a blade.

The gamblers dropped their cards at the ringing sound of Dominic's sword as he swept it from the scabbard. They gaped at him as he crossed the room in three long strides, ignoring the startled innkeeper who scrabbled under his counter and came up white-faced, balancing a heavy club across his sturdy shoulder. Scenting danger, the tension blurred into panic as the miners scattered like rabbits in the shadow of a hawk, abandoning their coins and cards. The door banged behind them, leaving a watchful, waiting silence.

Terrence Skinner eyed Dominic's angry approach with a passivity that bordered on the edge of insulting. He lifted one long, swollen, knuckled hand and waved the sword from Dominic's half-frozen grip, turning it in the air so it pointed back at him. Dominic spared the deadly tip not a glance as he glared at the powerful figure before him, blood boiling with rage. Power coalesced in his palms, itching to strike.

"Please do not bore me, Dominic," Terrence said. A bitter smile lingered under his long beard. "If you are going to kill me, do a better job this time."

Magical energy burned through Dominic's fingers. Eyes blazing, he used his gift to snatch the sword back and approached his uncle's table, heart pounding with fear and doubt. Terrence raised an approving eyebrow. "That's better," he said. "You've improved." He spread his hands wide, exposing the breadth of his chest. "Go ahead, nephew," he said. "I await your killing blow. I am sure you are under orders to carry out my execution. Prince Joran only ever tolerated my presence in the castle at his wife's behest."

He bared his teeth. Something malicious and foul lurked behind his dark-eyed gaze. He gestured at the cup on the table. "I'd be quick," he advised. "This is mostly heartsease, but the flagon is almost empty. As you know, its effects only last so long."

Dominic paused, glancing at the flask. He could smell the strength of the potion within it from where he stood.

"Shouldn't that also strip you of your magic?" he said, curiosity getting the better of him.

"'Tis a fine line," Terrence observed. He swirled the contents reflectively, his eyes gleaming at Dominic from beneath hooded lids. "Felicia has had plenty of time to perfect her talent with potions during her time at Traitor's Reach," he said.

Trembling, Dominic raised his palm again. "You should not mention her name to me," he hissed. "I will kill you where you stand."

"Really? You are taking your Gods-blessed time about it." Terrence took a sip of the potion, wiping his mouth fastidiously on the back of his hand. His own mage light revolved in his palm, flickering like starlight seen against the silhouette of winter branches blown by the wind. Alternately light and dark.

Caught in a welter of indecision, Dominic lingered agonisingly on the sharp edge of a nightmare. Joran's command resounded in his soul, demanding loyalty and obedience. It clashed with the force of steel against his lonely heart, aching for news of Felicia and his once proud love of his uncle and tutor. And he had questions. So many he hardly knew where to start.

A flicker of compassion crossed the older man's features, quickly lost beneath a colder expression. "'Tis hard, is it not?" he remarked. "I'd sit were I you. We have much to discuss and little time." He tapped the jug and pointed at the innkeeper, who flinched. "Mulled ale for my nephew," he said.

Dominic remained standing. "How do I know you are not Cerys?" he choked out, ashamed at the turmoil of emotion the sight of his uncle stirred in him. He blinked, holding back tears with the force of his will.

"Ask me something only you and I know," Terrence advised gravely. "Cerys can imitate anything, but she cannot know a person's memories or dredge the secrets of their hearts. Although I have to qualify that remark somewhat because what she doesn't know, she is quick to guess."

Dominic sifted through his memories, coming up with one that seemed to summarise their present situation. "Well then," he said. "The day you told me about the Dark Army in the Great Library. Do you remember that?" His uncle inclined his head. "I remember the day," he said. "What about it?"

"Just before then, you had cause to send Guildford and Felicia out of the library. Tell me why."

A weary smile lifted Terrence's features. "Ink," he said. "'Twas the day we discovered you had telekinesis. And very amusing it was, as I recall, watching that entitled brat, Guildford, land on his backside."

Dominic nodded. He sheathed his sword, careful to keep his Gods-blessed power stoked in his fist, still unwilling to sit.

"Your squire, where is he?" Terrence asked.

Dominic's eyes narrowed. "How do you know I have a squire?" he demanded. His uncle cast his eyes to the ceiling. "A Knight of Epera would not travel without one. In the stables, is he?"

"Aye." Dominic shoved his hands behind his back, clenching his fists to keep from trembling. His eyes darted over his uncle's face, noting the extra shadows beneath his deep-set eyes; the lines scoured deep into his flesh, dragging at his fine features. The innkeeper tiptoed over, holding out a tankard. Dominic seized it like a person dying of thirst, grateful for any sense of normality. Steam rose to tickle his nose with the scent of summer.

"Kill him!" Joran's voice in his memory razed shivers down his aching spine. He took a swallow of the apple-spiced ale, his teeth chattering on the rim. "I need answers," he said.

Terrence raised an eyebrow. "I believe you have something of mine," he said.

The contents of Dominic's drink spilt as he slammed the cup onto Terrence's table. "I won't go through this again," he said. "Cerys tried it just a few days ago, pretending to be you. I know you are here under her orders. You can save yourself the trouble. I will not hand the dagger over to you. Where is Felicia?"

Terrence sat back in his seat. Shadows claimed his gaunt features. "Safe, at present," he said. "But you are in way over your head, boy. Give me the blade and walk away with your precious honour intact whilst you still can."

"My honour?" Dominic spat the words back at him. "What about your own? I have orders to kill you. That is the price I must pay to prove my loyalty to the throne. Is torturing Felicia and me the cost of yours to Cerys?"

Silence. Shoulders hunched, his uncle dropped his gaze to the rough table. He took another sip of the potion, his hand shaking. "My soul is not my own, nor has it been since I was your age," he murmured. "But loyalty. Now, that is another matter. I do not expect you to understand the secrets of my heart. Nor should you."

Dominic skewered his uncle with his gaze. "I paid for this knife at Master Tingle's stall in Blade Market," he said. "I've since learned it was a keepsake. A love token. Between you and Juliana Tinterdorn. What made you get rid of it if it meant so much to you?"

His heart lurched at the bereft expression on the older man's face. Terrence's eyes darted to the dagger at Dominic's hip. One hand reached forward, then fell back to the table, clutching the goblet like a safety blanket. The gesture was so touching and simple it almost brought tears to his nephew's eyes. He hardened his heart with difficulty.

"I couldn't keep it," Terrence whispered. "Not once she changed it."

His tired eyes lifted to Dominic's, seeking understanding. "Cerys stole it from me on the night she discovered I am not her father," he said. "It was never the same afterwards."

Dominic blinked, startled. "Lionel Brearley said you thought she was your daughter."

"Oh, my boy, at the beginning, how I wished she was. But as she grew..." He shook his head. "Charming and wilful, like her mother..." His sunken cheeks lifted briefly in remembrance. "Patient and deadly, like her father. Like Darius. She looks like the Queen, her half-sister. Did she show you?"

"I first saw her on the night you tried to change the Grayling. The night Felicia..." Dominic swallowed. "Did you know Cerys was there, then?"

His uncle's shoulders lifted as he sighed. "In a manner of speaking. 'Tis hard to explain, the bridge of souls... And we didn't have the correct information. We needed the book."

"What?" Dominic took a step back. "What book? Darius' book? What are you talking about?" His skin crawled, remembering the strange, atonal chant Terrence had repeated, conjuring the Shadow Mage. The Grayling's frantic thrashing, battering his wings on the cage, trying to escape. Little Bird's shrill, childish voice. *"He's changing him, Dominic. He's hurting him! Do something!"*

He raised his sword and his palm, his power building. Every nerve spiked with energy. "You deserve to die for that, alone," he said.

Something altered. A shift in the atmosphere as the Shadow Mage gained control. Dominic's magical senses recoiled in alarm even before his conscious mind registered the change. His uncle glared at him over the table and upturned his empty flagon. Empty. Dominic's gut twisted in terror. "We were unsuccessful. Thanks to you," Terrence said, his familiar voice overlaid with ice. "You will not be so lucky next time. Give me that dagger, and I will ensure Felicia remains in good health. If not..." He paused, his eyes black as night, glittering with malevolent glee. "Well, let's just say she is not a stranger to torture. And your telepathic connection with her is serving us well at present." He held out his hand. The mark of the Mage undulated black as ink in the middle of his palm.

Appalled, Dominic's teeth clenched. He stood his ground on shaking legs. "I don't believe you. I will never give in to you. And neither will Felicia!"

Terrence raised one eyebrow. "Will she not?" he said. "Ask yourself this. How did I know you would be here tonight?"

His tone had all the effect on Dominic as a blow to the gut.

"No. You're a liar!" Shaking with frustrated rage, Dominic punched with his power and lunged with his sword simultaneously. More experienced, a twisted smile blurring his features, the older man was quicker. Dominic winced as Terrence flicked the cup of heated ale at him. It stung his eyes and blurred his vision. Propelled by the force of his uncle's mental power, the sturdy table collided painfully with his shins. He stumbled over it, and his sword thrust struck the thick wood of the settle, tearing his uncle's cloak. Terrence's speed on his feet took him by surprise. Dominic ducked under a barrage of coins swept from the gambler's table, swearing as one bounced off his cheekbone. His uncle laughed, eyes blacker than the deepest pit. One sweep of his arm elevated the tavern furniture to a frenzied dance of tables and tankards. Terrence dodged under the whirlwind, still laughing as Dominic struggled for an adequate response. Cursing, Dominic launched his own attack, batting the maelstrom away with a powerful twist of his own arm. But Terrence reached the door ahead of him. One hand on the latch, he blasted the furniture back to Dominic, trapping him with a barricade of wood and pinning him against the far wall. For a second, their twin powers fought each other. Terrence wrestled the door open. A blast of freezing air whistled into the room, a harbinger of the first storms of winter. Their eyes clashed. Loathing burned through every bone of Dominic's body. He tried to fight back, but Terrence's will pinned his hands uselessly to his sides, as they had done years before when he was yet a defenceless boy.

His uncle shook his head, his gaze almost pitying. "Too weak, still. Your power is there, but not the will to use it. Torture it is then," he said and slammed the door.

CHAPTER 29

"How now? What about my furniture?" The tavern master's wail sailed the air as the tense atmosphere calmed by degrees. He crept out from behind his counter, still trailing his club, and gazed at the mess, his round face crumpled in distress.

Blood boiling, Dominic shoved the barricade away with a clatter as his uncle released his mental grip. Ignoring the innkeeper's blustered protests, he marched to the door and wrenched it open. The blur of receding footsteps was already disappearing under a thin layer of snow. Aldric approached from the stables, his face stiff with cold, rubbing his hands together, his shoulder weighted with saddle bags. "What have you done to your face?" Aldric asked innocently before he caught sight of the devastated interior. He paused on the threshold and gazed around. "By the Gods, what happened to the inn?"

"Terrence Skinner happened to it." Dominic's tone was quiet. Laced with bitterness. He shoved the innkeeper toward the bar. "Drinks and food," he ordered brusquely.

"You owe me," the man began, slapping his club against his plump palm and wincing as he did so.

"Aye, mayhap," Dominic snapped. "Get the food."

Grumbling, the man shuffled away. Gritting his teeth, Dominic concentrated his mind on righting the furniture. Aldric watched, open-mouthed, as Dominic used his power to restore the tavern to order. A sweep and twist of his hand upturned the tables and rearranged the benches. He brushed the broken remains of a settle to a tidy pile near the fireplace. Aldric collected the littered Tarocchi cards. Dominic's face twisted at the sight of the Ace of Swords, clutched in his squire's hand as Aldric replaced it in the pack. His free hand wandered to his hip, where the enchanted blade still played its haunting tune and writhed against his thigh like a thing possessed. He huffed a bitter sigh, kicking himself for letting his uncle best him again. "Moving heavy objects," he muttered as he pushed a final bench into position with a savage rotation of his arm. "'Tis all I'm good for, after all. I'd be of more use as a servant, preparing the Great Hall on feast days."

"What happened?" Aldric asked again when they finally sat with bowls of rich broth steaming in front of them, taking advantage of the table by the fire.

Digging his spoon into his bowl, Dominic still trembled with a complicated mixture of rage and fear. "My uncle. My real uncle, this time, came for the dagger. They've got Felicia. They are forcing her to help them. But I still don't know what they plan to do with it." Staring at the lumps of vegetables swimming in the aromatic gravy, his face clenched with frustration. He pressed his hand to his cheekbone, wiping the thin smear of blood with his thumb as it trickled down his face from the cut under his eye. The enchanted blade danced at his hip. Taunting.

"What would happen if they got hold of it?" Aldric spooned his stew. Colour gradually returned to his ashen cheeks.

"I don't know. Terrence said they were trying to make a bridge of souls using the Grayling last time but failed because they didn't have the book. I'm guessing that must be Darius' book. Briana's diaries are full of it." He paused, staring across the room at the door. "What is Cerys trying to do? Does she think she can become Petronella somehow?" He scrubbed at his face.

"Where is this book? Any ideas?"

"None. Briana could never get near it while Darius was alive. It could be anywhere now he's dead. Destroyed, hidden? Who knows? Nothing makes sense."

Aldric took a sip of ale, his face thoughtful in the shifting light. "So, we are at war on two fronts," he remarked.

Dominic stared at him. "Aye. 'Tis what Master Ash said. Might and shadow magic, both," he said. "A secular war to distract us while she works her dark spells to get what she wants. Cerys is behind it all. If we find her, we can stop it."

Aldric's face was grave as he replied. "'Tis a risky strategy," he said. "You have the very thing she wants, and if Felicia is helping her..." He held his hand out to halt Dominic's automatic protest. "I said if..." he reiterated. "Gods know the girl wouldn't be doing it by choice." He took a sip of ale. "But if Felicia is using her farsight, you must admit 'tis a useful advantage. They know what you are likely to do before you do it."

Dominic's lips thinned. "Only if she tells them," he said. He smiled suddenly, remembering Felicia's wit and audacity. "And what she tells them," he added.

Aldric grimaced. "It takes a stern spirit indeed not to break under torture," he said. "I never knew Felicia, only what you say of her. Do not pin your hopes on her resolve under duress."

Dominic grimaced. "What they are doing to her is inhuman. I must find her." He took a mouthful of stew, hardly tasting it. Outside, the wind tossed the snow against the windows. The door rattled as it opened, and he coughed, waving away a billow of smoke as it blew back down the chimney. The gate guard, Cedric, slammed the door shut behind him and headed for the serving counter, nodding to them as he passed. "Gods greeting, Oswin, 'tis a foul night," he roared, slamming his hands on the board. "Where is everybody? Get your brother a drink!" An answering shout echoed from the back room. Dominic's gaze returned to Aldric, who was frowning in thought.

"They know you have travelled this far," Aldric said. "We had best be on our guard tonight and make some sort of plan."

"Aye," Dominic said. "I vote we sleep in the stables with the horses. Keep them safe. We'll move on in the morning."

Aldric wrinkled his nose. He glanced regretfully at the roaring fire. "Those stables are freezing," he said. "I put rugs on both our mounts."

"Aye, well, no doubt the barkeeper can spare a couple of extra blankets." Dominic waved at the tavern master, who was muttering to his brother at the bar. The man's head jerked around. His demeanour aimed at aggrieved and settled on fawning at the sight of Dominic's heavy purse as he dragged it from his doublet.

"Masters, how may I serve thee?" he asked, rubbing his hands together as he approached. His heavy jowls wobbled with his rolling gait.

"How far to Traitor's Reach?" Dominic demanded.

The rotund man cast a bemused gaze at the snow-crusted window. "In this weather?" he said faintly. "You must be mad. There's little travel in these parts now the winter's set in."

"But we have to get there," Dominic said. "How far?"

The man blinked. "'Twill take you a day, in fit weather," he said. "Now, you'd be lucky to get there in two days. If you managed it at all." His covetous gaze drifted to the purse. Dominic's eyes narrowed. "But you had a few miners here earlier this eve. And Hartwood is not a mining village. I wager there's another way, isn't there?" he said softly. "And you'll tell us what it is for a price, will you not?"

Eyes darting at his words, Oswin made nervous, shushing motions with his hands. He twisted around as his brother, Cedric, lumbered over, swiping foam from his lips. "Ah, 'tis you, have you warmed up?" the guard said. "Oswin said there was a little trouble here tonight, but all looks settled now, eh?" He took a seat at their table, planting his heavy elbows on the wood with the air of a man who aimed to remain in place for some considerable time.

Dominic's eyebrows raised at the alarm in Oswin's expression. He exchanged a mischievous glance with Aldric. "A little trouble? Terrence Skinner was here tonight," Dominic said. "A former member of the Dark Army with a powerful gift of telekinesis. We had an argument. Made rather a mess and broke a few things. Did your brother not mention him?"

Cedric's face screwed into a knot of confusion. "A former member of the Dark Army? One of them dark devils, here?" he asked. Under his beard, his cheeks turned white.

"According to Jon of Hartwood's description, he was the leader of the group who robbed and terrorised this village just a few short weeks ago," Dominic said. "He's one reason the Queen's troop are at Falconridge. Surely you recognised him if he entered by the gate?"

Cedric looked at first blank and then angry. "Didn't come in by our gates. Not by me." Scraping his chair from the table, he loomed over his brother. Oswin shrunk in on himself like a deflated pig bladder. "Oswin..." Cedric growled, thrusting his bearded jaw forward, "What are you about, you greedy oaf? Was it you who let them in?"

He extended a brawny arm and tangled his fist in his brother's collar. Oswin writhed in his grip, his face scarlet. As one, Dominic and Aldric rose, removing their supper and themselves to a safer spot against the wall.

"Well, this is interesting," Aldric murmured, tucking into his pottage again as Oswin shook free of his brother's grip and squared up to him, fists raised. "'Tis better than a mummers' show."

"Makes sense when you think about it," Dominic said under his breath. "Look how high the walls are. Hartwood is used to incursions, so it seems. But a traitor in their midst? That's not so easy to guard against." He flinched as Cedric's fist lashed out. Oswin grunted as it connected with his jaw, rocking him onto his heels, dangerously close to the piled hearth.

"How much did they pay you to let them in? Eh? I wondered about that new set of shutters on your windows," Cedric roared, his entire face contorted with disgust.

Oswin flinched. "You're not married to Helga," he whined. "Or you'd understand."

"Where's your loyalty? You're a disgrace to our good name. I'll be reporting you to Sir Jon," Cedric said.

"Nay," Oswin raised his hands in supplication. "Do not do that. I beg you, brother, he'll take my licence!"

"You'll not be letting any more of them vermin in. Where is it? Where's the entrance? Tell me!"

Dominic blinked, impressed by the gate guard's sheer strength as he hefted his brother by the shoulders of his tunic and shook him. Oswin's head rocked, his jowls lolling. "We'd like to know that as well," Dominic remarked, running his spoon around the last of the stew in his bowl. "We need to get to Traitor's Reach. Perhaps Oswin could take us?"

Face screwed in a mask of rage and frustration, Oswin turned his face with difficulty in their direction. "You don't want to go to Traitor's Reach," he ground out, his voice choked by the pressure Cedric was exerting on his windpipe. "'Tis a dark and dangerous place."

Dominic stood, one hand on his sword. "But we do," he said. "In the Queen's name. If there is a way to Traitor's Reach, you must show us. 'Tis a matter of life and death. And you must also show the way to the members of the Queen's troop who follow us."

Cedric released his brother, scratching his head under his helmet. "Those who follow you?" He turned his face to the door, his expression dubious. "They'll freeze to death out there," he said. "Once the snow starts around these parts, it rarely stops."

"They know to prepare for a cold journey," Dominic said. "They are but a day's ride behind us."

"Welladay, I'll let them through alright," Cedric said, "but there's no point you setting out now. Wait 'til they arrive. Rest. I'll charge my fellow guards to watch your mounts on their patrols tonight. You need not fear their safety."

"You'll not be able to ride," Oswin interjected. "Not where we're going."

Cedric's eyebrows formed one thick line on his forehead as he stared at his brother. "Just where are you going?"

Oswin shuffled his feet. "Mines," he said shortly.

"Nay. You can't mean it." Cedric took a step away. He turned to face Dominic, his mighty arms splayed wide. "Those tunnels were closed off years ago. The mines of Hartwood are all played out. No-one goes there now. 'Tis too dangerous."

Oswin shrugged. "They're not miners for nothing, those from Traitor's Reach," he said. "And my ale is excellent. Better than that piss poor brew they serve over the hill."

Cedric's eyes narrowed. "We guard the north gate well," he grunted.

A cunning smirk crossed Oswin's sweaty face. "Said, didn't I? They're not miners for nothing. Who said I let them in by the gate?"

CHAPTER 30

Cedric glared at Oswin and took a few more steps back, wiping his hands on his tunic as if contact with his brother soiled them. "You disgust me," he said, his voice aching with hurt. "A traitor in my family. I cannot believe it. And for what? Money? You have enough here. A good life."

Oswin lifted his head and glared defiantly back. "What do you know of my life?" he replied. He rubbed his arm, flinching a little as if the action caused him pain. "Do not judge me, brother."

Dominic bit his lip, glancing at Aldric. He nodded, and they moved across the room to the counter, giving the warring siblings some privacy.

"I almost wish I hadn't started that, now," Dominic said as the argument at the fireside continued. He wandered behind the counter and poured a jug of ale. "Here, let's sit," he said, grabbing a couple of clean tankards from the shelf.

"Loyalty." Aldric accepted his mug and folded his wiry frame onto the nearest bench. "'Tis a fragile thing. Easily bought and sold." He raised his drink, staring into the contents before he raised his gaze. "Let us wait for the others," he said, his voice low. "Rushing off now, before we have support, is a fool's journey. We'd be playing into Cerys' hands."

"But I can catch them off guard. Get in front of whatever they're trying to do," Dominic argued. "Every moment we tarry costs us dearly." He paused, his fingers closed convulsively on his tankard. "And make no mistake, I will fulfil Joran's mission," he said. "I watched my uncle claimed by the Shadow Mage in front of my eyes. 'Twas awful to see. I know in his right mind, he'd do anything rather than succumb."

"Aye, but he's not in his right mind, is he?" Aldric pointed out. "The Shadow Mage claimed him years ago. He's capable of any evil. 'Tis too dangerous, Dominic. Cerys is powerful."

"By the Gods!" Unable to sit still, Dominic lurched to his feet. He opened the door, peering out into the deserted street, shivering as the wind pierced his clothes with implacable fingers. "I hope the troop are safe," he said. "There was nowhere to shelter on the hills out there."

"They could still be in the forest. That will help," Aldric said. "At least for tonight. And the storm might blow itself out by morn."

The winter air nipping at their cheeks dragged the two older men from their argument. "Close the door," Oswin snapped, turning in Dominic's direction with a scowl on his face. He bent heavily to the hearth and loaded it with another log. Cedric heaved a sigh and left his brother stabbing moodily at the flames with a poker, his face downcast in the golden glow.

"'Tis sorry I am for Oswin's actions," he said as he crossed the room. "He gives no fine account of himself, but he will lead you through the mines as far as he's able." He shook his head as he stared at them. "You'll not believe what they've done," he said, his voice low. "There's an old well in the northern quarter. We closed it up when the water tainted. They've dug themselves a cunning little tunnel. Like thieving rats. Goes straight from there and into the mines. Oswin lifts the lid on the well when he gets a message from them. Simple." His lip curled.

"His fault is not yours," Dominic said, latching the door.

"Hah. That's what you think," Cedric said, his expression morose. He helped himself to ale and slumped to a seat next to Aldric. "A place like this, so small, with everyone known to each other... You can wager your entire purse on the scorn of our neighbours come the morrow. Might as well tell my wife we are leaving. She'll not like it."

He waved his flagon at his brother. "Oy, get these two your best chambers for the night," he said. "With some extra blankets. And you'll not charge them. 'Tis the least you can do."

Oswin grunted, shuffling past them. He avoided his brother's ire-filled gaze but flung Dominic a filthy look on his way out of the room.

Cedric shook his shaggy round head. "Always stubborn, Oswin," he muttered. "Hates being told he's wrong." He glanced at the two younger men. "All settled?" he asked. "You'll stay overnight and wait for your comrades?"

Aldric lifted his head, his searching gaze fixed intently on Domnic's face. "Well?" he said. "Will you wait?"

Dominic didn't reply. He wandered to the nearest window, rubbing his hand over the condensation on the glass, peering out into the snow-filled night. "Mayhap," he said shortly.

Chivvied by his brother, Oswin loaded their arms with blankets and led the way up the narrow stairs to the inn bed chambers. His lone candle flickered on the whitewashed walls, highlighting scuffs and scrapes caused by years of drunken patrons lumbering down the narrow corridor.

"Here," Oswin shouldered open a door and ushered them into a narrow room with a single gabled window, furnished with two low cots and a chamber pot. Frost coated the inside of the panes. The hearth was unlit. "I'll see to the fire," he muttered. "Take the candle."

Leaving them to their own devices, he slammed the door. His heavy tread vibrated the floorboards as he made his descent.

Dominic crossed to the window. The wind had eased outside. Snow fell as soft as whispers, filling the ruts and hollows of the road with dense clouds of ghostly silence. "What do you think you're looking for?" Aldric asked, dumping his blankets onto the straw-stuffed mattress. He lowered the heavy saddle bag to the floor and busied himself, arranging the covers.

Dominic shrugged. "Terrence, mayhap."

"He will have headed for shelter if he's any sense. The troop won't be here tonight, Dom."

Dominic cast a bleak gaze around the room. "I know," he said. "This blasted dagger is driving me mad." He wrenched at the buckle that fastened the blade around his waist, dropping the scabbard onto the bed nearest the window. They both watched as it writhed and twisted. "I can't leave it, and it's driving me mad to carry it," Dominic said. "And it never stops talking. Singing. Humming. Honestly, I swear it lives in my head."

Aldric's mouth twisted. "The blade that cuts both ways," he said. "Funny how the legend never said a word about how bloody annoying it is."

As if in response to his words, the blade stilled. They both stared at it. "Do you think it heard us?" Aldric whispered.

"By the Gods, Aldric, don't say that," Dominic breathed. He poked at the scabbard with a tentative finger and all but jumped out of his skin as the dagger lurched to life again. He glared at it, sure he could hear Cerys' laughter in his ears.

"Right." Jaw set, he grabbed it. He thrust it into his pack, burying the blade deep between the folds of his clothing, and kicked the bag under the bedstead.

"I challenge it to hear anything now," he said. "Let's get some rest."

He spread his own blankets out, glancing round as Oswin returned, laden with a bucket of coal, a bundle of kindling dangling from his shoulder, and another basket of logs tucked under his arm. "Blast this," he grumbled. "Fires at all hours. Shouldn't have sent the wench home so early. Thought we'd be quiet tonight."

He knelt at the hearth, loading the grate with an expert hand. The crackle of flames took the chill from the atmosphere as he took his leave.

"That's better." Aldric crouched to the warmth, blowing gently to encouraged the flames to spread. He returned to his cot and stifled a yawn. A slight smile lifting his lips, Dominic waited for his squire to sleep. It didn't take long. In repose, his friend's familiar features relaxed, his long eyelashes grazing his cheeks, his gangling limbs sprawled, taking up most of the mattress these days.

Dominic returned to his pack, dragging it from under his bed with all the stealth of a burglar. Glancing across at Aldric, he rummaged within until his fingers caught the edge of one of Briana's diaries. He slid it out. Her writing slanted across the page, almost seeming alive in the twisting firelight.

"He's done something heinous. I know it. Where is that book? I must find it."

It was her last entry. Below it, half a page of blank paper.

Crossing on careful feet to the fireplace, Dominic risked burning his hand and retrieved a charred twig. He winced as he tore the page from Briana's journal. Aldric murmured something unintelligible, rolling into a huddled ball on the mattress.

"My friend, Aldric," he scribbled carefully. The charcoal smudged across the page. "I must act now. The risk is too great to wait. Follow me with the troop as soon as you can. Trust that I am doing what I believe is right." He paused, biting his lip, heart pounding at the immensity of his actions. Shaking his head, his hand trembled as he ended the note. "Your friend, Dominic."

Gentle as a mother, he lifted one of his blankets, nestling it carefully around Aldric's hunched body. He left the note on the lad's pillow.

Nudging Oswin awake took longer than he thought. Deep in slumber, the man's shoulders shook with his snores. He jerked to life, sour with stale ale and resentment.

"Well, and what do you want?" he huffed, struggling upright, his nightcap askew.

"A guide," Dominic said briskly. "As you promised."

Oswin blinked, his clouded gaze darting to the ink-black night. "Now? 'Tis the middle of the night."

"Aye, now. Get up. There's no time to lose." Dominic waited, tapping his feet as the older man shuffled into his clothes, cursing as he pulled at laces and stamped his feet into his boots. "Catch me death," he said, glowered.

"Cloak? Gloves?" Dominic said, gesturing to each item and tossing them across the room at him.

"By all the Gods, you can stop doing that," Oswin said. "I'm coming, aren't I?"

"Not fast enough." Dominic bared his teeth in a mirthless grin.

It seemed an age until Oswin was ready, shrugging on a cloak that seemed large enough to cover the building, let alone its rotund owner.

Outside, the wind had dropped. The early winter storm, having bared its teeth, moved on. The village lay wrapped in ice and silence. Only the distant barking of a dog punctured the peaceful night. Boots crunching and sliding on the layer of the snow, Oswin grumbling into his beard, and the men tramped across the cobbles. The snow cast a secret, pristine spell over the everyday, wrapping each familiar object in a blanket of enchantment. Stars twinkled overhead between the drifting clouds. The moon sported a fragile halo of crystal.

Armed with his thick cudgel, Oswin cursed and muttered to himself as he led the way. Intent on the journey ahead of him, Dominic tuned him out, his mind churning with doubt. He glanced backwards to the Beaten Drum as it receded into the distance. Silently, he asked Aldric's forgiveness. Dread lay heavy on his heart. But the thought of

Felicia, alone and in pain, forced to aid Cerys' twisted plans, tugged him onwards. His hands fisted within the folds of his cloak. At his hip, the enchanted blade still danced. Loathe as he was to touch it, his fingers traced the edge of the hilt, his thoughts as dark as the night. "You'll taste Shadow Mage blood again tonight," he promised it grimly. "I swear it on my life."

CHAPTER 31

O swin cast a wary glance around as they crept into a shadowed courtyard by the north wall. More than one set of boots had dented the snow. A series of low-roofed, shuttered buildings rimmed the perimeter, either small shops or storage. Dominic caught the smell of freshly chopped wood. A heavy axe leaned against one wall, sporting a fluffy white bonnet, courtesy of the sudden storm. The well beckoned at the centre of the courtyard, its pitched roof sheltering the contents. All the footsteps led there.

Dominic's mouth thinned. "The snow does you no favours," he remarked.

Oswin's face contracted in a fierce frown. "This courtyard's owned by a friend of mine, the woodcutter," he rumbled. He nodded at the axe. "We have an arrangement."

"I'm sure you do."

With one hand on his sword, Dominic approached the well and leaned over the low wall. The void stared back, its single eye dark as the night. His nostrils wrinkled. The dank odour of decay crept from its belly like the breath of a dying animal. The rope carrying the bucket dangled into the column, twisting gently. No prizes for guessing how to get down. He grimaced and straightened to glare at Oswin, conscious of the tire ached across his shoulders and down his spine.

"You've travelled this way before?" he asked, his voice hoarse.

Oswin shrugged. "Once. Chasing a debt. The rope's sturdy. I replaced it myself if that's what you're worrying about. 'Twill hold your weight."

Dominic eyed him up and down. "Aye," he said, "But will it hold yours?"

Oswin took a shuffling step back. "I've done my part. You said you wanted a guide to the well," he said.

Dominic chuckled and unsheathed his sword. The fine edge glinted. "Oh no, my fine friend. You promised your brother to guide me through the mines to Traitor's Reach," he replied. "'Tis only fair that you earn your redemption by aiding the crown in its time of need." He gestured with his weapon to the noisome depths of the well. "After you," he said.

Oswin lumbered over, grumbling all the while. His heavy cloak dragged over the stone lip as he reached for the rope. "I can't do this," he said. His face tuned in supplication, white as milk. A sickly smile plastered across his sweaty forehead. "By your leave, sir, I'm no acrobat, and I'm injured." He tapped his left arm.

"Yet you will descend," Dominic bade him. "Or taste my steel." His lips twisted. "Pretend you're owed money," he said. "That should lighten the burden somewhat."

"Bastard." Oswin's face closed in a scowl. He rammed his club into his belt, took a better grip on the rope, and clamped his legs around it. "There's a platform about twenty feet down," he grunted. "That's where we're going. Don't go further. 'Tis deep. If you fall, I'm not getting you out." He gritted his teeth, peering up at the fresh air, took a huge breath, and lowered himself out of sight.

Clutching his sword in a sweaty grip, Dominic leaned over the drop. The rope tautened with the barkeeper's weight. Oswin's round face faded into the gloom, but his pained, muffled curses rose to greet his ears. A few short moments later, the rope swung free. "You can come," Oswin's rough tones echoed from below. "'Tis all clear."

Swallowing against his dry throat, Dominic sheathed his weapon and slung one leg over the lip of the well. His saddle bag, laden with a waterskin and provisions for the journey, shifted on his shoulder. He adjusted it, brushing his hands against his tunic for better purchase, and copied Oswin.

The rope ground harshly against his palms. He wrapped one leg in its length, grimacing as his weight stretched the sore muscles and semi-healed scars on his back. The enchanted blade strapped to his hip was a distracting presence. Somewhere far below, his ears caught the steady drip of water. Moist moss-tainted air billowed upwards, damp against his cold cheeks.

Slowly, steadily, he lowered himself, clutching fingers damp with sweat, terrified he'd miss the platform.

Oswin's voice looming out of the gloom nearly jerked his fingers from the rope. "Here," the older man said, tapping Dominic's foot. "A little further."

Blind in the darkness, Dominic slid down one more handhold. Oswin grabbed a handful of his cloak. "To me, lad," he said. He pulled the rope, and Dominic swayed as his feet touched solid rock. He teetered off balance on the narrow platform, and Oswin yanked him towards the wall, slimy with moss.

"Tis here, the entrance," Oswin said. A steady breeze crept towards them from the depths of the mountains. Dominic stifled a shudder as he felt the touch of its breath on his exposed skin. Working by feel, he dipped a hand into his sack of provisions and withdrew his lantern and tinderbox. Beneath his experienced fingers, the tinder caught on the second strike of his flint. Heart in his mouth, he transferred the flame to the lantern, lifting it high to reveal the tunnel. Damp earth trickled between the woven branches that supported the low roof. The light picked out the golden warmth of the wood. At their feet, the passage sloped gently downward, the earth pressed flat. Dominic shook his head, marvelling at the miner's ingenuity.

"By the Gods," he said, "Ingenious. Your beer must be good."

He swung his lantern so that the light touched the innkeeper's face. Oswin averted his gaze. '"Now, they might come for my beer," he mumbled. "In the days of the old king, when Falconridge gained control, this was a way out. Hartwood sprung up to service Traitor's Reach years ago when they rounded up the Blessed and sent them into the mines." He gazed around, his gimlet eyes troubled. "The old king sent a garrison of Citizens to guard them. That's what Hartwood was for back then. Lord Falconridge was obsessed with Blessed abilities. He used the prisoners. Experimented on them, trying to find out how their magic worked. Wrote it all down in his book. Of course, they tried to escape. The gibbets at Traitor's Reach were always full of the ones the guards caught. The Blessed lived in terror. They couldn't use their own abilities against the Citizens for fear of losing their gifts. So, they existed, never knowing who Darius would take next. For work or his experiments with the Shadow Mage. Or for his own pleasure. Any who resisted..." He shrugged and drew a sharp line across his own throat.

Brow quirked, Dominic stared at him. "How do you know all this?" he asked.

Oswin's heavy shoulders lifted. He stirred a random scattering of stones with his booted foot. "Your uncle's good company when he's himself," he said. "He was the first member of the Blessed ever sent here and one of the most powerful." He paused, gazing at the passage with a smile on his thin lips. "As a prisoner, he worked against Falconridge. He wanted to be an architect once, did you know that? Used his gift to build this. Darius found out and forced him to serve the Shadow Mage. When Darius eventually harnessed the Shadow Mage's power, he made Terrence the founding member of his Dark Army. The Dark Army grew and became the Blessed's guards. More deadly against their own than the Citizen soldiers at Hartwood. Over time, they forgot about this little rat run. It fell into ruin." He turned, his shadow stretching onward into the distant darkness. "When the queen freed the Dark Army, your uncle came back and repaired it. Just in case. They call it Terrence's Traverse."

"You speak like a man loyal to the Queen, but now you are using this tunnel to let people loyal to Cerys into Hartwood? By all the Gods, why?" Dominic rounded on Oswin, his ever-present frustration bursting out of him. Oswin's steady gaze flickered, morphing into something more haunted, laced with fear. He dropped his eyes. "Your uncle is good company when he's in his right mind," he repeated, his voice so soft Dominic had to stoop to hear him. "When he's not..." He held out his arm, shifting the folds of his cloak and pushing up his sleeve. A series of deep, half-healed cuts clawed his arm from wrist to elbow, oozing a foul-smelling pus. "He doesn't even have to touch me to do that," he whispered. "And he never lets them heal. Day and night, I have them. Itching, burning. When he's in his right mind, I don't think he remembers doing it. If I refuse to aid him, he cuts me again."

Dominic's horror-struck gaze matched the deep surge of fear in his gut. "By the Gods, if he does that to you, what is he doing to Felicia?" he breathed. He swallowed against the lump in his throat. His grip on the lantern trembled. Shadows writhed in the wobbling light.

"Aye, you're understanding now. Still want to go on, brave young warrior?" Oswin said, his voice laced with terrible, grim sarcasm. "Terrence has been merciful to you thus far, even under the dominion of the Shadow Mage. It will not last. Once you enter the mines at Traitor's Reach, you are risking your life and sanity and that of any who follow you." He gestured stiffly down the length of the tunnel with his injured arm.

Dominic's gaze followed his pointing finger and crept inevitably to the open wounds displayed so vividly in front of him. "Flayed," he murmured, remembering the fire of the lash against his own skin. His raging sense of injustice. The savage sting of humiliation. "Prince

Joran wants me to prove my loyalty to him by killing my uncle," he said, forcing the words through gritted teeth. "'Tis possible only I can do it."

Oswin lifted a thick eyebrow. "There's many would thank you for it, not just Prince Joran," he said. "Though 'tis a pity. He was a good man, once."

"Aye." Dominic touched the hilt of the enchanted dagger, where it danced and writhed within its scabbard. His palm tingled as his power blended with the blade, and he frowned as another thought found space in his troubled mind. "Perhaps there's another way," he muttered, half to himself. "If this blade does what I think it can do, mayhap I don't have to kill him. Perhaps I could save him."

He paused, tasting the words in the air around him as he uttered them. Trying to sense the wisdom of his own god. A memory of Aldric rolling a crown across his knuckles, face up, face down, crossed his mind. *"Which?"* he pleaded, sending out a desperate prayer for guidance. To the solid good sense of his friend. To the closed mental channel that led to the Queen. The Mage himself. *"Up or down. Tell me which."*

"Decide," Oswin said sourly. "Otherwise, I'm climbing that rope, and if you knife me in the back on my way up to civilisation, so be it."

Dominic's fingers closed on the enchanted blade. Despite his anguished plea, there was nothing there. No answers. No divine guidance. Only his own will. He raised his chin.

"We go on," he said.

CHAPTER 32

Terrence's Traverse sloped sharply downhill. The light from Dominic's lantern cast a golden light on the twisting lattice of interlaced branches braced hard against the hollowed walls. Sturdy logs and planks fortified the ceiling. A scattering of debris lined the path. Cast off tools, a worn pair of boots. Dusty bottles and jars that had, perhaps, once contained ale from the Beaten Drum. A steady breeze drifted from the distant mines, ruffling Domnic's hair. At the edge of his hearing, he caught the edge of distant conversations, blurring into the dusty silence. He glanced up at the ceiling as they travelled deeper underground. Packed earth gave way to solid rock. The soft plink of dripping water. Oswin strode ahead, although his gait grew more and more hesitant the further they walked.

"Here," he said, stopping so suddenly Dominic all but tripped over him. "Give us some light."

Pushing back his hood, Dominic shone his lamp over a row of old beer barrels standing on their sides against the damp stone wall. "Here?" he said, his voice loud in the narrow passage. "Are you stopping for a drink?" The breeze chilled his skin as he stood there. He glanced around, looking for an opening.

"Nay. Quiet now." Oswin bent to examine the barrels. "Now, which one?" he mused. "Ah. This one."

He turned the spigot of the container on the right. Dominic's eyes widened as the lid swung open to reveal another narrow, rocky corridor burrowed into the stone beyond. Oswin turned to face him. His eyes shone almost manically in the shifting light. "Well, there you go," he said. "The mines of Traitor's Reach. Good luck."

He turned on his heel. Dominic's free hand caught his cloak. "Oh no, you don't," he said. "You've been here before, yes?"

"Aye, I told you. Once. Years ago. And I don't want to go back," Oswin said. "Surely, I've done enough. If Terrence catches me down here, he will kill me. And you, too, probably."

"That's a chance I'm taking," Dominic said. "I have to go in. For Terrence, for Felicia, and for the Queen. I need a guide, and you are it. Don't make me force you. Also, you might consider this. There will be no escaping Prince Joran's retribution if he hears of your treachery."

Oswin eyed him with a dislike bordering on hatred. "And you'll make sure he hears, of course."

"Of a certainty." Dominic stood back. "After you."

Oswin glared at him. He stooped, forcing his bulky frame through the narrow confines of the barrel and into the inky murk beyond.

Glancing behind him, Dominic screwed up his courage and followed the man in.

The atmosphere changed immediately. Darker. Watchful. Oswin took a couple of steps and then faltered to a halt. The lantern light revealed a small, claustrophobic chamber, large enough for one person to stand upright. Dominic blinked as Oswin shuffled sideways, vanishing into a narrow space half-hidden behind another slim column of rock. The sound of the man's cloak ripping as it caught on the stone was loud in the eerie silence. "Come on," Oswin said, his voice muffled. "Quick now. 'Tis dark in here."

Dominic took a better grip on his light and followed the older man into the gap. His pack grated against the narrow wall, and he breathed in, squeezing himself around another narrow crevice, wondering how Oswin had managed it. All his senses craved space. He swallowed, conscious of the indifference of solid rock. The weight of the mountain above him. He frowned at the sound of a woman's voice singing the Prophecy of the Sword in his head. This time, adding words to the tune. Dominic frowned as he moved forward, shaking his head, trying to dislodge the song to no avail. *"The bearer walks a path unknown, through shadows thick and thin. For light and dark both mark the path, where destinies begin."* The tune tailed off. Light laughter pricked at his senses. He winced onward, trying to dispel the image of icy fingers clawing at him as he crossed the boundary into the realm of the Shadow Mage.

The oil lamp revealed a relatively wider corridor. Old lanterns, their candles long spent, dangled at intervals along the wall. A pair of rusting rails stretched across the puddled ground into the distance on each side. Glancing at the way they'd arrived, Dominic marvelled at the disguise. If his uncle had created this fissure in the rock, he'd done it with delicate skill. No-one looking at it would think it unusual. Biting his lip, he scanned the ground for something to mark it. He settled on a rusty pick. Using his gift to pick the tool up, he leaned it casually against the wall on the opposite side of the tunnel, pointing the way to escape. Oswin watched him with reluctant approval and turned to the right with a shrug. "If you make it out," he remarked. He didn't sound optimistic.

They travelled quickly, their boots kicking up dust, following the wagon tracks. Oswin continued to mutter. After a short while, Dominic picked out the rhythmic cadences in the man's low voice and huddled deeper into his cloak. The older man was praying. Begging the Mage for protection. He glanced around, tipping his head, trying to track the direction of the whispered conversations that trickled towards him from all sides. "Can you hear that?" he asked.

Oswin bit down on his lip, his shoulders drawn up to his ears. "Aye, a little. Just whispers," he returned. "It's starting already. Try not to listen." Head down, bullish shoulders hunched much in the manner of Mistress Trevis' oxen, he marched on.

Dominic froze at the touch of a hand on his face. He whirled, power blazing to life in his free hand. There was nothing there except the same girl's laughter. "Who is that?" he muttered out loud. "What do you want?"

"Don't listen," Oswin flung over his shoulder. "Ghosts, those voices you hear. Them who died here. Mad, they are."

"Ghosts?" Dominic rolled his eyes at the man's back. "You truly believe that? If I was a ghost, I'd choose better places to haunt."

"They can't leave," Oswin said, glancing at him. "Locked in here, aren't they? Still prisoners of the Shadow Mage."

The raw skin of Dominic's back crawled at his companion's words. He scrubbed his free hand over his face, shaking his head. The whispers grew louder, their tone menacing and sibilant. *"That's him,"* he heard one treble voice declared. *"That's the one she's waiting for."*

"Aye, so 'tis. Handsome, isn't he? Not like us, so white and cold," a deeper voice hissed.

"By the Gods, I wish they'd shut up," Dominic muttered, increasing his pace as if he could somehow outstride them. That same light, derisive laughter stroked his senses. *"Look how he runs,"* the treble voice said.

"Straight into trouble," the other agreed with malicious relish. Dominic clapped his free hand over his ear.

"Told you, don't listen, don't talk to them or about them," Oswin said. "That's what they want."

"My conversation?" Dominic blinked in surprise.

"Nay, you dolt. Your energy. They'll not bother too much with me, a simple Citizen. I can barely hear them. You, though..." He paused and cleared his throat, jerking his hand at the lamp glowing like a beacon of hope in Dominic's sweaty fingers. "To the likes of these lost wights, you shine like a thousand of them lanterns. They'll take all your energy, bit by bit, growing stronger all the while."

Dominic stared at him. The shadows cast by his light wobbled with the tremble in his arm. "You can't be serious," he breathed.

Oswin snorted and faced forward, his long cloak stirring the dust at their feet. "'Tis how the Shadow Mage works. Always has. The brighter the light, the quicker the fall into his darkness. 'Tis why Darius chose this place as a prison for the Blessed. He planned it once he realised the dark power under these mountains could serve his own ambitions better than the old king's."

Brought up short by Oswin's certainty, Dominic frowned. "You seem to know a lot about it," he ventured. "Talked to my uncle a lot, did you?"

Oswin shrugged. "Aye. Many's a long night we've had, speaking about the old days and the old ways in the last couple of years. He'd come to the tavern with his flask of heartsease. Most of the time, he left before it wore off. Other times... Well, you know the outcome."

They marched on. Talking to Oswin helped to keep Dominic's mind from the ghostly presences drifting around him. He flinched from time to time at a tug on his cloak or the quick shuffle of footsteps walking alongside him.

Up ahead, the path forked. Oswin stopped, tapping his fingers against his bearded chin. The rusty rails they had followed thus far split at the junction, leading to narrower passages. An abandoned cart stood forlornly in place, its interior full of ore. A mess of picks and shovels surrounded it. Dominic turned one over with his foot. "This is still useful," he said. "Not broken. And the ore is worth money. Why would they just leave everything?"

Oswin turned a pale face in his direction. "You probably don't want to know the answer to that question," he said, his voice hushed in the heavy atmosphere. "We go this way. The other passage is blocked off. Rockfall, years ago."

He led them into the right-hand passage. Dominic trailed his hand across the chiselled rock face. Here and there, low passages split away from the main tunnel, carved by long-ago miners chasing seams of ore. Shallow streams of grubby water splashed under their feet. The air was damp and dirty. Gritting his teeth, Dominic tried to tune out the increasing volume of voices in his ears. He shone his lantern into some of the tributary passageways as he passed, casting a lone light into the haunted corridors. At the edge of his hearing, he could swear he heard the rhythmic chink of metal on rock, the rumble of long-ago wheels on the rusty tracks. A low murmur of conversation. From time to time, his sensitive nose caught the odour of sweat and pipe smoke. A tang of tin. The sob of a tired child. Swallowing, he groped in his pack for a waterskin, jumping at every unfamiliar sound.

Face set, Oswin plodded on. "Come, 'tis not far now," he said when Dominic felt he'd been marching for several hours, chased by memories not his own. His stomach rumbled. The oppressive tunnels seemed to close in around him. Oswin turned left and then right again. All sense of time blurred. The darkness was disorientating. Whispering, malicious voices added to the dizzying unreality. He clung to the sight of Oswin's cloak tail, dreading the thought of losing him. The flame in his oil lamp danced. He screwed up his eyes to peer at it and gave it a shake. The remaining oil rippled at the bottom of the container. Nearly empty.

"Have we far to go? I'll have to stop and refill the lantern," he said.

Puffing slightly on the slope, Oswin inclined his head. "We should eat and rest a while," he said. "There's a likely spot up ahead."

He continued on his way. Dominic followed, fatigue lapping at his thoughts, wondering at the older man's confidence in this dim and fearful world under the mountain. He shook his head at Oswin's thick back. The innkeeper walked with a powerful stride, unerring in his direction. For a man who had only been this way once before, he was much too bold. Apprehension trickled slowly under Dominic's skin, chilling his blood. His hand tightened on his old dagger.

"Think he's realised yet?" the light female voice asked of her ghostly friend.

"Slow, isn't he?" the second voice replied. He felt her hands on his shoulders. A light tug and pat. The same way his mother had once woken him as a child. *"Wake up, Sir Skinner,"* she whispered.

"Hold." Dominic's voice rang out in the tunnel, chasing the ghosts away.

Oswin paused, only fractionally, but it was enough to underline his suspicion. "How now?" the man said irritably. "I said we'd stop for a bite anon."

"I said, hold." His heart racing, Dominic swept his sword from its scabbard. He placed the dying lantern on a handy ledge and took a fighting stance. Oswin whirled, eyes darting under their thick brows. They widened at the sight of Dominic's blade aimed straight at his heart. "Now, Sir Skinner," he blustered. "What's to do? Led you this far, haven't I?"

"Aye, and keenly for a man who has come this way but once be-fore," Dominic said. Blood thumped furiously in his head. Cursing himself for a fool, he took a couple of steps towards Oswin. The man moved towards him, raising his hands. "Here, what are you about? Think I'd leave you down here? How will you get out without me?"

"Where are we going, Oswin? Think carefully before you answer," Dominic returned. "If I have to stay down here keeping company with your ghost until my companions arrive, so be it."

"Huh," Oswin said. "They'll never find you. 'Tis a warren down here. A maze. All the tunnels look alike."

"They have Aldric," Dominic countered. "He's a tracker." He sounded more confident than he felt. "So, I ask you again, what are your orders? Where are we going?"

Oswin looked around, sweeping the dank tunnel with a practised gaze that sent prickles of tension down his back. A chilly breeze touched Dominic's cheek, drifting down the tunnel from the right. He winced at the sound of approaching footsteps, shaking his head, trying to sift reality from illusion. Oswin's face held all the satisfaction of the successful gambler. "Right about here, I reckon," he said cheerfully.

Terrence's attack took him totally by surprise. His uncle emerged from the narrow corridor and launched a blast of power that rocked Dominic off his feet. His head slammed painfully against the opposite wall. Dazed, he stumbled, dropping the sword, squinting at the two figures as they loomed towards him. One, a mountain of physicality, armed with a heavy club. The other, tall and thin. Old, but not weak. No, never that. Power coalesced in his own palm. Fighting his dizziness, he aimed it wildly at his uncle, twisting the man around and attempting to sweep him off his narrow feet. Terrence tightened his lips, his eyes alight with menace, and pressed him back against the damp rock. Beneath the malignant light of the Shadow Mage, sadness seared his expression. He wielded his magic with shaking hands. "Fight it, uncle!" Dominic yelled. "You know you don't want to do this. Please, fight it!" His words only heightened the grief on Terrence's lined face. The iron-hard pressure on Dominic's chest increased. He strained to breathe, let alone raise his voice.

Terrence didn't speak. Swearing, Dominic struggled against the magical force of his uncle's will, ever stronger than his own. Oswin closed, taking advantage of Dominic's distraction. He grabbed Dominic's arms in a hard lock, twisting them behind his back, where they could do little telekinetic damage. "That's the trouble with the Blessed," he huffed in Dominic's ear. "Always think magic will save the day, don't you?" He grunted as Dominic's lashing foot connected painfully with his shins and gave him a shake that ground his shoulders in their sockets. The abused flesh of his back flared to life. "Enough of that, now," Oswin said. "My mistress wants that dagger. And what she wants, I am happy to give her."

His plump hand pawed at Dominic's waist, scrabbling with the heavy buckle. His triumphant chuckle scoured Dominic's pride as he twisted and struggled within the man's expert grip like a bird on a wire. "Your queen sent a puny man to do her work, did she not?" Oswin said, releasing the buckle and dragging the enchanted blade from him. After so many weeks with the thing jolting at his side, his hip felt bare. Exposed. Oswin tossed it to Terrence, a fleeting expression of distaste trickling over his broad features as he did so. He followed up with a shove that smacked Dominic's head against the wall again and released his grip on his shoulders. Terrence stared at him from his position on the opposite wall, one hand out-flung, the sign of the Shadow Mage pulsing in his palm. The enchanted blade dangled from his free hand.

Dominic winced as he writhed in his uncle's mental grip. He reached out, straining every ounce of his will to overcome Terrence's control. All he could manage was a twitch of his fingers. Not enough to beckon either his sword or the enchanted blade to him. He bit his lip, anger and shame mixing into a noxious brew in his heart. Terrence surveyed him a moment longer. In the dull, flickering light of the lantern, Dominic could swear he spied a glistening tear tracking his uncle's age-ravaged cheek.

Mouth split in a gap-toothed grin, Oswin collected Dominic's lantern. "Thank you for your business, Sir Skinner," he said.

"Nay, don't leave me in the dark." Dominic whispered it. He couldn't tell whether the pair heard him. A frown crossed Terrence's face as Oswin raised his club. Dominic could do nothing to stop its descent. The blow scattered his wits. Stars burned before his eyes.

Together, they turned, retreating up the narrow corridor in the direction Terrence had come. The light bounced before them. A vanishing pinprick of hope. Shadows enveloped him, alive with whispers. He sensed the ghouls edging closer, a tangled mixture of clutching fingers and fascination at his plight. His head pounded from the force of its contact with the rough walls and Oswin's club. Blood trickled silent and hot from the gash on his temple. Terrence relaxed his hold by degrees, and Dominic stretched his fingers, aware of the tingle of power still trapped within them. He cocked his head, but his assailant's footsteps had vanished. And with them, any chance of retribution. Boneless, he slid to the floor, shrugging his heavy hood over his head, fighting the nausea that knotted his stomach. He lost the battle. His gut recoiled, and he groaned, gripping his head as vomit erupted from him to splatter the stony ground. He remained, clutching at the wet, acid-smelling soil as the darkness tilted all around him and his baffled senses swam. Something quick and light tugged his cloak and darted away. "Leave me," he muttered into the heavy nothing that was the dark mine. "Leave me alone."

"They have left you alone. All alone to die here. 'Tis a pity. You were so close." The phantom voice was hushed in his head, brushing his cheek with gentle fingers. Cool against his burning skin. *"A pity he didn't have more sense,"* the older voice argued crisply. *"And now Lord Terrence has your blade once more. Your beautiful, perfect weapon."*

"As it should be. 'Twas his, at the first. As I was. Always, and only his." The lighter voice was determined and sad. Dominic felt the ache of it deep in his soul, where his own loneliness lived.

Still arguing, their voices drifted in and out of his hearing. The pounding in his skull increased. Unconsciousness crept to claim him, pulling him down into the inky void of oblivion. "Juliana Tinterdorn," he whispered into the dirty heart of the mine. "Help me."

CHAPTER 33

It was the pain that woke him. A heavy, dull thud against his temple. He gained his senses by slow degrees, his thoughts sluggish and sticky like the damp muck of the mine floor. His lids fluttered in the complete blackness, seeking any shred of light. There was nothing. Teeth chattering, he pushed himself to his hands and knees, searching blindly for the nearest wall. His sodden cloak weighed heavily on his shoulders. How long he'd lain there on the puddled ground, he had no way of knowing. Finding the wall, he struggled to move the pack from his back. His frozen fingers fumbled for the straps. The most commonplace of actions seemed almost impossible. His hands felt like shovels, unwieldy and stubbornly disobeying the commands of his mind. Panting under his breath, he chewed his parched lips, trying to ignore the throb of pressure in his head.

There. Finally, the pack slid free. He pulled it between his legs and burrowed into the depths for his tinderbox and flint. Somewhere in there, he knew he had candles. Stuffed in as a hasty afterthought so many days ago.

He breathed a silent prayer of relief when his clumsy fingers closed on the lumpy shapes of them, wrapped in cloth at the bottom of the bag. Lighting them should have been the work of a moment, even in the dark. But dizzy, racked with shivers, and mouth dry with thirst, he tried six times before the flame caught.

By candlelight, the mine walls loomed over him. He blinked. His eyes watered as his vision adjusted to the changing circumstances. Beyond the gentle halo of light, nothing had changed. The whispers still scurried around him, hushed as dead leaves stirred by the wind. Turbulent. Restless. Tired beyond measure, he rummaged in his bag and found his waterskin. Half full. He'd have to ration himself. Another quick rummage produced some hardtack and jerky. He stuffed a portion into his mouth, forcing himself to chew slowly. Every movement of his jaw lanced pain through his head. Sipping water at intervals, he lifted the candle, shuddering with cold. The flame tossed and flickered in the draft from the tunnel opposite him. The tiny arc of light illuminated a loose stack of old boxes piled randomly against the wall. Conjuring his gift was hard. The crate he chose crashed to the ground and then evaded his mental command completely. The pounding in his skull made it impossible to concentrate, but he doubted his ability to stand without help. Grimacing, he willed the box to travel to him. It came reluctantly, jolting and scraping down the corridor. Struggling against its fate. Cursing under his breath, Dominic battled to keep the thing on an even trajectory. The effort it took was exhausting.

The wood was old and, thanks to the breeze in the corridor, relatively dry. He held the candle to a battered edge, wafting with the cloth that had contained the candles until a solid flame caught and flared. Dizzy with relief, he held his hands to it, huddling close to the warmth until some semblance of comfort returned to his battered limbs.

Immediate needs met, he sat cross-legged in front of the makeshift fire and burrowed once more in his bag for his flask of willow bark. The familiar tang of the brew, as it slid down his throat, brought grim solace. Corking the container carefully, he buried his aching head in his hands, trying to decide what to do. His thoughts jittered and skipped when he attempted to retrace the route backwards through the mine. The fork in the path marked by the abandoned ore cart was his waypoint; the path back out from there was relatively straightforward. But after that... He shook his head. Oswin had jinked and turned so many times there was no way he dared to risk retracing his steps. He was no tracker. That had always been Aldric's task.

His heart lurched at the thought of his squire kicking his heels back at the inn, cursing Dominic's name in a variety of colourful phrases. How long had he lain here, unconscious? Had the troop navigated the snow fields? He imagined Aldric would wait for them. Cedric would at least take them to the well. But did Oswin's brother know about the hidden entrance behind the beer barrels? His comrades could wander forever alone in the dark, just as he was, searching in vain until their supplies ran out. He'd failed to kill his uncle. Failed to find Felicia. Lost a powerful weapon. Lost himself. Fear shuddered through his body. The scalding wrench of guilt shook his soul. How well he knew it from days gone by. As close as his own shadow, dogging his every footstep. A dark, faithful monster.

He squeezed his eyes shut, rubbing his chest. A useless attempt at self-comfort. The watchful silence seemed alive, with dark shapes leaning inwards from the grim rock walls. The sibilant hiss of ghostly static in his head contained a note of alarm. Caution. Even fear. The phantom prisoners scattered, their distant voices vanishing, driven back by an older, darker presence. The breeze from the tunnel opposite chilled him to the bone despite the blaze. Dominic shuffled to the furthest corner of the damp rock, stifling a whimper. He grabbed his trusty old dagger, not trusting himself with the strength to lift his sword.

"Who's there? What do you want?" His attempt at a defiant shout sounded more like a shameful cry for help. He tightened his shoulders and levered himself painfully to his feet. The tunnel swayed around him as his stomach twisted again. His head weighed as heavy as a cannonball. Drying blood crusted his cheeks.

Nothing to see. But everything to feel. He felt the presence slinking forward. The hovering patience of an ancient predator as it prowled. Damp sweat prickled under his tunic. Panic twisted his gut. "No." His terrified whisper penetrated the thick atmosphere and was swallowed by it.

The Shadow Mage's chuckle at the edge of his hearing sent an icy shiver of dread down his back. He blinked, staring into the gloom, eyes darting, expecting an attack. His heart pounded, matching the heavy thump of pain in his head. Still nothing. Bit by bit, the biting chill receded. Gasping with fear, Dominic lurched back to the fire, crowding close to its warmth. A grasping motion of his fingers hauled another box towards him. Light and heat. Perhaps with both, he could keep the shadows at bay. His eyes flicked to the mound of boxes left. There were only two more.

CHAPTER 34

"*D*ominic, report!"

Slumped in an uneasy doze, Joran's unyielding tones jerked Dominic's head upright. He groaned, slanting his gaze to the dying fire. He'd run out of boxes. This was the last. Even as he stared at it, the wood collapsed into a pile of charred fragments. Smoke billowed. He coughed, clutching his cloak around him in the instant chill.

"*Master Ash tells me the troop has fragmented following your insurrection. You will report. Now! Where are you?*"

Dominic stared at the shifting embers, wondering what to say. "*In the mines near Traitor's Reach,*" he managed.

"*Where are the others? Are you alone?*"

He huffed an ironic laugh. "*Oh, aye. Alone, at present,*" he said.

"*Have you found Dupliss?*" Dominic raised his eyebrows, scraping dried blood from his forehead. So much had happened. He'd all but forgotten the troop's prime aim. "*Almost,*" he hedged. "*I am sure he is close.*"

Joran's exasperation bled down their mental connection. "*And your uncle? I hope that's who you are chasing in the mines at Traitor's Reach?*" The Prince's voice was hard as the granite against which Dominic sat. Remorseless and cold. Even in his weakened condition, Dominic could not miss the inflexion placed on the word 'traitor'. Familiar resentment flared briefly in his chest, but he was too tired to allow the flame of it to ignite.

"Aye. I have come close twice," he said. *"Both times, my uncle has bested me."* He hated having to admit it. The crackle of failure sent fissures of doubt through the shredded remnants of his self-belief.

Joran paused. *"Wait,"* he said.

His mental voice vanished. Dominic imagined him consulting with someone. Crossing his fingers, he hoped it was Petronella. Taking the chance, he opened his mental channels to her. This was no time to stand on ceremony.

"Your Maj," he blurted. *"I'm lost. The Shadow Mage is lurking here. What should I do? Do I go on or try to find my way back?"*

He strained his senses towards her, yearning for an answer. A guiding hand. Just a touch of kindness. *"I failed you..."* He whispered it; for her thoughts alone. *"When you needed me, I let you down. I'm so sorry."*

"Nay." Her connection with him was tenuous at best. Weaker than he had ever known it. His hands screwed into fists. She sounded ill. His whole being tensed with alarm at the thought of the Queen being in danger.

"Your Maj, what is wrong? How can I aid you?"

"Nothing you can do, Dominic. Be strong... Be true." He blinked. Her voice was almost as pale as Juliana Tinterdorn's phantom mutterings.

"How dare you talk to the Queen when she is ill!" Joran's roar of displeasure interrupted with a force that made Dominic wince. He grabbed his skull with both hands against the internal pressure. *"I did not give you permission."*

That declaration was more than enough. Despite his desperate situation, perhaps even because of it, Dominic's temper sprung from his battered heart like a winter blizzard. *"She didn't have to answer me. And she doesn't have to answer to you, either!"*

An ominous silence scraped his nerves. He could almost see Prince Joran grinding his teeth. *"I will see you pay for your insolence and your foolishness,"* he said.

Overwhelmingly tired, Dominic pushed a short laugh down the connection. It had no humour in it. *"No need to go to any trouble,"* he said. *"I'm already paying."* He closed the connection before the Prince said anything else.

Alone in the dark once more, he shuffled as close to the last warmth of the dying ashes as he could. The breeze from the corridor opposite him still blew against his grubby cheeks. The constant headache wound invisible fingers around his skull and squeezed.

He lifted the waterskin and shook it. Almost empty. There was still some willow bark. He drank it for water rather than pain and winced to his feet. The corridor swayed. He cupped the candle flame with his hand, peering back the way he had come, then up the corridor along which Terrence and Oswin had disappeared. Little by little, his incorporeal companions drifted back. He caught the shuffle of their spectral feet.

"Has he gone? Are we safe?" Juliana's voice.

"There's nowhere safe," her unknown companion replied.

"Nowhere safe," Dominic repeated in a dazed whisper. Stooping dizzily to the ground, he packed his slim belongings into his backpack and shrugged it over his shoulders. His cloak had dried. He huddled into its folds, pulling up his hood, and kicked dust over the remains of the fire by force of habit. Raising his head and fighting nausea, he looked both ways along the narrow corridors.

Then, with a fatalistic shrug, he shuffled up the windy passageway, following Terrence and Oswin. He'd almost reached the end of it when another mental voice blazed into his mind. Soft but strong and laden with savage wit.

"Wrong way, you idiot. Do you really want to die today?"

He stumbled, caught up in the wonder of her familiar voice at such a close distance. *"Felicia?"* He swiped at the rush of tears pricking his tired eyes. *"Is it really you? How can I know?"*

"Of course it's me. I had to wait until the heartsease wore off," she said, quieter now she had his attention. *"Cerys has some weak telepathic ability, but she's not a Seer. That's why I am useful to her. You must go back. I'll guide you. Trust me."*

"Wait. Please, you must prove it. I can't trust anyone anymore. Especially not myself," Dominic said. He could sense Felicia rolling her eyes. *"Very well,"* she said, *"hurry, ask me a question before Terrence returns and realises I have my senses."*

Choosing an appropriate moment took his dazed mind some time. He could hardly believe he was hearing her voice. Perhaps she was a mirage born of desperation. *"What did you say to Guildford that night in the garden in Blade?"* he said. *"Just before he beat me up."* His fingers clenched into tight fists as he waited for her answer.

Felicia laughed with little humour. *"You would have to ask me that, wouldn't you?"*

It took an immense effort to lift his chin. *"If it's really you, you'll know."*

She sighed. *"Alright. I asked him not to kill you."*

His shoulders relaxed for what felt like the first time in years. He put a hand out to the grimy wall, ashamed of the tremors that racked him.

"Dominic? Are you well?"

"Aye. No." His mental voice broke. *"I've been searching for you for so long,"* he said.

A pause. *"I know,"* she whispered. *"Listen, Dominic, we must get you back to your companions. I can guide you to them. You must not go further alone. Promise me."*

"Nay, I can't leave you now. Not when you're so close..." he began. *"Please, I must get to you. See you."*

"No. You must go back. Tell whoever has followed you that Dupliss and his men are with Cerys. They must be on their guard. Ask your healer for help if you have one. You are weaker than you realise."

"But–" he started.

She cut him off. *"No time,"* she said. *"Go back to where you had the fire. Take the next left, then the second right. Quick, or you'll miss them. And I'll have to take more heartsease soon. It's the only way I know to delay Cerys. I won't be able to contact you after that."*

"Ah." He nodded, knowing she couldn't see him. *"That's why,"* he breathed. Still talking to her, aching to see her face, he lumbered back down the drafty tunnel, dreading the endless, winding passages looming in front of him, following her directions.

"Have you been taking heartsease all the time?" he asked, ducking under a low-hanging rock, trying to ignore the tug at his cloak and the whisper of petulant ghostly voices that demanded his attention.

"Your uncle supplied it for both of us," she said. *"'Tis a strange thing, being both his captive and his fellow prisoner. We try to time it between us so the least damage is done. Cerys finds it highly amusing when she's not being vicious."*

Dominic's jaw clenched. *"Cerys,"* he snarled. *"I will kill her if it's the last thing I ever do."*

"Be careful what you wish for," Felicia replied. *"Don't underestimate her. Have you reached the passage with the tin drum at the entrance? If you have, turn left again."*

Limping onward, Dominic moved as quickly as he could along the shrouded byways until he reached the passageway he remembered, at the fork of the main tunnel where the abandoned cart mouldered. *"I know the way from here,"* he said.

"'Tis well." Felicia's voice was taut with tension. He caught her clutch of fear, even though she didn't voice it. *"Terrence is coming, and the Shadow Mage has him. I must go now, Dominic."*

Dominic put out his hand as if he could halt her departure. *"Nay, Felicia, not yet..."*

"Your friends are there, at the entrance to the mines. Be quick, or you will miss them. Listen for me again, Dominic. Stay true."

She closed her channel. Dominic almost fell over as she withdrew. He leaned against the old cart for strength, gathering himself for the final uphill push to Terrence's Traverse. Head throbbing, he supported himself against the walls, marvelling at Felicia's survival, reliving every moment of their conversation. He almost missed the rusty pick leaning against the wall. Breathless, every muscle in his body protesting, he squeezed himself through the narrow fissure, relieved beyond measure at the prospect of survival.

Arguing voices blistered his ears as he squatted low to navigate the narrow confines of the barrel entrance.

"By the Gods," Cedric said, his deep bass voice laced with impatience. "I don't know where he's gone. Just that this is the way in."

A ring of steel. "You'd better think again." Guildford.

"Put the sword away, your highness. If you swing it, you'll bring the roof down." Tom's rich tenor, his usual good humour overlain with fatigue.

Dominic pushed open the door and almost fell over them. Four tired, startled faces whirled, brandishing their weapons. He staggered upright, huffing breath after breath of good, clean air into his lungs.

"By the Gods, Sir Skinner," Aldric said, glaring at him down the length of an arrow. "Pleasant trip, was it?"

Chapter 35

Dominic staggered as Aldric flung down his bow and enveloped him in a hug.

"By the Gods, Aldric, leave off him," Tom said, hauling him off. He placed a sturdy arm under Dominic's elbow. "Come. Back to the inn," he said. "We need to get you seen to."

"Not back to the Beaten Drum," Dominic said. He grabbed the waterskin Guildford held out to him and gulped the contents. Guildford's head almost brushed the roof of the tunnel. He surveyed Dominic with a turmoil of conflict in his crystalline gaze.

"Oswin works for Cerys Tinterdorn," Dominic said, wiping his grubby face with the back of his hand. He swayed against the wall. "He led me into an ambush. My uncle has the blade." He glanced across at Aldric. His squire gaped at him. "You lost it? After all this time?" he said, disbelief plastered across his face. "That must have been some ambush."

"Enough talk," Tom said, a frown crossing his face. "We'll go to the other tavern. I'm sure Cedric can arrange something."

"Aye." Cedric passed a heavy hand across his brow. "I offer my apologies for my brother's actions, Sir Skinner," he said formally.

Dominic managed a huff of humour. "As if you could prevent a grown man from making his own decisions," he said. "There is nothing to forgive."

Together, the troop made their way to the narrow plinth and the dangling rope that marked the exit from Terrence's Traverse. Dominic swallowed as he looked up. He braced a hand against the slimy wall. "I can't manage that," he said, shamefaced. "Not right now."

"I'll go first," Aldric said. "Then Tom. Guildford can manage if you can hold onto him. 'Tis not far. We'll help you at the top. Cedric can go last, to steady it as Guildford climbs."

He didn't wait for their assent. Shouldering his bow, he leapt for the rope. "There's a lad eager for a drink," Tom said as Aldric vanished upwards. "Next," Aldric yelled, his voice echoing eerily back to them.

Dominic waited, still dazed, as Tom climbed. Guildford eyed him as he turned. "Sure you can hold on?" he asked, turning around. "Aye," Dominic hoisted his pack a little higher and clambered piggyback style onto the younger man's shoulders. For an instant, the action transported him years into the past. A tiny child astride his father's shoulders, galloping madly around the market square in Blade, demanding his father to go faster. His throat ached at the memory. He tightened his arms around Guildford's neck, desperate for rest.

The young princeling's grasp on the rope was firm. Even in his weakened state, Dominic marvelled at the ease with which he ascended. As if Dominic weighed lighter than thistledown. Light blossomed around them. The prick of chilly air grew stronger against his cheeks. At the top, Tom and Aldric hauled him from Guildford's shoulders and over the lip of the well to the frosty ground. He rolled over, blinking at the glare in the stone-cold sky, and gaped around him. "How long was I gone?" he whispered. The snow had all but vanished, leaving dirty, melting puddles over the cobbles.

"The storm blew out the night you left," Aldric said. He leaned over Dominic, offering an arm to help him to his feet. "And we've had a thaw. Cedric says it won't last." He paused, surveying Dominic with concern. Dominic shaded his eyes with his filthy hand. He could only imagine what he must look like. "How long?" he pressed.

"Two days. I waited for the others to catch up." Aldric bit his lip. "I wanted to come after you. I'm sorry."

The last to ascend, Cedric emerged from the depths. Brushing his hands against his cloak, he marched to the nearest building and returned with a heavy wooden cover balanced on his head. He heaved it across the top of the well and slid the thick iron bolts that secured it with grim satisfaction. "We are not going back that way," he announced to the waiting company. "And no-one else is getting out. My brother can rot in there for all I care. Come. We'll go back to the Mended Drum. I'm calling it mine now."

He stalked out of the narrow courtyard. Supported on both sides by Aldric and Tom, Dominic's bleary gaze darted away from the curious eyes of Hartwood's citizens as they went about their business in the cold, mud-trodden streets.

After his recent experience, the humble interior of the Beaten Drum oozed comfort and security. A cheerful fire burned in the grate. The low rumble of conversation and pipe smoke dominated the room. Its sheer normality almost moved Dominic to tears. Cedric ordered baths and food from a tiny, round-eyed serving wench. Overwhelmed by the height and bulk of the soldiers, she scurried to do his bidding. Murmuring apologies, citing the Queen's business, Cedric ushered the other patrons from the room. They shuffled out reluctantly, eyeing the armed group by the fire with narrow, suspicious gazes. Cedric beckoned another employee, a dark-haired lad laden with a tray of pots from the kitchen. "Go to the Queen's Head, tell Mistress Trevis and Will Dunn to make haste here," he ordered. The lad jerked his head and hurried out of the door. Cedric watched him go and locked the portal behind him. He served them drinks himself.

"Will and Mistress Trevis as well?" Dominic asked faintly.

Tom turned a bleak expression in his direction. "We left Sir Dunforde and the rest of the troop," he said gruffly. "They are still at Falconridge, with orders to guard the pass." His grass-green gaze drifted to the window; his narrow fingers clenched around his tankard.

Dominic stared at the table, marked with ancient gouges and sticky with spilt beer. "I am sorry to have led you away," he said. "'Twas never my intent. But I am grateful for your support."

Tom shrugged, his eyes narrowed. "Couldn't leave you," he said. "And the others insisted. Especially Will."

Dominic's heart twisted. "You shouldn't have brought him," he murmured. "This is not even half over."

Tom's heavy sigh acknowledged the truth of his words. "Aye, lad. I know," he returned. "But you need Mistress Trevis' help before we go any further. The way to Traitor's Reach is open at present. It might be our only chance before winter truly closes in."

Dominic was ashamed at the wash of relief that swept through him. "Over land," he murmured. "Thank all the Gods."

"Your bath." The tiny maid arrived at the fire, breathless with trepidation. Her narrow fingers twisted in her damp apron. "You don't need to fear us," Guildford murmured. "And you could have asked us to carry the water for you."

"Aye, my lord," she breathed. She tugged Dominic's sleeve. "Come. Before the water cools," she said. Aldric rose with Dominic. Cedric had arranged a more luxurious accommodation than that offered by his brother. A narrow copper tub steamed invitingly in front of the fire. Two comfortable beds awaited their occupants, warmed with scarlet blankets. The sign of the Mage decorated the whitewashed chimney breast.

"Do you need help?" Aldric asked as Dominic dropped his pack from his shoulders with a sigh of relief.

"Nay, but stay, won't you?" Dominic said. He stripped with difficulty, peeling his filthy tunic from his back, kicking off his boots, mired with filth. Aldric averted his gaze as Dominic took an unsteady step into the bath. "I'm not really sure you should bathe before Mistress Trevis has seen you," he said.

"I want to get clean." Dominic pressed his aching skull against the rim of the bath. He rolled his head in Aldric's direction. "The Shadow Mage is down there," he said. "I felt him waiting for me." His skin prickled with gooseflesh despite the heat seeping into his frozen bones from the steaming water. He reached a trembling hand for the thick cake of soap and grimaced as the water changed colour as he scrubbed.

"How did you get out?" Aldric strode to the window. He rubbed condensation from the panes and peered down at the street.

"Felicia," Dominic said simply, his heart lifting at the thought. "She's alive, Aldric. Truly alive."

"Did you see her?"

"Nay. She wouldn't allow me further into Cerys' lair. But she told me the way out. I would have died there without her."

"Mistress Trevis has arrived," Aldric announced, and his shoulders relaxed. He turned from the window. "The dagger," he said. "Is it really the Blade of Aequitas, do you think?"

"I know it belongs to Terrence. I could hear Juliana Tinterdorn down there as well. She was pleased he had it back."

Aldric's brow quirked. "She's dead," he said.

Dominic rolled his shoulders. "Dead and trapped," he said. "Like so many others. Oswin said he couldn't really hear them, but I could." He winced as he lathered his hair. The strong soap stung as it found the heavy gash on his temple.

"Careful, you'll start it bleeding again," Aldric said. He picked up a heavy water jug and rinsed Dominic's hair, shielding his face with his other hand, gentle as a mother.

Grateful for his ministrations, Dominic closed his eyes. "That voice that I hear, singing to me all the while. It sang the Prophecy of the Sword to me while I was down there," he murmured, half asleep. "At first, I thought it was Felicia, and then I wondered if it was Cerys. But I don't think it was, now. I think it's been Juliana all along."

Aldric put down the jug. "And so? What does that mean?"

"The prophecy says the blade contains both darkness and light within it. Juliana created it with love. Cerys tainted it with hate. Terrence struggles always between the darkness and the light." Dominic took the towel Aldric handed to him. "I don't think there is a question anymore. 'Tis the blade that cuts both ways. We don't know how, but Cerys intends to use it against the Queen." He glanced at Aldric from beneath the damp linen. Aldric's dark gaze was wide with alarm. He held out a hand. "Nay, don't say it," he said.

Dominic shook his head, dread clutching at his own chest. "I'm sorry, Aldric. I have to get it back."

He turned, wincing, as someone rapped on the door.

"That's Mistress Trevis," Aldric said. "Come, get out." He seemed relieved to let the woman in.

Struggling to process his thoughts, Dominic levered his battered body from the narrow tub and tumbled across the scarlet blanket on his bed. "Welladay. What a mess." Mistress Trevis rolled him over so she could look at the damage. "Nasty," she sniffed, touching the wound on his temple with gentle, probing fingers. Dominic flinched. "Nay, lie still. Let me ask. The Mage does not always agree…"

She pulled the heavy blanket over him, and he relaxed under her touch, his mind drifting as it had once before. Aldric moved quietly in the background, preparing potions and salves. The air filled with the earthy aroma of comfrey and the lingering scent of mine mud on his boots. "The Mage will let me help you," Mistress Trevis said after a pause. "Do you wish it this time?"

"I must be ready to face what is to come, so, aye, this time," Dominic murmured. "Only if he wills it."

Mistress Trevis placed her palms on either side of his head. Dominic felt the touch of her warm breath on his skin. His magical senses tingled. Beneath his closed lids, a night sky stretched into infinity, filled with the twinkling pinprick of a million stars. The healer's breathing slowed with the flow of her power. The voice he heard in his head was deeper and far older than hers. *"Have you learned, Dominic?"* The Mage's deep voice commanded his attention. He listened, breathless and humble, sheltered in the arms of his god. *"I have gifted you beyond many others. Be thou careful how you use my blessings. And have courage. The final reckoning is yet to come. You must be ready."* Bit by bit, the throbbing in his head faded. The tight and tender skin of his flayed back relaxed. Boneless, he sank deeper and deeper into the blankets beneath the Mage's stern, all-seeing eye.

"Aye," he whispered, half to himself as he tumbled into a healing sleep. "I know what I must do."

CHAPTER 36

"*Dominic... Dominic...*"

The voice in his head merged with his nightmares. He travelled a winding maze of twisting tunnels and stalking danger. His unconscious mind halted at a crossroads, confronted with a gibbet wreathed in flowers. A man's body hung from it upside down. Female voices drifted to him from every direction. Petronella from one road, Cerys down another. Felicia's voice beckoned before him, urging him on. Little Bird chased him from the rear, floating closer with every breath. All of them demanded his attention. His help. He revolved in place, uncertain, his boots embedded in bloody mud. Looking down, he noticed his foot caught in a lure, tethered fast to the rock, like the falcons in the mews at the Castle of Air. He tugged at it. The bond looked fragile, but it was as unbreakable as steel. Rocking gently, the figure of the dangling man turned. The features came into view. Terror clutched at his soul. The face was his own. Blank. Still. Except for the mouth. It opened wide. A yawning chasm into confusion and the howl of a winter storm. "Sacrifice," it said.

Stifling a gasp of horror, he lurched upright, bright-eyed and sweating in the shaft of moonlight that traced a silver line across his lumpy pillow.

"*Dominic!*" The voice was insistent as the pain of a rotten tooth. Only one woman of his acquaintance could nag like it. Grinding his teeth, he pushed himself further up the bed. "*Little Bird, are you well?*"

"Where have you been?" Her wail all but shattered his mental ears. *"I've been looking for you for days! The Queen is ill. You must hurry, Dominic. She needs you all back here!"*

Still chased by the visions in his nightmare, his blood ran cold. *"Slow down, Bird. What do you mean?"*

Bird's tumbled thoughts were hard to understand. He caught the words *"Fortuna"* and *"since yesterday"*.

"Bird! Wait, you must slow down. Take some deep breaths. Concentrate." He pushed the thought to her with as much command as he could muster and waited to discover whether she had taken his advice.

"Something happened to the Queen last night." He could sense Bird struggling to control her emotions. *"She was doing much better, but then she fainted at supper. The Grayling is going mad, Dominic. He won't settle at all. Took at least two chunks out of Thurgil's hand, and he won't eat. You must come home, Dominic. Quick, before he starves himself to death!"*

His mind whirled. *"Since yesterday? Are you sure?"*

"Of course, I'm sure!"

He swallowed. His fingers pleated the blanket. *"Does the Prince know?"* he said.

"Aye. He's been striding around her chamber, cursing the lot of you for your lack of progress. Especially you. Your name is coming up a lot. What have you done, Dominic? There are soldiers marshalling here. We can't move around the castle without bumping into them. Are we under attack? What's going on?"

He bit his lip, cursing the loss of the enchanted blade. Aequitas. The knife that cuts both ways. If he hadn't been sure before, he was now. Cerys had it. Either Terrence had given it to her, or she'd stolen it from him. And she was using it somehow to strike at the Queen.

"Listen, Bird. This is important. Tell Fortuna to go to the Restricted Section in the library and to find everything she can about the Shadow Mage and how his influence works. She needs to find any reference to an

enchanted blade called Aequitas. Petronella needs heartsease tea. Lots of it, to close her channels. She is not to open them. Not for any reason. To talk to Joran, or me, or anyone else. Do you understand? The Grayling may settle once she does."

Little Bird's confusion trickled across the void. *"Aye, but why?"*

"There's something we must do here," Dominic said. Lips thinning, he rose to his feet and grabbed the clean tunic and hose Aldric had left for him. *"If we are successful, the Queen will recover."*

A pause. *"What if you're not?"* Her mental voice was a mere whisper, but she may as well have screamed it at him. He jerked at the laces of his tunic and snatched up his dagger.

"We will succeed. I need to talk to Joran. Tell him to contact me tonight. 'Tis important."

"Very well."

About to close the conversation, Dominic caught the edge of Little Bird's plaintive question. One that she was asking on her own account.

"Dominic," she whispered. *"How's Will?"*

"I haven't seen him for a while," Dominic said, *"but I'm about to. Don't worry. I'm sure he's well. I will let you know."*

"Be careful. You will, won't you?"

He tried to convey reassurance to the girl. It was difficult when his own doubt pecked holes in the fragile threads of his confidence.

"I'll try, Bird," he said. *"Stay safe. Do what I said. 'Tis important."*

"Yay."

She withdrew, and Dominic marched to the door, deep in thought, his nightmare all but forgotten in the need for action. Only the barest ache remained of his previous injuries as he clattered down the steep tavern stairs.

Far from their usual roistering behaviour, a row of serious, tired faces greeted him as he joined his companions in the taproom. The battered tables sported only a sprinkling of decanters and tankards. His nose wrinkled in appreciation at the smell of food wafting from the kitchen. He pressed a fist over his growling stomach as Cedric approached, bearing a dish of pottage.

"Dominic!" Will shot from his stool. "Thought you were dead. Thank all the Gods." He took two quick steps forward, arms raised for a hug, before thinking better and offering his hand. Dominic clasped his arm. Man to man. "Well met, Will. Little Bird is worried about you," he said.

Will grinned. "When is she not?" he said, returning to his seat and helping himself to a lump of cheese from Tom's platter.

"By the Gods, you look better," Aldric said, "Thought we were going to have to bury you here."

Dominic bowed in Mistress Trevis' direction. "Thanks to our healer and her Blessed gifts," he said,

Mistress Trevis snorted. "Try not to thank me too much. You were lucky," she said. "The Mage denies my requests as often as not." She turned her attention to her supper, picking fastidiously at the nutty bread in front of her, removing the worst offenders before she dipped a morsel into her wine.

"I have news from Little Bird at the castle," Dominic said as he sat. "Cerys has wasted little time in attacking our queen."

He put his hands up to silence the immediate blare of questions and glanced at Aldric. "Have you told them anything?" he asked. Aldric shook his head. "Better from you," he said, raising his tankard.

"Well then. There is more here than meets the eye," Dominic said. "'Tis no longer a secular matter, if it ever was."

"Cerys?" Guildford said. Bewilderment creased his freckled brow. "Cerys, who was Celia, is attacking the Queen? How did she get to the castle so fast?"

Dominic sighed, settling his shoulders. He signalled the dark-haired lad tending bar to bring him a drink and prepared himself to tell a long story.

At the end of his account, Tom exchanged a troubled glance with Guildford. The young giant was picking at a tray of nuts, his tanned face thoughtful as he chewed.

"And this was Felicia you were talking to? Are you sure?" Guildford said. He took two walnuts and cracked them in his massive fist.

"On my life," Dominic said. "She is alive, Guildford, and she wants to help."

Guildford stared at him, hope blazed across his face. "Truly alive..." he whispered. "I can hardly believe it."

"'Tis true. I swear it," Dominic said.

Tom scrubbed his fists through his hair. "So, if we are to believe you, Celia, I mean Cerys, has been playing with us all along in order to make sure that precious dagger of yours was the blade she seeks. And now she wants to use it to attack Petronella with some sort of dark magic and take her throne? Have I got that right?"

Dominic spread his hands. "That's about it, aye. We must stop her. We might already be too late. Bird says the Queen fainted last night." He forbore to mention the Grayling's strange behaviour. Apart from Mistress Trevis, he doubted the present company would understand the delicate bond between Petronella and her falcon.

"If the Queen closes her channels, does that make her less vulnerable?" Aldric asked.

"To a point, I hope," Dominic said. "If Cerys is attacking her through her Blessed gifts, the best chance she has is not to use them. No matter what the circumstances."

"Something makes little sense, though," Tom said. "You say Cerys is gifted with the art of transformation and illusion and that she wanted the dagger."

"Aye," Dominic said. His legs twitched under the table. Already impatient to be up and moving.

"But she was alone with you on the way to Falconridge. Surely, she could have manifested an attack then?"

Dominic frowned, his thoughts returning to the bandit attack. "I think she did," he said. "'Tis possible she hired those former soldiers in Thorncastle to do her work for her. She seemed almost disappointed they failed to rob us. She must have realised Lionel wasn't much good to her in that regard. Before that, a mysterious maid ransacked our chamber. Aldric surprised her in the act."

Aldric rubbed his jaw in remembrance. "I understand that better now," he said. "I always thought the skinny lass I saw shouldn't have been able to lift that mattress the way she did."

Tom chewed his lips. "Pity she got the dagger," he said. "You were an absolute fool to take it with you into the mine."

Dominic huffed a sigh. "You think I don't realise that?" he said. He jumped from his stool, pacing the length of the room. "I had some stupid notion I could attack her with it. Use it against her, somehow, if I could only get to her." He drew to a halt, staring into the depths of the fireplace, seeking inspiration. There was little to be had.

"Felicia says Dupliss is with Cerys," he said. "If we go, we must be wary. My uncle is with her as well. She has protection. Both physical and mental. She has her lair in the mines at Traitor's Reach. 'Tis a dark and haunted place. I do not know what we will face there."

He turned to his comrades. "No-one has to do this," he clarified. "But, thanks to my stupidity, Cerys holds a weapon of terrible power. If we can retrieve it, we stand a chance to destroy the blade and Cerys both. Dupliss is with her. Joran's orders are to find and kill him. We can do that. I believe the Queen's life and the future of Epera depend on our ability to complete this task." He paused, his solemn gaze travelling from face to face. Tom, resolute and determined, Will's shining with youthful fervour and hero-worship. Guildford, resigned and grim, Aldric, chewing his lip, debating the odds, always sensible. Even Cedric, who had pressed close to hear his tale. One by one, they nodded.

Mistress Trevis picked up another morsel of bread and plunged it into her wine so fiercely that the contents splashed her sleeve. She stared at the blood-red marks, an irritated frown creasing her brow.

"Oh, the life of a soldier," she said.

CHAPTER 37

The road through the narrow pass from Hartwood to Traitor's Reach wound through a damp and sulky landscape. Freezing temperatures had stripped the autumn forests, leaving only the dark, winter-green pines. Mud and icy puddles claimed the rutted cobbles, where years of cartwheels had forged their own tracks. The sun had disappeared behind an iron-hard sky.

Glad to be on her way, Kismet frisked at the bit. Dominic rode easily. He kept his hand ready near his sword, his gaze sweeping the denuded forests and steep mountains for signs of attack. The countryside lay subdued around them, alive with the rusty voices of half-seen crows and the whip of wind scything a lament through the naked branches.

Trotting Hamil steadily at his side, Aldric shivered theatrically. "Bleak, this," he said. "Not a soul for miles."

Cedric glanced back at them, his heavy face set with purpose. "Aye," he said. "And you haven't seen Traitor's Reach yet. 'Tis no merry place, so close to the mines. The living there is hard."

Aldric's brow flickered as he processed the information. "Why would people stay?" he asked.

Cedric grimaced. "Don't really know," he admitted, scratching his beard. "But still they cling, burrowed into the cliffs below the mines, stubborn and proud." He paused, a furrow digging deep between his brows. "I suppose there must be rich pickings there for some," he said. "But 'tis a dark place. Full of ghosts. Not for the fainthearted."

Dominic's shoulders hunched. He glanced around the company, grateful for their solid support but terrified for their safety. Will Dunn, ever at odds with his mount, jogged uncomfortably in the rear, his square face remote. He'd said little since leaving the shelter of Hartwood. Mistress Trevis kept him company, eyes alert and watchful. She gave Dominic a thin-lipped smile as he hung back, waiting for them to catch up.

"Anything you'd like me to tell Bird, Will?" Dominic said.

Stirred from his thoughts, the lad glanced up across at him, his broad grin returning. "Aye, tell her I'll be home soon and not to torment Fortuna too much."

Dominic stifled a grin and opened his channels. Breathless for news, Bird answered with her usual enthusiasm. "She says to stay safe and that she's started making a hope chest," he reported a couple of minutes later. He laughed at the crimson blush that suffused Will's tanned cheeks under his freckles.

"Tell her she has my heart," he mumbled so softly that Dominic had to slow Kismet to hear him. Dominic's gaze softened, his thoughts leaping immediately to his own heart's desire. "Aye," he said.

"*Will says he adores you and will love you forever,*" he said to the maid. Her vibrant joy sparkled back at him. "*And I, him,*" Bird replied with simple dignity.

"*Bird, how is the Queen?*" he queried. "*Did she do as I asked?*"

"*Aye, I requested an audience through Fortuna. The Queen is very weak, but she is doing what you asked, although the Grayling is out of spirits. Mayhap not so much as before.*" Bird paused. Her mental voice lowered. "*She's pregnant, Dominic,*" she whispered. "*The fall from the horse nearly cost her the babe. But Fortuna has worked hard to look after them both. All is well.*"

"Ah," Dominic closed his eyes, muttering a thankful prayer to the Mage. *"By the Gods, I'm so glad to hear it. Tell her good fortune from me, will you?"*

"Please take care, Dominic. Remember your promise."

He closed his eyes. *"I will, Bird. Don't worry."*

Marvelling at the news of the Queen's condition, Dominic closed the communication, jogging to the head of the line, where Tom and Guildford were arguing over strategy. "I'll take Dupliss," Tom said. "I've a better chance of not turning soft at the wrong moment."

"Soft?" Guildford said, his eyes as hard as stone. "Not a chance of that. Who do you think you're talking to? My name's not Dominic Skinner."

"Thank you for your confidence in my ability," Dominic said, hackles rising. "If it comes to it, I'll take Dupliss, gladly."

"Lads," Tom remonstrated, "we'll have enough fighting on our hands without you two starting now. Let's get to Traitor's Reach. Find out what we face. You two can scout ahead. Dominic can look after the magic. Guildford, be on your guard."

He turned to Cedric. "Is there a tavern at Traitor's Reach? That's the best place for gossip."

Cedric's face wrinkled. He sniffed. "Not what I'd call a tavern," he said. "Drinking den's more like it. Just a ramshackle shed. Serves the worst ale in Epera, I reckon. 'Tis no wonder some of 'em risk the mines to get to Hartwood." He grinned as he took in Guildford's commanding presence. "Besides," he added, "I'd better be the one to spy. At least the owner there knows me and Oswin. No chance our two young nobles will get in and out without attracting unwanted attention." He winked at them. "The slatterns at Traitor's Reach will have you both for breakfast and rob you blind the while."

"'Tis well, then," Tom said. "We'll hang back and await your return. How far do we have left to travel?"

Cedric jerked his chin at the distant hilltop. "Just over there," he said. "You'll see when we arrive, but the rest of you will have to bide on this side, out of sight."

With little breaking the view, the distance was hard to judge. Wading through mud and shivering in the frigid temperatures, they tended their horses, broke a lengthy fast with strips of dried meat and hard bread washed down with small ale, and continued on their way.

"'Tis so quiet," Aldric remarked, tipping his head to note the position of the sun. "We could be the only people alive in the world."

"If Dupliss commands any troops at all, they are definitely not here," Mistress Trevis agreed. She waved a hand at the view. "We'd surely have spotted them by now. There's nowhere to hide out here."

"At Traitor's Reach, then," Dominic murmured. Impatience bit at him like a mutt snatching at his heels. He nudged Kismet to a brisker pace.

"None of that, young Skinner," Tom said, sharp-eyed. "You'll wait for my orders. We are doing this together, or not at all."

Dominic chewed his lip and shot the older man a glare. Tom laughed at him. "So eager to meet thy doom, stripling," he said. "Stay a while. Enjoy life a little longer."

Dominic scowled. "Do you think so little of our chances?" he asked.

Tom gave a fatalistic shrug. "Who knows?" he said. "We are a talented bunch, without a doubt, but whether we live or die is in the hands of the Mage. 'Tis the life of a soldier. To be sure, I will give my best in defence of our queen, and my comrades. On that, you can depend." He smiled. His teeth showed white in his tanned face. Reaching over, he clapped Dominic on the shoulder. "Chin up, young Skinner," he said briskly. "If the Mage wills it, we will all live to fight another day."

He trotted his mount forward. Dominic glanced at Aldric, who was squinting into the distance. "There's an old shack up there," the lad announced. "Can you see it? In the hollow between the rocks."

Cedric nodded. "Aye, that's the old goatherd's place," he said. "Used to belong to a fellow called Darton, if I recall rightly. Died the winter before last, he did. Good place as any to stop. We'll go there."

Aldric tugged his cloak more closely around his narrow frame. "Hope it's windproof," he muttered.

The sun was setting as they trudged up the last slope. Aldric's eyes had not deceived him. Sheltered from the worst of the wind by dint of having its back set into the surrounding cliff face, the cottage clung like a burr to the stony ground, protected in the front by an enormous boulder. A further shed attached to the side might once have housed the goats. Old and rundown as it was, the group dismounted, grateful for the slim shelter provided by its rough planks. Cedric remained aloft, surveying their tired faces with some trepidation.

"Stay here," he said, his voice hoarse. "I will ride into the village and say I'm looking for Oswin if they ask."

"What will you do if he's actually there?" Dominic said, his eyes narrowing at the memory of the man's broad back as he retreated into the gloom. His fingers clenched around his dagger.

Cedric chuckled with little humour. He flexed his fingers and then bunched them into a fist. "Well then, I found him, didn't I?" he said. "We have a score to settle, he and I. Either way, I'll come back with information. Do not move without me. We must get some idea of what we face."

"Aye." Tom nodded. "Fare well, friend," he said. "Mage go with thee."

Cedric nodded and turned his mount to the ridge, cloak fluttering in the fading light as he disappeared into the gloom. Aldric and Will took the horses into the former goat shed, leaving the knights to crowd into the shack. Guildford had to duck to fit through the door. "By the

Gods," he rumbled, staring round at the damp interior. "Did someone actually live here?"

It was a dark, narrow room, still dominated by the aroma of peat smoke. Flapping mournfully in the breeze, a dried goat skin served as the covering across the single window. Dominic shivered, automatically reaching for his flint box and candles. Aldric poked at the scattered circle of hearth stones in the centre of the room. The glare of Dominic's candle highlighted a neat stack of turfs lining the rear next to the narrow, stinking cot. Guildford eyed it and shook his head. "Not sleeping there," he said.

Between them, they piled the rudimentary hearth with blocks of peat, coughing as smoke filled the hut.

Tom huffed a sigh and pulled the goat skin away from the window. "By the Gods, give me wood," he said. "Even Sir Dunforde's pipe is preferable."

On pins, awaiting Cedric's return, Dominic warmed his hands at the budding flames only briefly. "Going outside," he said.

Tom eyed him. "Do not go far from the hut," he warned. "I will come looking for you."

Dominic threw him a glare. "I won't, but I can't stay here until that fire takes hold. The smoke is killing me."

He turned on his heel, rolling his eyes in the freezing dusk when Aldric followed him. "You don't have to come," he said. "I said I'd stay close."

"Aye, well," Aldric returned, refusing to fight. "Someone has to keep an eye on you."

The immensity of the landscape stretched around them, barely seen. Tendrils of mist tickled Dominic's exposed cheeks. They wandered into the shelter of the goat hut, where the horses munched peacefully on rations of grain. Kismet's ears flickered in Dominic's direction as he strolled over, running his hands over her coat. She removed her nose from the grain bag long enough to give him a nudge.

"Well, lady, at least you're happy out of the wind," Dominic murmured, tugging her ears.

He frowned, turning his face to the door. "Did you hear that?" he said to Aldric. Cocking his head, he listened again. Were those footsteps he could hear? Or just a trick of the wind?

Planting a finger against his lips, he drew his sword as stealthily as he could, balling up power in his fist. Aldric backed up against the wall, pulling out his own eating dagger. The horses tossed their heads as Dominic jerked the door open. There was nothing there. Only the insistent breath of the wind. On the verge of shutting the door and retreating to the warmth of Kismet's flank, Dominic changed his mind. Someone was lurking out there. Flattening himself against the rickety plank wall, he advanced, little by little, ears straining. He caught the scuff of Aldric's boot as the lad crept out after him. A shadow passed in front of the fire-lit window of the goatherd's cot. Dominic's eyes narrowed. His hand tensed on his sword, and he swallowed, forcing himself forward. Ready. His arm ached with the force of the power loaded within it.

The goatherd's cottage door exploded open. Guildford erupted from within it, sword raised, the light of battle sparking in his eyes. Tom followed, then Will. The jolt of argument and imminent violence shattered the tense silence in an instant, and Dominic launched himself into the fray, all his senses exploding into the joy of action.

"Stop!" His uncle's voice, hands raised, trembling above his head, "Please. You must listen! I want to help!"

Dominic skidded to a halt, wincing as his ankle turned on the ice of a frozen puddle. Terrence stood surrounded by a thicket of steel, all aimed at his throat. The creak of a bowstring behind Dominic showed Aldric stood ready to fire.

"Uncle?" His throat was dry. He blundered into the circle, straining his eyes in the darkness to make out the colour of the Mage light glowing in Terrence's palm. The colour of his eyes.

"Kill him." Guildford raised his sword, driving Terrence to his knees on the icy ground. Dominic's uncle stared up at Guildford, skeletal and pale with fear and determination. Guildford stiffened his jaw and lunged.

"Nay, wait!" Dominic flung himself in front of the blow. Deflecting it with his own weapon took all the strength he had. The strike glanced off his blade. In mid-thrust, Guildford stumbled.

"What?" he said, glaring at Dominic. "He left you for dead. Do you not have orders to kill him?"

Overcome with a fit of shivering, Dominic stared him down. "Not like this, when he's in his right mind," he said. "If he says he wants to help, we should let him. We need entry into the mines. What better guide do we have?"

CHAPTER 38

Mayhem.

Guildford recovered his stance and aimed his blade at Dominic's chest. "Move, Skinner. I'll despatch him if you will not!" he said, hatred flooding his eyes. "He's a traitor!"

Eyes blazing, Dominic continued to stand his ground. He raised his sword. Confused, Will's eyes flickered between the two of them. The lad took a step back, glancing instinctively at Tom for orders. The older man stood poised to intervene, his eyebrows clenched in a scowl. "Guildford, listen to me," Dominic pleaded. "He's an old man, and he can help us. The Shadow Mage does not hold him."

"The Shadow Mage does not hold him right now," Guildford sneered, panting. "How long do we have before he loses his mind to it? I say we don't take the chance. He'll only betray us." He lunged again. Power balling in his fist, Dominic flung his arm out. "Don't make me take that sword from you," he threatened.

On his knees, Terrence ducked. "Please, my lord Guildford," he said. The words emerged as a hoarse whisper. "Let me speak. You are right. I only have so much time before the Shadow Mage claims me, and then I am not responsible for my actions. 'Tis not my wish to harm you. You must understand. Let me aid you while I can."

For an answer, Guildford lunged forward, a snarl on his lips. Dominic blocked him with his own body. "You will not lay a finger on him," Dominic's voice rang in the night. "'Tis my affair. Mine and his."

Tom inserted his own blade between the two warring warriors and nudged them away from each other with a quick flick of his wrist. "We will not settle this in such a manner," he said. "There is more at stake here than your squabbling. Act like men, not children." He turned to Mistress Trevis. The healer had taken a position on the outskirts of the circle, her blade at half guard, her blue eyes narrowed. "Mistress, as a healer and someone experienced with magic and medicine, please give us the benefit of your wisdom."

Narrow eyebrows arching at Tom's request, Mistress Trevis knocked Guildford's sword arm away. He lowered the point reluctantly to the icy ground. She moved to stand in front of Terrence. "By what means do you keep the Shadow Mage at bay?" she asked.

"Heartsease. In large quantities when we can get it." Terrence glanced at Guildford from under his brows. Years of sorrow had ravaged his gaunt features. His hair hung grizzled and tangled beneath his hood. Stripped of his powers, kneeling uncomfortably on the cold earth, he looked every year of his age and more. "I share it with your sister," he said. "We try to use it to our best advantage. Felicia takes the drug, so her gift of Farsight is not available to Cerys when she demands it. But then, she cannot use her telepathy either. I take it to keep the Shadow Mage at bay and remain in control of myself. My thoughts and actions my own." His shoulders were hunched under the heavy wool of his cloak. "'Tis not always possible to get the herb," he whispered. "There are days when we run out, or Cerys is watching, and we dare not take it. Somehow, she seems to know, anyway." He shuddered. "Eyes. She is always watching," he murmured. "I wish I knew how she does it."

"When did you take your last dose?" Unmoved by the pathos in his tone, Mistress Trevis regarded him with distant, professional interest.

"Last night. 'Twas strong, but I have used it all. There is none left of the batch Felicia gave me," Terrence said. His searching gaze flicked around each member of the circle, settling at last on Dominic. "I am at your disposal, my lords," he said.

"How long before its protection is like to run out?" She took his hand, turning his palm over. "Blue, still," she murmured.

Terrence grimaced. "A few brief hours," he admitted. "I cannot predict it with any great accuracy despite Felicia's skill."

"Will you take us through the mines to Cerys?" Dominic demanded. "We have a duty to our queen. As you do. We must retrieve the blade of Aequitas and find Felicia of Wessendean before Cerys uses the blade to make another assault on the Queen."

"On the Queen?" Guildford's eyes bespoke his confusion. "How? What does this blade have to do with it?"

Dominic grimaced. "I don't know, Guildford. There is dark magic embedded deep in that dagger. Cerys put it there. Did you not listen to the Prophecy of the Sword the other night when Clem sang it?"

"The bard? Nay, not really. 'Twas just a song. Not a prediction, surely?" But the princeling shuffled his feet as he said it. Awkward and uncertain in the face of magic, like many other Citizen of Dominic's acquaintance.

"'Tis all true, Guildford," Dominic said. "The Queen is in terrible danger without a blow being struck or a cannon fired. We must act to help her."

Terrence lowered his bleak gaze to the ice-crusted ground at his feet. "I can take you," he said. "But we must be swift."

"Too risky," Aldric said from the darkness by the goat hut. He stepped forward to join them, an arrow still notched in his bow. "I won't let you hurt him again," he said. Dominic blinked at the ferocious expression on his squire's youthful face.

"Aldric, 'tis alright, put down your weapon," he said.

"Nay. I won't." Aldric's eyes shot sparks. "Would you let a wolf near your kin? A poisonous spider? He said himself he doesn't know when the potion will wear off."

"Aldric. Stand down." Tom's command was stern. "I will decide."

Aldric raised a pair of mutinous eyes in his direction but lowered his bow, although he kept the arrow held ready in his fingers.

"Mistress Trevis, your verdict, please?" Tom requested.

"As he says, Sir Buttledon," Mistress Trevis replied. "I have some heartsease in my pack. I can brew some more for him if you wish it, but it will take some time under these circumstances." She waved a hand that took in the tiny hut, with its meagre appointments and the massive, wind-blown landscape.

"Then we leave for the mines," Thomas said. "I take full responsibility. Master Skinner, you are under guard. You will lead us to Cerys. Quietly. The slightest hint of the Shadow Mage returning will be your end. With no redress or warning. Do I make myself clear?"

"Perfectly," Terrence said. "May I rise? The ground is no place for a man of my advancing years."

Glaring at Guildford, who was staring at Tom with rampant scepticism, Dominic thrust an elbow under his uncle's arm. Despite himself, his skin crawled at the clutch of his uncle's skeletal fingers as he levered himself to his feet.

Terrence shook out his tattered cloak, gaining a hint of his former dignity.

"That way," he said, nodding to the ridge. "Your horses are not required. But arm yourselves with weapons and supplies."

In short order, the company gathered themselves for travel. Dominic's heart lurched as he left Kismet with food, water, and a saddle blanket strapped over her against the penetrating cold. She humphed softly at him, blowing down her velvet nose. He pressed his forehead to hers, wishing he could take her with him. "I'll be back, lady," he whispered. "I promise." She nudged him to the door with a toss of her head. The action raised a bleak chuckle. "Aye, I know. No time to lose," he murmured. "Are you ready, Aldric?"

"Aye, ready." Aldric stood tall at his side, armed with his bow and dagger, his own sack of supplies occupying the remaining space on his back. "Dominic," he paused, "I meant what I said. If your uncle places you in a second's danger, I will take him down. I swear it."

Heart full of conflicting emotions in which hope and fear clashed in equal proportions, Dominic clasped his arm in a warrior's salute. "Aye, my friend," he said. "I know."

CHAPTER 39

Hunched in their cloaks against the bitter night, the group crested the ridge and marched down the road into Traitor's Reach. Cedric had not lied. It was a grim and forbidding place. The fitful moonlight showed a narrow valley truncated abruptly by the edge of a cliff. The cottages and workshops of Traitor's Reach perched precariously on the steep slopes like nesting birds. A sour smell dominated the place, part excrement, part the tang of smelted ore. A gallows, presently empty of occupants, stood to one side. The hangman's noose dangled from the crossbar, twisting in the breeze. A grim reminder of the price of dissent. Lantern light illuminated a few windows. Wooden stairways wended their way between the scattered buildings, and smoke hung heavy in the air from well-stoked fireplaces. Coal, at least, was readily available. A distant buzz of voices travelled to them on the tainted air. Exchanging glances, the group huddled together and marched onwards in Terrence's wake. He passed the low-roofed dwellings with nary a look, his tattered cloak sweeping through a light dusting of snow. Dominic's back prickled with goose-flesh at the whispers that drifted to him from every side. He opened his channels, scanning the ether for Juliana's light treble, but did not hear it. At the touch of another, deeper telepathic signal, he closed his own down in case Cerys was scanning the environment.

"Hide your breastplates," Terrence instructed as they crossed a narrow bridge slick with ice. "The mine guards know me, but they will not greet your arrival with any pleasure."

Dominic nodded at his uncle's back; his eyes screwed up at the sight of a broad, cloaked figure hurrying towards them from the village. "That's Cedric," he murmured.

"Welladay, that's a relief," the man puffed as he joined them. His breath carried the tang of rancid hops. "Wasn't looking forward to the climb." He stared at Terrence, his head cocked.

"You have a guest?" he hazarded.

"My uncle. Terrence Skinner. He's going to see us into the mines," Dominic said tersely. "What's the news?"

Cedric drew back, eyeing Terrence's cadaverous form with a caution more normally reserved for venomous insects. "That's an enormous risk, is it not?" he ventured, searching their grim faces.

"Aye," Guildford said. He cast a lowering glare at Dominic and fingered his sword. "Not all of us are happy about it."

"Report, Cedric?" Tom said before the argument could erupt again.

"Aye, well. No sign of Oswin, but there's a goodly guard in the mines. Seems our information is correct. Dupliss and some of his men are with Cerys, waiting on the outcome of her attack before he sends word further south." He grimaced, mouth twisting under his beard. "'Tis not much. There's only so much you can overhear of a conversation between two people. But the inn is quiet tonight," he said. He glanced around at the watchful valley. "Too quiet, if you ask me."

"No time to waste, then," Terrence said. He slanted a gaze into the night sky, where a full moon was rising. "This way. Make haste."

He raised his arm. One clawed finger pointing to a solid structure at the base of the cliff. "There, that's the entrance to the mines. In the old days, 'twas heavily guarded. Now..." He swept the company with a sardonic glance. "Cerys has her own methods. Beware. Her illusions are many and intricate. I cannot tell what you may face within. Only that you should think twice before trusting your senses. Dominic," he paused. Dominic's heart tripped to be the sole subject of his uncle's attention after so long. He glanced at the older man and then looked away. Terrence's memories, the sadness churning behind his eyes, were a stark warning of the dangers that lay before them. "As a member of the Blessed, you will hear and see things the others may not," Terrence said. "Be alert." His dark eyes flicked to Mistress Trevis. "You, as well, madame," he said. The healer nodded crisply in reply.

"Aye, we will." Dominic cleared his throat, aware of the stares of his companions. His shoulders twitched.

Warning given, Terrence turned, his gaze locking on the grim mountainside. An experienced old fighter who knew his enemy only too well. The icy breeze sighed itself to sleep. Even the faint voices from the drinking den seemed to halt. For an instant, no-one moved. Silence reigned. They stood, surrounded by the sparkling, distant stars as the heavens wheeled eternally onward, uncaring.

Terrence sighed. Dominic wondered if the man was praying. He seemed reluctant to take the last few irrevocable steps into the dark.

"Uncle?" he ventured. "Shall we go?"

Terrence shook himself. "Aye," he said, his voice hushed, as if it was coming from a great distance. He glanced across at Dominic, his dark, wondering eyes travelling across his features like a man memorising a route to an unknown destination. "So like your grandfather, 'tis uncanny," he murmured, almost to himself. He stood taller under Dominic's watchful stare. Commanding his attention. "You will take care using your gifts, lad," he instructed. "Remember who you are within those stone walls." He started forward, and the company fell in behind him. Their footsteps crunched against the silence, following the rutted cart tracks that marked the path to the mines.

No moonlight pierced the shadow of the entrance. A brick and timber structure formed a type of gatehouse flanked by iron-studded doors propped open. Up close, the gate to the tunnels loomed like a dark, open mouth circled with the frosted teeth of rocks. A single lean-to hut lodged against the entrance, inhabited by the burly presence of two armed guards, well wrapped against the cold. They glanced up from their dice as Terrence approached and scrambled to attention. Dominic frowned. The fear they displayed did not seem equal to the frail old man Terrence presented. A clipped discussion took place between them.

"Aldric," he whispered, as Terrence debated their entry within, "Do you sense Cerys here?" The younger man scowled. "Do I think she's disguised as Terrence?" He cocked his head, almost as if he was listening. "Nay, I don't think so."

Terrence snapped something at the guards that blanched their faces beneath their beards. They stood down, and the elderly mage gestured to the group, ushering them forward. Age had not dimmed his hearing. He favoured Dominic with a thin smile. "Cerys guards her treasure well," he said. "And it lies much closer to the heart of the mountain. Those two," he jerked his chin at the hut, "have known me for a long time. In both states of being. The Shadow Mage's talon within me scares them. As it should. Come."

Ghostly conversations began as soon as Dominic passed under the jagged outline of the mine entrance. The sullen atmosphere dropped over his shoulders like a mud-soaked cloak. Aldric gazed around at the damp black walls with deep uncertainty. Terrence lit a lamp from a cluster of those available on a rocky outcrop and gestured to Dominic to do the same. "Do not let your lanterns die," he said to the others as they followed suit, "but watch the flames. If they grow or flicker more than usual, 'tis a dangerous sign. Extinguish them immediately."

He held his own lamp high above his head. Far from the wooden palings and planks that had lined Terrence's Traverse, the roof here was heavily timbered with the split trunks of entire trees and buttressed with dark granite. Solid and unyielding as death itself. Rushlight flickered at distant intervals down the low, narrow passage. The air smelled heavily of damp wood, pitch, and stone. At their feet, a narrow timber rail led the way forward. Fear clawed at Dominic's spirit. He chewed his lips as they took their first hesitant steps in Terrence's wake. The lost voices of the mines' former occupants clamoured warnings at his mental defences, demanding his attention. He forced them away, his brow furrowed with effort.

"This doesn't seem too bad," Guildford said, striding onward with his usual blithe confidence. "'Tis just a mine."

"So you think," Cedric said. "Plenty of folk have gone mad in here."

"Nay, 'tisn't just a mine," Will said with a shudder. "I can hear whispers. People talking." He gazed around, fingers tightening on his army-issued sword. "'Tis like the night under the temple, isn't it, Dominic?" he asked and crept closer to Mistress Trevis. She exchanged glances with Dominic, her face grim. "I can hear them very well," she said.

"Aye," Dominic agreed, repeating Oswin's recent advice over his shoulder. "Try not to pay them too much attention. They want our energy."

The passage sloped downward and lowered the further they travelled from the entrance. Guildford's head brushed the roof. Aldric's face, brown in the lamplight, took on a sickly yellow hue. "I don't mind underground, ordinarily," he said, his voice hushed. "But this is...different. It feels wrong. Is it like where Oswin took you before?"

"Similar," Dominic said. "But this is more travelled."

The passage forked. Terrence led them to the left, down a separate tunnel lined with rough planks. Running water greeted their ears, and the walls grew slimy with moss. "Where is this?" Dominic asked.

Terrence turned, his face creased with tiredness. "To the cells," he said briefly. "Where they kept us when we first arrived. To acclimatise."

He bared his teeth in a skull-like grin that contained not a shred of humour. Dominic shuddered.

"I'm not going in a cell," Will said, his normally deep voice shrill with nerves.

"Me neither," Aldric said. Bringing up the rear, he'd notched his bow and walked stealthily as a cat, his eyes glowing golden in the rushlight.

"We're going past the cells," Terrence reassured the youngest members of the group. "Not into them."

The passage forked once more into another tunnel. So low that Guildford's helmeted head bounced from a solid beam with a clang that would have conjured a laugh in other circumstances. He cursed out loud. Terrence turned his head and pressed a stern finger to his lips. Guildford glowered and carried on, his soft swearing mixed eerily with the voices still competing for Dominic's attention. He battened down his magical senses with all the force at his command, but the spectral fingers reached out to tug his cloak or twitch his hood. Trying to tug him back. There were other emotions mixed in with the chatter of voices, forming a toxic mix in the oppressive atmosphere. Anger, fear, loneliness. Confusion. Pain. Loss. He could name each one as they sloughed into being, melting against his chilled skin, seeking and finding his own matching moods. "Don't," he muttered. "I don't want it…"

Malevolent laughter dominated the other emotions. It swirled around him, conducted by a master of manipulation. "He's close, here," Dominic managed, swallowing against his dry throat. "The Shadow Mage is watching us."

Terrence jerked to a halt at the head of a flight of steps. His lantern light illuminated yet another branch tunnel, even lower than the one in which they stood. "Down here," he said. "Watch your heads."

Through the rocking shadows cast by their lamps, Dominic gaped at the shallow caves hewed roughly into the solid rock, each shuttered by a heavy iron gate. Some chambers contained low platforms carved into the solid rock. Traceries of wax lingered. Dark, shiny rivers hardened on the walls from niches where candles had once stood. The air here was fetid and rank with deprivation. Though they were empty now, Dominic's mind provided him with image after image of tattered figures, stretching thin arms desperately through the bars of their prisons, begging for food, and light, and warmth. Their screams of pain and fear and frustration bounced in the echoes. Burrowed into the bleak rock walls like a seam of poison to remain part of the atmosphere forever. Abandoned and alone. His skin crawled, and he pressed one hand to his empty belly, fighting nausea.

Here and there, people had attempted to mark the passage of time into the walls. Dominic's heart ached for one last prisoner, who had kept a faithful tally for what seemed like years, only to stop at some point, his scribing tool ending in a savage scribble of despair. As if he'd simply given up.

He caught Terrence's eye. His uncle gave a single nod. Moisture glinted on his cheeks. "Mine," he said. "That's how long it took for Darius to break me."

Relief flooded the company as Terrence led them up a stairway at the end of the prison corridor into relatively clearer air. Dominic caught the huff of Aldric's breath as the lad breathed more deeply. Will moved slightly away from Mistress Trevis' strangely comforting presence. Their collected light showed a large cave. On first inspection, the place seemed less grim and forbidding than the prison floor. The roof stretched high above them. A majestic temple of stalactites dripping water onto the puddled ground. Guildford raised his head thankfully, stretching his long limbs. Tom gazed round, a light frown twisting his brow as he surveyed the surroundings. But within a heartbeat, Dominic's magical senses caught the rush of fear and pain. He flinched as his gaze took in the number of shackles around the space.

Cedric jangled a pair of rusty manacles bolted deep into the wall. "By the Gods, what did they do here?" he breathed. Terrence stared at him. "Mostly, we screamed," he said in a tone of ice. Cedric ducked his gaze and dropped the iron with a rattle that penetrated the darkness and seemed to stir its bitter memories to life.

"What's that?" Will said. He pointed a stubby finger into the gloom. Dominic followed Will's terrified stare to the centre of the chamber. A plinth of black granite stood there, part of a natural outcrop. Aldric stumbled to a halt on one side of him, Will on the other. The sight was familiar to all of them. They had seen something just like it two years before, under the Temple of the Mage in Blade. An altar dedicated to the darkest of Gods. Unable to help himself, drawn by an inexplicable compulsion, Dominic wandered towards it. Aldric's hand shot out to catch his sleeve. "Don't go near it," the lad warned, his voice high with fright.

Dominic shook him off. Entranced. Sure he could hear Felicia. See her, even; a shadow in the darkness on the other side of the cave. A ripple of blue fabric. The memory of her voice lingered in his mind. The sight of her gathering her skirts to leap into the towering spiral of black energy, only to vanish from his life like a ghost. "She must be here, she must," he murmured as he crossed to the altar like a sleepwalker, moonstruck and unable to stop.

"Dominic!" Guildford closed the distance between them in six quick strides and snatched at his arm, wheeling him around. "Where do you think you are going? There's nothing there," the princeling said. "This is empty. Just a cave. Part of the prison."

Dominic shook him off. "She's here," he insisted. His voice didn't feel like his own. The words left his lips as slurred as if he'd been drinking for hours.

"There's nothing here! Nothing! Snap out of it!" Guildford gave him a shake that bounced his brain against his skull. Dominic struggled from his grip. "You don't believe me. You should," he gasped.

"When she's right here. Look. Look!" He pointed. Felicia stood opposite him, just beyond the slab of granite. Dirt and bruises marred her thin face. Her hair, a tangled, dirty mess, was bound roughly in a scrap of grey cloth. Her eyes burned into his, beseeching. Lost.

"Felicia!" he yelled. All the anguish at their separation echoed into the tense atmosphere, adding to the screams of the many other deluded souls already trapped within its walls. Guildford grabbed at his arm again. Dominic twisted away, sprinting across the cavern. Felicia was all he could see. All he had dreamed. He skidded to a halt when his crazed progress fetched up against solid rock. Dazed, he recoiled, his wits scattered. His ears splintered with Dupliss' battle cry as the man raced into the cavern, followed by a score of men and more. Dominic whirled, with Cerys' mocking laughter tearing at his senses. The air was a dizzying melee of swords, scuffling feet, and frightened, panting breaths.

It took him only a second to identify the last of these as his own.

CHAPTER 40

Dizzy and terrified at his loss of control, Dominic wasted precious time struggling to decide if the new enemy was truly there.

For Guildford, there was no question. Delighted at facing a real foe, at last, the young giant roared into action. His sword flashed in a ring of steel; a grimace of exhilaration and fierce determination plastered his dusty face. Dupliss' narrow face was an iron mask of equal purpose. Tom stood his ground against him, wielding his own weapon with his customary dextrous grace, a deadly combination of speed and agility. Dupliss fought back. Elegant and contained. As poised as a snake ready to bite. Aldric scrambled above the fray onto a tall boulder, firing arrow after arrow at the enemy, while Will and Mistress Trevis fought back-to-back. Youth and experience. A devastating tornado of wisdom on the one hand and Will's berserker fury on the other. Stolid Cedric used a combination of brute force and sly tavern tactics to best his opponents, wielding his sword, feet, and fists to useful purpose. But to Dominic, Dupliss' forces seemed in endless supply, pouring into the chamber from several directions at once. Shaking his head, trying to free himself of illusion, Dominic stumbled into the skirmish, mage power collected in his fist, only to find that his magical skills were useless. There were no Blessed here. These were Dupliss' men. Soldiers all. Well drilled and determined. Forbidden by the Mage to use his Blessed gifts on the Citizens, he drew his sword, planted his feet, and jabbed fiercely at the nearest assailant. His blade took the man in his ribs. Panting, Dominic withdrew, wincing at the grate of steel against bone and thrust again at someone else. A blow rang off his chest guard, alerting him to danger, and he whirled, remembering Sir Dunforde's grunted advice from so many weeks before. "You'll not beat them on your own. Work as a team."

He joined forces with Will and Mistress Trevis, circling the outskirts and picking off those rebounding from their efforts. Sweat ran into his eyes. His mouth was dry with nerves. Blood pounded through his veins in the heat and confusion of battle. The boulder-strewn floor was a dangerous obstacle course of hunched bodies and dropped weapons. Heaving breath into his lungs, he tripped on a discarded shield and found himself on his knees, trapped by Aldric's boulder at his back. He looked up in horror at the flash of a blade raised high above his head. His assailant's mouth twisted in a sneer as he bunched his muscles for the strike.

Unable to move, Dominic stiffened himself in acceptance of a killing blow, gritting his teeth at the laughter mocking him from the ether. Breaking from Mistress Trevis, Will launched himself toward the wild-haired warrior, shouting his fury, dark eyes burning with rage. His sword swept low, aiming for the soldier's hamstrings. Alerted by the boy's shout, the man responded with a swift change to his original intention. He whirled, changing his grip on his heavy sword. Dominic groped for his dagger, but he was too late. The enemy blade smashed backhanded into Will's stocky body, sweeping him to one side. Will grunted, eyes wide with shock. Dominic's breath left him in a rush. Cold with horror, he lunged to his feet and buried his sword in the man's chest. Aldric's arrow followed a second later. It took the man straight in the eye. Tall and heavy, Dominic's blade buried in his body up to the hilt, he almost took Dominic down with him as he fell.

"Will, Will!" Dominic gestured frantically to Mistress Trevis. Unable to leave her own battle, she spared him only a pitying glance. His gaze clashed with Aldric, who leapt from the boulder to the ground and flung himself to Will's side. "I've got no more arrows," Aldric gasped, snatching rags from his pouch. Teeth bared, he waved Dominic away. "Fight," he said grimly. "I'll look after him."

"There are hundreds of them," Dominic said. He staggered to his feet. His sword arm felt heavy with defeat. Will's face was white. His blood pooled darkly on the ground beneath him. A vision of Meridan's hunched body flashed into Dominic's mind, filling it with remembered grief.

"Nay, there are not," Aldric said, a frown on his brow. "Cerys is still playing tricks. You are not seeing true. There are only ten left. Go."

Only slightly heartened, Dominic joined Mistress Trevis, buttressing her fading strokes with quick, sure ones of his own. Dupliss had vanished from the scene. Tom took on the remaining troops, his face tightly controlled, white beneath his soldier's tan. Guildford rampaged around the chamber, his blood well and truly up, seeking every crevice for those who might be hiding. Dragging one cowardly ruffian by his hair, he dropped his sword, took out his dagger and slashed the man's throat, dropping him to the ground like a dead rat. Cedric disappeared and reappeared from the chamber like a court jester, checking for Dupliss' reinforcements in the connecting corridors with a complete disregard for his own safety.

After the noise and fury of battle, an oppressive silence settled on the chamber like a smothering blanket. The air was thick with the salty smell of spilt blood. Locked in silent accord, Tom, Cedric and Guildford patrolled the perimeter, shooting grim glances at the knotted group by the boulder. Mistress Trevis dropped to her knees at Will's side, her long braid dangling over his face. Aldric was sobbing. The desperate sound of it cut Dominic's soul like a knife. He slumped to the ground, taking Will's grubby, flaccid hand in his own. Dread lodged a hand in his heart and squeezed. He could hardly breathe.

"Will, wake up," he said, "Please, you can't die. Not now. Bird is waiting for you. She needs you. What will I tell her?" He knew he was gabbling. His voice trailed into the silence as Mistress Trevis closed Will's staring eyes with a gentle touch of her fingers and returned to brush the tears from his own cheeks.

"He can't hear you now, Dominic," she said, her normally brisk voice softer than a sigh. "Let him go."

Her words didn't penetrate. Dominic stared at her, unseeing. "No," he said. "He can't be. You must bring him back. Ask the Mage." He took her arm and shook it so hard Mistress Trevis' blood-crusted braids danced. "Please, you must," he said.

She let out a breath. "Too late," she said, removing his clutching fingers. "Even the Mage cannot return those who have passed over the threshold into his grace."

Her words sent Aldric into a renewed frenzy of weeping. Dominic bowed his head. A pit of grief and guilt opened in his heart. A grave yet unfilled following the deaths of his parents and brother. His mind's eye watched in numb disbelief as his young friend found a place there. "'Tis the suddenness," Will had said just weeks ago. "No warning. No time to prepare or say goodbye." Dominic bit his lip until it bled, welcoming the slight, stinging pain. Forcing his raging tears down, down, lest they destroy him utterly. He gave Will's lifeless arm a last squeeze. A warrior's salute. Man to man.

"We will honour you," he said fiercely. "And we will win this battle. I swear it on my life. I will avenge you."

Every muscle in his body protested, and he creaked upright, supporting himself on his sword. Cedric lumbered over, wiping sweat and blood from his brow, and bowed his head. "Welladay. A strong fighter and a loyal friend," he said. "There are many older than him who passed from this life boasting of less."

Guildford and Tom joined them, sheathing their swords. Guildford stared down at Aldric, whose shoulders still shook with the force of grief. He bent and helped the slighter lad to his feet. Aldric rose, swiping tears from his cheeks. Guildford clamped an arm around his shoulders, gave him a rough hug, and let go.

"Come now," he said hoarsely. "We should honour his memory. A stern and merry spirit both." Aldric's throat jerked on another sob. His hands trembled as he reached for his bow. Nodding at the group, he trailed around the battleground, collecting arrows, wiping them fastidiously on the bandages he'd dragged from his bag to help his dying friend.

Sorrow punched Dominic in the ribs, watching his squire on his lonely task. He raised heavy eyes to Tom, who was looking around the cavern at the carnage.

"Where's your uncle?" Tom said suddenly. "What happened to Master Skinner?"

CHAPTER 41

Dominic dragged his exhausted gaze from Aldric and searched the dim cave for some sign of Terrence's narrow figure. Tom was correct. He'd gone, vanished like a rat down one of the many tunnels leading from the central chamber. His spirits, already low, sunk to his blood-splattered boots. The man could be anywhere.

"It isn't over," he said, forcing the words from his throat. "We still have not got what we came for. What happened to Dupliss?"

Tom jerked his chin at a narrow fissure in the rock, half hidden by shadows. "I wounded him." He grimaced, tugging at his hair. "By the Gods, the man is quicker than a cat, despite his age," he said.

"Then we follow," Dominic said, surveying the remains of the troop. "We have not fulfilled our mission."

Guildford smacked a fist into his opposite palm. "Aye. We should," he said. "I'm not half done yet."

Tom raised his eyebrows at the show of youthful bravado. "Take a moment to rest," he said, reaching into his pack and withdrawing a wineskin. "We have had little sleep and a fierce battle. We will follow, but first, let's drink to our fallen friend and comrade. Come," he commanded. "Open your rations. We cannot fight on empty stomachs."

Dominic understood the admonition, but his stomach had closed. Eating was the last thing on his mind. Gulping his water ration, he roamed the chamber, his reluctant gaze marking every warrior frozen in their death throes. He channelled his Blessed gifts to lift each fallen body and place it, still trailing gore, in a neat row against the far wall. There was no way to bury them. He piled stones around them the best he could. They would have to rest where they were, a feast for rats. Glancing back at Will's lifeless figure, now resting with his hands clasped loosely across his battered torso, draped with his own cloak, he made another decision. Whatever the cost to his Blessed energy, he would see Will Dunn buried with honour. In a marked grave.

Munching on jerky, Guildford's roaming, sombre stare caught his. The younger man nodded as if he could hear Dominic's thoughts. "I will help you carry him," he said. His voice echoed against the rock. "We will do it together."

Dominic jerked his chin. His hands twisted at his sides, seeking work to do. Some sort of distraction from the haphazard confusion of his thoughts. Finally, the rough meal over, the group gathered in the centre of the chamber.

"We will follow Dupliss," Tom said, marking the distant passage with a grim nod. "But we cannot risk all our small forces. Mistress Trevis, Aldric, and Cedric remain here. Guard our backs and our fallen friend. Guildford and I will go with Dominic. If we do not come back, return to the surface and send word to Joran and Sir Dunforde of our failure. Do not follow us." He paused, staring at each of them in turn. "Are we agreed?"

Mistress Trevis' eyes narrowed. "Aye," she said after a pause that contained an unspoken argument. Cedric nodded robustly. "I'll look after this lad," he said. Dominic drew comfort from the older man's statement. Cedric had glanced at Aldric as he said it, not poor Will. Wrapped in his own misery, his face pale, Aldric stared into space. Dominic doubted his squire had even heard Tom's instructions. He nudged him. Aldric turned his way but said absolutely nothing. "Aldric, did you hear Tom?" Dominic asked. "Aye," Aldric said, his eyes hollowed with pain.

Dominic sighed. It would have to do. "Come, then," he said, shoving his waterskin back into his pack. "Let's go." He clasped Cedric's hand and made the sign of the Mage over his chest towards Mistress Trevis. "Aldric," he said. "Stay here with Cedric. I will return."

"Mayhap," Aldric whispered, his face taut with shock and grief. "Mayhap."

The knights left the quiet, death-filled chamber as quickly as their tired legs would move them. The passageway taken by Dupliss wound snakelike into the darkness. Black as pitch in the wide spaces between flickering rushlights. They felt their way, hands tracing rough, chiselled stone, alert for signs of attack. Dominic found himself trapped in a strange, dreamlike state that seemed at once both part of his reality and completely detached from it. The ghostly voices of the mines, silenced during the din of battle, returned in full measure to batter his senses. He didn't bother closing his channels. A frown screwed across his forehead as he marched onwards. Conviction was growing in him that Cerys was here. Close and watching. If she picked up his energy, so be it. He hoped she also caught a sense of his anger and bitter contempt.

"By the Gods, this place is weird," Guildford said a few minutes later as the passage wound uphill. "I'm so tired. I feel like someone is pushing me over. And where are those whispers coming from? There's no-one here."

Dominic rolled his eyes. To his mental ears, the voices had dispensed with whispers. He was trudging along in a chorus of shouting. A thousand different voices clamoured for his attention. All of them chanting variations of the same phrase. *"Go back."*

Tom said nothing. Leading the way with his face set, he, too, walked with a stoop as if he was forcing himself against a heavy wind.

"'Tis the spirits trapped here," Dominic muttered. "They want us to stop."

"Too bad," Guildford said, renewing his efforts. "I'll kill my step-father if it's the last thing I do."

The slither of steel leaving a scabbard stopped them in their tracks. Dominic peered around, noting the brush of fresh air on his cheeks from an unseen passageway. "Attack!" he yelled, raising his blade as another set of enemy soldiers raced from both sides. Shouting their battle cries, they converged on the weary trio like a flood of muddy water. There was little room in the narrow corridor. Dominic kicked out at his assailant and skewered him to the rocky wall with a blade through his throat. A whirl of power blasted him off his feet. He stumbled, rolled, and came up with his own energy glowing blue in his fist. He punched it forward blindly, intending to delay. A muffled shout and the thud of a body hitting the wall told him he'd used more force than was strictly necessary.

Fighting using his gift filled him with savage joy. These members of the Blessed, fuelled and twisted by the Shadow Mage, had no compunction about using their magic against Citizens. Tom yelped as a loosened lump of masonry crashed towards him. Guildford screamed his rage as a fistful of stones zipped through the darkness to batter his cheeks. The indifferent rock walls hampered both their movements and the attack of the enemy. Disdaining his sword at close quarters, Guildford lashed out with feet and fists. Tom's dagger flickered in his palm. He hissed in pain at the slice of a strike. Chills pricking his skin, terrified that they would lose Tom as well, Dominic launched a ferocious joint attack with Guildford. The sullen darkness filled with the gasps of men fighting for breath, shouting their pain and anger. On the edge of exhaustion, his energy nearly gone, Dominic finished the last warrior. The man's face twisted in malice, crushed by rough contact with the ceiling, and stared at them from beneath the rippling torchlight. Exhausted, Dominic collapsed to his knees on the cold earth. They'd fought the length and breadth of the corridor, but no more troops tumbled from the unseen corridors to join the fray.

Clutching his arm, Tom leaned against the nearest wall, his bearded cheeks haggard and his eyes washed with pain. Even Guildford drooped over his sword, coughing for breath. Fatigue swept over Dominic. He recognised it now for what it was; the draining of his God-blessed power. Straining his eyes in the gloom, he staggered against Tom as he struggled to his feet. The older man winced. "Mind my shoulder," he muttered. "Some bastard just knifed me."

"There's a light down there," Dominic said. Even pointing a finger felt beyond his strength. His entire arm trembled as he raised it. Concentrating on his mental ability was hard. The day's battles had all but wiped him out.

"Felicia, are you there? Can you hear me?" The thought floated like mist through the ether, lacking both power and direction. His head sank to his chest, overwhelmed by the effort.

"Save your strength…" the whisper echoed back to him. He frowned, trying to determine the owner of the voice. Felicia? Or Juliana Tinterdorn? Or her daughter, the Mage-forsaken Cerys? Light laughter tinkled back at him. Not Felicia. Mayhap Juliana, her doughty shade watching from the blackness beyond the veil. Forever trapped. *"My blade,"* he heard her say. *"My blade…"*

"By the Gods!" He pounded the wall with a bunched fist. Rage at his inability to tell dark from light burned through him like a lightning strike. "Stop playing with me!" His cry rang through the tunnels. A howl of frustration and pain.

Guildford grabbed his fist before he could injure himself more. "Peace, Skinner." The leather under his filthy armour creaked as he pushed himself away from the wall. "Action. That's what we need. Felicia is near." At Dominic's confused look, the princeling's lips lifted. His teeth shone white in the torchlight. "What? She's my twin," he said simply. "I need no magical bond to tell me when she's close."

Dominic used the offered arm to stand upright. "You said you thought she was dead," he reminded Guildford, struggling to keep his eyes open.

"Aye, well. That's before you proved she wasn't," Guildford replied. He tugged Tom from his pained crouch. "Got any bandages in your pack?" he asked.

"Aye, likely," Dominic said. He waited like a packhorse as Guildford rummaged through his haversack and fetched out some wadded cloth. "This it?" he asked, shaking it out under Dominic's nose.

"Mayhap 'twill do," Dominic muttered. Together, they wound the makeshift dressing around Tom's upper arm and shoulder. "How do you fare? Can you continue?" Guildford asked Dominic, his freckles standing out like plague spots on his tired face.

"Aye." Dominic fixed his gaze on the distant lamplight shining in the distance. "I'll go first," he said. "If Cerys is short on soldiers, she'll use whatever magical tricks she can. At least I might catch her at it before you do."

"Welladay, Tom can go in the middle. I'll stay behind to pick you both up." Beneath Guildford's cheer, Dominic sensed the younger man's strain. Shaking his head, he limped towards the light like a sleepwalker, dreading the thought of another pitched battle. He bent his head as he moved forward, picking up speed as the pressure against his chest altered. Now, it was a surge of energy behind him. Urging him on. His lips tugged upwards in a faint, ironic smile, and he renewed his grasp on his sword, tightening his fingers on the hilt, stretching his shoulders. Ready.

The rushlights shed crazed shadows on the walls as they passed beneath their sulky light. Their own and others. Unseen and all but unheard by his companions, the ghosts of Traitor's Reach marched with him.

CHAPTER 42

The ghostly voices died to an urgent muttering as they approached the circle of light emanating from a low doorway at the end of the passage. Dominic flattened himself against the near wall, creeping along it as quietly as he could. He cocked his head at the indistinct murmur of voices from within. The constant drone of a familiar chant sent shivers up his spine. He'd heard it years before, under the temple in Blade. A man's voice. The strange, atonal wail of it turned his skin cold. He clenched his fists. "'Tis Terrence," he whispered to his companions. "He is calling the Shadow Mage once more. Be wary."

There was no door, just a low hollowed archway of black granite carved with the sign of the Mage. Someone had lined the etched design with a cunning mosaic of glittering black diamonds. His heart pounded as he ducked beneath it. The Shadow Mage lurked here. Alive within that black stone. Darius had worn a ring set with a large piece of it. Dominic remembered it glittering on the man's finger from his days as a boy soldier in the army. Even then, not knowing what it was, he had cringed at the sight of it. He glanced up as he crept into the shadows, quieter than a ghost, expecting instant retribution the second he passed across the threshold. Unseen eyes bored holes in his back, and he pressed against the wall, grateful for the brighter light in the centre of the room that allowed him to linger without detection.

More jet-black, glittering stone lay everywhere he looked. Huge chunks jutted like rotten teeth from the chamber walls in a continual seam at floor height all the way around. The surrounding air chilled his ankles even through his heavy boots. His breath frosted, and he dragged up his hood to conceal his presence. Despair and guilt tugged at his emotions, dragging him downwards until it seemed hands reached into his heart to tether him to the solid rock face. Chained there by the weight of his own thoughts. An invisible force snapped his head back against his will, directing him with malicious intent to the circle of figures at the centre of the room. He fought against its dreadful weight but found himself trapped. Unable to move.

His uncle still chanted, his head flung back, his thin arms spread wide. Dominic clamped a hand to his mouth to stifle a gasp of horror at the familiar figure lying on the black altar in front of him. A tall, slim form clothed in midnight blue. Her dark, moon-streaked hair trailed nearly to the floor, her pale oval face twisted and restless. The silk of her gown outlined the faintest hint of her pregnancy.

"By the Gods, 'tis the Queen!" Tom whispered. He took a painful stride forward, every limb trembling with the effort it took, and then slumped back, overwhelmed.

Looming over Petronella's prone figure, completely immersed in the ceremony, Cerys could almost be her twin, so closely did they resemble each other. She raised the Blade of Aequitas. In the hands of its owner, the blade glowed a rich, dark crimson, staining the runes that covered it. Even looking at the thing from a distance made Dominic's gorge rise. His head rang with its familiar, eerie song.

He fought to pull free of the enchantment that kept him prisoner, fighting a grim, silent battle with the Shadow Mage in the depths of his mind. Ever present guilt rode his shoulders. Will's heroism. The awful knowledge that he had yet to tell Little Bird the news that would break her. His failure to fulfil his mission to Joran and the Queen. At his side, Guildford and Tom remained frozen, unaware of the dark force working its spells on their own thoughts. Guildford took a powerful step forward and then stopped, bewildered, clamping a hand to his mouth. His shoulders heaved as he battled his own stomach. "Blood. 'Tis all I can see," he said, choking.

Tom twisted restlessly, confused. Perspiration dotted his forehead. "What is it?" he groaned under his breath. "Why can't I move? All I can see are the faces of the women I've loved and left and the men I've killed. Every one of them, demanding to know why."

"The Shadow Mage," Dominic hissed back. "His presence fills this chamber with the worst of our own nightmares. 'Tis the source of all Cerys' power. We must fight it!"

Desperate to reach the Queen, he dragged at the restraint, unable to break free. Despair claimed him at his failure.

Cerys glanced at Terrence, her broad white brow twisted in a scowl. "Where is the power?" she demanded. Her voice was as clear as mountain crystal, scything the darkness. "I must strike now while I hold her firm in my mind."

Dominic blinked. His frantic gaze raced around the room. There was no spiral of dark energy gathering to churn the ether and claim its next victim as it had before.

Terrence halted his chant. The echoes of the evil song faded into the cavern walls. "The power takes time to conjure without the book, my lady. Be patient but a little longer, we will try again," he said. Taking a breath, his questing gaze bored across the cavern to where Dominic stood, snared by his own doubt. Terrence's eyes widened in recognition. He took a subtle step to the right, and Dominic caught the ripple of a blue cloak in the shadows behind him. Struggling to see, his heart thumping like a battle drum, he craned from the wall. "Please," he prayed, "let it be her. Not another illusion." He craned to his left just a little more and glimpsed Felicia's tangle of dark blonde hair. A flash of her spirited, grey gaze. His eyes flooded with tears. "Felicia," he whispered. His spirit sank as he realised the girl was not alone. Dupliss stood close by her side, his sword drawn, his thin face alight with purpose and grim satisfaction. Dominic's eyes flicked back to Terrence, who held his gaze but a second longer before spreading his hands once more. The chant echoed around the room. Louder this time. But there was no dark force behind it. Under Terrence's fingers, scattered objects raised from the ground. Pebbles and dust, grey with age. He rotated his fingers, a subtle movement that spread the dirt like smoke in the air. A dark spiral. An illusion of his own. A sly smile caught the edges of his thin cheeks as Cerys raised her blade again, locked in her grim purpose. Satisfied he had captured the woman's attention, Terrence nodded to Dominic.

"By the Gods, he's still on our side!" Hope blazed through Dominic's senses like a shooting star, lighting a thread of energy. He stretched out a hand, praying as he'd never prayed before for the blessing of the Mage.

"By the might of the Shadow Mage, I claim this soul and sever her bond to the light!" Cerys cried. "Dark lord, come to me! Fulfil your promise!" She lunged with her knife.

Conjuring every morsel of magical energy at his disposal, Dominic swept his arm towards Cerys as she struck. Her scream of frustrated rage rebounded against the obsidian walls as the dagger twisted from her grip. The force of it spun her around. Another sweep of his arm, and Dominic reversed the dagger. The power of his own momentum, propelled by hope, released him from the rock face. He stumbled away from its iron grip. His face contracted in a mask of hatred; he launched the dagger like an arrow into Cery's fragile chest. She screamed, staggering against the altar, her eyes wide with shock. The illusion of Petronella drifted into nothing as she fell.

"Strike!" Dominic yelled. "Our enemies lie in front of us, not in our minds!" He struggled to ignore the fatigue that cascaded through him with the draining of his power. Scrabbling for his sword, he raced across the chamber, vaguely aware of Guildford's heavy footsteps behind him as he launched himself from the wall, bellowing his sister's name. Tom followed, and together, they sped across the space, intent on death. Dominic batted Felicia beyond Dupliss' grip with the last shred of his magical energy. She stumbled to the ground, her grey eyes wide with alarm, as Tom and Guildford closed in. The clang of steel and the grunts of effort punched holes in the shadows as they engaged in a flashing whirl of bruising metal against Dupliss.

Dominic's God-blessed power drained from him. Sword flashing, he turned to face Cerys, his legs wobbling as the familiar fatigue swept across him. A vicious smirk of triumph on her face, Cerys clasped the Blade of Aequitas in both hands and dragged it, squelching, from her chest. She rose slowly to her feet. The knife dripped with her blood. "Do you really think to use my weapon against me when 'tis my blood that lives within it?" she hissed, her black eyes narrowed with hatred. She raised the dagger, stalking him, pushing him backwards to the walls. "You're a fool to come here, Dominic Skinner," she said, taunting him with its gory edge as she approached. "'Tis about time we ended you."

He glanced at Felicia. She raised on her hands and knees, watching Cerys' approach like a hawk, and attempted a mad scramble backwards as the woman feinted with her blade and grabbed her arm. Cerys drew the girl, struggling, to her feet, holding the blade close to her throat. Poised to strike, Dominic halted in mid-lunge. The sudden silence scraped at his nerves as the battle with Dupliss ended. The commander collapsed to the ground, blood gushing from his mouth. Panting, the two knights turned to stare at Cerys. Tom's arm dripped blood through his makeshift bandage. Guildford's eyes widened in terror at the fear on his sister's face. He raised his weapon. Cerys faced them down, her face white with rage.

"One move, and she dies," she said, sliding Aequitas in a delicate line across the younger woman's throat. Felicia closed her eyes as a thin seam of blood oozed from the cut. "I'll do it," Cerys warned. "If you move a single muscle."

"Don't listen to her!" Felicia screamed. "Get the blade, Dominic. You must get the knife!"

Cerys tightened her grip. She took a step backwards, dragging Felicia with her. "Kill them!" she ordered Terrence. "Do it now!"

For a second, no-one moved.

Dominic's skin crawled as he felt the twist in the atmosphere that marked the approach of the Shadow Mage. He clenched his fist, but the pulse of the Mage power in his palm had drained. There was nothing he could use in their defence as Terrence took a step in their direction.

His eyes jerked to his uncle's face. Terrence bared his teeth, his skeletal frame racked with tremors. Even in this dim light, Dominic could see the battle he fought to stay in the light. "Please," Dominic breathed. "Fight it! By all the Gods, you must fight him!"

"Can't..." Terrence muttered, still shaking. His arms raised. "Can't..." Dominic froze. At his side, Tom and Guildford could do nothing as Terrence's blessed gift of telekinesis swept over them all, pinning them in place to await his killing strike. "No!" Dominic said. "Please, uncle..."

"Can't..." Terrence said again. His throat worked. The Shadow Mage's presence flickered in his pupils, first brown, then black. Agonised, Dominic could only watch the battle play out. Guildford's head drooped. His grey gaze locked on his sister. Tom's face as he turned to look at Dominic held only sadness. Felicia's sob pierced anguish into the depths of his soul.

"I'm so sorry," Dominic said before the end could come.

"Can't..." his uncle shouted once more. He whirled in a cloud of dust. His scream of triumph blasted the air in a single clarion call that pierced the weight of the atmosphere like a shining silver blade.

"I can't let him win!" His arm moved in a sudden blur of speed that took them all by surprise. Felicia tumbled from Cerys' grip to land on the ground. Released from Terrence's grip, Dominic dropped to his knees, gathering her into his arms, pressing his face against her filthy, matted hair.

"Traitor!" Cerys struck with her dagger, and Terrence collapsed under the onslaught, buried beneath the weight of her body.

"No!" Dominic watched in horror as his uncle fell, clutching Felicia to him in an iron grip.

"Get the dagger! You can't let her keep it. Quick!" Felicia hissed.

He struggled from the ground, all his instincts fighting to keep her there with him. Safe. "Get the blade." Felicia gave him a push. She was so weak he barely felt it.

Weary beyond words, he raised his steel. Guildford and Tom moved with him. Together, they advanced on Cerys, who skittered away from Terrence like a spider, all arms and legs. The action bred a savage disgust in Dominic's soul.

"You," he advanced. "Give me that weapon."

"Never!" Cerys' lips bared in a snarl. "'Tis mine. I will never rest until I take back what should be mine! The crown and the kingdom, both!"

They stalked her. She backed off. Closer and closer to the thrumming dark heart of the Shadow Mage's energy, trapped in the walls. "Don't go too near," Felicia warned, her voice soft. "She'll trap you with it, like before."

"Dominic..." His uncle's voice was weak. Dominic cast a glance at Guildford. "We'll hold her," he said roughly. "Go to him."

A few quick strides took him to his uncle's side. The older man lay on his back, wheezing, the wrinkled skin of his cheeks wet with tears. Glancing at Cerys as she weaved a dance with the edge of Aequitas, hoping to lure Guildford and Tom closer to the walls, Dominic crouched, holding his uncle's wizened hand with his own.

"The book," Terrence whispered. "She cannot complete the ritual without the book..."

"Where is it?" Dominic murmured. Terrence's eyes closed. "Please, uncle, you must tell me where it is."

The man's hand slid from his, boneless. "You know where it is..." Terrence said.

Dominic waited, his heart in his mouth, but his uncle had slipped away between one breath and the next. His baffled, exhausted stare clashed with Felicia's.

She shuffled over and took his uncle's lifeless hand in her own, resting her grimy forehead against it. "Help the others," she said. "We must get that blade."

A shout of frustration from the far reaches of the cave snapped his head up. He staggered to his feet, searching the dim recesses of the cavern for Cerys' slender, deadly figure. He could see nothing, but the echoing remains of her laughter nudged his mental ears.

"By the Gods!" Guildford's sword raised sparks as he swung it wildly at the nearest boulder. "One minute she's there, the next, nothing!"

Dominic felt Felicia's alarm. It pecked at his senses with no need for words. "You should have got the blade," she said.

He shook his head. "My uncle said she cannot use it without Darius's book," he said. "And Dupliss lies dead. We will find Cerys and stop her before she can do any more damage."

Felicia laid Terrence's hand carefully on his chest, drawing his cloak around him, and rose unsteadily to her feet. Guildford caught her as she stumbled, holding her upright. "Sister," he rumbled. "Thank the Gods." He enveloped her in a rough hug. She patted his broad back but then stood back, pointing into the shadows at Dupliss' fallen body.

"We haven't stopped her." He frowned at the sadness in Felicia's eyes as she glanced across to the commander's corpse. Dominic's mouth fell open. The man lay on his back, his thick cloak bloody, his face plump and still. Twisted in death.

Not Dupliss. Oswin.

Tom and Guildford looked at Dominic with such dismay his heart thumped in his chest. His frantic gaze sought Felicia's, the familiar sense of failure tugging at his heart. He wanted to take her home. Marry her. Keep her always safe.

Reading his thoughts, she shook her head and cupped his cheek in her grimy hand. He turned his lips to it. Kissing her palm. "Please, don't say it..." he whispered. Her fingers turned, pressing gently against his mouth, stopping his words with a feather light touch. She was so close to him, he could see the flare of Farsight as it ignited in her eyes. Fire under ice.

"Dominic, she has the blade, and Dupliss yet lives. If she finds that book, we are done."

THE END

Also by Christine Cazaly

Tales from the Tarot:
SAGA OF THE SWORDS
Seer of Epera
Queen of Swords
Page of Swords
Knight of Swords
King of Swords (due for release December 2024)

Books in development:
WAY OF THE WANDS
Page of Wands
Knight of Wands
Queen of Wands
King of Wands

KING OF SWORDS

Coming DECEMBER 2024

"The distance between justice and mercy is the width of a blade."

King in all but name, enigmatic Joran of Weir holds the future of Epera in the palm of his hand.

But Joran's troubled and turbulent past has left him a man full of misgivings, only too aware of his dual nature and the potential deadliness of his own power.

As Epera faces the manipulative might of the Shadow Mage, Joran must unite his divided kingdom to save the soul of his beloved queen.

It falls to him to banish the Shadow Mage for once and for all. But can Joran face his own demons to claim the Ring of Justice?

Join Joran and the full cast of Saga of the Swords in the gripping finale to Saga of the Swords.

Watch out for it this winter!

COMMENCING 2025
VOLUME 2 OF TALES FROM THE TAROT
WAY OF THE WANDS
Set in the harsh desert world of Battonia, Way of the Wands is a series of epic tales full of passion, adventure and romance. It all kicks off with Domita's story in Knight of the Wands.

Knight of Wands Way of the Wands Book 1

A fantasy adventure romance set in the scorching desert land of Battonia. Feisty Domita Lombard fights for her right to love as she wishes. And her battle threatens to alter the entire fabric of society.

Follow me on:

amazon.com/Christine-Cazaly/e/B0BBJW5VWS?ref=sr_ntt_s rch_lnk_2&qid=1661516964&sr=8-2

facebook.com/christinecazalyauthor

bookbub.com/profile/christine-cazaly

goodreads.com/https://www.goodreads.com/author/show/22 759981.Christine_Cazaly

Facebookhttps://facebook.com/christinecazalyauthor

GoodreadsChristine Cazaly (Author of Queen of Swords) | Goodreads

BookbubQueen of Swords (Tales from the Tarot) by Christine Cazaly - BookBub

Instagram https://www.instagram.com/christine_cazaly/

AmazonAmazon.com: Christine Cazaly: books, biography, latest update

For updates, recommendations and give-aways, join my newsletter and get Carlos and the Mermaid, a FREE short story, set in Oceanis, the Kingdom of Cups. It's inspired by the tarot card Five of Cups. You can join my newsletter at https:/christinecazaly.com

Join my newsletter for progress updates and to be notified when my next books are due for release!

Acknowledgements

My thanks go, as ever, to my wonderful editor, Natasha Rajendram, of Scott Editorial. I couldn't do this without her eagle eyed comments, cheerleading and enthusiasm.

Likewise, thanks to my super fans, Joy, Gail and Aly. It fills my heart with joy to know you are hanging on the next adventure! Equal credit to my loving husband, Jim, who does so much to keep the wheels turning while I am absent exploring the content of my imagination. Darling, you are my rock.

And last, but not least – to everyone who has discovered Tales from the Tarot, and purchased one of my books.

My undying gratitude. May the gods bless you. Don't forget to review. It helps more than you can possibly know!

CC x

Printed in Great Britain
by Amazon

44517037R00189